For more than forty years,
Yearling has been the leading name
in classic and award-winning literature
for young readers.

Yearling books feature children's
favorite authors and characters,
providing dynamic stories of adventure,
humor, history, mystery, and fantasy.

Trust Yearling paperbacks to entertain,
inspire, and promote the love of reading
in all children.

THE HORSES OF OAK VALLEY RANCH

The Georges
and the
Jewels

Jane Smiley

with illustrations by
Elaine Clayton

A YEARLING BOOK

Text copyright © 2009 by Jane Smiley
Illustrations copyright © 2009 by Elaine Clayton

All rights reserved. Published in the United States by Yearling, an imprint of Random House Children's Books, a division of Random House, Inc., New York. Originally published in hardcover by Alfred A. Knopf, an imprint of Random House Children's Books, a division of Random House, Inc., New York, in 2009.

Yearling and the jumping horse design are registered trademarks of Random House, Inc.

Visit us on the Web! www.randomhouse.com/kids

Educators and librarians, for a variety of teaching tools, visit us at
www.randomhouse.com/teachers

The Library of Congress has cataloged the hardcover edition of this work as follows:
Smiley, Jane.
The Georges and the Jewels / Jane Smiley.
p.   cm.
Summary: Seventh-grader Abby Lovitt grows up on her family's California horse ranch in the 1960s, learning to train the horses her father sells and trying to reconcile her strict religious upbringing with her own ideas about life.
ISBN 978-0-375-86227-4 (trade) — ISBN 978-0-375-96227-1 (lib. bdg.)
ISBN 978-0-375-89414-5 (e-book)
[1. Horses—Training—Fiction. 2. Ranch life—California—Fiction.
3. Family life—California—Fiction. 4. Christian life—Fiction.
5. California—History—1950—Fiction.] I. Title.
PZ7.S6413Ge 2009
[Fic]—dc22
2009006241

ISBN 978-0-375-86228-1 (pbk.)

Printed in the United States of America

10 9 8

First Yearling Edition

The
Georges
and the
Jewels

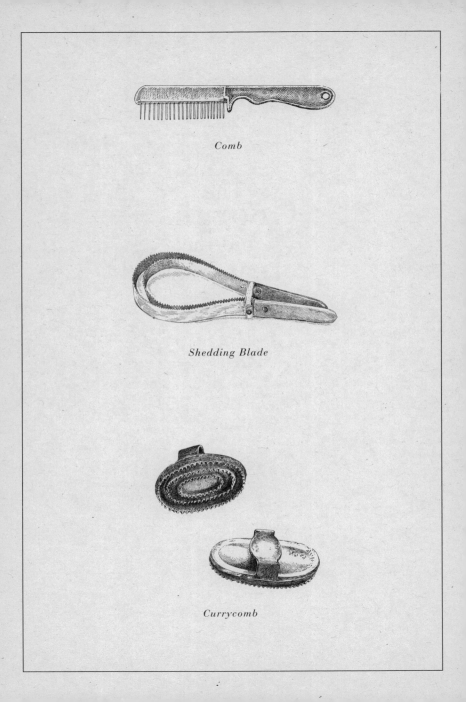

Comb

Shedding Blade

Currycomb

Chapter 1

Sometimes when you fall off your horse, you just don't want to get right back on. Let's say he started bucking and you did all the things you knew to do, like pull his head up from between his knees and make him go forward, then use a pulley rein on the left to stop him. Most horses would settle at that point and come down to a walk. Then you could turn him again and trot off—it's always harder for the horse to buck at the trot than at the lope. But if, right when you let up on the reins, your horse put his head between his knees again and took off bucking, kicking higher and higher until he finally dropped you and went tearing off to the other end of the ring, well, you might lie there, as I did, with the wind knocked out of you and think about how nice it would be not to get back on, because that horse is just dedicated to bucking you off.

So I did lie there, looking up at the branches of the oak tree that grew beside the ring, and I did wait for Daddy to come trotting over with that horse by the bridle, and I did stare up at both their faces, the face of that horse flicking his ears back and forth and snorting a little bit, and the face of my father, red-cheeked and blue-eyed, and I did listen to him say, "Abby? You okay, honey? Sure you are. I saw you bounce! Get up, now."

I sighed.

"How am I going to tell those folks who are looking to buy these horses that a little girl can ride them, if you don't get up and ride them?"

I sat up. I said, "I don't know, Daddy." My elbow hurt, but not too badly. Otherwise I was okay.

"Well, then."

I stood up, and he brushed off the back of my jeans. Then he tossed me on the horse again.

Some horses buck you off. Some horses spook you off—they see something scary and drop a shoulder and spin and run away. Some horses stop all of a sudden, and there you are, head over heels and sitting on the ground. I had a horse rear so high once that I just slid down over her tail and landed in the grass easy as you please, watching her run back to the barn. I started riding when I was three. I started training horses for my dad when I was eight. I wasn't the only one—my brother, Danny, was thirteen at the time, and he did most of the riding (Kid's Horse for Sale), but I'm the only one now.

Which is not to say that there aren't good horses and fun horses. I ride plenty of those, too. But they don't last, because Daddy turns those over fast. I had one a year ago, a sweet bay mare. We got her because her owner had died and Daddy picked her up for a song from the bank. I rode her every day, and she never put a foot wrong. Her lope was as easy as flying. One of the days she was with us, I had a twenty-four-hour virus, so when I went out to ride, I tacked her up and took her down to the crick at the bottom of the pasture, out of sight of the house.

I knew Daddy had to go into town and would be gone for the afternoon, so when I got down there, I just took off the saddle and hung it over a tree limb, and the bridle, too, and I lay down in the grass and fell asleep. I knew she would graze, and she did for a while, I suppose. But when I woke up (and feeling much better, thank you), there she was, curled up next to me like a dog, kind of pressed against me but sweet and large and soft. I lay there feeling how warm she was and smelling her fragrance, and I thought, I never heard of this before. I don't know why she did that, but now when Daddy tells me that horses only know two things, the carrot and the stick, and not to fill my head with silly ideas about them, I just remember that mare (she had a star shaped like a triangle and a little snip down by her left nostril). We sold her for a nice piece of change within a month, and I wish I knew where she was.

But Daddy names all the mares Jewel and all the geldings George, and I can hardly remember which was which after a while.

The particular George who bucked me off had a hard mouth. I did the best I could with him for another twenty minutes, but Daddy said that probably he was going to have to get on him himself, which meant that we weren't going to turn this one over fast, because a little girl couldn't ride him yet. Which meant that Daddy was in a bad mood for the rest of the day.

We took the George back up to the barn, and while Daddy threw out the hay, I brushed the George off. He didn't mind, but he didn't love it like some of them do. Then I picked out his feet and took him out and put him into one of the big corrals. We didn't keep horses in stalls unless we had to, because Daddy said that they did better outside anyway, and if you kept them in stalls, well, then, you spent your life cleaning stalls rather than riding. Was that what I wanted?

I always said, "No, Daddy," and he ruffled my hair.

In the winter, though, it bothered me to think of them huddled out in the rain, their tails into the wind and their heads down. Of course that was what horses were meant to do, and ours had heavy coats, but I would lie awake when it rained in the night, wishing for it to stop.

It was worse in Oklahoma.

Oklahoma was where we came from, where Daddy and Mom grew up and had Danny, then me. We moved to California in 1957, when I was four and a half. I could barely remember living there, though we went back once or twice a year to see my grandparents and buy some horses. In Oklahoma, there could be real rain, and real snow, and real ice. Daddy had seen a horse slide right down a hill once, just couldn't stop himself, went down like he was on skis and right over the edge of a crick, fell on the ice, and had to be pulled out with a tractor. Couldn't be saved. At least in California we didn't have ice.

It was only five when we got into the house, not even suppertime, but it was January and the days were short. Christmas was over and school would start again on Monday, which meant I could ride two horses in the afternoon at most. Now that my shoulder and my arm were starting to hurt from my fall, I didn't

4

mind a break from the riding. It was just that I was sorry to be going back to school. Seventh grade. I've never heard anyone who had a single nice thing to say about seventh grade.

The next day was church. We went to church twice on Sundays—from nine to twelve in the morning and from two to four in the afternoon—and also Wednesday evening. Daddy was an elder in the church, and the place we had found, that we called our chapel, was really just a big room in a strip mall, with a cleaners on one side and a Longs drugstore on the other. Daddy and Mr. Hazen were looking for another place, maybe a church that was for sale (you'd be surprised at how many churches get sold when the congregation decides it needs more room), but they hadn't found one yet, so between noon and two, we kids wandered around that strip mall and went into Longs and looked at the comic books (until we got caught) or the toys or the makeup or the medical supplies, whatever there was that might be interesting. Sometimes Daddy drove me home to check on the horses, and sometimes he went by himself. Mom always offered, but Daddy said she had enough to do, setting up the lunch for the brothers and sisters.

The brothers and sisters were mostly fairly old—older than Daddy and Mom. Only three families had kids, us and the Hollingsworths and the Greeleys. We had me, the Hollingsworths had Carlie, Erica, and Bobby, who were all younger than Danny and older than I. The Greeley kids were four, two, and one. Sometimes, on a really unlucky day, Carlie Hollingsworth and I would be told to watch the Greeleys, and then our hands were full, because those Greeleys, even the baby, could run. What Mom said, if I made a face, was "Sally and Sam need a break, so you can do your share."

The only thing I liked about church, though I didn't say this to Daddy or Mom, was the singing. To tell the truth, I never knew what songs were really hymns, because Daddy, Mom, Mrs. Greeley, and Mr. Hazen were ready to sing anything, and some Sundays we would sing for an hour at a time, more like a songfest than a church service. On those days, Daddy always came home happy. We sang "Farther Along" and "When the Roll Is Called Up Yonder, I'll Be There," "Abide with Me," and "Amazing Grace." We didn't have hymnals—Daddy said we might get those next year—but someone always knew the words anyway and would teach the others. It wasn't right that the singing would push into the preaching of the Gospel, but sometimes it did and I didn't mind. On the days when there was more preaching and less singing, Daddy came home in a worse mood.

That Sunday after I fell off, I was still a little stiff, so rather than wander around Longs, I stayed with Mom and helped her serve the food. She had macaroni and cheese, baked beans, some broccoli and carrots, a loaf of bread, and a wedge of cheese. For dessert, Mrs. Greeley had made an applesauce cake, which I liked very much. The younger women always made a lot of food, because, Mom said, for some of the old people, this was the biggest meal they got all week. "You know you are going home to a nice supper, Abby, so you watch what you eat, because Mrs. Larkin doesn't have that, and neither does Mrs. Lodge." I watched what I ate, but I especially watched myself eat a piece of that applesauce cake.

The second service was more like Sunday school. The grown-ups went to one side of the room and studied the Bible, and the kids went to another side of the room and did things like read Bible stories and color Bible coloring books. There was also a felt board that Mrs. Larkin sometimes brought, on which she did felt shows. There would be a cutout of Joseph, say, made of white felt, and then a bunch of cutouts of his brothers, and some felt palm trees that represented Egypt and a felt house that represented Israel, and she moved the felt pieces around on the board while telling us the story. I think she had pieces for six or eight different stories. For the most part, everyone at church was nice.

This was not true of seventh grade. Monday morning, I got on the bus. Because we had horses to feed and water before school, I was always the last person on the bus, and fairly often the driver had to stop after he had already started and open the door again for me. The impossible thing was deciding whether to get dressed first and then do the work or to get dressed, do the work, and change again before going to school. If I slept in, even a little, I could not get dressed twice, and so my shoes would be a little dirty when I got on the bus. Sometimes the other kids started yelling, "Hey! What's that smell? Hey, what smells so bad in here?" and sometimes they didn't, but I always expected them to. I didn't have any friends on the bus, so I tried to read a book or look out the window.

The best thing that can happen to you in seventh grade, really, is that you float from one classroom to another like a ghost or a spirit, undetected by the humans. I thought maybe it would be possible to do that at one of those big schools in a big town, but our school was small, the seventh grade had forty kids divided into two classes, and everyone had a slot. My homeroom teacher was Mr. Jepsen, the math teacher. It did not help that numbers made my head hurt. If I could sit by myself at night and work out my homework problems, I almost always got them all right, but Mr. Jepsen was the kind of teacher who likes to interrupt. "So, Abby, what's the square root of sixty-four?" and then, just when you are opening your mouth to say, "Eight," he says, "Cat got your tongue today? Are you thinking?" And then when you open your mouth again, he says, "Well, what's the square root of sixteen?" and now you're in this rhythm—every time you have the answer, he asks you another question, until he gives up on you and finally says, "Billy Russell?" and of course, Billy Russell has been sitting there for five minutes, thinking about the answer, and he pipes up, "Eight!" as bright as he can be, and Mr. Jepsen says, "Good boy!"

Or, if you happened to look out the window, as soon as your eyes went in that direction, Mr. Jepsen would say, "Abby, is the great outdoors that much more fascinating than this classroom?" and of course you couldn't say yes, you had to keep your mouth shut. Most of the other kids seemed to like Mr. Jepsen, at least they laughed at all of his jokes. Even so, I had a B in math—A on homework and tests, C on class participation—and that was good enough for Daddy, who didn't expect me to be going to college anyway.

In our seventh grade, there were only thirteen girls. Eight of them were in the other section. The four girls I liked least—the Big Four was what they had called themselves since fifth grade—were all in my section, and Gloria, who had been my friend since kindergarten, was in the other section and I didn't see her much. All day I wondered if, at the end of the day, she would still be my friend or whether those seven girls in the other section would finally capture her. We had one new girl this year, Stella Kerkhoff, who had come into seventh grade from another school in the district. She had tried to be friends with almost everyone in the class and discovered what we all knew—that there was no room in the Big Four for a fifth wheel, that Maria, Fatima, and Lucia kept to themselves, that Debbie Perkins (who I was friends with in third and fourth grade) was not only amazingly quiet, but also lived on a ranch at the furthest end of the school district and could never come over or have guests, and that the Goldman twins, even though they were friendly, really were twins—it was hard to tell them apart (and they didn't mind playing tricks about that), they didn't really need another friend, and anyway, they were so smart they took half their classes with the eighth graders.

So Stella had decided before Christmas that Gloria was the one—Gloria's backpack was always filled with folded-up little notes from Stella, and at lunch Stella made it her business to sit between Gloria and me whenever I didn't get there first. For the month between Thanksgiving and Christmas, I did what Mom told me and pretended not to know what was going on. Gloria did, too, so it was impossible to tell who was winning. That Monday, I was so stiff from my fall (you're always more stiff the second day than the first) that of course Stella got in there, no problem. And then they went to the girls' room together, and I was just sitting there until the bell for sixth period rang. So, it was a bad day.

And then the bus broke down on the way home and was stuck for an hour while it was getting darker and darker, and so I knew we weren't going to get any training in, and Daddy was going to say, "Well, the hay was wasted today, since the horses don't know a single thing that they didn't know yesterday."

All of this is just a prologue to the thing that happened next.

Bridle Without Reins

Braided Rope Reins

Whip

Chapter 2

THE NEXT MORNING, TUESDAY, OF COURSE, I HAD MADE UP MY mind not to get caught by the school bus, so I got up really early. It was dark and pretty cold. Even by the time I was dressed and ready to go out and start with the hay, Daddy and Mom were still in bed. I didn't mind that—I did the morning work by myself fairly often, and I liked hearing the horses nicker to me, seeing them standing by the gate looking for something to eat. Even horses who don't know you or don't like you are happy to see you if you have an armload of alfalfa.

I hayed the Georges first, the littler George (chestnut), the George who had dumped me (named, as far as I was concerned, Ornery George), and the pony George. Then I went back in the barn and came out with hay for the Jewels. We only had two mares at the time—Daddy had just sold two to a ranch up in the valley, nice horses and pretty enough so that he could get a little extra for them. He always said, "Even the most dried-up old cowboy will pay for a good-looker, and don't you let them tell you different. You could have the greatest horse in the world, and if it had a head like a bathtub, I couldn't sell it for beans."

But only one of the Jewels was standing by the gate. That was a bad sign, and I was glad that it was starting to get light in case there was something out there in the paddock that I had to look for and report back. I threw down the hay in three piles, the way you're supposed to, one more than the number of horses so they won't fight over it, and then I climbed the gate. Most of the mares' pasture wasn't visible from the gate—it ran in a gentle slope down to the crick. For a while I didn't see anything. Then, over to one side, I saw the second mare, standing under a tree. She turned her head toward me. She wasn't down and she didn't look like she was in trouble. When I got a little closer, I saw that she had something with her, and then, when I got closer than that, I saw that that something was a foal. The foal was standing next to the mare, and when it saw me, it skittered around to the other side of her and peeked at me under the mare's neck. When I got even closer, I could just see its legs and its nose.

You never know with a mare, no matter how friendly she is on her own, how she will react to you when she has a foal at her side, so I stopped and stood there. After a minute or two, the foal came around the mare again, gave me a look, and then began to nurse, his back end to me and his little tail switching back and forth. He looked to me to be at least six or eight hours old, which meant that maybe he was born before we went to bed and we just missed the mare in the dark. When you don't know a mare is pregnant, I guess it never occurs to you to wonder whether she is having a foal.

This Jewel was one of three horses Daddy had bought right after Thanksgiving. One he had sold already, and the ornery George was the third one. What with Christmas and all, we hadn't done a lot with her or even paid much attention to her, though I thought she was nice, and I always gave her a few extra pats. She was pretty without being distinctive—no white on her at all, not too big, not too small, good head, decent feet.

Now it was getting to be day. I took one step toward the mare, watching her, and then another and another. She looked at me, but she didn't pin her ears and start switching her tail, and so I took another step. The foal kept nursing, his tail turned to me. He didn't have any white stockings that I could see. I took another step. The foal's head popped up and he ran around the mare again, so that she was between the foal and me. Now I was fairly close, close enough to lean forward, stretch out my hand, and touch the mare on the neck. I watched her, though, before I tried. She still gave no warning signs, so I stretched out my hand, leaned forward from my hips, and touched her, then I touched her again, just a little stroke, down her neck. I took one step closer. Then I was very still. The mare's tail moved slowly back and forth, and the face of the foal appeared. Its little dark ears were pricked and its nostrils wide, and it was staring at me. No white on the face. Prominent forehead. "Hey, baby," I said softly.

13

And now there was a shout from up the hill—"Abby! AAABBYYY!" Daddy's voice. "Ruth Abigail! You out there?" He only calls me by my full name when he's worried or mad.

I was backing slowly away from the mare and foal, not wanting to shout and startle them.

Daddy appeared on the brow of the hill. I could see him out of the corner of my eye. Surely from there he could take it all in—me, mare, foal. I backed up two more steps. There was a silence. Then I heard him say, "What the—" He never finished this sentence, because he never spoke the name of the Lord in an idle fashion, but sometimes he came close.

I turned and ran up the hill.

He said, "Is that a foal?"

"It is, Daddy. It's so big and pretty."

We stood there for a minute, and Daddy said, "Well, I'll be—" And then, "It's always one trial or another."

"Should we bring them in?"

"And put her where? Those stalls aren't clean enough for a foal. They're better off out here."

"But it's cold."

"Well, she should have thought of that before foaling out, don't you think?"

I looked at him. We were walking up the hill, almost to the gate by now.

"Mares can wait, you know, not like humans. You ask your mom about it. I've heard of mares going three hundred eighty days, just because the weather's no good." With every word he said, I sensed him getting less and less happy.

I said, "It's so cute, Daddy. It doesn't have a speck of white on it. It's got a pretty head."

14

"What can I do with a foal? What can I do with a mare who has a foal? Can't wean it for five months, then it'll take another two months or so to get her in shape. That's seven months of burning hay before we can even begin to sell her. That's probably why they sold her to us in the first place—they knew she was in foal and they didn't want to deal with it. Woke up one morning and one of the stallions was out with the mares, or something like that, so they crossed their fingers behind their back and threw her in with the others just to get rid of her."

Mom was at the door. "What? What is it? Is everyone okay?"

"Got a foal is all," said Daddy as he went past her into the kitchen.

"A foal!" She put her hands on my shoulders. "Do they look okay?"

I said, "It looks great, Mom!"

"Should we call the vet?"

Daddy said, "First, we'll call the Lord. The Lord will decide."

I kind of did not like that, because in my experience, the Lord didn't always decide as I would have.

Daddy said, "Abby can help me outside. She's already missed the school bus."

Mom looked at the clock and said, "Well, she has."

That was the second good thing to happen that day, and it was only seven a.m.

We had some toast and went back out. The first thing we had to do was clean the biggest stall and put all new straw in, and lots of it. I was happy to think that the Jewel and her foal would be able to snuggle down into the bedding and stay

15

warm. Then we took a halter down to where the mare was. We approached her carefully, but she was friendly, just the way she had been before she foaled. After I put the halter on her, Daddy stood looking at the baby. It was now full day, and even I could see that he was a colt, and a nice one—strong, with a well-set neck and an alert look about him. He wasn't crowding against the mare, either—he already had a mind of his own ("Not a good sign," said Daddy).

The colt would turn away from the mare and stare out over the crick or up the hill, then leap into the air and kick out or trot around in a little circle, and she would nicker at him, but not sounding as though she was worried. More of an "I'm here" than a "Watch out!" In the end, we didn't try to touch him, we just walked the mare slowly up the hill, letting her stop and call him anytime she wanted to. He came along, but not without jumping and frolicking. I couldn't stand the idea that we might name him George, but Daddy was strict about the names because he said I already got too attached to some of them. If he let me name them, then I would pine for them after they were gone. So I didn't say anything.

When we got to the top of the hill, Daddy held the other mare so that she wouldn't try anything, and we went through the gate. The Georges were all eyes and ears, too. Every one of the horses was whinnying.

The hardest thing was getting the colt into the stall. The way we did that was, I held open the stall door as wide as it would go, Mom stood inside with Jewel, and Daddy ranged around behind the foal, not driving it, but being a barrier if it wanted to go away. The key was to let the mare call him and let him find her. Even though it took a few minutes for him to make up his mind to go through that scary doorway, and even though her nickers got just a little louder and more nervous, neither one did panic, and pretty soon we had them locked in the stall. If you ask me, the mare looked relieved. She had a nice clean bucket of water and she drank about half of it. The colt gave us a stare and then started to nurse.

Mom said, "Did you look around down there?"

Daddy shook his head, then said, "You two should do that. It's time she learned."

"What?" I asked.

Mom said, "We've got to go down the hill and look around for the bag and placenta. We've got to see if all the placenta came out."

"I guess you'll tell me what that is when we get there."

"You know what that is. It's what feeds the baby through the umbilical cord when it's inside the mother. If any of it stays inside the mare, she can die."

"Let's go!"

But the placenta was there, lying crumpled in the grass. Mom carefully laid it out, fitting together the pieces we could find the way you would a jigsaw puzzle. "Seems complete," she said. "We had a mare once—" But then she decided not to tell me that story, and so I knew it was a bad one.

"Daddy doesn't like the foal."

"A foal is a lot of work. And a colt is more work. A big lively colt is the most work."

When we got back up the hill, Daddy said, "Well, I guess if you aren't going to school today, you'd better start riding."

I rode the pony George first. Daddy said that there usually wasn't much market for a pony, but when someone needed one, then a pony was exactly what they needed and the only thing. Our pony was medium-sized—he came up about to my chin (all the horses were taller than I was by at least an inch or two). Once the spring rolled around, Daddy thought he could sell that pony to some people who had an English riding school out on the coast. In the meantime, no pony burned much hay—in fact, you had to be really careful about giving a pony too much feed or it would founder, which is when a horse's feet get hot and swell inside the wall of the hoof, except there's nowhere for the feet to swell to but down through the sole, so the horse (or pony) can get crippled and die.

I rode the pony around the ring with the English saddle, walk, trot, canter, turn right, turn left, back up, go in a big circle, go in a little circle. Three days a week of this was enough for the pony. Once I had untacked him and picked his feet and put him back with the other Georges, I went and peeked in the stall.

The foal was lying down, his back legs folded underneath him and his front legs stretched out. He had his nose on his knees and his eyes closed, but then he lifted his head and looked at me, his ears flicking back and forth. The mare nickered to him, a low ruffling sound, and he put his nose up to her. She touched it with her own, then took another bite of her hay. Behind me, Mom said, "Now, it's okay to look at them, but you let him and her get to know each other for three or four days before you introduce yourself. Sometimes if you get between a mare and a foal and get your smell on the foal, she'll reject him." The foal flopped over and stretched out in the straw. His legs looked incredibly long and thin, loose, like noodles. If I hadn't seem him jump around on them, I wouldn't have thought such a thing was possible.

After the pony, I rode the other Jewel, then the chestnut George. They were little girl material all the way. Then Daddy said, "Okay, Abby, get up on that one again." He tossed his head toward Ornery George.

"I thought you were going to ride him a couple of times."

"My back hurts. My feet hurt."

"I don't believe you."

"I think you'll do fine. I don't want him to get used to me. Sometimes when a strong man pushes a horse around and makes him do what he's supposed to, then he's worse when the girl gets back on him. You rode him fine before. Let's just try it."

I knew better than to say I didn't want to try it.

But in spite of how nice the pony had been and the other two horses, it made me nervous to put my foot in the stirrup, and then when he stepped away from me and pinned his ears, I felt my mouth get dry. That was a new one for me. Daddy came up behind me and threw me into the saddle and said, "Now go forward. Don't give him a chance to think about it."

I kicked his sides and he squirted forward, then went off at a trot. I tried to remember what my goal was—Daddy said I was to have a goal every time I got on. After thinking hard about my goal for a few seconds, I decided that it was only to be less nervous. I took some deep breaths.

"What are you all stiffening up for? You look like you're riding a pogo stick."

I made my hips loosen up and I straightened the small of my back so that I sat more deeply in the saddle. He said, "That's better."

When we got to the end of the ring, we trotted back, then did a few circles in both directions. George seemed half asleep. Daddy said, "Stir him up. He's ignoring you."

I slapped his sides with my legs, and there he was, kicking out. He kicked out so high that he nearly tossed me over the front. As it was, I got the saddle horn in my stomach. He stopped, I kicked him on, he kicked up again, I pulled him up.

"Now he's got you," said Daddy. "He's got your number and he's dialing it. He's saying, 'Abby, I don't want to go and you can't make me.'"

"I can't."

"You can."

"I can't."

"You have to. *You* have to. It doesn't matter if I do. It's your number he's got, not mine."

While we were talking, he'd come over to me, and now he was standing, looking up at me, his hand on the pommel of the saddle. I could feel that I was shaking now, both because Daddy was giving me his sternest look and because I could feel George beneath me, ready to take off again. I took some more deep breaths and said, "I can't." Then I said something I hadn't ever said before: "And I'm not going to."

Daddy wasn't always as strict about sassing as he thought he was—you could say, "I would rather not," or, "No, thanks," and sometimes he would give in. But I had used "a tone" with him, so now I looked down, so as not to have him stare at me anymore, and jumped off. I handed him the reins, then walked away, back toward the barn, where I couldn't resist peeking at the colt. But then I went out the other end of the barn and around into the house without letting Daddy see me. I went up to my room and closed the door. There was always homework.

Anvil

Hoof Pick

Horseshoes

Chapter 3

MY BROTHER, DANNY, DIDN'T GET KICKED OUT FOR TALKING back to Daddy, but that's how it started. We call him Danny, Mom and I, but Daddy has always called him Daniel, because that was the real biblical name. Daddy wanted Danny to grow into his name—Daniel. There was a time when I was a little kid when Daddy and Daniel were "just like this!" as Mom would say, putting her forefinger and her middle finger together and holding them up for you to see. But after Danny turned twelve and got to be as tall as Daddy, they went from being "just like this" to being "cut from the same cloth," and it was a rough, tough cloth. Neither one of them could say anything that the other didn't disagree with, which meant that Daddy considered Danny "ornery" and Danny considered Daddy "stubborn." It didn't help that they looked pretty much alike and could stare each other down, eye to eye. The whole thing made my mom very sad, but there wasn't a thing she could do about it. She would say, "It's hard to be a man in the Lovitt family," and then shake her head.

I remember on the day Daddy kicked Danny out, which was before Halloween, I was in my room with the door open, braiding a set of reins. I heard Mom go into Danny's room and start in with him. She said, "Honey, it's fine for you to read any book you want, especially if it's a schoolbook, but you don't have to discuss it with him or even tell him what's in it. You know it will make him mad, so just keep it to yourself."

"He should know about evolution."

"He does know about that."

"Then why didn't he ever tell me? So that when I raise my hand in science class and make my contribution, as Mr. Freer wants me to do, they can all laugh at me? It's a good thing I'm bigger than all those guys, or I would have gotten beat up over lunch period."

"Well, your dad and the science teacher disagree about a few things, but you can learn what the science teacher has to teach you and read the book and make up your own mind without getting into it with your dad."

"I can?"

"You can. I wish you would."

Danny generally did what Mom told him, so what happened at the table wasn't precisely about the science class thing. However, it was about breaking rules. It was Saturday-night supper. Because Mom had to cook for church the next day, we were having something simple—just some minute steaks and gravy with rice and string beans. It was good. Then Danny said, "I'm going to the movies with Frankie Horner. He drives and he's picking me up. I've got the money myself."

"You're not going out with a pack of boys alone in a car."

"It's not a pack of boys. It's me and Frankie and one other guy. We're going to a movie."

"What movie?"

"It's just *Frankenstein Meets the Space Monster*. It's—"

"It's a piece of foolishness, I'm sure."

"Well, yeah, but the other kids said it was good. It's been out for weeks. Everybody's seen it—"

"And if every kid in your class—"

Mom and I gave each other a look.

"Poked a rattler with a sharp stick—"

Danny started scowling and then said in his own sarcastic voice, "Would you get in line to poke it, too?"

Daddy slammed down his knife and fork. Danny had never talked quite like that before. Mom said, "Danny—"

I said, "Daddy—"

And then Danny said, "Goddammit." And he said it in a voice that you would only use if you had said it before, more than once, and if you were used to saying it, not as if it was the first time.

Daddy said, in his extra-quiet, you-better-watch-it tone, "What was that?"

I don't know that Danny had realized what he was saying

before he said it, and maybe he was sorry, but it was clear as day that he wasn't going to back down, and then he said, "I said, 'Goddammit.' What I meant was, 'Goddammit to hell.'"

"So," said Daddy, "some boys who taught you to take the holy name of the Lord in vain are going to pick you up and take you to see a fantasy movie about evil and hate. Am I right?"

Danny backed down a little here, and he said, "It's harmless. I'm s—"

But now Daddy was madder, because the way it works with him, something starts him off, and at first he's not so mad, but then he thinks about it a little and he gets hotter and hotter. Usually he has to go in his room and pray and seek the righteousness of the Lord before he calms down (though Mom said it was worse before I was born). Anyway, Daddy didn't hear Danny begin to back off, and so he leaned forward across the table and landed a blow, the chastisement of the Lord, which was a punch across the jaw. This knocked Danny out of his chair, but he came up swinging and crawled across the table, putting his knee in the green beans, and returned the punch, and then the two of them fell off the table and were rolling around on the floor, yelling and hitting. And truly, I had never seen anything like this in my life. My mother jumped up and was shouting, "Mark! Daniel! Mark! Daniel!" but they didn't pay one bit of attention to her.

Finally, Daddy had Danny pinned because after all, he did outweigh him quite a bit, and by this time Danny was crying. Daddy let him up, saying, "Dear Lord forgive me!" but Danny wasn't going to forgive him, and he went into his room and packed a bag, and when those boys arrived in their car, even though Daddy was shouting, "Don't you go with them, young man! Don't you do it or you will find yourself in very hot water!" Danny walked out the door with his bag and never looked back.

He came home a couple of days later for more stuff, and he and Daddy haven't spoken since, though Mom goes and sees Danny from time to time and takes him things like biscuits and bread and probably money, though he doesn't need money, because he works for the horseshoer, Jake Morrisson, and even though Jake shoes our horses and Danny doesn't come over when Jake does, Daddy doesn't mind that he has a real job and a hard job.

One night, I heard him say to Mom, "It's just as well that he doesn't go to school anymore, because the higher you get in school, the more they teach you that's against the Lord." But they won't speak until Danny is moved to come forth with a humble and sincere apology and reaffirm the authority of his father, which I don't think is going to happen. Daddy and Mom pretend that everything is fine. Daddy even said once that he himself left home at sixteen and started supporting himself, and what's wrong with that?

What's wrong with it was that everyone was so angry and that Danny didn't help me ride the horses anymore. Daddy pretended that everything was the same as it was the previous year when we had ten horses waiting to be sold and they were getting ridden every day and really working. Ten horses in the late winter was good. Along about March, just when you'd gotten them ready, spring came, the flowers bloomed, and the buyers started feeling like they needed new mounts, or better mounts, or prettier mounts. Daddy could make enough in March to be a nice cushion for the whole rest of the year. This year we had five horses, and now it was four, until the foal was weaned.

These were not the things I was thinking about when I refused to ride Ornery George, but I thought about them later, that night in my bed. Danny and Daddy had been "cut from the same cloth" for so long that our house was quieter and more peaceful without him, and sometimes I was glad of that, or at least relieved. But Danny had always been fun for me— never (well, hardly ever) the kind of brother who hits or teases, more the kind of brother who teaches you to play checkers and pick-up sticks, or helps you saddle your horse, or lets you have the last cookie if you really want it. I missed him, but it was hard to get to see him, so I tried not to think about it. Daddy said that it was the job of the prodigal to return, not the job of the righteous to go after him.

The next day, of course, I had school again. I sat through math (unilateral equations), science (the cell), English (*Hard Times*), social studies (the Pharaohs), health (protein, fats, and carbohydrates), and homeroom. Through all of these classes, the Big Four (Linda, Mary A., Mary N., and Joan) sat in a single row in the front, passing notes when Mr. Jepsen wasn't looking and poring over their books when he was. They weren't actively mean to me, but I had known since fifth grade that they would be if they thought I was acting "weird" or "stupid," so I sat across the aisle from them, beside the window, not looking out, but thinking of the foal. Already, after only a single day, he was stronger and more inquisitive. When I went out to feed that morning, he had been peering over the top of the stall door, just to see what he could see, and though I didn't touch him, he looked as though he would have let me if I'd tried. His eyes said, "Who are you? What do you want?" I just murmured in a low voice, "You'll see, little buddy, you will certainly see."

Stella and Gloria sat with me at lunch, no problem. Stella was extra nice to me. "Oh, Abby. I know you like oranges, and I don't care. Here's mine. I'll eat your apple." While I was sharing the orange with Gloria, Stella leaned toward us and said, "He called me again last night. We talked for half an hour." She glanced over her shoulder at Brian Connelly. Brian Connelly was a boy Gloria and I had known since kindergarten, who had spent the first four years of elementary school picking his nose. He was now kind of good-looking. His mom let him grow his hair long, for one thing, and he also liked to talk to girls, which was a rarity among the boys we knew.

She whispered, as if it were a secret, "He says he got a stereo of his own for Christmas! So did I! We both thought that was such a coincidence. And I got a Dusty Springfield album and he got a Rolling Stones album. And you know, Dusty Springfield and the Rolling Stones are *both* English, so we thought that was a coincidence. He doesn't like the Beach Boys at all."

Gloria rolled her eyes, but discreetly, as if she were sort of laughing at Stella, but not really. At my house, at any rate, we didn't listen to the Rolling Stones or Dusty Springfield or the

Beach Boys. More Bob Wills and Porter Wagoner on the radio or on Mom's old record player that only played 45s. Danny probably listened to all of those English bands now, but I didn't know. Even so, I said, "My brother likes Dusty Springfield."

"She's really pretty," said Stella.

"Yeah," I said.

Gloria made a face.

Stella went on, "I love the way she does her makeup."

"Let's talk about something else," said Gloria.

I said, "We had a foal."

"What's that?" said Stella.

Gloria snorted, but I decided to be nice. I said, "It's a baby horse."

"I thought that was a colt or something."

"It is a colt. Our foal is a colt. A colt is a male and a filly is a female, and a foal is just a baby."

"Is it cute?"

"Really—" But the foal wasn't cute, I thought, he was . . . stirring. I said, "I don't know if—"

"You know what Brian told me?"

"What?" said Gloria.

"He said that Martin Selden likes you."

"Who, me?" said Gloria.

Stella nodded excitedly.

"I think I'm going to puke," said Gloria.

I said, "Right now?"

"If I have to."

"But—" said Stella.

Gloria turned her back on Stella and leaned toward me. She said, "Can I come home with you on the bus and see the foal? My mom wouldn't mind. She'd like to see it when she picks me up. I can call her from your house."

Over Gloria's shoulder, I could see Stella looking a little surprised. I didn't know what I thought about that. I would have expected to be happy, but I wasn't, really. Gloria could be pretty mean if she lost patience. I said, "Not today. Not till he's three or four days old, my daddy says."

Gloria flipped her hair over her shoulder, practically in Stella's face, and said, "Okay, we'll come over the weekend, then. That will be fun." She didn't say a word about Stella coming along, and neither did I, since it was Gloria's idea. But when the bell rang, and they went to their sixth period, they were laughing.

That afternoon, I rode the pony, the chestnut George, and the Jewel. All three were extra good, and Daddy even dragged out some poles and tubs and had me jump the pony over some cross-poles. Every time the pony jumped, Daddy laughed and said, "Look at those knees! Right together and up around his chin." Then he went inside and got a tablecloth. To tell the truth, it was the very one that we were eating off of that week, but Mom must have been somewhere else. Anyway, Daddy set a pole so that it was straight across two of the smaller tubs and draped that tablecloth over the pole so it fluttered a little in the wind. He said, "Now take him over that."

I was sitting on the pony about twenty paces from the jump, just beginning to wonder whether I liked that idea, when the pony picked up a trot and trotted right down toward the fluttering cloth. I sat tight, not knowing what he would do, but I didn't kick him or turn him off. I just looked over the top of the jump at the peak of the barn roof, and sure enough, he picked up a canter and popped over that square of fabric like he'd done it a hundred times. Daddy said, "I bet this little guy'd jump anything, really."

I knew what that meant.

Now Daddy got a bee in his bonnet. For the next few days, he went looking for anything you could possibly jump. Not only the tablecloth, but a couple of kitchen chairs, a row of wastebaskets, the wheelbarrow, a low clothesline hung with dish towels, a length of picket fence, two hay bales with a place setting of dishes on them. The pony jumped everything. Daddy got happier and happier and said that in the spring, he would take me to the coast, where they had the English-style horse shows, because that pony was like gold coins in the bank, and he was pretty, too, gray with black points and a black mane. Every day I was to brush him all over and then rub him with a folded-up piece of an old woolen sweater to make him shine.

The pony didn't seem to mind the foal, so after I rode, when I was doing the extra grooming, I cross-tied him in the aisle outside the stall where the mare and foal lived. The foal would stand there, looking at us and flicking his ears back and forth and ruffling his nostrils. He had a high whinny that made me laugh, and sometimes he just whinnied all at once for no reason, even though his mom was standing right behind him, eating her hay. Then the foal would give a high squeal and lift up on his hind legs for a moment and toss his head like he had more energy than he knew what to do with. But I still didn't go up to him or pet him, even though it seemed to me that he was saying, with every look and every whinny, "Come here! Come here! I want to get to know you!"

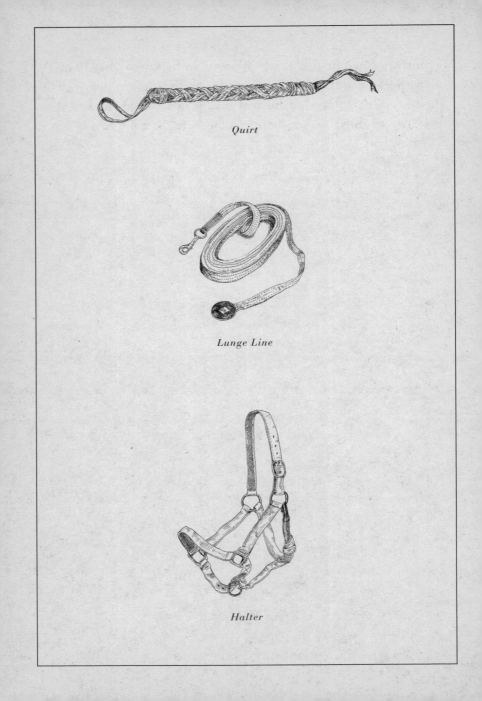

Quirt

Lunge Line

Halter

Chapter 4

ON SATURDAY MORNING, THE FOAL WAS FIVE DAYS OLD. IT WAS a nice day—not wet and almost warm—so after breakfast, we went out to the barn, all three of us. Mom got a halter and lead rope and took the other Jewel out of the big mare corral and led her into one of the stalls. Then she put the halter on the foal's dam, opened the stall door, and brought her out. Daddy and I stood to either side of the door, ready to guide the foal if he went the wrong way. Mom stopped with the mare about ten feet out into the yard, and we waited for what seemed like a long time. The foal stood in the doorway with his nose poked into the sunlight, snorting. A couple of times, he struck out with his front hooves, as if he were a big tough guy, and then he jumped through the doorway, jumped up to the mare, and pressed himself against her for a moment before Mom led her on to the corral. The mare went quietly. The foal leapt and bucked in the breeze. His ears flicked back and forth. After we closed up behind him and then shut the gate to the corral, he reared straight up into the air and galloped for about ten strides. I guess he just couldn't believe how free he was. The mare trotted after him, nickering.

Even though I had horses to ride, I stood by the fence, watching him play and laughing. Finally, I heard Daddy say, "Abby! I'm talking to you! If your friend is coming over, you'd better get started."

I turned to him. "I don't want to name him George."

"'Little George' is fine. We'd know him perfectly well by that."

"No, Daddy. He's not a George. He's too bright and—"

"Cocky?"

This was a dangerous word. Daddy hated a "cocky" horse, but I said, "Well, yeah."

Daddy sighed, took out his handkerchief, wiped his nose. Then he said, "Okay, child, I see the handwriting on the wall."

The handwriting on the wall was something in the Bible. It said, "Mene, mene, tekel, upharsin," and I didn't know what it meant really. In our family it meant "Watch out, you're in trouble." But Daddy put his handkerchief back in his pocket and said, "If we've got him, we'd better do a good job with him. So name him what you like."

The colt skittered around the mare, his feet fluttering. He stopped dead and stared at us, leapt up again as if we were just too much, and then settled down and began to nurse. We both laughed. I said, "Jack is okay. Jack is better than George."

"As in Jack Sprat could eat no fat, his wife could eat no lean?"

"No, as in Jack be nimble, Jack be quick, Jack jump over the candlestick."

"Okay, but let's go for Little Jack Horner, who said, 'What a good boy am I.'" Daddy ruffled my hair, and I gave him a hug.

The pony had been jumped a lot, so we gave him the day off. The chestnut George had a long work—walk, jog, lope, a few sliding stops, some spins, and some gallops around the barrels, though not at top speed. It was fun. I worked on his manners—sidestepping to the gate so I could open it, going through, sidestepping the gate closed and waiting until I was ready to go. He was supposed to wait quietly, no shuffling his feet or trying to put his head down, and he did. He was ready to sell, really. He was just waiting for a buyer, and truly, a little girl could ride him. After I got off him, Daddy took him over to the washstand and combed out his mane and tail, which were long and full, then he trimmed his whiskers and the hair in his ears. You could just see him in a parade down Main Street, his tail flowing behind him.

In the meantime, I got on the other mare. At first, she kept taking me to the end of the ring nearest the corral where the foal was. She would stop and prick her ears. She had that stiffness in her body that sometimes means a horse is going to pull away and run off, but she didn't. She got used to the foal, and pretty soon, she was passing that end of the ring without a look in the foal's direction, though if he squealed or whinnied, she would flick her ears. She had her normal work. She wasn't as far along as the chestnut George, but she was willing enough most of the time. When I kicked her or flicked the quirt at her,

her usual response was "Do I have to, well, okay," which is fine for a riding horse. That means more people who don't really know what they are doing feel safe. She was already starting to shed, so when I was finished with her, Daddy and I each took currycombs and curried off the dull winter hair. Underneath, that Jewel had a regular bay coat, red enough. She had a kind eye and a very pretty head that would make her valuable.

So, we put her away in the stall and looked at each other.

Daddy hadn't made me ride Ornery George after I refused. Probably he complained about me to Mom, and she recommended patience, because look what happened with Danny, and Daddy didn't know how to back off, and I would change my mind in a few days—I knew all the arguments. Now, as we looked at each other, I was trying to decide how stubborn he was going to be, and he was trying to decide how stubborn I was going to be, and, to be honest, I myself didn't know how stubborn I was going to be, but then he said, "Let's put him on the line."

This meant we would take him into the arena with his saddle and bridle on and run a long tape through the ring of his bit and then up over his head behind the ears and attach it to the ring on the other side. He would then trot or canter around Daddy and get rid of some of his extra energy. Usually, Daddy wasn't a big fan of using the line, because he thought it just made them fitter and fitter without teaching them much, so I knew he was exercising mercy—after some time on the line, Ornery George would be too tired to buck, and we might get a session in during which he didn't misbehave. Part of the problem with a misbehaving horse was that the more he misbehaved, the more he got into the habit of misbehaving, and, as Daddy often said about just about everything (but mostly about smoking, which he had once done), "Old habits die hard."

Ornery George looked okay. He was a brown horse with a smallish head, good legs, an arched neck, and a short back. He had great feet, which was why Daddy had liked him in the first place—no foot, no horse. He didn't have to be shod at all, just rasped every six weeks. But he didn't ever look at you, or if he did, it was only secretly, when you weren't looking at him. Most horses, when they came from the sale barn, didn't make eye contact for a while, but then, after days of hay and grooming and talk, they would begin looking for you and at you—not only did you have feed or a carrot, but also, what were you doing? But Ornery George didn't seem to care. The whole time I was grooming him and tacking him up, he pretended that I wasn't there.

Daddy led him into the ring and went to the big end, which was empty. He stood there with the looped line in one hand and a long whip in the other, and he flicked the whip so that Ornery George would turn and trot away, which he did. The way he trotted away showed us pretty clearly that he knew what he was supposed to do, and for one circuit, he did it. But then, as he was coming around the second time, he threw up his head and spun outward with his shoulder, taking the line through Daddy's hands, then trying to gallop to the other end of the ring. Daddy dropped the whip, set his heels, and leaned back against the line. Ornery George came to a stop and tossed his head again.

"Now, Abby," Daddy called, "this is a perfect example of

why you always wear gloves when you are working a horse on a line." He pulled Ornery George back to him and returned to the end of the ring, where he got George on a shorter length of tape and made him go around in a smaller circle, closer to the fence so that the fence could control him a little. Ornery George looked grumpy, but he went around on the line, making quite a few circuits. After a while, Daddy changed the attachment and sent him in the other direction. Then he said, "Well, he doesn't make you happy to be in his company, does he?"

"His jog is smooth. In fact, all his gaits are smooth. I like that part."

"He has his good qualities. But I admit they aren't mental ones. He's quiet now, though. You want to get on him?"

This wasn't a question.

"We'll stay at this end of the ring. Just do a few things to remind him what a good horse is like."

The worst thing that could happen was for a purchase to be a complete bust. It was bad for us, because it was a loss of money as well as hay. And it was bad for the horse, because if he was untrainable, he might have to go to the knackers. That was where horses were killed and turned into dog food and other things. We had only ever sent one horse to the killers, a mare that was given to Daddy as a last resort, for a dollar. She was fine for a few days, and then, after she reared up on the cross-ties and struck out at him with both front feet, Daddy took her out to the ring and put her on the line. The first thing she did was not, as Ornery George had done, trot off. That mare had backed up and then run toward him where he was standing in the center, her teeth bared and her ears pinned. When he put his arm up to protect himself, she bit him through his jacket. It was kill or be killed with her, and she went off two days later.

I didn't think Ornery George would ever be like that. But if a little girl couldn't ride him, then I didn't know what would happen to him. He was the first one Daddy bought after Danny left that a kid, namely me, had not been able to manage.

I stepped up to the horse, took the reins in my left hand, put my palm on top of his neck, and bent my knee. Daddy threw me into the saddle. Ornery George didn't do anything, but he gave me a look out of the corner of his eye—"Oh, it's you." I settled into the saddle and gave him a little nudge. He walked a step or two but then stopped. Daddy had his back turned, rolling up the line. I gave Ornery George another nudge and, when he didn't move, a little kick. Then *he* gave a kick, just a little kick out with his right foot, quick. What it said was, "I'm the boss. Watch your step." I kicked him again, and he started walking forward. By the time Daddy was watching, Ornery George was going along. Daddy said, "He looks okay today."

So, Ornery George and I had a secret. It was that he was going to do things his way, and I was going to let him, and we were going to get along more or less on that basis. This is not a good secret to have with your horse, because it gives him the upper hand. You always know that there might be something you could ask him to do that he would say no to, but you don't really know what it's going to be, and you're a little afraid of finding out. But I was too chicken to argue, either with Ornery George or with Daddy, so I kicked him into the trot and went around well enough while Daddy said, "He's not a bad horse. Good-looking, nice mover, a little on the dull side. I think I made a good deal for him. He'll work out."

Secretly, Ornery George and I said, "I guess we'll see about that."

Everything we did, we did just enough. His jog was just lively enough. His walk was just energetic enough. He took the proper lead at the lope, but I had to think about making him do it. He dropped into the halt, but not in a balanced way, more as if he weren't bothering to go forward any longer. A halt, as Daddy always said, is different than just stopping. A halt is as much of an exercise as a lope or a jump. You want the horse to think about it, set himself up, and then come to a standstill. Ornery George just stopped. A horse that just stops is doing what he wants to do, not what you want to do. He reined back. He was okay at that, though his ears flattened to show he was unhappy.

I did some figure eights at the trot, trying to make nice circles. When I tried it at the lope, dropping back to the trot to change leads, he bunched up a little for a buck or two but didn't actually do it, even though at the thought he might, my heart began to pound a little. After about twenty-five minutes, Daddy was satisfied, and I dismounted. As I led Ornery George back to the barn to be untacked and groomed, he and I continued to have our secret about who was the boss, but tomorrow was Sunday, I thought, and I wouldn't have to deal with him again until Monday afternoon.

When I was putting him away, Gloria's mom's white Impala turned into our road, and pretty soon here they were. Gloria jumped out of the passenger side, and Mrs. Harris opened her door more slowly and then got herself out of the driver's side.

Mrs. Harris was a big woman, at least a head taller than Mom, and older, too, I think. Gloria was an only child, and Mrs. Harris had always treated her, Mom said, like she didn't know the first thing about children and was afraid of them to boot. But she was nice in her awkward way, and she always talked to me as if Mom and I were about the same age. Now she walked over to me and said, "Good morning, Abby. I hope you're well. It's wonderful to see you." She held out her hand, and I offered her mine to shake. She was wearing sunglasses. "I understand you have a new foal, and I would love to be introduced to the young man." She picked up one of her feet to show me her cowboy boot. She always wore red cowboy boots when she came out. I don't think she'd ever been on a horse.

Gloria had always been about my size, that is, not short and not tall, not fat and not thin. I sometimes wondered if we would look like our moms when we got older, and if so, when her future size would kick in, but it hadn't so far, even though lots of the girls had gotten their growth, as my mom would say. Gloria was wearing jeans, a jean jacket, and sneakers. She seemed excited, and that made me excited, too. I said, "They're out. Over here!"

We walked over to the gate, and in a moment, Mom joined us. She and Mrs. Harris had a little hug.

It was quite sunny and warm by now, and the grass in the mares' corral had greened up nicely, because only one mare was out there much. The foal's dam was eating calmly and the foal was stretched out on his side, sleeping, though his little tail

43

flicked against the grass from time to time, and his little ears flicked, too. Mom said, "Follow me. It's time to get acquainted." She opened the gate.

As we walked toward the mare, she looked up at us and then moved around the foal so that she was between him and us. "Perfect," said Mom. She pulled out a handful of carrot pieces. She said, "Okay, girls, now each of you can take some carrots, and we're going to go up to the mare, not the foal, slowly but confidently, and we're just going to feed her some carrots and pet her and pretty much ignore the baby for a while." We did this. The Jewel ate the carrots quite happily, Gloria and I petted her on the face and down the neck, and Mom slipped the halter on her. She said, "Just keep petting her, all over. As if you were brushing her with your hands." We did this, a little carefully, in case she might change her mind about whether she trusted us, but she stood quietly, keeping her eye on the foal but enjoying the petting.

After a little bit, the foal rolled up onto his chest, blinking a little. His eyelashes were really long. He even yawned, which was very cute. Then he got to his feet. This was a production. First he used his front feet to lever himself up, then he got his back feet under him and pushed off and sort of jumped into the air. Then he shook all over and yawned again. Gloria started laughing and her mother said, "Oh, how darling!" but we just kept petting the mare until after a moment, she walked over to him. Mom followed her, holding the lead rope. The foal started to nurse. Mom said, "Okay, now come over here, nice and easy, and start petting her again, on the side away from him, just petting her. We'll see how she likes it."

She liked it fine. The foal nursed and we petted the mare, Gloria and I at the neck and shoulders on the side away from the foal and Mom in front, stroking her face and head. Mom inched her way to the side the foal was on, and then every so often, she let her hand drop smoothly to his shoulder. Then she stroked him lightly but smoothly, so as not to be mistaken for a fly. He did shiver his skin, the way horses do to shake off flies, but after a few minutes, he even stopped doing that. Then she said, "Okay, Abby, trade places with me." I did and then did just what she had done.

The foal's coat wasn't smooth and soft, like the mare's. It was rough and thick, to keep him warm. And he was warm. Because he'd been lying in the sun, his coat was almost hot. I let my fingers stray through it, but smoothly, like Mom had done. At one point, he stopped nursing for a moment and realized that I was next to him. He jumped a little bit, as if startled, which made me jump, too, and that made Gloria jump, and we laughed. I switched places with Gloria. By this time, the colt was more or less used to us being around and even to us petting him, and he didn't seem nervous. In fact, he got bored and walked away, over toward the George corral, just to look at the geldings. Then he jumped in the air and galloped around for a minute or two.

"Now's the test," Mom said. She followed the mare again when the mare followed the colt. We stood there quietly, just the way we had done before, petting the mare and giving her some more carrots. Finally, the colt turned around and looked at us, all standing there. He snorted and jumped, then stopped and looked. Then, the best thing, step by step, he came toward us, toward his mom. His tail kept flicking back and forth. He stopped, took a step or two, stopped again. But finally he was back beside the mare, him on his side and us on our side. He peeked under her neck at us. Mom's hand moved toward his neck and then stroked it. His skin shivered, but he stood still. "Smart boy," said Mom.

"Oh, how lovely," said Mrs. Harris.

"I think that's enough for one day," said Mom.

"I love him," said Gloria. "You are so lucky, Abby."

I knew I was, but I said, "Daddy says that a foal is a terrible responsibility."

"I have every confidence that you are up to it," said Mrs. Harris.

Mom smiled. We went inside for tea, and Gloria and her mom stayed almost until supper. Gloria had a *Seventeen* magazine with her, and we went into my room and sat on the bed and leafed through it. She pointed at a couple of the models and said, "Did I tell you my cousin Emily saw them in Florida at Christmastime? They were sitting together in the restaurant of the hotel where she was staying, and they all had matching outfits on."

"They must have been doing a shoot."

"I guess. Don't you wonder how much they make?"

"I heard it was like a hundred dollars an hour."

"Wow." We stared at the models cavorting in the snow (this was, after all, the February issue), and then Gloria read me the dating column that was written by the guy they had. It was about whether boys like popular girls best or not. As far as I could tell, he wished that they didn't, but he knew that they did. All in all, Gloria and I had a nice afternoon, just the sort of afternoon we had been having ever since we first played Chutes and Ladders in second grade, ever since we got coloring books and her crayon box (forty-eight colors) was always in perfect order. If she broke one, her mom taped it together so all the tips were the same height. My crayon box would be half empty because even though I only liked certain colors, Daddy said I had to use all the colors before I could have a new box. So Gloria would loan me hers and we would color all afternoon. They went home before supper. We hadn't said a word about Stella, and I didn't know if that was good or bad.

Truck and Horse Trailer

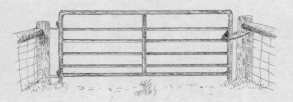

Farm Gate

Mounting Block

Chapter 5

NOW WE COULD MAKE FRIENDS WITH THE COLT, AND WE DID. THE path to a colt's heart is through his mom, and the first thing I did was to make friends with the Jewel (whom I called "Pearl," just between us, as in "Hey, Pearl! Hey, sweet thing! What a good girl you are, Pearl!"). Every time I passed the stall or, if they were out, the corral, I called to Pearl and gave her a couple of pats or a bit of carrot. Pretty soon, she was looking for me and nickering to me. She and the colt stayed out more and more as the weather got better. Mom was cautious about putting the two mares out together with the foal, but the other Jewel didn't mind staying in and eating hay most of the day and then going out at night. I was happy we didn't have any more mares, because that would have meant more stalls to clean.

Daddy started talking about going back to Oklahoma and buying more horses. Horses were cheap in Oklahoma, and there were plenty of them, but now that Danny was out of the house, Daddy hated to leave Mom and me on our own. Then he started talking about whether his brother, Luke, in Oklahoma might bring us some horses, but then Luke would have to be cut in on the profits, and anyway, Luke had a different idea of a good horse from Daddy's idea. Luke was older than Daddy, and though they got along, you never knew whether that would last. Sometimes they didn't fight for a month and sometimes only for a few days. Luke hated for Daddy to "boss him around" or "tell it to him straight" (whichever of these it was depended on your point of view). Whenever they had a fight, Mom said that Daddy felt a strong obligation to witness to Luke, but older brothers, in particular, didn't care to be witnessed to by the boys they had spent a lifetime beating up and bossing around. So, for the time being, there were no horses from Oklahoma. The other thing my mom said once in a while was, "Mark, you should make things up with Danny."

"He needs to work at a hard job for a while and see what life is like."

"If he works long enough, he'll never come back."

"If it's hard enough, he'll learn his lesson."

"You never know what lesson he's learning."

They went round and round like this. But it was a touchy subject, and Mom was careful to not bring it up very often. I think she thought that the idea of horses from Oklahoma and the idea of making up with Danny would come together of their own accord, and better not to push them together before Daddy was ready. In the meantime, she said to me, "You know your grandfather and his brother Eben didn't speak for thirteen years because once Eben got drunk and drove home in the wagon, forgetting your grandfather in town. I don't think the family ever stopped arguing about what that *meant*. When you argue about what things *mean*, they just get bigger and bigger."

The good thing, other than the weather, was that we got a call from a lady who had horses at the biggest riding stable on the coast. A girl wanted a pony. The girl was nine, an "advanced beginner" but small. The lady, who had seen Daddy's ad in the newspaper, wanted to come out, but Daddy insisted that it would be his pleasure to trailer the pony to the coast, and then we spent three days getting ready, which meant not only cleaning up the pony and me getting out my nicest English-style riding clothes, it also meant Daddy washing the truck and the trailer.

"Now, Abby," he said as he did, "this is something you should know, a business practice. If this lady were to come out here, she would see our place and she would think that we really couldn't possibly have a pony that would be good enough for her client. If we drive there, though, and we are all cleaned up and shined a bit, then she'll look at our old truck and trailer and say to herself that she's getting a deal on the pony, but the fact that everything is spic and span will tell her that we are *economical* rather than *poor*. She'll be sure she's getting a good deal on the *right* pony." He suggested that Gloria come along, and that was fine with me. I knew her mom would dress her up so that she would look good at the fancy stable.

I'd been polishing the pony with the sweater every day, and even though a gray doesn't shine up as brightly as a chestnut, he looked good and felt good—his coat was as slick as a piece of silk. Daddy could hardly contain himself. He even made Mom iron his jeans on the Friday night before we left.

The stable was about an hour away. I had heard of it but never been there. It wasn't on the way to anywhere, but rather off by itself under a big stand of pines. You had to go through a gate and down a special road to get there. Daddy would have had to pay a dollar just to drive down that road, except that he told the guard he was taking a pony to the stable and the guard waved him past. We drove for a while on the road through a forest—with the windows open, you could smell the pines—but it wasn't cheerful. Fog wafted here and there, and all of the houses were behind big walls and gates. There were, needless to say, no kids playing in the streets. It was like the country but not country. Walls, houses, lawns, and gardens but no animals or fields. Even so, Gloria and I picked out houses—or, rather, mansions—that we thought were pretty.

The lady, who introduced herself as Miss Slater, was waiting for us at the gate to the stable. She was small, not much taller than I, but a little on the wide side. She was wearing copper-colored English-style riding breeches that were wide on top, brown tall boots, and a brown wool jacket. Even though it wasn't that cold, she had gloves on. Daddy stopped the truck and she came to the window with a big smile, which made her look prettier than I thought she had been, and she told us where to park and unload the pony. She gave Gloria and me a nice smile and said to me, "So! You must be Abby! You're going to show us what this pony can do!"

I said, "Yes, ma'am," the way I was supposed to. Daddy opened the back of the trailer and went in. A moment later, he brought out the pony. Miss Slater said, "What's his name?"

Daddy said, "George," with a perfectly straight face.

"Hello, George," said the lady. She put her hands on her hips and stared at the pony while Daddy stood him up. The pony's ears were pricked, and I might have said he was nervous, but he did stand quietly while she walked all around him, then went up to him and picked up his feet and opened his mouth. In the meantime, Gloria and I pretended to be perfectly well-mannered girls and that we were just standing there doing what we'd been told to do, but really we were edging closer and closer toward the gateway to the inner court of the stable so we could get a look.

The whole stable was painted white, and all of the stall doors and windows were painted with dark green trim. Horses' heads looked out over every door, and the courtyard was full of people—some of them were girls or women dressed like Miss Slater, and others were men in overalls who were cleaning stalls. Miss Slater said, "Not bad." I looked at Daddy, who had his poker face on. "Let's see the little fellow go."

I held the pony while Daddy got out the English tack, and Gloria helped him saddle up. When I went to get on, though, the lady said, "Abby, did you bring your hard hat?"

"No, ma'am."

"We'll lend you one. Why don't you lead the pony through here."

We followed her into the courtyard. Everyone there stopped what they were doing and stared at us. The first hard hat she handed me came down over my eyes; the second one sat on my head like a mushroom cap. Gloria started to laugh, but I poked her a good one. Finally, Miss Slater found one— nice black velvet—that fit me. I was relieved. We walked the pony to the mounting block and I got on. Then we went out of the courtyard and over to the arena.

There were five or six horses and riders in the arena—no ponies—and all of them looked at us as I rode George in. Of course, some of the girls said, "Oh, isn't he cute! Look at him!" but I pretended not to hear them. I walked across the arena and then turned left and walked along the rail. The pony flicked his ears here and there, but he minded his manners. After two circuits, we made a little U-turn and went back the other way. Miss Slater called out, "Abby! Please pick up a trot." And so we did. Some horses get into a ring full of other horses and they don't like it because the other horses come too close. Others think that if the ring is full of quiet horses, then every- thing must be okay—no mountain lions anywhere nearby. That was how the pony was. He liked other horses and liked feeling that he didn't have to keep his eye out.

After we had shown off the walk, trot, canter, halt, rein back, and a few turns in either direction, she motioned me into the center, and we trotted over a few poles. Daddy was standing by the rail, chewing on a piece of straw and talking to one of the ladies. I was sure he was putting on his Oklahoma accent so that everyone would think he was the biggest hick in town. We jumped a few low jumps, and then I pulled him up in front of her and said, "Ma'am. Just so you know, he'll jump about anything. Daddy had him jumping over two chairs draped with a tablecloth the other day. He didn't look right or left."

"Hmm," said the lady.

I could tell that she was trying to look undecided, but she seemed happy underneath that, so I knew she liked the pony.

Now she took the rein and led us to the fence, where a girl in fancy riding clothes was sitting. The lady said, "Abby, this is Melinda. She's the girl who's looking for a pony."

Melinda had white eyelashes and big eyes, which made her look like she had just seen a ghost. She reached out and put her fingers on the pony's neck, then she said, in a very low voice, "Is he nice?"

"Oh, sure."

"Is he *always* nice?"

"Well, we've only had him for about six months, but he's always been during that time."

"You're a good rider."

"But he's well behaved anyway." I waved toward Gloria. "She can't ride very well, and he's always fine with her, too."

"My dad thinks I should have a show pony."

I jumped off.

Getting Melinda onto the pony was a big job, as she was practically limp. It was like she could hardly hold herself up as soon as she stepped inside the ring. For one thing, she acted like she was sure one of the other horses might come running at us, and she kept flinching and looking over toward them. The lady gave her a leg up, but as Melinda bent her knee, she sort of crumpled. Finally, since Melinda was small, the lady just put her hands around her waist and set her on the pony. It was Gloria and I who put her feet into the stirrups. The lady fixed the reins in her hands. Melinda closed her eyes for a moment, took a deep breath, and gave the pony a kick. He walked away. He looked a little surprised to see me standing there, knowing that someone was on his back.

The thing was, she wasn't a bad rider. Her heels were down and her thumbs were up and and she sat in the middle of the pony and went with the motion. It was hard to figure out why she was so scared. The pony understood the words "walk," "trot," and "halt" perfectly well and followed every one of the lady's commands. They didn't try a canter. I saw that a life here would be just what a nice pony deserved—not much to do and plenty of time to do it in.

After Melinda got down, Daddy and the lady went off to one side and parleyed for a while, and then he waved me over. He said, "Miss Slater would like to ask you a favor, Abby, dear."

I adopted my most respectful look. She said, "Well, you know, Abby, Melinda's dad would like to see the pony as a good investment, and he is a good investment, but I think he'll need to be shown before Melinda will be ready to show him, so I wonder if you would mind coming over from time to time and taking him in our shows?"

I glanced at Daddy, then said, "I haven't shown English before." I showed western pleasure as a rule.

"But you're a good rider and you say you've jumped the pony a lot, so we can try it. If the pony can't show, I'm afraid that Melinda's father—"

Won't go for it. They didn't have to tell me that. So I nodded. Daddy said, "Miss Slater, that's very kind of you. Abby is eager for all kinds of experience—" and they shook hands. We spent another half an hour with Miss Slater. She gave the pony a real going-over, including holding each leg up really high and then having the pony trot off as soon as she dropped it, but the pony trotted off sound. She looked at his eyes and his teeth again and peered into his ears and ran her fingers the wrong way in his hair to check for funguses or parasites. She even spread apart the hair on the dock of his tail because if a horse has worms, he'll rub his tail. But she didn't find anything, and so she wrote Daddy a check, which he put in his pocket with a serious shake of the hand. It wasn't until we were practically to the gate of the whole area that he started whooping and grinning. Of course, how much he got for the pony wasn't my business or Gloria's, but I knew he'd start bragging about it at some point. All he said to us was, "Well, girls, we can say a prayer of thanks, because the Lord has been good to us today."

Gloria had been my friend for so long that even though she didn't go to our church (and Mom said that, really, they didn't go to any church, unless you called dropping in at St. Dunstan's from time to time "churchgoing"), she never blinked at anything Daddy said about the Lord. All I said was, "Okay." What I was thinking about was going to that horse show to ride the pony. I had heard about it—beautiful horses, and a lot of Thoroughbreds, and everyone perfectly dressed. The horses would have braided manes and tails and sometimes checkerboard patterns combed into their shining rumps. The people would all be wearing velvet hats and their boots would be clean all the way down to the soles, because grooms would prepare the horses. The whole thought made me nervous and excited all of a sudden, especially since I had said yes without really thinking. I let myself imagine it while we were driving through the pines, but then I put it out of my mind as just one of those things that grown-ups say but don't mean.

Daddy was in a good mood for days after the sale of the pony, but I missed the little guy. I didn't think that the girl Melinda felt comfortable enough to really take a liking to him, but I hoped she would at least pet him and give him treats.

In the meantime, now that Daddy had three thousand, five hundred dollars from the sale of a pony he had paid four hundred dollars for, he couldn't wait to get back to Oklahoma and buy some more horses. During this period, he gave me a lot of business tips. For example, when the amount he got for the pony finally came out, he said, "Now, Abby, that extra five hundred dollars we got was because he was gray. Don't forget that. A working horse who's going to live outdoors shouldn't be gray, because that just means that he's going to look dirty all the time—no rancher has the time to wash that horse enough to keep him looking good. But a show horse, and especially a show pony, should be gray, because the judge can't help watching that one just a little longer. A gray show pony stands out, and that's why we got some more money for him. That's a 'premium.'" I don't know that Daddy expected me to go into the horse business when I got older—his sisters got married and never kept up with their riding—but he didn't have Danny to give his tips to any longer, so he gave them to me.

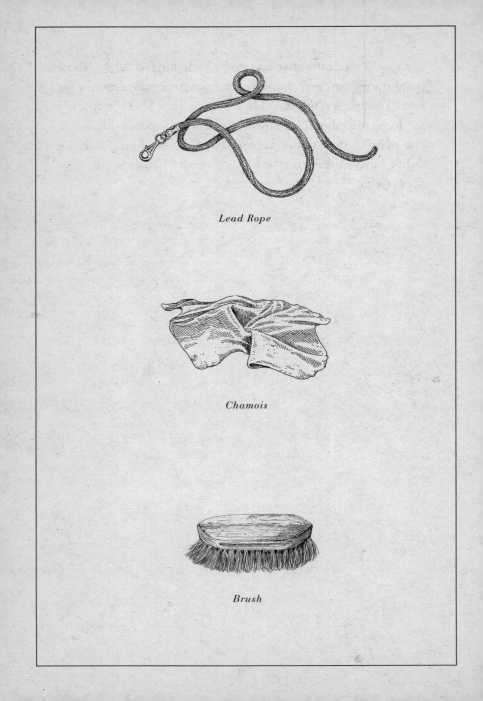

Lead Rope

Chamois

Brush

Chapter 6

WELL, THE MARE DIED. LITTLE JACK WAS A MONTH OLD TO THE day, Daddy was in Oklahoma getting ready to bring the horses back, with Uncle Luke to help him. Mom and I got up Saturday morning to feed the horses.

It wasn't a bad morning—a little chilly, but dry. The first thing we said when we went out the front door was, "Is it too cold for him?" We had left the mare and the foal out for the night. We had done it twice before, because he was getting a little too big for the stall. We decided that it wasn't too cold— he was a big boy and still furry with his foal coat. But as soon as we looked toward the mares' corral, Mom said, "Uh-oh." Normally, they would have been at the gate, waiting for their hay. I said, "Maybe it's all right. Maybe there's enough grass so that she isn't that hungry."

But it wasn't all right. As soon as we got to the top of the hill and looked down, we could see the dark shape of the mare, lying stretched out on her side in the grass, and the foal standing above her, by her rump, poking at her with his nose. While we were running down the hill, she flopped her tail and lifted her head, then tried to lift her front end, but her head fell back into the grass. Jack gave a loud, high whinny, and that was when I started to cry, but we had to keep running anyway.

Mom did some things to try and figure out what was wrong with her—like kneeling down and listening to her belly sounds—but all I did was sit by her head and start to pet her. Even though it was cold, her neck was crusty with dried sweat. Another bad thing was that the hair around the top of her head was worn off, meaning that she would have been rolling around in pain for a long time. But she liked the petting. I stroked her face and ears, and she gave a few grunts and sighs. Mom said, "I think she colicked in the night. Rolling around with the pain might have given her an intestinal twist. Oh, dear. She has no gut sounds at all." Horses always make gut sounds because their digestion is always working.

"She seemed fine when I gave them the hay last night." I always did that around six.

"Oh, there's no telling," said Mom. "What a business." Then she said, "Hey, darlin', does your tummy hurt?"

I kept petting Pearl's head and her neck, and she closed her eyes. In the meantime, the foal came over to me and began to nose my shoulder. I felt his breath on my cheek and twisted around to pet him, too, but he moved away and went back to pushing on the mare and whinnying to her.

"I'm sure he's terribly hungry," said Mom.

"Are you going to call the vet?"

Daddy hated it if we had to call the vet, even though sometimes we did. He maintained that he knew almost as much as most vets, and when they came and said, "Well, Mark, I don't really know what to tell you," you still had to pay them anyway.

Mom was stroking Pearl on the belly, long, kind strokes that the mare seemed to like. At any rate, her eyes were still closed. She said, "Abby, sweetheart, I don't know what the vet could do. Look how swollen her belly is. That means the gases have already built up and the poisons have started to break down her insides. There's nothing he could do that would save her. Honey, I hate to have to tell you this, but she's going to die, and what we have to do is just keep her company. Do you understand that?"

I said, "Yeah. Yes, I do."

She nodded. After a moment, she said, "Okay."

So, we knelt by the mare for a few minutes, Mom stroking her belly and me stroking her head, and she seemed to quiet down and relax. I played with her mane a bit, too. Horses like you to scratch them lightly at the base of their manes, because that's a spot they can't reach themselves. But we couldn't do anything with Jack. He was restless. He kept pushing at her and pawing the ground. Once in a while, he would take a few strands of grass between his lips, but then he would toss his head and spit them out. All the time he was making noise—

little whinnies and nickers and grunts. He went around her a few times.

At one point, he stood behind her tail, reaching across her back leg, trying to nurse from her. He knew where the spot was, but since she was lying down, he couldn't make it work. I was just on the verge of saying to Mom, "Maybe I should—" but I didn't know what I should do, when the mare lifted her head and her shoulders. Mom and I backed away—there was no telling what she would do—and she heaved herself up, shoulders first. She rolled up on her breast and got her front legs under her and then made herself stand up. She gave a huge grunt, almost a groan. When she was up, she spread her legs to each side and kind of staggered in place. Mom was behind me, and she put her hands on my shoulders as if I were going to go and help the mare and she was going to stop me.

The mare stood there with her head down and her ears flopped, and the foal went to his accustomed spot and started to nurse. But it only lasted a minute. She couldn't do it. She began to collapse, and the foal jumped out of the way. When she hit the ground, her eyes were already closed, and I think she died a minute or two later. By that time I was crying so hard I couldn't see, and Mom was crying, too. We got down next to her and petted her and petted her. The foal kept whinnying.

After a little bit, Mom leaned over and listened to her chest, and then she sat up. "Honey, I'm going to get the foal's halter."

When she was gone, I sat back on my heels and looked at the mare. What had happened to her was invisible. Everything about her looked nice—her furry ears, her hooves, her shiny coat, her long tail. I thought of Daddy saying, "The Lord works in mysterious ways." That certainly seemed to be true in this case. I wiped my eyes with my sleeve a couple of times. I couldn't believe two things—how fast it all happened and how soundly we had slept all night when a hundred yards from the house, the mare was dying and the foal was—what? Terrified? Out of his mind? I didn't know.

Mom came back with the halter and the lead rope. It took her a while to get the halter on Jack, because he was throwing his head and putting his nose down to touch the mare—he was very upset—but Mom was patient, and she talked to him in a low voice. She tried over and over, but when it didn't work, she just kept talking and trying. When she finally had it on him, we had to lead him uphill away from the mare. He didn't want to go. He would turn his head and whinny or stop and try to go back, but Mom wouldn't let him. She didn't exactly pull, but she didn't let him go back, either.

My job was to walk alongside him, pushing him a little if he needed it, but otherwise just petting him and keeping him company. We had taught him to lead, so he went along well enough, but there was a terrible racket of whinnies and nickers, and I couldn't believe how sad the sounds made me. I hated to leave the mare by herself down there, even though, as Daddy would have said, she was "happily departed." We got Jack to the top of the hill, through the gate, and into the stall. Then Mom went into the house and brought out a big metal bowl and a half gallon of milk. I was standing outside the stall, leaning against the door, watching him rocket around in there, if anything more panicky than he had been.

We hadn't taken his halter off, so Mom set down the bowl and the milk outside the stall and went in and caught him, snapping the lead rope back on his halter. Then she brought him to the door and said, "Pour some milk in the bottom of the bowl. Not too much. And bring it in." Jack stood next to her, but he kept nodding. I don't think he knew what he was doing.

Mom held him while I brought the bowl to his lips. As soon as I touched the milk to his muzzle, he started smacking them together, but then he put his head up. Mom said, "He doesn't realize that milk is for drinking—he thinks it's for suckling. He's a baby. He'll learn, though. Just hold it still." The bowl wasn't heavy, and there wasn't much milk in it, so I held it as steadily as I could. For the first while, every time Jack got a taste of the milk, he would root upward, but then he learned to drink it (he had already learned to drink water, of course), and pretty soon, he had taken all the milk. Mom said, "Pour out some more. We'll give him a little. But he has to get used to cow's milk, so we can't give him all he wants just yet."

In the end, he probably drank about half a quart. Then Mom brought him some nice grass hay, not so much for him to eat, though a month-old foal would have tried a little of his mom's hay from time to time—but more for him to play with.

By the time we had fed the Georges and the other mare (who was plenty interested in what was going on), I was exhausted. Mom was, too. All we had for breakfast was some Rice Krispies and an orange to split.

There was no calling Daddy—he was somewhere between Oklahoma and California with Uncle Luke and six horses, and unless something went wrong, he wouldn't call us. Mom didn't expect him until Sunday night. And she didn't expect the truck from the rendering plant until Monday morning. "At least it's pretty cold," she said.

We went down the hill with a couple of old horse blankets and laid them over the body of the mare.

We fed Jack a little more of the milk. Otherwise, I stood outside his stall and watched him. He continued to be restless, and much of the time he just stared over the door of his stall, which he also kicked with his knees. I was sure he thought she would be coming up the hill any minute. When he was standing still, I approached him very quietly and started petting him on the neck, first little tickles and light brushings. He seemed to like that, so I made firmer and smoother strokes, down and down and down, and all the time saying, "It's going to be all right, little guy. You'll be all right." I did it on one side of his neck and then on the other. He seemed to like it. I liked it. I didn't really want to do anything else. Even though I had three horses to ride and my room to clean before the end of Saturday, I didn't want to do anything but be with Jack.

When Daddy and Uncle Luke got home, with two geldings and four mares in Uncle Luke's big rig, Daddy was not happy about the death of Pearl, but since he didn't see it, he was more mad than sad. He wasn't mad at me or Mom—we had done our best—he was just mad, or mad again, at the man who had sold him a pregnant mare in the first place.

During the course of the month since Jack's foaling, Daddy had come around to accepting the colt and agreeing that he was a pretty boy—a very pretty boy. He had also looked under the mare's upper lip and found a tattoo, which meant that she was a registered Thoroughbred and had run in races. There was no telling what her real name was, but if we wanted to, we could use the tattoo number to trace her and find out who her sire and dam were and if she had won any money. That was fun to think about, and once Daddy even said, "So maybe we've got another Whirlaway here." Normally, he never let himself think like this about a horse, because gambling was a sin and in lots of states a crime, and horse racing itself was as "crooked as your elbow" (though some of the tracks were very beautiful), but he would never deny that Thoroughbreds were a sight to see, whether they were running or jumping or just romping around in the corral, like Jack. But now the mare had died, and if the whole foal thing had been upsetting before, now it was a real pain in the neck.

And, of course, until the rendering truck came for Pearl, there was no place to put the new mares other than into stalls, which meant straw and cleaning and restlessness—after such a long ride, what they really needed was a chance to walk around and eat some grass. Daddy had planned to put the Georges and the mare and foal in for the night, divide up the new set into mares and geldings, and let them have the pastures until morning, but he didn't want the new mares seeing the dead mare. When I asked him why, he said it was "just not good. Bad way to introduce them to the place." And so there was more work—the geldings outside and six horses in for the night, including Jack, who was still staring and whinnying, but not as badly. We had fed him the milk ten times by then and watched him closely. He seemed okay, but the vet would have to look at him, just to be sure he was all right with it, and all right in general, when he came out to give all the new horses a once-over.

Uncle Luke was not born again. He and Daddy had always gone to the same church, and then Daddy accepted Jesus into his life and went to a different church. Uncle Luke didn't quite understand the difference between the churches or didn't care about the difference. Daddy felt a call to witness to Uncle Luke, but most of the time he kept it to himself. Uncle Luke was older than Daddy by about four years (Uncle John came in between them; he had died as a boy when a mule kicked him in the head), but he was shorter than Daddy by about four inches. He was bowlegged and almost bald. He always wore a bandanna tied around his head and a Stetson on top of that. He had a big silver buckle he'd won roping in the rodeo. His boots had purple morning glories tooled into the leather, and he always wore them because he said that you didn't want to die before you wore out your best pair of boots.

On Monday morning, after the truck came and took the mare away, and after we gave the foal some milk, and while we were waiting for the vet, Uncle Luke said to me, "Abby, let's see you ride a couple of these cayuses." I knew I was going to have to ride all day, because it was a teacher conference day at school, and we had the day off.

I got on Jewel first (Jewel Number 1, since now we had Number 2, Number 3, Number 4, and Number 5, which we named Red Jewel, Blue Jewel, Star Jewel, and Roan Jewel). I showed off her gaits, her stops, her spins, and her figure eights. Uncle Luke leaned on the fence smoking a cigarette. Each time he finished one, he stubbed it out with the toe of his boot, picked it up, broke off the tip, ground the tip between his fingers to make sure it was cool and put the cigarette butt in his pocket. Then he lit up another one by striking a kitchen match against the fence. He blew on the tip of the match until it was cool and broke off the tip and put the two halves in his pocket, too. Finally, I pulled the Jewel up right next to him, and I said, "Uncle Luke, it looks to me like smoking is a full-time job for you. I don't see why you just don't quit."

He laughed. "Quitting would kill me, Miss Abby. I know it, so why chance it?"

"Daddy quit."

"And that was a sight to behold. Put me off of quitting for good. Go get on that other bay. He's a lot better-looking than this nag."

"She's nice."

"I didn't say she wasn't, darlin'. But she's got no spark. Let's see that bay. What's your Dad call the geldings?"

"George. But he lets me call the foal Jack."

"That's big of him."

I ignored this and went to get Ornery George.

While Daddy was gone to Oklahoma, Ornery George and I had gotten along well enough by me skirting all the issues between us. If he was willing to trot but he didn't want to put in more effort to trot out, I let him go at his own pace and more or less got him to go a little faster when he didn't seem to be paying attention. It worked like this—we would be walking. I would kick him up into a trot and he would poke along. If I pushed him, he would pin his ears and switch his tail. Then we would come around the corner of the arena so that we were heading toward the barn, and he would pick up speed, at which point I would give him another kick, and since he was already going faster, he would give me a little extra, which would last almost around the far end, too. Or if I smacked him with the quirt and he kicked because he didn't like it, I would pretend that he really didn't need to be smacked with the quirt again. Riding him made my stomach hurt, but I kept that to myself, another secret Ornery George and I had together.

I went and got him. Uncle Luke helped me brush him off and tack him up, taking a ten-minute break from smoking to do so. Then he offered me a leg up and threw me into the saddle. He said, "Honey, you are light as a feather."

Ornery George started out in a pretty good mood—it wasn't that he was always lazy, it was that he always wanted to do things his way, and then sometimes his way and my way coincided. We did a few of the same exercises that I had done with the mare—walk, jog, lope, some stops, a spin one direction and then the other direction, and then a fairly large figure eight, with lead changes in the middle. Uncle Luke said, "He's a good-looking thing, but he doesn't have the happiest expression on his face. From that I take it that he's not the most eager-to-please animal in the world."

I shook my head. I thought we were having a fairly good day, though. Just then, Ornery George tried to veer for the gate, because he had decided that he was finished. The veer wasn't much, and I pulled him over, but then I gave him a smack with the quirt, just because, ordinarily, that's what you would do to say, "Not yet."

At that, Ornery George started bucking, and he leapt and twisted like a rodeo horse, at least seven or eight big bucks and kicks, with his head between his knees. When I jerked his head out from between his knees and pulled it around, he got it back down there and kept going. I had to hold the horn of my saddle and sit back, but even then he almost got me off. He hadn't had me off in over a month. Finally, Uncle Luke managed to get to us. Ornery George was almost finished, anyway—I could feel it in his body. Uncle Luke grabbed the reins just below the bit, and he said, "*What* the hell do you think you're doing, Mr. Horse?" He gave Ornery George a jerk, and the horse's head shot into the air and he started to back up. Uncle Luke gave him another jerk, and he stopped. His eyes were big and his ears were forward. Uncle Luke said, "Someone doesn't know who the boss is."

"That's true. I—"

"Honey, it's not your job to tell him who the boss is. Your daddy should have made that clear to him months ago."

"He said that wouldn't work."

"Oh, sure it will—"

Just then, Daddy came around the barn and shouted, "Vet's here! Need some help!"

Uncle Luke said, "You walk him out now, and he and I will come to a little understanding tomorrow or the next day when your dad's away for a bit. You got school tomorrow?"

I said, "Yeah, of course."

"Well, we'll have a little school after school."

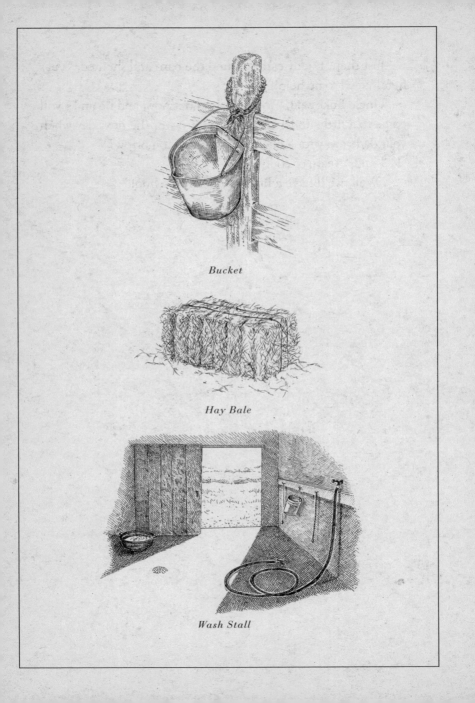

Bucket

Hay Bale

Wash Stall

Chapter 7

On Tuesday, we couldn't ride because of the pouring rain, and on Wednesday, both Mom and Daddy were gone to the chapel to set up chairs for the evening service, which every family had to do in turn—it was our time about once every eight or nine weeks, though if one of the old ladies had to do it, Mom would go and help.

It was therefore a perfect day for Uncle Luke to take Ornery George in hand, as he said. I rode Jewel Number 1 and gave the foal some milk as soon as I got home, and then Uncle Luke helped me with Ornery George. We had a lot more horses to ride now, but the plan was to let them get settled until Friday and begin them Saturday. Uncle Luke was to stay through the weekend and help with that, then go back to Oklahoma. That was why he had brought his own saddle.

It took us about ten minutes to get Ornery George brushed and tacked. Uncle Luke led him into the arena, stood him up, and stepped up on him. Ornery George flicked his ears. He knew perfectly well that he had a different rider, and I knew perfectly well that he would put Uncle Luke to the test sooner or later.

They got on fine for about fifteen minutes. Uncle Luke made George walk up briskly and trot in both directions. It wasn't until the first lope, to the right, that George gave any trouble—I saw him do it. When Uncle Luke asked for the lope, George flicked his ears backward and humped his back. Uncle Luke smacked him with the end of the reins and said, "Get on, now." George didn't respond. This time, Uncle Luke both flicked the reins and spurred him. George pinned his ears, stuck his head down, and bucked. Uncle Luke spurred and smacked him again. George bucked some more. At that point, Uncle Luke did something I'd heard about but never seen—he vaulted out of the saddle, landed on his feet, bent his knees, and set his heels, pulling the horse around with one rein. He made the horse go around a couple of times, and then George stopped moving. But he looked happy. He looked like he thought Uncle Luke had come off because he'd bucked him off.

Uncle Luke walked the horse over to me and handed me the reins. He said, "Bit of a rogue. But we'll work it out of him."

He went into the barn and came out with a coiled rope.

Both Daddy and Uncle Luke had learned how to rope cattle when they were boys, but Daddy hardly did it at all anymore. Uncle Luke, though, still hired out to do ranch work, and he roped cattle all the time. Now he came over and held out his hand for the reins. Then he led George into the center of the arena. George went along nicely.

"Now, Abby," said Uncle Luke, "this is a horse who's had his own way over and over. And underneath that is some stubbornness of temperament. All horses have something—stubbornness or fear or selfishness. Ideally, you'd fix that early on, but a horse who's had several owners, that's a sign that the stubbornness or whatever never got fixed. This horse thinks he's the boss now." He uncoiled a loop of the rope and laid it on the ground. It was big enough so that a moment later he could lead George forward until he had both hind feet in the loop. Uncle Luke then lifted the loop up and brought it over George's tail and haunches so that it came to rest around his loins, just behind the saddle. He slipped off George's bridle and hung it on the fence. Now Uncle Luke tightened the rope. George stood there, his ears flicking suspiciously. Uncle Luke tightened the rope again and pulled on it. All of a sudden, George pinned his ears, gave a big buck, kicked out, put his head down, and started throwing himself around as if the rope were a mountain lion on his back and he had to get it off.

Uncle Luke hung on to the rope and George pulled him around the arena with him. Every time the horse bucked, the rope tightened around his belly. The idea, I could see, was to make bucking so painful that the horse would stop. But George was stubborn, and it took so long I began to get scared. They kicked up a lot of dust. Uncle Luke's hat fell off.

By the time they were finished, the horse had bucked thirty times or more. The saddle was cockeyed, and both of them were panting and sweaty. Uncle Luke pulled the bandanna off his head and wiped his face, then went and picked up his hat.

George just stood there, his sides heaving and his head down. Uncle Luke took a deep breath, coiled up some of the rope, pulled once on the horse. George didn't move. Uncle Luke went over to him with the bridle and put it on him, then he loosened the rope and lifted it over his tail. When it was a loop on the ground again, he stepped the horse out of it, picked it up, and hung it over a fence post. Then he uncinched the saddle and straightened it, cinched it back up. George didn't move except when asked. Uncle Luke walked him around in a couple of small circles, then stood him up and mounted again. He gave George a kick and said, "Move off, now."

George moved off, and I let out my breath. He was still breathing hard—his nostrils were flared and his sides were going in and out. They must have walked about, here and there, for ten minutes. Uncle Luke even had a cigarette, right up on the horse. I was about to go into the house and get a drink of water when Uncle Luke urged George up into a trot and then into a lope. George gave him about a minute, and then he put his head down again, dropped Uncle Luke over his shoulder, spun on his haunches, and galloped to the other end of the arena, leaving Uncle Luke sitting there. Uncle Luke got up and went and picked up his hat. I was beginning to get scared.

Uncle Luke had a smile on his face, but he wasn't happy. He went over to George, took the rein that was dangling down, and brought him over to where I was standing. He handed me the rein.

I said, "Uncle Luke, are you mad?"

"Course not. But I am resolute. You'll never get anywhere with a horse if you get mad."

He went over to the fence and took the coil of rope.

Then he came back to me and said, "You ever see your dad lay a horse down?"

"You mean for the vet?"

"No, I mean to teach him submission."

I said, "No."

"Well, it's an interesting thing to watch."

In the meantime, George was the one who was watching, and as soon as Uncle Luke took the reins out of my hand, he started backing away. Uncle Luke just followed him, but as he was doing so he uncoiled his rope and all of a sudden flicked it over George's foot so that it caught him around the ankle. George noticed this and stopped, just for a moment, but then he backed up another couple of steps. Uncle Luke tossed the rope up over the horn of the saddle and then pulled on it a little so that George had to pick his foot up. At this point, George reared up and struck out with the untied foot. Uncle Luke ducked out of the way. George was snorting. He reared up again, and when he came down, Uncle Luke pulled up his foot with the rope and George fell over onto his side. He struggled once to get up, but Uncle Luke kept hold of his foot with the rope and he couldn't manage it. When George was flat out, Uncle Luke went over and sat down on his shoulder, right in front of the saddle. George lifted his head but then dropped it down again. After that, they just sat there for a few minutes.

The dust settled in the arena.

Uncle Luke pulled out a cigarette and a match and lit up, sitting there. Then, while he was smoking the cigarette, he sang, "Old Stewball was a racehorse, and I wish he were mine. He never drank water. He always drank wine." The song had about four verses. When Uncle Luke had sung all of them and finished his cigarette and put his match and his butt back in his pocket, he stood up.

George lay there quietly, making no effort to move, and Uncle Luke then patted him on the head and said, "There's a good son. Just like that." Finally, he shook the reins and the horse got to his feet. He was trembling, and he looked exhausted. Uncle Luke walked him around again for a minute or two, then mounted him. He didn't ride him much—a little walk, trot, and lope, but George did as he was told. When he got off, Uncle Luke called me over. He said, "Now, Abby, look at his eye. He doesn't have that balky look anymore. This horse was keeping himself to himself all along. That's not his job, and, as he showed you, it's dangerous to boot. I think now he knows who's boss."

I nodded, the way you do when adults tell you something. I surely didn't think I would ever be able to do that to a horse. By the time Mom and Daddy got home from setting up the church, we had George cooled out and brushed off and put in the gelding corral with the others, who all seemed to be getting along well enough.

While Mom cooked dinner, I went into Jack's stall and did a thing I had started doing, which was to pet him all over, ears to tail, just long firm strokes along his neck and back and sides. He stood stock-still for it. I didn't know why I did it, except that he seemed to like it—he didn't move away—and I liked it. I wasn't picking up his feet or trying to get him to do anything or training him. It only took five minutes or so, but I did it every time I gave him his milk. On this particular day, I told him that he was never going to be the sort of horse who needed to be laid down. He was going to be a good horse from the beginning, which was right that minute.

In the days since the death of the mare, Jack had settled down for the most part, but it was still a question what to do with him. He was just over a month old, and he needed a friend. Daddy said that maybe the pony could have been his friend, but the pony was gone. None of the mares or geldings could really be trusted. The mares would probably not like him, and if they didn't, they could kick him hard and really hurt him. With geldings, you never knew. And, he said, "It's not like I have time to sit and watch them all the time and make sure nothing happens. And neither do you."

But Jack couldn't go on the way he was, which was living in a stall and going out into one of the corrals for an hour every day while the others were brought in. Foals on stud farms were out all the time, at least in nice weather. I even heard Daddy tell Mom that we should give him away, but I saw her shush him, and then I suppose they prayed about it.

Jesus was merciful, because, at least for the time being, we didn't give him away. Instead, Uncle Luke, seeing our predicament, proposed that he and Daddy spend a day building a new corral—not as big as the others, but big enough for three or four horses to trot around in for a bit. "Give you way more flexibility. And the ground's soft enough. We can get those postholes dug in no time." To me, Uncle Luke said, "Your daddy didn't get to be this stubborn all by himself, so I feel obliged to do what I can for you, Abby, because I know you like that little guy." When I came home from school Friday afternoon, they had all the posts in the ground, and while I was riding the mare and working around the other mares, they ran the woven wire fencing.

They worked until after dark, and we had a late supper. I would say that everyone was happy. Daddy let Uncle Luke smoke at the table (though Mom opened the kitchen windows so the air blew through), and the two of them talked about snakes back in Oklahoma. They both had stories. Daddy had found a rattler in a bag of grain. Uncle Luke had found a rattler in his bed. Daddy had gone for a swim once in the crick below their house, and a cottonmouth had swum right alongside him, round and round. That was nothing, Uncle Luke had been climbing a tree and saw a rope hanging from a high branch, and when he reached up to grab it, it was a rattler. If Uncle Luke thought that was something, well, Daddy had roped a snake. How about this, Uncle Luke had *used a snake as a rope*. Of course, by now we were all laughing, it was really late, and pretty soon we went to bed.

In the morning, first thing, I gave Jack his milk and his petting session, and then I put him out in the new pen with some hay and a water bucket tied to a corner post. He romped and played and seemed to know that this was all for him. I still wished he had a friend, though.

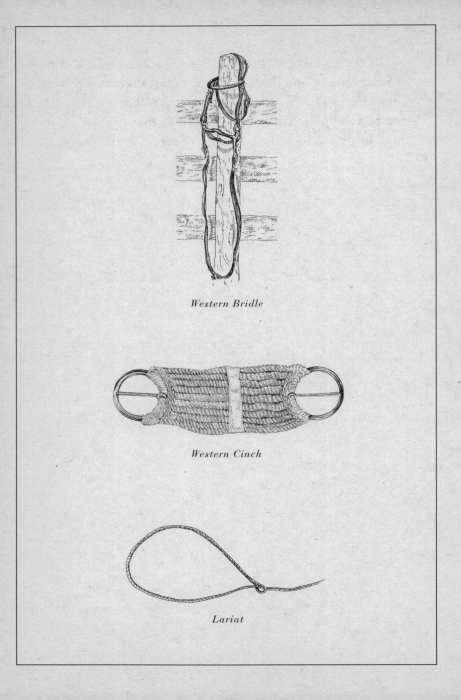

Western Bridle

Western Cinch

Lariat

Chapter 8

OVER THE WEEKEND, WE WORKED WITH THE NEW HORSES. I could tell they had been pretty cheap, because all the things you could fix needed fixing—they all required shoeing, or, if they didn't have shoes, their feet were broken and untrimmed. Their tails were tangled and their manes were too long, and most of them were only partly shed out, with dull, uneven coats that we had to scrape with the shedding blade or, according to Uncle Luke, a farrier's rasp, but we didn't have that. The vet had checked their teeth—two of them would have to have their teeth worked on, which meant that the vet had to come back out and file off sharp corners. It was a time-consuming job, but afterward, they would be more comfortable eating and would get the benefit of their feed, which, since feed was expensive and no one wanted to buy a horse in poor condition (except Daddy, who could always see beneath the surface), was worth it in the end. Still, they seemed well mannered enough.

And they looked different Monday morning from how they looked Friday morning, because we worked all Saturday, and then Uncle Luke declined to accompany us to our church on Sunday. He said he would go to the regular Baptist church in town, but there was no way to tell whether he had or not. Even so, he didn't mind working Sundays, and so he did pull manes and give baths all afternoon. Daddy might have said something about it being against the Lord's day, but, as he pointed out, it wouldn't have made a difference, anyway.

It was good to have Uncle Luke around, but when he drove away in his big rig early Monday morning, we were happy to see him go, because he did make it a point to do things his way and to be sure that Daddy knew he was doing things his way.

That afternoon, I got on Ornery George for the first time since his session with Uncle Luke. Daddy was grooming one of the new geldings—we called him "Black George"—so that I could get off Ornery George and right onto that one with only a switching of the saddle. He didn't see that when I threw the saddle onto Ornery George's back, he pinned his ears and reached around as if to bite me. He had never done that before, but anyway, he didn't bite me. He was just showing me that he could. I led Ornery George to the mounting block. I put my foot in the stirrup, grabbed his mane, and began to hoist myself on when Ornery George leapt away from the block and deposited me in the dirt. I was okay except I sat on my left hand. I jumped up. I still had Ornery George's rein in my right hand, and I gave him a jerk. He started backing up and pulling me with him. I gave him another jerk. Daddy tied Black George to the bar and came trotting over, and when Ornery George kept backing up, even though I was jerking the rein, he took the rein out of my hand. Ornery George stopped and stood still.

Daddy said, "What's going on with you, buddy? Got a thorn in your cinch?" He leaned down and put his hand inside the cinch and felt around. George flinched away from him. Daddy said, "Come on, buddy, come on, buddy," and started leading him forward. George walked along nicely enough. Only when Daddy turned toward him did the horse throw his head. Daddy walked him over to the arena, opened the gate, took off the bridle, and let George go. George bucked like mad all around the arena, stopping only a little bit in order to run a few strides and start bucking again. Daddy leaned on the fence. Finally, he said, "Well, you've got to wonder what's got into him."

As for me, I couldn't help thinking that it was rather interesting that what Uncle Luke had done with George had never been mentioned in the five intervening days, certainly not by me. Daddy often said, "All secrets are guilty secrets." I said, "Did Uncle Luke tell you he rode the horse?"

"No, he did not," said Daddy. "I did not give him permission to ride the horse. Did you?"

"I didn't know he needed permission."

"Well—" He looked at me. "Did he sack him out? Lay him down?"

I said, "I guess so. He said he needed to learn his lesson."

"And then he left before you could find out what lesson, exactly, it was that he learned."

I said, "I guess so."

"Well, Abby, it looks to me like the horse learned the wrong lesson. What do you think?"

"I don't want to ride him."

"I don't blame you."

"Are you mad?"

"Not at you."

"At George?"

"Of course not."

All of this time, George had been bucking and kicking out, but now he settled and stood across the arena with his head down. Daddy whistled with his fingers between his teeth, and George looked up. Then he turned toward us and walked, then trotted, to the gate. Daddy said, "Put a halter on him and walk him around the arena for ten minutes, because now we have to start all over with him." He stopped, then said, "Abby. He's not a bad horse. I'm going to tell you something about the horse business. You see how we are giving this horse another chance?"

I nodded.

"It's because he's good-looking. When you go to buy a horse someday, you make sure he or she is good-looking. They live longer because they get more chances to redeem themselves. You hear me?"

"Yes, sir."

"And another thing. Anything you saw your uncle, bless

his soul, do with this horse, you just forget it. Put it out of your mind. Got that?"

I nodded at that, too.

While I was walking Ornery George, he behaved well enough. But he was jittery and I had to go so carefully to get the saddle off that it took me ten minutes. The Ornery George I knew had been grumpy. This Ornery George was nutty.

I rode Roan Jewel and Blue Jewel. They were nice enough. Then I went to the pen and gave Jack his milk. After he drank it, he stood with his head down and his ears flopped while I ran a chamois over him, head to tail, on both sides. We often used the chamois on the horses just to shine them up, but on him I used the rough side, which seemed to give him a nice scratching. While I was doing this, standing back by his shoulder, his head came around my body. I thought he was looking for something, a bit of hay, maybe, but he didn't seem to be. I finished rubbing him with the chamois and picked up the bowl. He followed me to the gate, and I patted him on the nose after I had let myself out. Later, when we were giving all the horses their alfalfa for the night, Daddy said, "That foal gave you a hug."

"He did?"

"That was a horse hug."

I thought about that later, in bed. Horses normally show their appreciation by nickering at you, or pricking their ears when you come, or, to be frank, getting inside your space and crowding you, and then you have to shoo them away, because they have to respect you even though you weigh about a tenth of what they do. I had never felt a horse do that thing before that Daddy said was a hug, just that steady pressure for a moment or two that said something like, "Be next to me."

That kid, Brian Connelly, was now calling Stella every night and talking to her for at least forty-five minutes. Every day at lunch, she bragged about how she hardly had the time to do her homework because he was bothering her so much. And then, first thing in the morning, he would stand with her by her locker while she sorted her books for the day and talk to her some more. Gloria and I sometimes found ourselves waiting for her, and for the life of me, I couldn't understand why he talked about all the things he did. For example, he would have watched a show on TV the night before, something everyone watched, like *Dick Van Dyke*. I was the only person in my class who didn't watch *Dick Van Dyke*, because we didn't have a TV. But Brian wasn't talking to me, he was talking to Stella, and he would tell her everything that happened in a show that she herself had seen, including all the jokes, which he would laugh at with his mouth open. Or he would tell her what he had for breakfast (usually Wheaties but sometimes a crispy fried egg "because I don't like it all runny").

Gloria and I would stand there watching Stella while Brian talked to her. She kept this happy expression on her face all the time and nodded. Gloria once said to me, "Look at her, she's nodding to the rhythm, like he's singing a song. I don't think she's hearing what he's saying." After that, I couldn't see the nodding in any other way—though when you asked Stella what Brian had said, she knew.

I can't say that he wasn't interested in her, because sometimes he asked her questions—what shows had she seen the night before? What had she had for breakfast? What was that thing she was wearing called (in this case, a "dickey," which was a knitted turtleneck that you could wear under your shirt to keep your neck warm, and you didn't have to have the whole sweater, but in that case, what was the point, I thought), or what was the plaid of her skirt called? When Brian was in a question-asking mood, he asked questions until you wanted to pop him one. And, in fact, when we were in elementary school, he had been popped more than once, which at the time had made me feel sorry for him.

Now that he was so interested in Stella, though, I could kind of see Brian the way those mean kids had seen him back then. Fact was, Brian was big now, and those kids weren't, yet, so Brian did pretty much what he pleased. He also got good grades, always sat in the front row in class, and always "contributed," so the teachers liked him. Stella said, "He's kind of important, isn't he?" and Gloria and I didn't tell her any different. In fact, I would say that Stella saw herself and Brian as the most popular couple in our grade, which didn't sit well with the Big Four. From my point of view, Stella's concentration on Brian meant that she expected me as much as Gloria to listen to the "Tales of Brian" and learn something. What we learned about, mostly, was getting dressed, since she was very careful to dress nicely every day, and she never wore the same thing more than once in two weeks. One of Gloria's jobs, which I didn't have to share, was to go shopping with Stella and her mother, looking for more and more clothes. These were clothes that she could offer to share but didn't have to, since she was two sizes bigger than both Gloria and me. At our school, nobody wore very nice clothes, especially in the winter, when it was cold, rainy, and muddy. I could see the Big Four looking at Stella and rolling their eyes, but I didn't feel I could say anything to Stella. Gloria shrugged and said that they should mind their own business.

One day, Stella wore stockings.

It was only March and way too chilly and damp for stockings, and anyway, girls in the seventh grade didn't wear stockings to school. We wore loafers and kneesocks in the winter and sneakers and kneesocks or ankle socks in the warmer months. At that point, I had never even worn stockings, and Gloria had worn them only once, to her cousin's wedding, with a pair of dyed satin flats. Stella wore them with flats, too—navy blue with little bows on them—and a knee-length navy skirt, a round collared blouse, and a navy cardigan with little red cats all over it.

Brian, of course, noticed the stockings right away, and he kept looking at them. First thing in the morning, I heard him say, "Those look nice," and Stella just smiled and rubbed her hand down her calf, as if smoothing the nylon. She said, "They're warmer than they look, really." She pranced around in them for the rest of the morning.

But then, as Stella was walking into the lunchroom, with Brian right behind her, Mary A. ripped her stocking with a pencil point, and then said, "Oh! Look what happened! I am so sorry!" But Stella's stocking had a big gaping hole in it, and now it sagged down. Mary A. was grinning.

Stella jumped back and said, "You are not sorry! You did that on purpose!"

"How dare you say that!" exclaimed Mary A., and then the other three started exclaiming, too—how dare she, what a thing to say, who did she think she was, all that sort of thing meant to make Stella out as the bad one and Mary out as the good one. Brian wasn't saying anything for once, just standing there gawking, and I stepped forward, but Gloria poked me and shook her head. She was right. It wasn't a good idea to attract the attention of the Big Four, especially when they were in full cry already. Stella dropped her tray on one of the tables and ran out of the lunchroom. After a moment or two, Gloria and I went after her. I saw Barbara and Alexis Goldman watch us leave the lunchroom and then turn to each other and shake their heads. Stella was in the girls' bathroom, and she was bawling.

There wasn't any blood, and at first I didn't understand why she was crying like that. The Big Four had been mean, and maybe that was enough, but what Stella was saying was, "Look at it! It's ripped! It's terrible! I have to go home, I can't wear this. They're ruined!"

I said, "The other one's okay."

"It isn't!" exclaimed Stella, and then she pulled up her skirt. That was the first pair of panty hose that I ever saw, and yes, if one leg was ruined, the whole thing was ruined. Then Stella said. "My mom is going to kill me, because she bought these for going to my aunt's wedding, and they were *exPENsive!*"

"Well, you better take them off," said Gloria. "You can't wear them that way."

The bell rang for class. Nobody else came into the girls' bathroom. Stella made us wait until all the noise in the hall was gone, and then we came out of the bathroom together. Stella and Gloria went to their math class, and I went to English. We were reading *Adam Bede*. It was so boring that the teacher was having us read it aloud in class just to make sure that we read at least part of it. The Big Four ignored me when I came in, and I ignored them, too. But I knew that whatever was going on with them wasn't over and that it was going to include Gloria, me, and Brian, because we were on Stella's side and they were the other side. That was the way things worked in seventh grade.

Gloria called me that night. I was allowed to talk to my friends for ten minutes, and I had to do it in the living room or the kitchen, because that's where the phones were, so I couldn't really ask questions. What I learned was that Stella got in trouble with her mom and was grounded for a week for "sneaky behavior," that she couldn't talk to Brian for more than ten minutes anymore, and that she had had to go to the principal's office for calling Mary A. a bad name right out in the hall by the front door. What made her mom extra mad was that while she was in the principal's office, the bus left without her, and her mother had to come pick her up. And she had left her book bag in her locker, so she couldn't even do her homework. Gloria said she felt sorry for Stella since, "Nothing was her fault to start out with," and I said that I felt sorry for Stella, too. After I hung up, Daddy said, "What's that all about?"

"Nothing, really."

"Must be something."

I shrugged.

He stared at me. I idled around the living room for a minute, then went up to my room. Once upon a time, I would have told him all about it, just because it wasn't me who was in trouble, and it was all pretty interesting. But I knew what he would say: "Pride goeth before destruction, and a haughty spirit before a fall." I didn't think it was as easy as that.

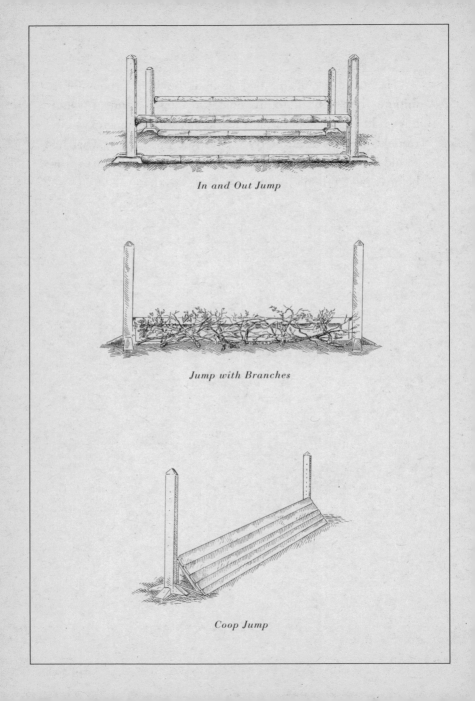

In and Out Jump

Jump with Branches

Coop Jump

Chapter 9

WITH ALL THE NEW HORSES, IT WASN'T HARD TO LEAVE ORNERY George alone. And March was a busy month. First, Daddy sold Jewel Number 1 as a ranch horse, which was a nice enough life for her. She was good with the cows and never afraid of them. She could get by on hay and no grain, so they liked her for that. And later we learned that one day, she was out on the ranch with the owner, an old man, looking for a stray calf. He asked the Jewel (they kept her name, Jewel) to cross a dry riverbed, and she refused. Even though he hit her with the quirt and spurred her, she balked. Well, by that time, the owner was pretty mad, but he got off and went around to lead her to show her there was no problem with the river, except that there was—it was quicksand, and he sank up to his knees before she pulled him out by backing away while he held on to the reins. After that, of course, she had a home for life and a friend for life. We heard this story because the man called Daddy up and told him, and thanked him for selling him "a brainy one," and all things considered, well, she had been cheap at the price. When he was telling us about this over dinner, Daddy said, "I never would have known she had that in her, but who can tell? Thank you, Lord."

"Amen," said Mom.

The chestnut George got sold as a trail horse to a big hotel, and Daddy said that he might live a long time. When all a horse did all day was walk along at an easy pace, he could live to be thirty or more. And, of course, since he was at a big hotel, in a fancy barn right beside the golf course, they would keep him clean and shiny. In the summer, they were going to put him in a camp for little kids. So, all in all, Daddy was happy in spite of Ornery George and the death of the mare. Other years had been worse, and I knew not to ask about them.

The new horses were in full work now. Daddy and I rode horses until sundown every night and fed after dark. Jack was eating hay now, but he still had to be fed his milk, with bran mixed into it, in a bucket, several times a day, which was time-consuming. Mom was good with the horses because she was good with all animals, including baby birds and lost dogs, but she didn't ride unless she was going on the trail and the horse was old and quiet. I made myself extra work, rubbing Jack with the chamois so that he would always be happy to see me. In other words, we were busy, but when Miss Slater called and said the horse show was coming up and could I come and ride in a few classes, it seemed as easy as you please to get out my English riding clothes and brush them off, then shine up my jodphur boots and drive over there. I had never shown in them before, but Daddy had gotten them secondhand somewhere and had always told me they would come in handy. Daddy picked me up after school. The truck was clean, too, and Daddy was wearing his good hat.

I was to ride that afternoon, just to get the feel of the pony again, and then the next morning, Saturday, I was to take him in three classes—pony hunter over fences, two feet; pony hunter over fences, two feet, six inches; and pony hunter hack (no jumps). This time, Miss Slater said, Melinda would watch and learn. Maybe next time she would try it herself.

When I got there, Melinda was nowhere to be seen, and when Miss Slater saw me looking around for her, she said, "Poor Melinda. She's home with a tummy ache. I'm sure it's not serious."

I said, "Does she ride the pony much?"

"You mean Gallant Man, here?"

"Is that what you named him, Gallant Man?"

Miss Slater smiled. She said, "The original Gallant Man was a racehorse some years ago. He was quite small. When my dad took me to the Belmont Stakes that year, he put a bet on him for me, even though he himself preferred another horse. Gallant Man won, and in record time. So when I saw what a nice pony we had here and how he is ready to do anything we ask of him, I thought it would be a cute name for him. What did you call him?"

"We called him George. But that's what we call all of them."

"So you won't get attached."

I nodded.

She didn't say anything about Melinda. I then mounted the pony. He was completely accustomed to the stable now, so he was as calm as he ever was at home, though there were flags flapping and horses and riders and grooms and trainers everywhere, and tents, too. Riders were showing in the main ring, in front of the biggest tent, and in another ring behind the tent. Miss Slater led me to a smaller ring that was fairly distant from all the brouhaha, down toward the trees. Daddy waved us off and went into the stands to watch the action.

Eight jumps were set out in the ring, and we had it to ourselves. The jumps were a fair selection, with white poles, brushes in boxes, and branches arranged like hedges. There were two chicken coops and two gates, too. The pony didn't look at anything. He had seen it all in the month or so since coming here.

Miss Slater had me walk, trot, and canter both directions, with a few small circles, some halts, some shortened strides, and some lengthened strides. After that she had me warm up over some crossbars and some plain poles, the way we would warm up for a show round the next morning. Finally, she called me to the center of the ring and gave me a course. It was simple enough—I was to go to the right, jumping the white gate, then the white poles. After that, I was to cut across the ring diagonally, jumping one of the coops. Then I was to make a short left turn, take the other white poles at the end of the ring, then the one-stride in-and-out on the far side, finishing up over the other gate. The last exercise was to turn the pony in one nice circle on the proper lead and come down quietly to the trot and the walk.

It wasn't as easy as it looked.

I can't say that Daddy and I ever thought in terms of "courses" of jumps. For one thing, we didn't have very many standards or poles and for another, we weren't in the jumping horse business. That was probably why I lost my way after the third jump, turned right instead of left, and was faced with the first jump again, even though I knew that was wrong. We jumped it and then I pulled Gallant Man to a halt. Miss Slater came over. "Mixed up?"

"Yes, ma'am."

"Okay, try this." She had me just go around the outside of the arena, jumping each of the seven jumps as they were set, including the in-and-out, which was two fences set one stride apart. You jumped twice, but it counted, for scoring purposes, as one effort. This, too, was harder than it looked, but I made it. When I came back to her, she said, "Abby, that wasn't bad."

I knew there was a *but* coming.

"But you seemed a little out of control. This time, I want you to go more slowly, sit up more in the turns, and not let the pony lean to the inside."

When I did it again, I realized how bad the previous time had been by the fact that I actually felt the pony canter to the jumps this time in a balanced way and jump them in a balanced way, without leaning to the inside. The last thing you want your pony to do when he's jumping is take them tilted.

She said, "I would like you to think about the jumps that

are coming up when you are going *into* the corner of the arena rather than coming out of it."

I tried this the third time around. It was much better.

This time she said, "You're a fast learner. And a good rider. Try the first course again."

She stood with me in the center of the ring and gestured to demonstrate the course again. I was to fix the turns in my mind first and the jumps in my mind second.

I repeated the course back to her.

She said, "That's right. One other thing."

"What?"

"Look where you are going to be ten strides ahead, not two or five strides ahead."

It was easy.

In fact, that night in bed, I lay there for a fairly long time, trying to figure out how it had gone so quickly from being impossible the first time to being easy the last time. I pictured the jumps in my mind, one after another. I realized that the most important thing was not that I was jumping jumps, but that I was riding a route from one spot to another, just like on a map. If I remembered the map and sat up, we would get there.

When we arrived at the show the next morning, Daddy went right up to Melinda's father, Mr. Frederick Anniston, held out his hand, and introduced himself. Mr. Anniston was wearing a tweed jacket and another coat and a dark-colored hat with a green feather in the band. He had on gloves and seemed to be cold; Melinda was pressed against him and looked as though the weather had shrunk her down to nothing. Melinda's mother didn't seem to be around. Mr. Anniston didn't speak to me, but he watched me.

There were six other ponies in the warm-up area, which was fairly large, and six trainers calling out to six riders. Two of the ponies were very fancy—they almost looked more like reduced-size horses than ponies. The other four were just ponies. Gallant Man, the only gray, was prettier than all of those four. I wove my way among the other ponies—this part wasn't hard. After we warmed up, Daddy held Gallant Man, and Miss Slater walked with me around the course, step by step, so that I could learn it on my feet. The course had more than two turns—it had four—and more than seven fences. If you counted both halves of the in-and-out, it had nine fences.

I got back on Gallant Man. One of the girls and her pony were jumping the jumps in the warm-up area, a crossbar, a single bar, and an oxer, which was two bars parallel to one another, the back one a little higher than the front one. Her pony was one of the plain ones. He was willing, but he looked dull to me. The girl counted as she approached every fence—"One two one two one two one two"—and then they jumped. The other thing she did was lift her eyes higher and higher as she got closer to the fence, so that when she was over the top, she was looking up into the trees. This made me smile.

We warmed up by trotting the cross-rail, then cantering it. He kept me right with him, and by the time we were ready for a real jump, I couldn't wait. But I did. One thing I knew (and there weren't many of those) was to wait. I took slow breaths. I could see Mr. Anniston standing by the rail, staring at us. Melinda was pressed up against his leg. Neither one was smiling.

Now we did the oxer—first small, then bigger, then big. I did my best to think, Slow. Level. Slow. Level.

Then they called my number and Miss Slater walked me to the gate into the arena. I stood there until the previous pony came out. The jumps looked like an absolute jumble. They were all plain, natural brown or white, no colors. That made it worse. I walked and then trotted the pony to the other end of the ring, and then, completely panicked, I asked him to start his canter circle. I wasn't panicked about the jumping—the jumps were small. I was panicked about the feeling that I was in a sea of jumps and had no idea how to make my way around it. But I did know where the first jump was and the second. After that, I saw the third, which was a white chicken coop, and then it was one jump after the other, and all too soon, we were done and doing our final canter circle. The trot. And then we walked out of the ring. I was filled up with the thrill of the whole thing, the cantering, the turning, the jumping. I could have gone around all day.

Miss Slater met me at the gate. She said, "That was fine, Abby, for a first round. Next time, just a degree slower. Do you have a rhythm? Think the same rhythm, but slow it down." She glanced over toward Mr. Anniston. He still wasn't smiling, but he nodded. In the meantime, Daddy trotted over to us now that we were back in the warm-up area, and he kissed me on the cheek. When I took off my hard hat, he ruffled my hair. I was really glad he was my daddy rather than Mr. Anniston.

I walked the pony around, and Daddy walked with us. He was saying, "This is fun here. This isn't bad at all. You know Black George? He could do this. Most of these horses look just like him but don't have as pretty a head. Yes, this gives me an idea. Yes, yes, it does." Then he went off and got me a hot dog, and I ate it sitting on the fence, holding the pony. Daddy had a lump of sugar for him, which we sneaked to him when Miss Slater wasn't looking. I didn't know for sure that she was against treats, but I suspect she would be that type, as she was very neat.

We got a ribbon in the class—fifth place out of ten ponies. I took it over to Melinda and gave it to her, and she smiled and said thank you, but she held it limply in her hand, like she was going to drop it any second. I guess I had never really seen anyone like Melinda before. She was scared of her own shadow.

The sun came out in time for the second class, which was a hack class, no jumping. All we had to do was walk, trot, canter, turn around, trot again, halt, canter again, according to the commands that the judge called out. A fancy pony who wasn't very nice pinned his ears and bucked once while the judge was looking right at him. Some of the other ponies had trouble with their leads. However, Gallant Man was easy and perfect, and he won the blue ribbon.

Afterward, Daddy said, "You know, I've been walking around, pretending I'd like to buy one of these horses, a show horse like these—not necessarily a pony, because a good pony is just luck—anyway, some of these horses cost ten thousand dollars. All of them five to ten." He was grinning.

Now it was past noon and time for the third class. I thought it was silly that the first class and the second class were equal, with the second class being so easy, but it was true, and the pony was in contention for a champion award. The course for the third class was almost like the first course but with one less turn and higher jumps. Miss Slater and I walked it. Melinda went with us, leaving Mr. Anniston standing by the fence.

We walked from jump to jump, right from the back middle of every fence to the front middle of the next fence, Miss Slater taking steady even steps. She said to me, "This is your path, Abby. Think of it as a red line going around the course. You just stay on the red line and slow your rhythm a little bit and look right between that pony's ears all the time, okay?"

"Okay."

Then Melinda took my hand for a moment. The first thing she said all day was, "He's my pony."

I said, "I know that, Melinda. I'm not taking him back."

"But if he's not good enough, Papa will sell him and get another one."

I realized what she meant. I said, "How many chances does he get, Melinda?"

Melinda looked up at me. "I don't know. Not many. I'm scared of another pony."

Miss Slater glanced at me. She said, "Well, let's not think about all of that now. He's a good pony. Do you understand the course, Abby?"

I nodded. I understood the course and everything else, to tell the truth. My own opinion was that even if Melinda just wanted the pony to stand around and eat carrots, that's what she should have. I went back to the barn, and the groom brought out Gallant Man. I mounted at the mounting block and went into the warm-up. The whole time, it was like the eyes of Mr. Anniston were freezing a hole in my back. It made me mad. It made me sit up and lift my chin. I knew that Miss Slater liked the pony a lot, and if something happened, she would find the pony another home. I knew also that it wasn't my worry or Daddy's, but anyway. I sat up. I made myself float around the warm-up as if the other ponies were not worth looking at.

The bell rang. I heard my name. I passed the previous pony in the gate. We trotted to the end of the ring and did our circle.

This time, the jumps were higher, and so they were more fun. I could feel the pony curling underneath me, rising under me and then landing and cantering on. The jumps, the very centers of the jumps, came up one by one right between the pony's ears, right between my ears, too. The other thing that the pony had to do correctly in order to win, which was change leads in the turns, he did perfectly well. He was automatic at that and it didn't worry me. It was the pace and the style that would tell the tale. We came over the last jump. I asked the pony for his circle, then for the trot, then for the walk. I dropped the rein contact and lifted my chin. As we exited the ring, I took a deep breath, as if I were Mary A. or one of those other girls at school, ignoring everyone who didn't make any difference. I pretended to be Mary A. all the way back to the barn. Miss Slater and Daddy clapped for us.

The pony came second, after a blond fellow, whose round I didn't see. We got reserve champion. Since it was the pony who was being judged, not the rider, Melinda went into the ring, leading Gallant Man, wearing her best riding clothes. They gave her a long red and yellow ribbon and a silver dish for mints. She came out smiling and hugged me. I glanced over at Mr. Anniston. At last he was smiling, even though it was a small, only semi-happy smile. It got bigger when Melinda ran over to him. He picked her up and gave her a kiss on the cheek, but it all looked fake to me—not as if he didn't love her and wasn't happy for her, but as if he had lots of ideas and keeping the pony was only one of them. I saw his eyes follow the blond pony, who had won champion. But nobody knew those people, and Miss Slater said they were from down south. As we were untacking the pony, she said, "You can't believe what horses cost down there. It's a crime. It really is."

On the way home from the show, I reported this to Daddy. He said, "Is that so? Is that so, indeed?" When we got home, he pulled Black George out of the paddock and had me stand him up so that his feet were square and his head was up, ears pricked. Then he walked around him, peering at him. After a few minutes, he said to me, "Now, Abby, look how he stands. His back legs are set right under his haunches and his front legs are set just a hair behind the straight, but his knees are a smidgen bent. That's called being 'over at the knee,' and it's not a bad thing. His croup has a nice slope, and his neck comes up out of his withers. And his throatlatch, where his head is attached to his neck, that has a nice curve to it. The Lord himself only knows what he was doing for a living in Oklahoma, given how bad his feet were and what a job it was to do his teeth, but I know what he's gonna do for a living, so your job tonight is to write down everything Miss Slater said to you, and then we'll read it over together and see if we can learn something."

My paper had seven things on it. Daddy read it over a couple of times and said, "This is a nice puzzle. I think we're going to have a good time."

Seven things:

1. Ride the course, not the jumps.
2. Keep the horse level, especially through the corners.
3. Look ahead ten strides, not two or five.
4. Ride to the middle of every fence.
5. Wait.
6. Maintain a rhythm.
7. Look up, never down.

Gate Jump

Ribbon

Flower Box Jump

Chapter 10

SOMETIMES A LUCKY THING HAPPENS, AND FOR US IT WAS THAT Mr. Tacker, the old man who had Jewel, decided he needed two more ranch horses, so he came by to look at what we had. Of course we had Black George and Ornery George. The other George was a chestnut with two white socks in front, so we called him Socks George. We also had the mares. The old man bought Red Jewel right off the bat—she was well broke and, now that she'd been with us for a month, neatly shod and a deal fatter than she had been. He didn't want any of the others, but he looked twice at Ornery George. Then he looked again. He said to Daddy, but glancing at me, "Your girl ride this one?"

Daddy said, "She has been. What with the new shipment,

we've given him a bit of a rest. . . ." He shrugged. Not exactly bearing false witness.

"Well built."

"He is a stylish one," said Daddy. "Looks like a reining horse, if you ask me."

"Has he been around cattle?"

"Supposed to have been, back in Oklahoma. I can't guarantee . . ."

"What would you say to a tryout?"

"I don't know about that. I'll have to think about that."

Now, the fact was, Daddy didn't mind a tryout. As he said, his horses had nothing to hide, and generally they were just the same if they went away for a week as they were at home. But then, that very thing would be the problem with Ornery George.

Daddy stuck his hands in his pockets. He said, "Mr. Tacker, I don't want to say no, but I can't really say yes at this point." He gestured toward Red Jewel, who was standing quietly with her head down. I stepped over to her and scratched her beneath her ear. She cocked a hind foot. Very relaxed. He said, "I think you're gonna like this mare. She's a useful animal."

But he could see the light in Mr. Tacker's eyes, and so could I. I knew that when he was taking off his boots to go to bed that night, he would have a picture of Ornery George in his mind, not one of the very useful and sedate Red Jewel. I said, "What are you going to name the mare?" I said this in that bright way you say things when you are trying to distract the grown-ups from what they are thinking.

Mr. Tacker looked down at me. He said, "What's her name, Red Jewel?"

I nodded.

"Well, that looks to me like 'Ruby.' I'm sure she'll do fine." And he led her off toward his trailer. Of course, he looked back at Ornery George two or three times before he got her into the trailer and drove away. He paid eight hundred dollars for her. What with the shipping from Oklahoma, two shoeings, and the teeth, Daddy had about four hundred into her, so he was happy at supper. He said, "He wants to come back next week, but I put him off. And then he's going out of town for a week, up to a cattle show. So that's maybe two and a half weeks we've got to figure something out."

Mom set down the early peas, put her hands on her hips, and said, "Figure what out?"

"How to get that horse right so he can ride him. Those two mares—"

I interrupted, "Jewel and Ruby!"

"—are fine for him, because even though he's old and a little stiff, he used to be good on a horse. And he still thinks he is."

Mom shook her head and then shook it again. "Mark," she said, "that's a dangerous game."

"It was him who noticed the horse and asked me about him. I had to answer his questions, didn't I? I couldn't be un-friendly about the horse. That makes people suspicious."

But we all knew that wasn't the right response. And I knew Daddy would have me up on Ornery George sooner or later, most likely sooner, and what he would say about it was, "Let's just give it a try and see what happens," and I would know what was going to happen perfectly well, and it wouldn't be good. The funny thing was that I could ride all the others without any problems and I had gone to the horse show and done something new with-out worrying, but I couldn't stop fretting about Ornery George.

Mr. Tacker had come by on a Thursday. On Friday, Brian Connelly ate lunch with Mary A. and Joan. Five minutes after he
sat down, Stella got up, took her tray to the trash area, and
dumped everything, including the plate, into the trash bin.
Then she walked out. Gloria put her hand on my knee and
muttered, "We should listen in and tell her everything they
say," so we did.

Brian talked about his lunch. He opened his brown paper
sack and took out everything and lined it up on the table. He
had a peanut butter and bacon sandwich on white bread, a
navel orange, six carrot sticks, a gingersnap, a napkin, and a
carton of milk. His lunch, according to him, was full of protein
and vitamins (especially vitamins A and C). A gingersnap was
the only really nutritious cookie there is. The two girls didn't
say anything, and I secretly watched Mary A. and Joan while he
was explaining this. They kept exchanging glances, which included some raised eyebrows, but when they finished with their
lunches, they waited for him. As they passed our table on the
way out, Joan said, "Oh, hi, Gloria. Is Stella sick or something?"

Gloria shrugged. Joan and Mary A. both gave me big show-
off smiles and then they frog-marched Brian out of the lunchroom and down the hall. When they were really gone, we
jumped up, got rid of our trays, and ran to look for Stella. We
found her in the bathroom, of course. Gloria started in. "You
can't believe what they talked about."

"He described his whole lunch to them, and it was sitting
right there on the table in front of them."

"He told them about the difference between plant protein
and animal protein."

"He said he didn't have quite enough B vitamins, but he would have more at dinner."

"It took him about an hour to peel his orange. He had to peel the whole thing in one piece."

But it didn't work, because she started crying. The bell rang, and we went to class, leaving her there. I guess sometime after that, her mom came and picked her up, and she was counted absent for the rest of the afternoon. The Big Four paid no attention to me, but they were loud, and Joan and Mary N. got sent to the principal's office for passing notes. By the end of the day, I was tired of school all over again.

I can't say I'd planned to defy the righteous authority of my father. Although I had refused to ride Ornery George before, I wasn't all that clear in my own mind whether my refusal still stood. I rode Blue Jewel and Black George with no problems, one in my western saddle and one in my English saddle. We weren't yet jumping Black George, but I was trying to make him go around the way the pony had in the hack class, even and smooth, going into the corners and never leaning to the inside. I practiced holding a rein in each hand, bending my elbows, thumbs up, heels down, back straight, body square.

When I got off Black George, I saw that Daddy had Ornery George tied up and groomed and my western saddle on him, all cinched up and ready to go. Ornery George looked at me out of the corner of his eye, but he didn't turn his head. I put my hand on the stirrup, and he switched his tail. Daddy was bent under him, picking his foot and talking. "He's not a bad fellow. Willful, a bit, but not actually unkind. You'll do . . ." Daddy let the foot drop, and George shifted his weight toward me. This was another sign, him pushing his haunch at me. I could read these signs just as easily as another horse might—they meant, I'm the boss. They also meant, as far was I was concerned, that he was ready, and even eager, to show me a thing or two. That was the difference between the old George and the new George—with the old George, you had to go and find the resentment, but with the new George, he had it out ready to show you.

I said, "He seems a little grumpy."

"You can work him out of that."

"If he's going to a man, you should work him out of it yourself."

Daddy stood up and looked at me, frowning, I'm sure, at my "tone," but all he said was, "Could be. But if I get on him, we might end up going down the trail that your uncle Luke blazed for me. I don't want to go down that trail. He needs to return to where he was with you."

I wiped my mouth with the back of my hand, because I knew I was about to say something more sassy. I said, "Where he was with me was that I refused to ride him."

Daddy threw the hoof pick into the brush box and blew out his lips. Then he said, "Flat refusal?"

"Well, I—"

"Defiant refusal? Defiant refusal to even try?"

"Look at him!"

"What's wrong with him? He's just standing here."

"He was switching his tail. He—"

"He what?"

"He gave me a look."

"You defiantly refuse to get on him because he gave you a look?"

"I don't . . ."

"Yes or no?"

"Yes, I refuse, or no, I won't ride him?" If I was going to get in trouble, I wanted to be sure that we both agreed on what I was getting in trouble for.

"Listen, miss—"

"No, I won't ride him. I don't want to get bucked off again and I don't trust him." Rather than look at Daddy's face, I turned away, picked up a halter and lead rope, and went to get Socks George. When I returned, Daddy had put Ornery George in the pasture. He helped me with Socks George, and we finished for the day after dark, as usual. He was very polite at dinner, the way he could be when he had given up on you and turned you over to the Lord. After dinner, I did the safest thing and went into my room and did my homework, as I always did on Friday night, because I wasn't allowed to do homework on Sunday, and Saturday night I was often too tired. I knew Daddy was giving me more leeway than he had ever given Danny, but even thinking that made me so nervous that I just kept reading *Adam Bede* until I lost the thread of the story completely and fell asleep. Mom came in late to help me out of my clothes and into bed. If I hadn't been so groggy, I would have talked to her, because even though she never went against him, she sometimes told me how he worked.

The next day was Saturday, and Daddy was already up and the hay was already delivered to the horses, and he was already gone by the time I opened my eyes. I found out the reason during breakfast—the shoer, Jake Morrisson, was pulling through the gate in his truck, and my brother, Danny, was with him. Mom popped up and ran out the door, and when the truck stopped, Danny jumped out and gave her a big hug. I swallowed the last of my toast and hurried out, too. Usually Jake came during the week, when I was at school. This time, he'd been busy all week, and Saturday was his only spot. It had been six weeks since all the new horses had been shod, so here they were. Danny grabbed my shoulders and kissed me on the forehead, and Mom put a wrapped package into the passenger side of the shoeing truck. All of this reminded me that what had happened with Danny—six months, now—was really bad, and even though we acted like everything was okay, it wasn't. While Mr. Morrisson was setting up his anvil and his forge and all, Mom took Danny aside and looked at him and asked him questions, but I didn't hear what she asked or what he answered. When things were set up, he gave her another hug and came back over to put on his apron.

He said, "I heard you showed those society girls a thing or two with that pony a week ago, missy."

"Only a thing. Not two."

He laughed.

"It was fun. But now there's work to be done."

"I'm sure there is."

Before, I had come up to his chin. Now I came up to his shoulder. And his shoulders were big, too, no doubt from learning to shoe horses. In his leather apron, he looked bowlegged and grown up. Jake Morrisson said, "Who's first?"

We got through Blue Jewel and Socks George. They behaved themselves and were reset all around.

Ornery George, however, needed new shoes. I went and got him while Danny stoked up the fire and Jake looked in his shoe stock for the right size to begin with.

Out in the gelding corral, Ornery George could see me coming, and no doubt he could put two and two together—the shoeing truck was here, two horses had come and gone already, and he was next. Therefore, he went around behind the other horses, and when I passed through them and tried to catch him, he threw up his head and trotted away. I walked after him. Normally, I didn't have this problem, but there was plenty of hay in the corral, he had eaten his fill, and the only thing I meant to him was taking time out from his day to do yet another thing that humans demanded of him. He trotted off again and again every time I got anywhere near him.

Finally, Danny called from the gate, "What's wrong with this one?"

"At the moment, he doesn't want to be caught. Normally, plenty else, too. He wasn't very nice, and then Uncle Luke got on him and . . ."

"And that was that!" Danny laughed and pulled the gate latch backward. He came in, closed the gate after himself, and held out his hand for the halter and lead rope. I said, "With pleasure."

But Danny didn't head for the horse. He walked along the fence with his head down and his arms by his sides, and after a few steps, several of the horses were looking at him. Then he turned toward Ornery George, and when Ornery George looked at him, he waved the halter and lead rope so that Ornery George backed up and then trotted off. After that, he walked toward George, still making him trot away. Then he put his arms down and turned left again, into the group of other horses. At the far end of the corral, George had stopped and was looking at him. Now Danny turned right and walked

119

along the fence, not toward Ornery George or away from him. When he saw George was looking toward him, he waved him off again, and George turned, tossed his head, and trotted away. But he looked back.

Now Danny seemed to ignore George, and George walked toward him. When Danny stopped among the other three, George was looking as hard as he could, possibly wondering why the other three were so interested in Danny. When George approached the others, Danny let him get fairly close, then he waved him off and walked toward the gate. The others followed, and George followed them. Pretty soon, he was standing at the gate with the other three. Danny didn't do a thing that showed he cared. He just walked down the line of horses, giving each of them a word and a pat, same with Ornery George, nothing special. Then he patted each one in turn again, but when he got to Ornery George, he slipped the lead rope around his neck. Then he stroked his neck for a long time, then he traced figure eights around his eyes. He eased the halter on. It seemed as though Danny was in no hurry at all.

Pretty soon, Danny walked briskly out into the middle of the corral, the lead rope in his right hand and Ornery George following behind. When they got into the center, Danny walked him in a couple of circles, then sent him in a circle in each direction. When the horse was finished doing this, Danny turned abruptly and walked back toward the gate. George followed. He looked a little confused, or maybe that's not the word. Just not quite sure of what was going on and why. I opened the gate. Danny and George walked right past me and over to Jake Morrisson. He stood up for the shoer and gave no problems. When Danny put him back in the corral, he led him through the other horses and out to the middle. There he sent him in a circle in each direction again, then he had him turn and come to him. He waited. Ornery George looked around, his head up and his ears pricked. Danny just stood there. It wasn't until George lowered his head that Danny took the halter off, and when he did, he sent the horse away rather than letting him trot away on his own.

When Danny met me at the gate, I said, "You've got to come back."

"Why is that, sis?"

"Because that horse is going to kill me."

Danny laughed. "No, he's not."

"Yes, he is, because Daddy has made up his mind that I'm going to ride him, and every time I do, he tries to buck me off. And he's a good and dedicated bucker."

"Don't ride him."

"He's been here almost six months. He's got to get sold."

Danny knew about the six-months rule. The six-months rule was that after a horse had been here for six months, even talking about him made Daddy mad.

"I've never seen you be afraid of a horse before."

"You always rode the hard ones. You know what he says—how can I—"

"Say that a kid can ride this horse if you can't ride it?"

"A little girl. That's what he says now."

"What did Uncle Luke do with the horse?"

"Laid him down."

"With the rope?"

I nodded.

"Sat on his shoulder?"

"And sang four verses of 'Stewball.'"

"'I bet on the gray mare, I bet on the bay, if I'da bet on old Stewball—'"

Listening to Danny sing made me miss him like crazy, but I just chimed in, "'I'd be a free man today.'" Then I said, "Yeah. That one."

Danny ruffled my hair. "When do you have to ride him again?"

I shrugged. We walked the horse out of the pasture. Every time I had seen Danny since he left—this was the fourth time—I knew just by looking at him that he wasn't going to pay the price he'd have to pay to come back. Daddy and Danny and everyone we knew could deplore pride and a haughty spirit until they were blue in the face, but that didn't make either pride or a haughty spirit go away.

Jake Morrisson was finishing up on the last horse, the third mare. Danny now helped him put all his things away, and pretty soon, they were loaded up. But I didn't think Mom was going to leave it at that, and of course she came out of the kitchen, wiping her hands, and invited the two of them to stay for lunch—she had some brisket and homemade bread and, amazingly enough, she had just baked a lemon meringue pie! Danny's favorite, imagine that, so we went in and everyone washed up, and we all had lunch, but Mom didn't really eat. She just sat in her place at the end of the table, with Danny catty-corner from her, and she talked and joked while we ate and asked Jake Morrisson if Danny was doing a good job, and Jake said he was, he was especially good with the horses, and someday he would figure out what the business end of a hammer was, Mr. Morrisson was sure of that. We all laughed.

While Mom and Mr. Morrisson drank cups of coffee, I took Danny out to Jack's corral to have a look at him.

Jack was over two months old now and big and strong. Normally, he trotted right over to me as soon as he saw me, but now we could see him over in the far corner of the corral, with his nose down and his ears pricked. Though there was some fresh grass in the pen, he wasn't eating it. I said, "What's he doing?"

"He's watching something."

He seemed transfixed, so we crept around the outside of the corral, quietly but not sneakily, since we didn't want to startle him, but nor did we want to distract him. Whatever he was watching moved, and Jack took a step to follow it, then he pushed his nose down farther and sniffed. By this time we were close to the corner, and Danny squatted down and peered through the wire mesh. Then he laughed. "He's watching a gecko."

The gecko must have run off at that point, because Jack snorted, threw up his head, and leapt into the air. Once he did that, he put his nose down again, right where the gecko had been, but finding nothing, he flicked his ears and walked over to the fence. When he got to me, he stuck out his nose. I said, "The other day, he followed a stray cat all over the corral, that orange cat with one ear."

"That big tom," said Danny.

"Jack would follow him, sniffing at him. The cat wasn't scared at all. At one point, the cat was lying there and Jack reached his nose down and the cat suddenly sat up and batted him. Jack just jumped. It was so funny."

We stroked the side of his face for a bit, where the foal hair had begun to be replaced by the silky dark coat the color of black walnut that would be his adult color. He had no white on him, except for four white hairs in the middle of his forehead. I put my hand on his neck, and he stretched over the fence. I started stroking him firmly along the length of his neck, the way I did with the chamois. Air ruffled in his nostrils.

"He's going to be a nice horse," said Danny, fingering Jack's sparse little black mane.

"I love him."

"Mom told me what happened to the mare."

I didn't say anything.

"Ab, you know that orphan foals rarely come to much and can be very dangerous."

"No, I didn't know that." I kept stroking.

"Who's going to push this little guy around, the way his dam would?"

"I don't know."

He took his hat off and waved it in Jack's face. Jack jumped back and trotted off a few steps, his tail high. Then he tipped forward, kicked out twice, and took off across the corral, giving two or three high-pitched whinnies. He bucked a couple of times. When he came to the fence on the far side, he executed a sharp left turn and galloped five strides before dropping back to the trot. Then he trotted toward us, his ears pricked and his nostrils wide. He was snorting, looking for the hat, which Danny had put back on his head. Now came the funny part— when he got back to where we were standing by the fence, he stuck his nose out and sniffed Danny's hat. Danny obligingly cocked his head forward so that Jack could sniff to his heart's content. When he was done, he gave a big sigh and his ears went floppy again. I started stroking his neck. Danny said, "Did you see how quick and self-confident he is? He needs someone to be telling him what to do, and it isn't going to be you."

"You don't know how he is. He's really sweet."

"I'm just saying, don't count on anything."

"Well, now you do sound like Daddy."

A scowl, but only a little one. He fixed his expression almost immediately and said, "Maybe so, but I'm just saying."

"I heard you."

I felt grumpy as we walked around the barn, but then Danny said, "I don't know what the mare looked like, but he's a Thoroughbred for sure. Abby, he's a beautiful colt. And he's going to be a beautiful horse." He glanced at me. "But don't get your hopes up."

I don't know what Jake Morrisson and Mom were talking about all this time, but I'm sure it was plenty, since not only did Danny work for Jake, he also lived above his barn, where his ranch hands had once lived when he still had the whole ranch. But they sorted everything out, and Jake called us over. Danny got in the truck, everybody waved, and they drove off. Afterward, Mom seemed happy enough. All she said to me, though, was, "No evidence that he's doing anything stupid."

I said, "That's good."

"He bought his own car."

"Well, I'm sure he did. What kind?"

"Fifty-six Chevy convertible."

This made us both laugh, but then Mom said, "I think a convertible would be fun, even if it is almost ten years old. We can get him to take us for a drive."

Tack Box

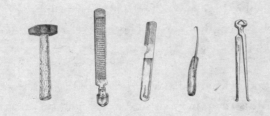

Farrier's Tools

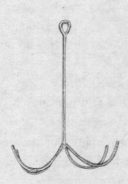

Tack Cleaning Hook

Chapter 11

THERE WAS NO RIDING, THANK YOU, LORD, ON SUNDAY, AND MY favorite cook, Miss Larrabee, brought supper to church. We had chicken with dumplings, homemade bread, and because she and her brother were avid gardeners plenty of homegrown asparagus with a sauce made from their homegrown lemons. The Larrabees swore by rotted horse manure as a fertilizer, so they came by our place several times a year and carted off part of the manure pile. Over supper, they said that their strawberries looked better this year than they ever had, and everybody at the table kind of sighed at the thought of the strawberry shortcake to come.

There were two different theories about shortcake in our church—Mom and Daddy and some of the others preferred something like a sweetened biscuit, crumbly and crisp on the bottom, split and filled with strawberries and whipped cream. Miss Larrabee and her brother and some of their side preferred a dense, sweet pound cake shaped like a crown, with the center of the crown filled with berries and topped with ice cream. All of the kids liked both kinds equally, and we looked forward to the first strawberries of the year, which made a sort of celebration of our church. I won't say that Daddy and all of the others agreed about everything they thought and talked about, but I will say they never argued about the strawberries.

Eating the chicken and dumplings and thinking about the strawberry shortcakes to come reminded me that things at church had been very peaceful lately—even the Greeley children were willing to sit quietly three out of every ten minutes, or however long it took to read one picture book. The one they liked best was *The Little Engine That Could*, which had nothing enlightening in it about the Lord, but it was the one that kept them quiet, so that was the one Carlie and I read to them, over and over, six times apiece on that Sunday alone.

And then Monday and Tuesday, it poured rain, so I kept Daddy happy by cleaning and oiling all the tack. On Wednesday, the arena was soaking wet, and Thursday, Daddy had to go into town for the entire day, not my fault. When we finally got to ride on Friday, we had to do all the easy horses first, and by that time, it was dark.

On Saturday, it was sunny as you please. The footing in the arena was perfect, and I was sitting over my French toast, dreading the morning. In my mind, Ornery George had gobbled up all the others, and I dreaded riding him so much that I didn't look forward even to Black George, who was turning out to be quite nice. It was seven a.m.; we were getting a bright and early start, and just as Daddy pushed his chair back to stand up, there was a knock at the back door.

"Who could that be, I wonder," said Mom. But she said it in a funny way, as if she didn't wonder at all.

The man at the door took off his hat as soon as she opened it. They spoke for a moment or two, and then she brought him in, with a smile. He wasn't a very big man, what Daddy would call wiry rather than rangy, and he had on faded brown pants and very old boots, with a blue denim shirt and leather vest. He said that he was pleased to meet us. Daddy shook his hand, because you never knew if someone came to your door whether it was Jesus or not, and in fact there was a Greek myth about this very same thing. The man said his name was James Jarrow, called Jem, and he had heard from Jake Morrisson that we had some nice horses for sale.

"We do, indeed," said Daddy, and he got his business face on, which was simultaneously friendly and efficient. He said, "Let's go look, shall we?"

Mom said, "Abby has finished her breakfast. She can go along," which was the first clue that she had something up her sleeve. However, I put on my jacket and my boots and followed the two men out to the corrals. The horses were eating their hay. Jack was eating hay, too, even though we were still giving him some milk, usually mixed with bran. I had already fed him that, and he had licked the bucket clean.

Jem Jarrow was not a talkative person. He went with Daddy to each corral, stood by the gate, and stared at the horses. He didn't fidget in any way. Next to him, Daddy looked like a jack-in-the-box, jumping up and down and making noise, but Daddy was just normal. It was Jem Jarrow who was different.

It must have taken him twenty minutes to stare at all the horses, including Jack. Finally, he went back to the gate of the gelding corral and pointed to Ornery George and said, "That's a nice one. Well built. Good eye."

I later found out that he didn't prefer Ornery George at all.

"He's not for a beginner," said Daddy. "Which is not to say—"

"Does your girl here ride him?"

"She has," said Daddy. At this point I fully expected to be told to mount up.

Jem Jarrow said, "Mind if I feel him over?"

"Not at all," said Daddy.

"Mind if I catch him up?"

"You seem like an experienced horseman."

"Done ranch work all my life."

"I guess it's okay, then. If Jake Morrisson recommends—"

"Lemme get my headstall."

He came back from his truck with a rope halter attached to an especially long lead rope. He opened the gate and let himself into the gelding corral. Black George, Socks George, and Ornery George noticed him right away, but after a moment, they went back to eating their hay. He stood there. Pretty soon, one by one, they looked up from their hay. Black George came over to him, and he stroked his head by the eye and ear and down the cheek. Black George let out a snuffle. Now Socks George had to see what was going on, and since he was a little bossy, he came over and pushed Black George out of the way with a quick pinning of the ears. Black George stepped

130

back. Jem gave Socks George a few strokes, too, but when Socks George pushed at him with his nose, he used the head-stall he had in his hand to wave him off.

In the meantime, Ornery George was standing off at a distance. After watching for a minute, he moved around so that his rump faced us and went back to eating. Jem lifted his hand. The other two horses, who had been nosing him, moved off, and then, with Socks George in the lead, they trotted off and swept around in a big arc. It was as if they didn't want to get too far away from Jem. When they came close, he waved them off, but when they got to a certain distance from him, they turned. Pretty soon, he had moved away from the gate toward the middle of the corral and they were going around him in a ragged circle. After they made one circuit, they swept up Ornery George, who just couldn't seem to resist. Now all three trotted around in a leisurely way, not afraid or excited, just, it appeared, willing to move. Every so often, one of them kicked out at another, but not as if he really meant it. They actually seemed to be enjoying themselves.

After they had gone around maybe four times, Jem started stepping backward and to his right. Almost immediately, Black George turned toward him, his ears pricked. The other two were clumsier, but they followed his lead. Then Jem stepped to the left, switched his rope hand, swung his rope, and they were off again, trotting around him, this time going the other direction, Black George in the lead. Two times around, and he stepped back and let them relax. As soon as he did, they came right up to him, and he put his hand on Ornery George. The other two tried to push in, but he lifted his hand and they backed off.

All this time, Daddy was trying hard not to say anything. I

could see all of the thoughts running through his mind—these are my horses, what's he doing, I don't know if I like this, it seems okay, should I stop him, should I ask a question, hmm. Then Jem Jarrow slipped the headstall over Ornery George's head, turned, and walked briskly toward the gate, with Ornery George right on his heels. He stopped once, lifted his hand, and Ornery George stopped, too, and lifted his head. After that, the horse kept his distance a little better. When Jem got to the gate, he said to Daddy, "Would you mind, just for a few minutes, if I used that pen where the colt is? Just to feel this fellow out a bit. I never like to get on a horse until I get to know him a little."

"That makes sense," said Daddy, then, "Abby, put the colt in the first stall."

That's what I did. I was proud of the fact that Jack met me at the gate and walked quietly enough to the stall. I took him all the way in and turned him around, then gave him a few strokes before taking off the halter. As soon as I went out of the stall, he put his head over the door and stared at Jem and Ornery George. It was as if none of the horses could get enough of Jem Jarrow.

Ornery George and Jem were standing in the middle of Jack's pen. George was facing me, and Jem had his back to me. He had his left hand on the lead rope, a few inches below George's chin. The other hand was holding the other end of the lead rope, and maybe a foot and a half of it hung down. What Jem did now was to lift George's chin up and back, toward his (George's) shoulder, while swinging the other end of the rope. George stood there, twisted awkwardly for a moment, and then his hind end moved to the right, away, so that he was more comfortable. Jem released the halter hand, petted George once on the neck, and then did it again. This time I was looking at them from the side. I saw that after the moment of hesitation, what happened was that George's hind foot, the one closest to Jem, stepped under his belly and crossed in front of his other hind foot. Then the other hind foot stepped over, too. It was like a dance step, where you step over your left foot in front of your right and then bring your right foot around.

Jem asked Ornery George to do this three more times. On the third time, as soon as he lifted the hand near the halter, George stepped over behind. Jem said, "There's a fellow," and gave him a good pat down the neck. Then he went around to the other side of the horse, switched hands, and did the same thing but in the opposite direction. George was better at it in this direction and moved over twice, with hardly any pressure, almost immediately.

I had never seen any of this stuff before, and I watched as carefully as I could, because I knew without being told that this was what Mom and Danny had worked out between them.

Now Jem waved the end of the rope, and George went around him in a tight circle, a few times one way, then a few times the other. He was clumsy at it and stiff. Jem had to insist, but eventually, he got it, and he got less awkward.

Jem led the horse to the gate.

I looked at Daddy. He looked like he didn't quite know what to say. Jem said, "Athletic horse, Mr. Lovitt. Nice-made horse. Don't know much about using his body at this point. How old did you say he was?"

"He's six."

"Young, then."

Now he stood George up and ran his hands down his front legs, feeling his knees and fetlocks and hooves. Then he ran his hand down George's spine, pressing here and there. At one point George flinched and tried to step away, right when Jem had his hand where Uncle Luke's rope had been. I thought Jem might ask a question or say something, but he just ran his hand farther down and pressed again. Then he put one hand over George's nose and the other hand on his neck and shifted his head back and forth. He didn't once look at his teeth. All the horses were staring at him. Jack called out from his stall, as if to say, "Look at me! I'm here! I'm the important one, don't you know that?"

Finally, Jem Jarrow walked over to the gate. He said, "Mr. Lovitt, what are you planning to do with this horse, if I might ask?"

"Well, we're getting him ready to be sold, so—"

But really, of course, he didn't have an answer for this question.

Jem said, "I'd like to ride the horse, but I'm wondering if I might come back another day, say, Wednesday? And, if you don't mind, you might just leave the horse alone until then."

I said, "We don't mind."

Daddy said, "Wednesday, Mrs. Lovitt and I will be at the church, setting up—"

I piped up. "I'll be here. I can watch for you, Mr. Jarrow, and help you with whatever you need."

"That's fine. That would be fine," said Jem Jarrow, and even though Daddy didn't look one hundred percent happy about it, he was stuck. And so he smiled and made the best of it.

It was fine with me not to ride Ornery George for another four days.

In the meantime, school was no better than home. In fact, school was so bad that the only thing I enjoyed about it was things we were doing in class—in history we were studying the missions, and I was making a clay model of the mission at San Juan Bautista with one of the boys in my class, Kyle Gonzalez, the sort of kid who is very quiet and always does a good job. In English, we finished with *Adam Bede*, to everyone's relief, and we were reading *The Witch of Blackbird Pond*, which was pretty good. In math, we were making graphs. This is how bad things were with Gloria, Stella, and the Big Four—anything that was a break from them was good. I even tried being friends with Alexis and Barbara and Debbie, but Debbie and I had been bored with each other for four years. Alexis and Barbara were nice enough to me, but they were much more interested in a play they were trying out for at the community theater. It was called *Twelfth Night*, and they were hoping to play a set of twins—Alexis would play the boy and Barbara would play the girl. They couldn't stop talking about this play, which I had never heard of, and they were both afraid of horses, so we didn't have much to say to one another.

As for Stella and the Big Four, you could only call it a war. Brian Connelly was the prize. I couldn't figure out why it should be Brian—there were several boys in our class and in the eighth grade who were cooler and better-looking, but he

135

was the one they were fighting over, and he made it worse by trying to be nice to everyone—he must have talked to some grown-up about it, and that's what they told him to do. Every morning before class, he would stop at each locker—each of the Big Four, Stella, Gloria, and me, for sure, but sometimes also Debbie and Maria and Alexis and Barbara—and say something or other, even if it was only that today, his mom had fixed him tuna fish salad, with celery but not pickles, because he didn't like pickles at all. Our lockers were alphabetical, so his progress ran Mary A., Joan, Stella, Maria, Linda, the twins, Gloria, me, Mary N., Debbie, Fatima, Lucia. Stella and the Big Four kept track of how long he spent with each girl. Of our group, he spent the shortest time with me, and that was good. Usually, he said, "Hey, Abby, how ya doin'?" and I said, "Fine, thanks." It was this, and only this, that prevented the Big Four from focusing on me. If Brian wanted to talk to Stella about *The Munsters*, which was one of his favorite shows, then he might only say a word or two to Mary A. and Joan about what he'd had for breakfast and not even get to Mary N. For the rest of the day, the Big Four would monopolize Brian, and also criticize Stella, by saying things like, "Do those socks match, Stella? In this light, they look different," or, "Did you know you have a little zit, Stella, right there beside your nose? I'm just telling you in case you didn't know." This would be said in a loud voice.

If Brian spent more time with Mary A., looking into her lunch box and admiring what her mother had sent, and didn't get to Stella, then Stella (and sometimes Gloria) played their own games, and one of these was to ask Mary N. if she was losing weight. "You look thinner in the face," was what Stella said, knowing perfectly well that the very thing Mary N. wanted above all things was to look thinner in the face—she had dimples in both cheeks. When they were really mad, they said, "You should wear your skirts shorter." We all knew that Mary N. had fat knees. They said these things in a sweet way, as if they wanted to be friends with Mary N. Since she was the least big of the Big Four, she was the easiest to pick on. Once, when Gloria went to Stella's house for a sleepover, she and Stella called Mary N. twice and asked, "Is your nose running? Better catch it!" They disguised their voices, then laughed and hung up. Gloria told me about this when she called the next night, Saturday. I knew I was supposed to laugh, but I didn't. I didn't like the Big Four, but I wasn't sure who was being meaner. Even so, I didn't think there was anyone to be friends with besides Gloria, and if she liked Stella, then I was stuck with her, too, wasn't I?

On that Monday after Jem Jarrow, everything was quiet for almost the whole day. Even at lunch, they sat at their table and we sat at ours, and the two tables might not have even been in the same universe. Brian had begun his day by chatting with Mary A. and Joan about watching *Mister Ed* the night before. I had never seen *Mister Ed*—even if we'd had TV, the show was on Sunday—but I knew Mister Ed was a talking horse. I had heard Brian say that they got the horse to move his lips by rubbing peanut butter on his gums, and I thought that was interesting. Worth a try, too. But apparently, this conversation was so involving that Brian never did get to Stella, even to say hi, and so she was mad about it for the rest of the day. Then, when Brian came a little late into the lunchroom, Joan and Mary A.

waved at him and moved over to make a spot. Brian hesitated, but he didn't actually look at us. He just sat down.

The problem came in study hall, last period, which normally our class did not have. But our science teacher was sick, so we were sent to study hall with the other seventh graders—no doubt they didn't trust the boys to leave the gas jets alone in the absence of the teacher. Anyway, about five minutes after the bell, our group filed into the study hall and took whatever seats were available, and by the time Mary A. and Joan got into the room (they had been brushing their hair in the girls' bathroom), there was one chair by the window and another by the door, and that one was right next to Stella. I had snagged a chair just behind Stella, and we had already passed our first note—something from her to me, which I hadn't had time to open yet. Joan sat in the chair near us and gave me a look, then gave Stella a look. Then she sighed and opened her science book and began writing a note, which she passed to Debbie, who passed it to Jesús Valdez, who passed it to Fatima, who passed it to Mary N., who passed it to Mary A. So far, so good.

But when Mary A. had completed her response, the teacher just happened to get up and walk around to make sure we were all doing our work, as she sometimes did, and so there was a new challenge. Mary A. and Joan met this challenge by deciding to sharpen their pencils, which they were allowed to do without asking permission, and so they both got up, pretending not to be paying any attention to one another, and headed for the pencil sharpener next to the blackboard. As soon as Joan got up, I saw that Stella was fiddling with something, and then, before Joan even got to the pencil sharpener,

I saw what it was—she had removed the cartridge from her fountain pen (black ink, because we were required to turn in final copies of our papers in black ink) and leaned over and set it on Joan's desk chair.

Now Joan sharpened her pencil, exchanged her note with Mary A., and headed back to her seat. I was looking at the cartridge. I was sure she would see it—it was sitting right there as big as anything. But she was too busy making faces across the room at Mary A. and Linda, and so she turned around, twisted her body, and sat right on it. And then she slid around to get more comfortable. I looked at Stella, who was smiling and reading her history book. Stella didn't look at me. Everyone else was studying hard. Even Debbie had her nose so deep in her book that I couldn't see it. I didn't know whether Stella knew that I had seen the cartridge.

Joan wasn't wearing a white skirt, but it wasn't black, either—she had a new mossy green wool skirt with pleats that were sewn to about four inches below the waist, and then flared out. It was pretty, and her sweater matched it. She also had on a white blouse. When the bell rang and she stood up, she had a long streak of black ink running across her skirt and then down. When she reached around to smooth her skirt after standing up, she got the ink on her fingers and then on her sweater. It was then she noticed the ink. She screamed and started cursing. She said the G word attached to the D word, and more than once. Very bad. Stella made no sound or gesture. She didn't even ask what happened. She just wandered out of the room with the boys. The boys didn't care, but all the girls except Debbie, who was already out the door, gathered around Joan and looked at her skirt, her hand, and her sweater. "Oh, it's ruined!" cried Joan.

Linda found the ink cartridge under the desk chair. The desk chair had a streak on it, too. Joan insisted that someone had left it there on purpose, but the other girls didn't believe this—any one of the boys, they thought, could have forgotten that he dropped the ink cartridge or dropped it without realizing it. It could have been there for hours or all day.

I was the only one who knew that Stella had put it there on purpose.

After school I was waiting for the bus with Gloria, who had been sitting in her usual seat in the front of the study hall, under the gaze of the teacher, and so didn't know anything about the skirt incident. She and I were watching the other girls. Stella had, once again, gotten picked up by her mom. Gloria said, "I don't see why it's such a big deal. She got ink on her skirt, so what? Her mom will take it to the cleaners."

I said, "I guess it was a new skirt."

"Stella said that. She said they were talking about it at lunch, that it was a new skirt from some store in San Francisco."

"She heard that?"

"She said she did."

I said, "You know, I—" but I said it quietly, because I wasn't sure how to tell Gloria about Stella. Gloria didn't even hear me. She exclaimed, "Forget them! Can I come see the colt this weekend? I saved him some apples."

"He doesn't eat treats yet."

"Well, I'll give them to the others, then. But we can do something after. I'll get Mom to bring me out for a while, then you can get your mom to let us go someplace for the afternoon."

"I'll ask."

So, I didn't say a word about what I'd seen, but all the way home on the bus, I thought about how mean Stella had been. I wondered if the ink on the skirt equaled the pen tear in the stocking. I also wondered when Joan was going to realize that Stella had done it on purpose and whether Stella wanted Joan to know that. After all, what good was it, in terms of the war, if Joan thought it was an accident?

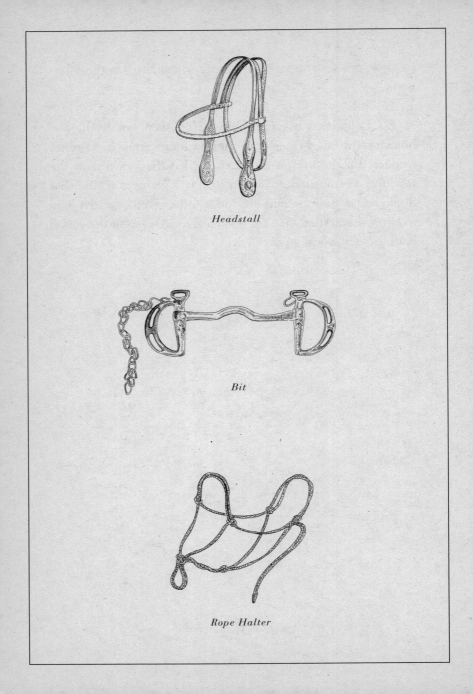

Headstall

Bit

Rope Halter

Chapter 12

ON WEDNESDAY AFTER SCHOOL, I CHANGED INTO MY RIDING clothes right away and was on Black George when Daddy and Mom left for the church. As soon as they turned right out of the driveway, I jumped off him and put him back in the gelding corral—he was a willing horse, and Daddy always said, "Some days, ten good minutes is enough."

I still didn't quite know what was going on about Jem Jarrow, but I had some suspicions—Danny worked for Jake Morrisson, Jake Morrisson knew Jem Jarrow, Jake Morrisson and Mom had had a long talk, Mom had hurried Daddy out to the church, telling him something that I didn't understand about the chairs, and maybe the windows needed cleaning, too, since no one had touched them since the fall, and cleanliness was next to godliness, and when Daddy said, "Why today?" Mom said, "Next week is Mrs. Larkin and Mrs. Lodge doing the chairs, and after that the Greeleys, so if we don't do it, it won't get done." They packed up the Windex and some rags and off they went.

Jem Jarrow's truck turned in the driveway moments later. I ran to meet it.

Jem Jarrow wasn't much of a smiler, but he had a cheerful face. When he got out, I saw again that he was small—maybe half a head taller than I was at the most—I had forgotten that and been thinking of him as Daddy's size. And you could see the horizon between his knees, as Daddy would say. Being bowlegged was, according to Daddy, the first sign of a horseman, because to get that way, you had to fit your legs around the horse from an early age. Jem said, "How do, Abby. Been well?"

And I said, "Yes, sir, how about you?"

"Can't complain," said Jem Jarrow.

That was it for the formalities. I followed him out to the gelding corral. The horses all looked up at once and stared right at him. Just as before, but for not quite as long a time, he stopped and watched them.

I said, "What are you looking for?"

"How they are. How they feel about each other."

"What do you make of that?"

"Well, first off, I'm just curious. Always been curious. When I was in school, they told me not to ask so many questions, so I learned to keep my mouth shut and my eyes peeled. But more than that, right now, I wonder how this gelding we're working with gets along with the others. I see both this time and the last time that he's quick to take offense. That other one, the dark one, he's more easygoing, but he's more athletic, too. So, all in all, I suspect that the dark one—"

"That's Black George."

"—is the boss of the three of them, but he spends less time thinking about it than our friend."

"Some kids are just cool."

"That's right."

I laughed.

By now, we were standing at the gate, and Jem opened it and walked in. The first thing he did was wave the horses away and walk to the center of the corral, where he got them going around him again. They all did it more smoothly than the last time, to the right and then to the left and then back to the right. By the time he let them turn in toward him, they were one hundred percent relaxed, as far as I could tell.

Ornery George didn't act as though he knew this session was about him. He was just curious and sniffing, like the others, until Jem put his hand on his neck, and then the horse's ears flicked backward and his eyes sort of narrowed. But Jem acted as if he didn't notice this and put his hand on the bridge of George's nose, about halfway between the nostrils and the eyes. They stood there. Jem didn't pet George as I would have done. He just stood there with his right hand on George's neck and his left hand over the bridge of George's nose. After some time, George's neck loosened and his head dropped. Just then,

Jem gave him a pat on the neck. While George's head was still lowered, Jem pulled up the headstall and fastened it together. Then he turned and walked briskly back to the gate. George followed him. George had a look on his face that wasn't willingness, I would say, but also not grumpiness. More than anything, it was curiosity. I shooed the other horses back and held open the gate. Man and horse walked through and headed to the arena.

Jem and George went about a third of the way into the arena, to the most open spot, and at a wave of Jem's hand, George started trotting around him in a tight circle, tighter than in the corral, just right around Jem. Since the other horses weren't with him, though, he must have decided that it wasn't much fun, because he kept trying to stop. Jem wouldn't let him. Every time he tried to stop, Jem waved him forward again with his free hand while lifting the hand that was holding the rope. Jem wasn't going to let George stop until he did something, and what that thing was, I saw a moment later, was that dance step—cross his inside hind leg over the outside hind leg and bring his hindquarters around to the outside. When he did that, Jem let him stop, then he waved him in the other direction, in the same tight circle. Once again, he was reluctant to move and awkward until he crossed those hind legs, inside to outside. At the same time as the legs crossed, George's head and neck dropped and relaxed, and his progress around the circle was easier.

I climbed up on the fence. I was glad I had my hat on, because it was a sunny afternoon, nice and warm across the top of my back. I could see from there that the geldings and the mares had decided that whatever was going on didn't concern them, and so they had gone back to eating their hay, but Jack, in his pen, was all eyes. He stood with his chest against the fence and his ears pricked. A couple of times when George changed direction, Jack snorted and humped his back. It was cute.

After a couple of minutes, Jem let George stop trotting around him. Now he stepped up right beside him again, where he was standing, and he used that lifting motion on the rope. George had to step his hind end over as soon as he felt the upward pressure, but I have to say that he didn't learn this smoothly, or without protest. Especially when he was stepping to the left, he tried more than once to pull his head away or simply to stiffen and wait until Jem Jarrow would give up.

But Jem Jarrow was a patient man. That was the complete difference between him and Uncle Luke. You had the feeling that Jem would stand there all day with the rope lifted, waiting for the horse to put two and two or, for that matter, one and one together. If he did, he got a pat. If he didn't, he didn't get anything—they just waited. Uncle Luke, I knew, and maybe even Daddy, would have said something, or batted the animal, or given him a push. I could see that Jem Jarrow wanted George to think of this thing himself, to not be told every time what to do.

They must have worked on this for five or ten minutes. Another thing they did was Jem just put his hand over the bridge of George's nose and pulled it around so his neck was curved to the left and down. A couple of times, Jem released his hold, and George's head popped back to the front, as if on a spring. But then he did the right thing—he just relaxed and kept his head turned even after Jem had taken away his hand. It was then that George got the pat.

I shouted, "What's that for?"

Jem said, "The horse doesn't know how to soften."

"Is that because people were mean to him?"

"Don't know."

"But—"

Jem stopped working the horse for a moment and waved me over to him. I jumped off the fence. The sand in the arena was moist and springy. Perfect, really. When I got to the two of them, Jem didn't do what I thought he would do, which was to ask me if people had been mean to the horse, he said, "Here's how I think of it, Abby. When the horse knows how to soften and go along and be happy doing it, then it won't matter to him what happened before, and if it doesn't matter to him, then it doesn't matter to me, either."

He handed me the rope.

I was to stand just to the side of George's neck with my hand up by the halter and the rope coming up through it like a rein. At the same time that I lifted the rope, twisting the horse's head and neck upward a bit, I was to put my other hand on George's shoulder about halfway up to the withers and push steadily, but not hard. As soon as I felt George's shoulder loosen and release, I was to stop everything and give him a little pat. To be frank, I didn't see the point of this, but I did it three times and then a fourth. Each time, I felt George's body start out stiff and then soften up. Jem said, "See all these muscles, from the chest to the tail? All along the shoulder and the ribs and the flanks? And then this other set, all down his back and over his croup?" His hand feathered along George's spine for a moment. "If all those muscles are loose, he'll be easy to ride and he'll enjoy himself. If they're all tight, he'll be hard to ride and dangerous, too, because even if he doesn't go against you, his balance won't be good, and his mind won't be on what you want him to do. He'll be looking for a reason to rebel, or to spook, or to stumble."

"How can he look for a reason to stumble?"

"If his body is stiff, he won't pick up his feet very well, and so a little something on the ground that he would be aware of if he were supple will cause him to stumble."

He showed me how to get George to come around me, and then I set myself up so I could feel the other side tense and soften. He said, "When he steps his back feet under and across, he has to use all those muscles I was telling you about, especially the back muscles. It's easier to use them if they're supple, not stiff, so he learns to soften them when you ask, because he really wants to do things the easy way. And it's actually easier for him to get along with you and do what you say and not buck you off, but you have to show him how to do it before he knows that."

He took the rope back from me and went right in front of George, maybe three feet out. He said, "Here's another little test." He raised both his hands, both his index fingers, and waved them at George, as if to say, Naughty, naughty. But what he wanted George to do was step back. George wasn't

149

sure that he himself wanted to step back, so he leaned back and then leaned farther back, without moving his feet. His ears were out to either side and a little back, what Daddy and I called "I can't hear you" ears. When Jem put his hands down, George stood up straight again. This time, Jem raised his left hand and then, with his right hand down low, used the lead rope to suddenly pop George under the chin. George threw up his head and stepped back. Jem patted him on the forehead. Then they did it again. It took three times, but on the fourth time, Jem lifted his fingers, and George stepped back one step without being popped under the chin. Jem said, "Horses don't like to back up, generally. There's no eyes back there."

I laughed.

"But when he backs up, once again, he's got to be soft all over to do it. So it's a good test. I don't get on without giving him that little test. If he won't back up, then we work a little more."

"Don't you ever get on a horse without giving him tests?"

"Not unless we're good friends of long standing."

The next thing Jem did was hand me George's rope and go get the tack. I just stood there, because I didn't want to do the wrong thing, and I noticed that George just stood there, too, which was an accomplishment for Ornery George. I gave him a little pat on the nose. I couldn't help myself.

Jem was small, but he carried his saddle like every cowboy I'd ever seen, over his hip, with the cinch folded over the seat of the saddle and the stirrups hanging. A western saddle is heavy. Daddy always carried his on one side one day and on the other side the next day so as to exercise his back evenly. When Jem swung the saddle up on George, George stepped away. Jem took it off, swung it up again. George stepped away. Jem took it off, swung it up again. George must have seen that resistance was futile, and so the last time, he stood there. Jem went around and arranged the cinch, then he came around again and gestured for me to hand him the lead rope. When I gave it to him, he laid it over his forearm. I saw that he wasn't going to make George do anything at all, but instead, he was going to have him stand there of his own accord while Jem was going about his business. After the saddle was cinched up, Jem asked George to make some tight circles again, this time with the cinch tight and the stirrups flapping. At first, it was hard for George—he was stiff and kind of mad, but then he got used to it. I ran to get the bridle.

When I passed Jack, he whinnied at me, and I stopped to give him a pat on the neck. His neck was almost shed out, and his coat was dark and shiny.

Jem went about getting George to take the bit in the same way he had done with the halter—he put his hand over the bridge of George's nose. George was to bend his neck and drop his head and relax so that Jem could slip the bit into his mouth and pull the crown piece over his ears. It took a minute or two to get this done, but not as long as before. I said, "Is he smart?"

"All horses are smart. How else would they be able to work for a living? They've got jobs to do, and most do them."

"Daddy says they only understand the carrot or the stick."

Jem laughed. He said, "Generally, I don't use either a carrot or a stick. Seems like most horses remember the stick better than they remember the carrot."

"What do you use, then?"

"I use curiosity."

I could see that.

"A horse is a curious fellow. Even when he knows he shouldn't go look at something, chances are his curiosity will get the best of him, and he will at least walk toward it. Hardest horse to train is a horse who isn't interested in anything new or is always afraid, but this horse isn't like that. He's of two minds."

"Mom says curiosity killed the cat."

"When does she say that?"

"When someone is asking too many questions."

"Someone like you?"

"No. Someone like Danny."

Jem laughed again and said, "I can see that."

Then he said, "But horses aren't cats. Horses in the wild have to keep an eye out and be ready to investigate and know what should be in their world and what shouldn't be. They have to make up their minds. So they're always looking, and that's a sign of intelligence. Lots of people don't give them much credit for intelligence, but I don't agree with that. If your horse is curious about you, then the first step is made. When he satisfies his curiosity and finds something interesting and fun going on, then likely he'll want to join the fun."

After softening George in the saddle and bridle in the way that he had previously done in just the halter, Jem squared him up and mounted. He mounted with no apparent effort— it was like he had springs in his heels. Just watching that, I knew that getting on and off a horse was as automatic for Jem Jarrow as walking. Then he didn't ride off immediately. It was only after sitting there for a moment that he asked George to walk on.

Stepping over, stepping over, stepping over, that little dance step—for a while, that was all they did. Finally, they trotted around in a circle. George had his head low and to the inside, and his inside back hoof went in the print of his outside front hoof. They went around a couple of times like that and then turned, step step step, the hind legs crossing, and went back the other way. Then they cantered. George was good for about halfway around the arena, and then he remembered who he was and started to put his head down. Just then, Jem used his inside rein to lift George's head up and to the inside. George softened, turned, and cantered on, no longer thinking of bucking. This happened twice. Otherwise, they wove around the jumps and barrels in the arena, at the trot and then the canter and then back to the trot, always changing what they were doing, what direction they were going. Ornery George, I could see, had given up.

When they were walking around, catching their breath, I said, "But a little girl can't ride him."

Jem Jarrow smiled. He said, "Maybe not today. But soon."

I believed him. But I was glad that "soon" wasn't "now."

We cooled George out, and brushed him down, and put

him with the other geldings. Jem shook my hand and thanked me, got in his truck, and drove off. I didn't know what the next step was, but I was sure Mom had a plan. I watered and hayed all the horses and gave Jack his rubdown. It was getting dark when Daddy and Mom drove in.

We had to eat supper in a hurry because we had to get back to the church. Mom made pigs in a blanket and coleslaw. While we were eating, Daddy ran down the list: did I check the horses' water?

Yes.

Did I give everyone their hay?

Yes.

Were the stalls clean from the weekend?

Yes.

Was all the tack put away?

Yes.

Were all the gates closed and locked?

Yes.

Did this fellow Jem Jarrow look like he was going to buy the horse?

I glanced at Mom, who lifted one eyebrow but didn't say anything.

I said, "He went nicely for him. He wasn't ornery at all."

"Hmm," said Daddy, smiling. But then he said, "He doesn't look like he can pay much. Mr. Tacker—"

But Mr. Tacker hadn't called. I said, "We didn't talk about that."

"I didn't expect you would."

There was a silence, and then Daddy said, "Well, you can't

count on a thing. For every buyer, there are ten lookers. I wish I'd been here for the tryout, though."

"It went fine," I said.

For the rest of the week, Daddy didn't say another thing about Jem Jarrow. I suppose he figured that Jem was just another buyer who'd gone elsewhere.

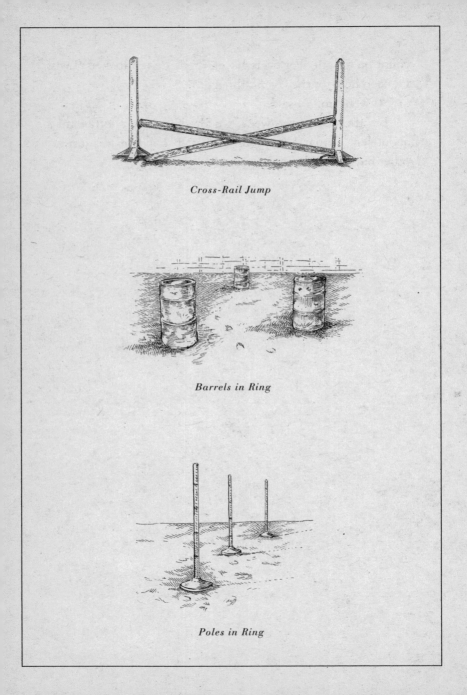

Cross-Rail Jump

Barrels in Ring

Poles in Ring

Chapter 13

ALL THAT WEEK, THERE WAS A LULL IN THE WAR AT SCHOOL. FOR one thing, lots of kids were out with a virus, including Brian Connelly and Mary A.

Kyle Gonzalez and I worked steadily on our model. There was going to be a big display of all the mission models in the cafeteria lasting for the rest of the school year. Ours was the only one made of clay. We finished the church and the walls around the courtyard and the bell tower. The art teacher gave me a piece of green cloth for the grass in the courtyard, and I cut trees out of cardboard and colored them on both sides. Kyle found some little Christmas bells somewhere and set them into the arches of the bell tower with bent pins. If you hit one of them with your pencil, it would ring. When we were finished on Friday afternoon, everything was painted a light color—not white, because Kyle didn't think that white was the right color, but sort of a pinky-gray-cream that was the best we could do.

The missions would be set up in the lunchroom in order, south to north, on a long map of California cut out of brown paper and laid across three tables. The first one was San Diego de Alcala, and the last one was San Francisco Solano. San Juan Bautista was number 15. I didn't know a thing about saints or missions, but I thought all the models were pretty. I had thought all those places—San Jose, San Luis Obispo, San Francisco—were just cities, but they were people, too. In our family, we never talked about saints or missions or Catholics, really, so I hadn't thought much about it.

There was going to be a parents' night during which everyone was supposed to come to look at our models of the missions, but that would be on Wednesday, so we wouldn't be able to come, and so I didn't tell Daddy and Mom about it at all. I wondered if, four years ago, Danny hadn't done the exact same thing.

In the meantime, at home, I rode all the horses other than Ornery George and I did my jobs and everything was quiet. On Friday night, the phone rang, and it was Miss Slater, inviting me to come to their barn. Melinda, she said, wanted to see me, and Miss Slater thought we might have fun—Gallant Man was in great shape. I would have a jumping lesson on him (there was a show in two and a half weeks) and then Melinda would have a little jumping lesson on him, too. She could watch me and then try it herself.

Gloria was never opposed to going out there. When I called her, she said her mother would drive us. That way, we could stop for supper at her house, and they would bring me back about nine. Mom and Daddy agreed to all of this, as long as I rode Black George, Blue Jewel, Socks George, and Star Jewel first thing in the morning.

Gloria and her mother showed up about eleven. They had on cowboy boots and cowboy hats, and bandannas around their necks. They wore matching shirts with bucking horses and lariats all over them. They waited while I changed into my English riding clothes, and we got into the car.

It was a beautiful day. Even the pine forest around the stable was bright with sunshine. Gallant Man was all tacked up, and he looked really cute, so cute that after I was on him, Gloria's mom took pictures of us (then she took pictures of everyone else, including Miss Slater, who sat sideways on the fence with a whip in her hand and her tall boots crossed at the ankles) and Melinda, who was perfectly turned out, as always.

My part of the jumping lesson went fine. Miss Slater was in a good mood, and Gallant Man was very gallant. He trotted or cantered down to every jump with his ears pricked, and he came up under me each time in exactly the same way. The only bad thing he did was after the second and third jump, when he bucked a little bit and tossed his head. I knew it was from high spirits, so I just turned him and went on. He didn't do it again.

Once was enough. When I brought him over to Melinda at the side of the arena, she shook her head. Miss Slater kept smiling and said, "Come on, now, Melinda. You rode him yesterday, and you said you liked it."

"He wasn't bucking yesterday."

"He's not really bucking today, is he, Abby?"

"He was happy," I said. "That's all."

"I don't want him to be happy." Then she changed her mind. "I mean, I don't want him to be extra happy."

Gloria said, "You're a good rider, Melinda. I saw you. You're way better than I am, and I would ride him. You don't have to worry."

Melinda didn't say anything.

I gave Gallant Man some pats. He snorted away a fly, which startled Melinda, but he was otherwise being good. What I really wanted to do was ask Melinda what had happened that had made her so scared, but I remembered Jem Jarrow saying that things that have happened don't really matter to a horse, so I thought, well, maybe the same thing worked for people. I took Melinda's hand and said, "Let's walk around with the pony awhile." Miss Slater caught my eye and smiled. I said to Melinda, "You go on the left side and I'll go on the right, and the pony will walk between us."

We did this, both of us holding a rein, with Melinda also holding the end of the reins so that they wouldn't drag on the ground. When we were at the far end of the ring, as far as we could get from Miss Slater, Melinda suddenly said, "It's only when I get here that I get afraid. When I'm at home, I always think it's going to be great. You can't believe how many pictures I've drawn all over my notebooks of Gallant Man and how much I think about him, but the closer I come to him, it's like I want to scream."

"That's funny. Not funny ha ha."

"I know."

"Do you come out here every day?"

"Every day they let me. That's almost every day. My mom says I'm too grumpy if I don't come out."

I said, "You're weird, Melinda," not as if I meant it, but as if I were just joking with her, and Melinda gave me a big grin.

160

She said, "I know that." We walked on. At the end of the arena, we turned and headed back toward Miss Slater and Gloria. Melinda said, "If I get on now, will you walk along with us? You don't have to lead me."

I gave her a leg up. Once she had settled into the saddle and I had shortened the stirrups, she sat up and put her heels down. Her position was very good. We walked along. The pony behaved himself. Finally, I said, "Has the pony ever done anything bad?"

"No."

"Then why do you think he will?"

"I don't know."

"I don't think he will. He never did anything bad with me, either. Some horses just don't do anything bad. It's like a habit that they don't have."

"Like not sucking your thumb."

"Yeah. Exactly. Kids who don't suck their thumbs just don't suck their thumbs." I stepped a little away from the pony and let her handle the reins. She turned him, and I followed. I thought that was a good sign. Then she turned him again. She was riding him, but it was like she didn't even realize it. She said, "I've got pictures of him on the lid of my desk, so when I open it, there he is. And I wrote two stories about him for school." She was smiling. A moment later, she trotted away, but then she stopped because I didn't trot after her.

I trotted after her. Then I got an idea.

She was looking at me. When I trotted past her, she nudged the pony up into the trot again, and they followed me, about ten feet behind. I jogged down the long side of the arena, then rounded the corner. They were right behind me. I jogged diagonally across the arena. They were right behind me. I turned right. They turned right. I turned right again and trotted over a tiny cross-rail, not more than six inches off the ground. They were right behind me. I didn't even look back, I just swung around and trotted over it again, then I turned right and trotted over another one. By this time, I was out of breath, so I stopped. Melinda and the pony came up to me. I thought of Jem Jarrow and how he gave George one pat but didn't make a big deal. I said, "That was good!" but nothing more. It occurred to me that when you make a big deal rather than a little deal of someone doing something, maybe they think you're also telling them that you never thought they could do it.

I walked over to Gloria and Miss Slater and Gloria's mom, where they were standing together watching us. Miss Slater was grinning, but as we approached, she calmed down, gave me a nod, and walked toward the center of the arena. Melinda and the pony followed her, and then they started having a regular lesson. Melinda did fine and seemed happy. It was like she had been under a spell, and now the spell was broken. Anyway, the lesson even included trotting back and forth over the two sets of cross-rails. We just watched. Melinda's mom smiled but didn't say anything. She must have thought it was very cold, because she had a black wool coat on, gloves, and a fur hat.

Miss Slater was beaming. After the groom came out and led Melinda and the pony away to be untacked, she held out her hand to me and said, "Abby, my dear, you are a natural. I want to thank you."

I held out my hand. She shook it and put her other hand on my shoulder.

It wasn't until we were in the car that Gloria and her mom

started talking about Melinda. I gathered that while I was riding the pony, they had learned a lot about Mr. and Mrs. Anniston. Melinda was an only child. Mr. Anniston was twenty years older than Mrs. Anniston, and he had children from his first marriage who were almost the same age as Mrs. Anniston.

Anyway, the really important thing that they had learned from Miss Slater, who obviously was "talking out of school" as Mom would say because she didn't like gossip, was that the Annistons were "estranged."

I couldn't imagine what this meant. Certainly Melinda was strange, or "weird," but she seemed proud to be weird. As I listened, I learned that one symptom of being estranged was that one parent lived in the "vacation home" and one parent lived in the "primary residence," but according to Miss Slater, with the Annistons, you couldn't tell the difference between the two—one was in Los Angeles and the other one was here, and both were very splendid.

"One of them has to be sold, though," said Gloria's mother, "to pay for the divorce. Martha Slater says that Melinda doesn't know a thing about it yet."

"I won't tell."

"I didn't think you would, dear, but a word to the wise is always the best policy."

After that, we didn't talk about it.

But neither did we talk about school. I thought we would. In fact, I thought that Gloria had set up this whole invitation so that we could figure out what to do about how awful everything was. Instead, she worked on her model of her mission (San Juan Capistrano), which she was making with Debbie and a couple of the boys. The only thing she had left to do was make little origami birds to represent the swallows. I made a couple for her, but they weren't very good, so she said she would glue them in the back. "Debbie isn't very good at that, either," she said. "But she wrote out the history in fancy writing with red capital letters. That looks nice." We played records on her new hi-fi set. When you folded the turntable up into the box and unplugged the cords, it looked sort of like a suitcase with a handle, so you could take it with you places if you wanted to. Her grandfather had sent it to her for no reason at all, just because he saw it in a store, and he had also sent her two albums, *Beatles '65*, by The Beatles, and another record by a group called The Searchers. I was kind of amazed that a grandfather would do something like that. When my grandparents gave us things, they were old— pictures of what Oklahoma looked like in the early days or a silver belt buckle that had been passed down in the family.

We had fried chicken for dinner, which was very good, a special recipe including cornflakes. It came to me maybe three times to tell Gloria about Stella and the ink cartridge, but in the end I never did. It felt too much like tattling, and anyway, it was possible that Gloria knew all about it and wasn't telling me.

Nor did I tell Mom when she came into my room at bedtime that night. When I told her about Melinda, she said that maybe Melinda was afraid because her family was keeping things from her, so she suspected that there was a lot going on that she didn't know anything about. She said, "Children always know more than you think."

I didn't know if this was true, because I didn't know what Mom and Daddy thought I knew.

I told her about the fried chicken and the origami birds and the new record player.

Just when I thought she was going to leave, she said, "Jem Jarrow had stopped by while you were gone."

"He did?"

"Yes, and your daddy was all set to sell him a horse, but he said that he was never in the market for a horse, and he thought maybe he should clear things up."

"What did he have to clear up?"

"Well, Abby, Danny and Jake sent him over, and I knew about that. It was me who told Jake that you were afraid to ride the horse."

"I told Danny that, too."

"I know. The thing is, Danny has been working with Jem. Jake has known Jem Jarrow for forty years, working around at one ranch or another, and Jake always thought he was the best hand with a horse in the area, but Jem wasn't hiring himself out before. He and his brother had a big ranch, but now they've sold some of the land and some of the cattle, so he thought he would go out and see if there was a living to be made training horses."

"What did Daddy say?"

"He said, 'Not much of one.'"

I sighed. I said, "Daddy never did ask me what happened."

"I think he thought you just stood there while Jem tried the horse. He didn't know that Jem actually did anything with the horse."

"Does he want to know now?"

"Yes."

"Can I tell him tomorrow?" I was really tired.

"Tomorrow is Sunday. What I came up here to tell you, Abby, is that if you would like Jem Jarrow to come back, I think you'd better make your case tonight, before your father has his own thoughts about it and they get set, if you know what I mean."

I knew what she meant. I threw back the covers and put on my robe and slippers. She went out of my room, and I followed her downstairs.

Daddy was sitting at his desk, reading the Bible, when I came in. He always had to do that on Saturday night in order to have a lesson to talk about on Sunday, because our church didn't have a pastor or a minister—the men in the church took turns "talking" about things, which meant that each Sunday, each of them would do a short lesson. The short lessons were supposed to add up to something about as long as a regular church service.

Daddy closed his Bible and pushed it away from himself. Then he turned his chair toward me. I hoped that the lesson he was working on was about forgiveness and mercy rather than justice and wrath, but there was no telling ahead of time. He said, "So, Abby. I guess Jem Jarrow never came to actually buy the horse. I guess your mom and Jake played a trick on me."

I said, "I guess."

"I can't say I like that, but I recognize that 'God resisteth the proud, but giveth grace unto the humble.'"

I guessed that that was going to be his text for the following day. I wasn't quite sure whether he was referring to himself or Ornery George, so I said, "Well, George acted pretty humble after Jem—I mean, Mr. Jarrow—worked with him."

Mom said, "I think it's okay to call him Jem."

Daddy said, "How did he work with him?"

I decided that it was still not the best thing, especially if we were talking about pride, to mention Danny, so I mixed the two up together a bit. "Well, first he got George to do things that he wanted him to do without making a big deal of it. If the horse was coming toward him, he waved him away and made him keep going until *he* said George could stop. Whatever George did, he never let him think it was his own idea. If he wanted to go, Jem made him go faster. If he wanted to stop, Jem didn't let him stop until he had gone farther than he wanted to."

"Hmm," said Daddy.

"Another thing was, he didn't focus on him at first. He worked all the horses together so that George couldn't prepare himself to be ornery. By the time he singled him out, George was ready to do something."

"Why?"

"Well, according to what he said to me, because he had aroused his curiosity. He said horses are very curious."

Daddy opened his mouth to speak.

"And you can use that to get them to do what you want to do. I guess like making something a game."

Mom said, "That always worked with you kids. If you were fussing or crying and I went over and started doing something in your toy box, pretty soon you would stop fussing because you wanted to see what I was doing."

"Like that," I said.

"Hmm," said Daddy.

"But once he got on George, he did make him work. It's just that the work started out with a lot of turns. He said that the horse had to learn to soften and step his hind foot over the instant you asked for it, and if he did, he would be less likely to get stubborn or to stumble." I thought again. "When he was loping and George started to buck, he pulled him up with one rein and over to the inside, not very hard, and George went around a little bit and then loped off. He only tried to buck that one time."

"Well, he's a good rider. He's been riding and working cows all his life, they say."

"I know. But it didn't look that hard."

This was a statement I soon came to repent of.

"I wish he would buy the horse and we could dispense with the whole problem." He sighed.

I said, "I don't want to dispense with the whole problem."

"You don't?"

"I want to try it a couple more times. I want to see if it only works for him."

"Well, I—"

"It was interesting. I watched the whole time." To myself, I added, and I watched Danny, too, and that was interesting, too. I said, "He came twice, right?"

"Yes."

"Well, it seemed to me that the horse learned something from the first time to the second. I always thought that the horse is supposed to do what he's told, but this was different— he did more than what he was told. It was like he remembered what he was told before and didn't have to be told again, only reminded. I bet if Jem came another couple of times, the horse would do what he was told without being told."

Mom said, "You mean he would learn something."

"Yes, that's what I mean."

Daddy said, "I don't really think of horses as having a body of knowledge, but maybe they do."

"They do," I said. "I mean, when George doesn't want to get caught, he's acting like he knows something bad is going to happen, and so he isn't going to cooperate."

"Well, even so, I'm sure Jem Jarrow doesn't train horses for free."

I knew what that meant. It meant that was that. Because if you put a lot of money into a horse, then you couldn't make much of a profit, and if you didn't make much of a profit, then you couldn't buy more horses. Or anything else.

Thinking of Ornery George made me think of something else, though. I said, "Mr. Tacker really liked George. He looked at him three times while he was loading Red Jewel into his trailer. You always said someone will pay more for a pretty one, and he's the prettiest, except for Black George."

"I doubt if Mr. Tacker would think Black George is prettier. Ornery George is about as pretty as they come for a ranch horse. Or a parade horse."

Now was when I buttoned my lip. Because I could see the wheels turning, even though as a little girl, I wasn't supposed to see the wheels turning. Mom said, "Okay, Abby. You go to bed now. I know you're tired."

But I stayed awake for another hour or more, waiting to hear Daddy and Mom go into their room. By the time I fell asleep, they were still up. If they were still up, they would still be talking. If they were still talking, then Daddy hadn't yet said, "I've made up my mind," or, "Who's the boss around here?" If he hadn't said that, then Mom was going to have her way.

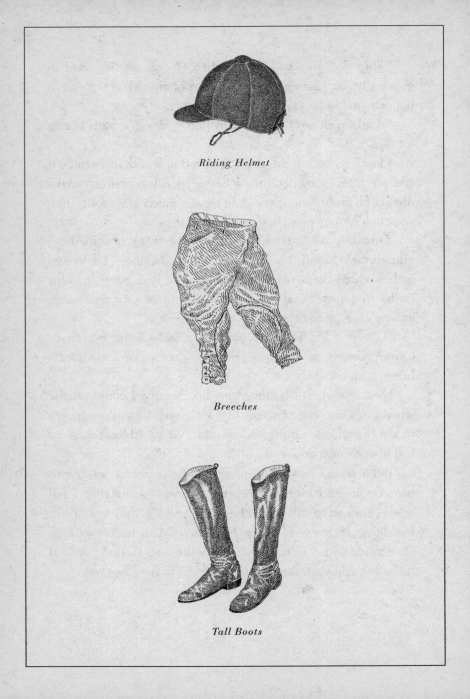

Riding Helmet

Breeches

Tall Boots

Chapter 14

TRAINING SESSIONS WITH JEM JARROW WERE TWELVE DOLLARS apiece, for forty-five minutes. He agreed to come on Monday and Tuesday and then on Saturday. This gave me something to look forward to during school.

After lunch on Monday, the tables in the cafeteria were moved into their new arrangement, six of them in a long line over against the back wall, away from the windows. The teachers then laid out the long sheet of brown paper with the outline of California on it. At each of the spots where the twenty-one missions were to sit, someone had drawn stars, and because some of these were rather close together, someone had drawn arrows to different places on the paper where we were to place our missions. Barbara and Alexis Goldman had made the San Diego

Mission entirely of corks that were cut into chunks and glued together. Two of the missions were made of Lincoln Logs. One was just a pile of stones, and the label read, *The Mission La Purisma was destroyed by an EARTHQUAKE in 1812.* There were some plastic cows and pigs set around the rubble. I doubted that the boys who made that model were going to get As.

Joan, Linda, and the two Marys had gotten permission to collaborate on one mission, Mission San Carlos, in Carmel, because it was big, beautiful, and important. The model sat in the middle of the whole display, about half again as large as any of the others. There was the church, the bell tower, with steps going up around it, and a courtyard. Everything was inside a box, and on the outside of the box, the girls had pasted color photos of things like the garden and the interior of the church, with information about Father Serra and Monterey typed on cards. The buildings were glued together from plywood, with designs painted on them. It took two girls to carry the mission from the social studies room to the lunchroom, and we all had to make way.

Unfortunately, Stella and one of the boys, Larry Schnuck, had constructed Mission San Antonio out of cardboard. It was the next one down from Carmel and looked very poor and small by comparison. And then Miss Albers, who was homeroom teacher for the other seventh grade, said, "Stella, we'll just move yours a little bit to the side so that we can fit Carmel in here." I didn't even have to look at Stella to know what she thought of that.

I made Gloria meet me in the girls' bathroom during study hall. After we pushed on all the stall doors to make sure that no one else was in there, I took her over by the sinks, where we could see someone come in, and I said, "Were you looking at Stella when Miss Albers made her move her mission?"

"No. Some of my birds fell off—"

"Well, she was plenty mad. Her face turned beet red." As I said this, I felt sick to my stomach.

Gloria said, "So what?"

"So what if she does something to that mission?"

"Oh, pullease. You're crazy."

"No, I'm not, but I can't tell you—"

"Well, if you can't tell me, then so what, again. Why can't you tell me?" Her eyebrows lowered and she stared at me. Right then, I knew she knew all about the ink cartridge.

"I saw something that nobody else saw."

Now she looked at me. "What?" But it didn't seem as though she was asking a question. More like she was making a dare—daring me to tell.

I made up my mind right there that Gloria wasn't on my side anymore. "I can't tell." And then I made up my mind that she was.

"Abby, if you brought me in here, you have to tell."

"I haven't told anyone."

"You're kidding. It's that bad?"

It seemed like two halves of me were certain of what I should do. Unfortunately, each half was certain of a different thing. One half was certain that if I told Gloria, she would be shocked at what Stella had done and help me prevent Stella from hurting the Carmel mission. The other half was certain that Gloria and Stella were in on things together, and in that case, I had no idea what I should do. I didn't know if Gloria was more in favor of Stella doing something bad or more against it.

I didn't say anything, and finally, Gloria said, "Oh, for heaven's sake. Who cares?" She sounded fed up. She washed her hands and dried them with some paper towels, then walked out. After that, I sat on the edge of the sink rubbing my stomach in circles, trying to make the feeling go away. I actually said, out loud to myself, "Don't make such a big deal of it! It's not a big deal!" But my stomach thought it was a big deal, and so I was late to algebra. I didn't see Gloria for the rest of the day.

Thanks to Kyle, of course, our mission was one of the best—very neat and colorful and important-looking, because of the clay and the bells. It got a lot of compliments.

That afternoon, Jem Jarrow stayed for an hour and a half. Daddy was somewhere with the truck, getting the carburetor fixed, so he didn't get to see Jem right from the beginning. The first thing Jem did was to work with Ornery George in much the same way that he did the previous Wednesday. Jem was on him within about ten minutes. But then he was off him again. He waved me into the arena. When I got to him, he said, "I forgot to tell you the most important thing."

"What's that?"

"When you're working with an unbroke horse, never be too lazy to get off."

I laughed.

Jem smiled, but then he got serious and looked me in the eye. He said, "I mean it, though. This horse gave me a sign. I felt it. His back is still tense and he's still distracted. Instead of being lazy and thinking that I'll ride him through it, I made up my mind to get off and do a few more things with him before I try him again. Sometimes I don't get on a horse at all during a session. It doesn't do me any good if he hurts me, and it doesn't do him any good, either."

"Daddy says they have to know who's boss. If you get off, then you're giving them their way."

Jem asked George to step over and then step back, then step over the other way, then step forward. George kept looking off toward the gelding corral as if he didn't care one bit about Jem Jarrow, and then Jem raised his hand and made him speed up, and George suddenly tucked his head, curved his body, and looked really beautiful. It was startling. Jem let him come to a halt, and then he gave him a pat. He said to me, "I don't get into a fight with them just to let them know who's boss. Most horses, if they win a fight, it scares them, and if they lose a fight, it makes them resentful."

"After George and my uncle Luke had it out, George was worse."

Jem Jarrow didn't say anything to this. He didn't seem to be an "I-told-you-so" sort of person. After a bit, he got on George again, and this time the horse did all his movements with his ears up and his head and neck relaxed. Also, his hocks were under him, and his response to all of Jem's signals was practically instantaneous. I realized that I had never seen him before without that grumpy look on his face. Jem never let him do the same thing for more than ten or fifteen steps. He turned or halted or cantered or trotted or walked with long steps or made a little circle or figure eight or galloped off and came to a sliding halt or did a neat rotation around his hind feet, first one direction, then the other. He cantered from the halt without bucking.

After they had done all of these things, Jem walked George around, and George continued to look pleased with himself. When they passed me where I was sitting on the fence, I said, "He's a well-trained horse."

Jem said, "He knows a lot of things, yes, but he isn't a well-trained horse until it's his second nature to soften as soon as he's asked to do anything."

"At which point a little girl will be able to ride him."

"I expect a little girl will be able to teach him to do that." He pushed his hat back on his head. He said, "You like that dark one?"

"Yes. That's Black George."

"Well, why don't you go get on him and let's see how he does."

"It's been forty-five minutes."

"Has it? That's fine. Let's try him out."

I put the western tack on Black George, which I hadn't done in a month and a half.

I would have said that Black George was a very good horse. He never bucked or spooked, much less reared or bolted. But after I had taught him, with Jem telling me what to do, to step under in both directions and to drop his nose to the inside and quietly bring his hip around, it was like I was riding a different animal. At the walk, his body was relaxed and loose and I could feel his stride lengthen or shorten every time I asked. At the trot, it was as if the saddle rode his back like a little boat, and I could feel each of his hind legs step under my seat like a little wave. He covered a lot of ground, too. But the canter! The canter wasn't like anything I had ever felt before, rocking and comfortable, but strong and dynamic. I knew that what made it good was right in the shoulder, right in front of my hands. And when I looked at his head, I could just see the bulge of his inside eye; I could also feel his inside hind leg stepping underneath me and launching us, and yet all of these little bits of things I noticed came and went in what seemed like a whoosh of speed. I made small circles and large circles; I asked for a gallop and he leapt forward; I asked for and got a neat halt. The feeling in my stomach had vanished, and school seemed very small and far away. It seemed like I would never make a big deal about anything at school ever again.

Daddy was standing by the fence with Jem. I waved. They talked.

I went over to them. Daddy said, "That looked very nice, young lady."

"He's so comfortable."

"Music to my ears, darling." He shook Jem's hand and walked away.

After Jem left, I tried what he'd taught me on Socks George and the two mares, but what he had taught me, even though I could remember a lot of the very words he had used, was like a refreshing fog that slowly lifted and wafted away. After a while, I had no idea whether I was doing the right thing or not. But he was coming back the very next day. With luck, I thought, Jem might stay two hours.

* * *

In the morning, as soon as we got off the bus, the principal, Mr. Canning, sent us into the lunchroom to have a look at the missions. He and Miss Rowan, the art teacher and Mr. Jarek, the history teacher, stood at the end of the table by San Francisco Solano, smiling and clapping and exclaiming that we had all done a wonderful job, the best ever. The display was more elaborate now—the sixth graders had added some things to the map, just as we had done the year before, when we were in sixth grade—mostly cutouts of cattle and sheep and some fish and whales out in the ocean, as well as two models of sailing ships. The photos of the missions "as they are today" were taped to the wall. Miss Rowan had brought a plate of peanut butter cookies, and we all had one.

Out by the lockers, while we were waiting for the bell, Stella looked happier than she had looked in weeks. And she was also nicer to me. While she was smiling at me and asking how my horses were (she never asked this, normally), her eyes kept drifting toward Brian, Joan, and Mary A., who were talking about bologna sandwiches in loud voices. I said that the horses were fine, and then I said, "Stella, listen to them! Why do you even care?"

"Care about what?"

"About him. Or them. Any of it."

"What makes you think I care?"

"You're looking at them."

"He's just wearing a very strange shirt is all."

He wasn't, though.

At this point, one of the eighth-grade boys walked by, a kid I'd been riding the bus with since kindergarten, named Dougie Wilder. Stella gave him a big smile and said, "Hi, Dougie!"

He looked at her and walked on without saying anything.

I said, "Why do you speak to them?"

"Why not? I'm a friendly person."

"You say hi to them and they don't answer back."

She waved her hand, then she said, "My mom said I could have a party. A boy-girl party. But I have to invite everyone in the class. Can you come?"

"My mom will say yes and my dad will say no, so it depends."

"On what?"

"That's what I don't know."

"Your family is so weird, Abby."

"Well, yeah," is what I said.

"Anyway, if you come, you have to wear something nice" is what she said. She made her voice sound like she was telling me a friendly secret, but I knew she was being mean.

After lunch, when we were at our lockers, Kyle came up to me and said, "You got any glue or Scotch tape or anything like that in your locker?"

I had some Elmer's. I handed it to Kyle. He said, "Some of those trees you made fell over. I'm going to make little stands on the bottom of them. I already colored them brown, but I want to glue them, not just slot them in."

"Okay. But what about your next class?"

"It's gym. I hate gym."

"Don't they care if you're late?"

"Not if you're working on your mission." He took the glue and turned away.

I went to science. We studied barometric pressure. After science, I went back to my locker, thinking solely of showing Jack to Jem Jarrow and finding out how to make him perfect starting right now. I was rummaging around in the bottom of my locker for my colored pencils, and someone bumped me from behind and made me hit my head on the back of the locker. I stood up. Kyle said, "Oh, sorry. I didn't mean to run into you. Here's your glue." He held it out to me, then he said, "I worked on those trees until they were practically growing, waiting for her to go away. She walked all over the place and looked at every mission about six times. I reset the bells. I did everything I could think of."

"What are you talking about?"

"I'm thinking she was going to spill her root beer all over it."

"Who?"

"Your friend Stella. She kept walking around with it and taking tiny little sips and looking over at me, but I didn't look at her, I just kept doing stuff."

"What happened?"

"Well, the bell rang, and then she stood around for a while, and then she left."

We looked at each other. I'm not sure that Kyle and I had ever looked at each other for more than half a second, but now we were both thinking about the same thing, so we looked at each other. Then he said, "But the evidence is only circumstantial."

"What does that mean?"

"It means we could report her only if she really spilled her root beer."

I got that feeling in my stomach again. I said, "What about Gloria? Was she around?"

"No." Then he shrugged. "I did reset the bells. They ring good now."

Jem Jarrow was already there as soon as I got off the bus, and the first thing he said to me was, "Mind if we have a look at the colt?"

Of course not. Jem already had his rope halter out, and he followed me to the pen.

Jack had his head up and his ears pricked, looking right at me. He always did when I came down the road from the school bus. Most of the time, he whinnied or squealed, too. What I did first when I saw him was to pet him on the head and neck, both sides. No treats. Almost every adult in the world that I knew said that treats make a horse nippy, though Daddy would give a trained horse a bit of something once in a while. Sometimes, I picked a handful of grass and let Jack take that between his lips, especially if it was green and moist.

Jem said, "Show me what you do with him."

I went and got the halter and the chamois. Jack stood nicely for putting on the halter. Once he had it on, I started leading him around, and he was okay for the first while, but then he got balky and distracted. I turned him and led him a little bit more. He stopped, threw his head up, and started backing up. Then he came with me again, but when we got back to the gate, I was disappointed and thought that he could have behaved himself better, but then I thought the other thing I always thought, which was that he was just a baby and he would get better as he got older. I held the lead rope with one hand and rubbed the chamois over him with the other, first one side, then the next. He stood quietly for that.

Jem said, "How old is he now?"

"Almost three months."

"He's a big colt."

"He might be a Thoroughbred."

"Looks like it. Why don't you let him go for a minute." This was not a question. When I let him go, he trotted off, his neck arched and his ears pricked. All of a sudden, he reared up a little and pawed, as if he had an imaginary enemy to scare away. He leapt into the air and ran a few strides, then he kicked out. A lot of his foal coat was gone now, and the dark, shiny coat underneath looked sparkly in the sun.

Jem said, "It's going to be a big job, raising this colt."

"That's what everybody says."

"His dam would normally be doing a lot of the work for you."

"I know."

"My suggestion, you turn him out with the geldings."

"I'm afraid he'll get hurt."

"He might, with the mares. Less likely with the geldings, but there's always a risk. First thing, though, he needs to know what they all need to know—how to step over and get out of your space when you ask him to."

Jack had by now come back over to us, his neck arched and his ears pricked, just as interested as he could be. Jem let him be close but not too close. If Jack pressed into him, Jem lifted the halter in his hand and waved it a bit. When Jack then backed up a step, Jem stepped toward him and gave him a pat. Two times, he made the colt back up three or more steps, then he gently touched the side of his face and asked him to turn his head. When his head had turned pretty far, Jack unbent by stepping over. Jem gave him a pat. He said, "One good thing is, if a horse is curious, a colt is twice as curious. If a horse wants to play, and horses do, because otherwise why would they do most of the things we ask them to do, a colt wants to play all the time. Your job is to teach him not to play rough. That's what his dam would do."

I said, "I never thought of what horses do as playing."

"Sure it is. You seen a horse work a cow? That horse is going to tell that cow what to do, pretty much the same as two kids playing tag. My feeling is, the more the horse likes the game, the less the cow does." He smiled and waved Jack away more energetically. First, Jack threw his head up, snorting, and pricked his ears, then he spun and galloped across the pen with his tail curled over his back. After that, he arched his neck and trotted around in a circle, snorting even more loudly and staring at Jem and his rope. He lifted his feet high, then halted again and whinnied. He was tremendously cute. Jem said, "Every move that colt makes, he makes because he enjoys it and it expresses something. He wasn't afraid of the rope when I shook it—he took the shaking of the rope as a reason to move, and then he enjoyed himself moving."

"And we enjoyed watching."

"Well, there you go. Showing, going in parades, working cattle, racing, you name it, if the horses didn't enjoy it, they wouldn't have given humans any ideas about what a horse could do for them."

"Plowing?"

Now Jem really laughed. He said, "Oh, you are something, Miss Abby. You make me laugh. But who says a plow horse doesn't enjoy pulling the plow? How are you going to make him if he doesn't want to do it?"

I was sure that there were ways, and of course, I had read *Black Beauty*, but I liked the way Jem thought of it, so I didn't talk back.

In the meantime, Jack returned to us as if pulled on a rubber band, and this time, Jem put the halter on him while I went and stood outside the gate. Jack acted as if he were a little insulted by the halter and started trotting away, but Jem held on, and Jack came around. Jem waved the end of the rope at him as he got close, and Jack went on past him, pretty soon taking some steps in a circle around Jem but still tossing his head a little. Then, very easily, Jem put some pressure on the rope, and Jack, without even seeming to realize what he was doing, stepped his inside hind leg in front of his outside hind leg and turned smoothly inward. His ears were flicking back and forth. He hesitated. Jem now lifted his left hand, and when Jack moved away from that a little, he found himself going the other way, trotting to the right around Jem's little circle. I saw right away that with a colt even more than with a horse, your job was to give him a little suggestion more than a strict command. If he was playing a game, then you wanted the game to be fun but to also have rules. Jem did this with him for only five minutes or so, just as if it were a game. When Jack was standing quietly, Jem called me over. I opened the gate and closed it behind me.

He handed me the rope and said, "Jake seen the colt?"

"I think he's coming this week."

"Good, because you got to keep a colt's feet in good trim so his feet and legs will develop right. Let's pick his feet up."

"Sometimes I do that when I'm rubbing him down. I rub the chamois down his legs to his feet and then I pick the foot up."

Jem did the same thing, only with his hands—he rubbed from the shoulder downward, down the forearm and then over the knee. When Jack seemed uncomfortable, he stopped his hands moving, but he didn't move away, and then Jack would relax, and Jem would move his hands downward again. He didn't get all the way to his feet at first, just a little closer every time, until after a few tries, he reached a foot and asked Jack to pick it up and stand for a moment on three legs. It was a short moment, though. And then he would drop the foot.

Jem stood up straight and looked at me. He said, "Now, you don't put the foot down. That can be irritating to him. You just let the foot go and he'll stand up on it." He worked his way around the colt, doing this with each foot. I think because of what I'd done with the chamois, Jack didn't mind, really. By the time I did it myself, Jack was standing up like a pro and letting me hold his foot up for maybe thirty seconds. Thirty seconds is a long time when you are holding up a horse's foot and waiting to drop it.

After that, we petted Jack and let him go. Jem said to me, "You've done a good job with him so far, Abby, because he likes you and he lets you be around him. He's half doing what you say because you say it and half doing it because it's interesting to him. That's not bad. But soon he's going to be a big fellow, and you're going to want to rely on him to behave himself—not to get distracted or worked up about things that happen. So you need to work with him every day and give him good habits."

I nodded.

"Let's put him in with the geldings and see what happens."

I must have looked shocked, because he smiled and said, "There's only three of them. If they seem overbearing, we'll grab him and take him out. But he needs to understand other horses, or he'll live a sad life."

I could see this all too well. It was rather like seventh grade.

All we had to do was stand there in order for Jack to come back to us, looking for something, as always. When Jack got to me, I patted him while he snuffled my hands and my hair. Then I slipped the halter on, showing off a little that I could do it smoothly rather than roughly. Then I turned and walked away, and Jack walked along with me toward the gate. Jem said, "Pause, just because you feel like pausing. He should pause, too." He did. But when we went out of the gate, the colt was all eyes. And when he saw that I was leading him toward the gelding pasture, I felt him fill up, sort of like a balloon, and begin to jog. Jem said, "Turn him. He doesn't get to do the most interesting thing unless he can contain himself." As we were passing the hay barn, Jem grabbed a few flakes of hay.

The three geldings were maybe a hundred feet out into the pasture, nibbling grass, but they looked up as soon as they saw us coming, and Socks George threw up his head and gave a whinny. Jack answered. Luckily, though, they just stood there staring as I brought Jack to the gate, and Jem opened it. Jem said, "Pretend there's nothing important going on. Just walk him through the gate and out a ways, and then turn him and get him to lower his head so you can take off the halter." I did.

Jack stood staring at the big horses, his ears pricked, and then, when they came toward him, he started smacking his lips together, which made a little noise. His ears went from being pricked to simply flopping to the side. He dropped his head a little. Jem said, "See what his lips are doing, the way he's showing his teeth a little? He's saying to them, 'I'm a baby.'"

"He never seems to think of himself as a baby."

"Well, he is, and he knows it. And they know it, too, so they expect him to act like a baby."

"What do you mean?"

"Low man on the totem pole."

"Oh."

Now the geldings came over to him, Black George in the lead and the other two right behind him. Then Black George first, Ornery George, and Socks George sniffed noses with him. They sniffed the rest of him while he stood quietly, occasionally flapping his lips. He didn't jump or move or kick out. He tried to sniff their noses, too, but carefully, so as not to cause offense. Ornery George gave him a little bite on the neck. I gasped, but the bite didn't seem mean exactly, more like he was trying it out. Jack flicked his ears backward, but he didn't pin them, as if he were saying, "Okay, bite me if you have to."

Then he made a wrong move, as if he couldn't contain himself and just didn't know what he was doing. He leapt up and struck out with his front hoof. Black George squealed and his ears went back. Jack lowered his head immediately. I said, "They're kind of bossy."

Jem said, "Not really. The three of them, it's more of a club than a dictatorship." We continued to watch, but Jem made no move to go in or rescue him.

As for me, I did want him to fit into the club, but I knew that the club could change—would change, if Daddy had his way, and that the members of the club could get meaner. One thing I loved about Jack, and one of the reasons that I watched him sometimes, was that he didn't know what the rules were. He ran, he leapt, he snorted, he stared at geckos and ground squirrels, he pawed things and investigated. He whinnied and squealed and came running, or went running. He was willing to try anything out, and he looked beautiful doing it. His neck arched, his feet lifted, his tail went up, his nostrils flared. A breeze might get him going, or a bird taking off from a branch, or the sight of the other horses galloping. He was by himself, so he had to make his own fun, and we all knew that the fun that kids sometimes make for themselves isn't that good for them. Still, he was the only creature on the place who did what he wanted to when he wanted to do it. I liked watching.

Jem said, "Well, it's going pretty well, I think."

Black George seemed to lose interest. He walked away. The others followed. Jack stood there, then he followed.

Jem said, "If he follows, he's saying that they are the bosses. And that's what we want him to say. The bosses pretend not to notice the underlings, and the underlings show that they are always aware of the bosses. That's how horse herds work. So you watch for a bit. You'll see that now they will all pretend to ignore him, but they'll test him a little bit to see if he's paying attention." And it was true—just a bit after Jem said that,

Socks George trotted past Jack, kind of close to him, in fact, without seeming to notice him, and Jack stepped back to let him go by and then turned toward him. Jem said, "The chestnut just showed who was boss, and Jack just showed that he understands that."

I said, "What if they gang up on him—"

"My thought is that these horses aren't going to do that. They're pretty consistent, and they have a pretty stable group—"

"Club."

"Yeah. I don't think they'll kick him—that's why I didn't put him in with the mares. Mares kick more than geldings. He looks like he knows his place. That's not to say that later he won't decide that he isn't a baby anymore. But he knows he's a baby now, and they will remind him of that fact with a nip here and there, so don't be surprised if you come out and find a few bites on him." He turned and looked at me. He said, "The geldings are doing a job that you would have to do, Abby. It's a job that has to be done, especially with a bright colt like this fellow."

"Like school."

"Like school."

He said, "Okay, now let's give everyone some hay. It's almost feeding time, and at feeding time, horses get a little worried. Once they all have plenty of hay and the colt doesn't bother them at theirs, then everyone will settle down."

We set out five piles. Jack started out at the farthest-away pile, mouthing the hay and eating a little. Then he moved to the next one closest to the other geldings. Ornery George looked at him once and flicked his ears backward, but then they all settled to eating, and I let out that long breath I had been holding.

Western Saddle

Western Stirrups

Farrier's Apron

Chapter 15

Jem left shortly after that, and I felt his reassurance all through supper and all through my homework (and anyway, I went out to check on the geldings two or three times before I went to bed). After she fed Jack his bran mixture, Mom came in and told me they would be all right, and Daddy said that if I was worried, then I should turn it over to the Lord, because then the best thing would happen. I nodded, but we both knew that the "best thing" could always be a trial of some sort, which I frankly didn't think I was ready for. But even in the morning everyone was fine. I got up early and watched them before school. I saw that Jack did his romping and playing a little off by himself, but the geldings watched him with pricked ears, like indulgent uncles. He watched them, too. When they got their hay and settled down to eat it, he stood in the line like they did, switching his little tail (I always set the hay piles out in a long line, each pile about ten feet from the others). Perfectly relaxed.

But I was so tired from waking up in the night and worrying about him that I fell asleep on the school bus, which I would have thought was an impossible thing to do. When we got to school, I woke up, but I was sleepy all through homeroom and first period. And it wasn't until I went to the girls' bathroom during the break that I realized what I looked like. My hair was flat on one side and sticking out on the other side and my blouse was wrinkled, too, because I had picked it out of my closet without really looking at it in the dark. What a mess. No wonder Stella wanted to make sure I would wear something nice to her party.

By lunch, I had more or less fixed myself. At least Stella and Gloria didn't say anything. They were talking about the mission open house and potluck that night. Gloria's mom was going to bring steamed artichokes with a special sauce and Stella's mom was going to bring the safest thing, chocolate chip cookies. Stella told Gloria that her mom was weird and Gloria shrugged, as if to say, Well, we all know that. Then Stella got up to go to the girls' bathroom to do something, and even though I expected Gloria to follow her, she didn't. She leaned toward me and said, "Guess what?"

"What?"

"Remember that ink thing? When Joan got the ink on her skirt?"

I sat very still and said, "Yeah, sure."

"Somebody sent Joan an anonymous note and said it was Stella, that she did it on purpose with the cartridge from her pen, and Joan's mom showed the note to Mr. Canning."

I decided to be very careful. I said, "Do you think Stella did that? It's a really mean thing to do."

"Ha!" exclaimed Gloria, tossing her head. "I bet Joan wrote the note herself and sent it to herself, then showed it to her mom to blame it on Stella. That's what I think. I wouldn't put it past her."

She sounded like she believed that, but really, I didn't feel like I could figure anything out anymore. I said, "Don't you think things were easier before Stella came into our class?"

Gloria shrugged. She said, "Not as fun, though. More boring." We got up, put away our trays, and went into study hall. While I did my work, I thought about the fact that Jem Jones would be coming for one more day, on Saturday. It seemed like a treasure to know that.

Everything was normal that night, which was a Wednesday. We went to our chapel, and I gave thanks that I didn't have to talk to Daddy about the missions and whether I had witnessed to Kyle and the other kids about the wrongful history of the Catholic Church and all of that. That Wednesday, we happened to sing a lot. Daddy sang one of my favorites, one called "Deep River," that he didn't sing much. Then Mr. Hazen sang one called "Lonely Road" that I hadn't heard before. And we all sang all the verses of "Amazing Grace," including the one about the earth dissolving like snow. On the way home in the car, Daddy and Mom did a duet of "How Can I Keep from Singing?" which is one of my favorites of all time. When we checked on the horses before going to bed, everyone was quiet and happy, and Black George was standing by Jack, as if he had decided the colt was his boy.

No one was happy when I got to school in the morning, though. The Big Four were gathered around Joan's locker, gossiping in low tones, Brian Connelly was absent, and Stella and Gloria didn't have much to say. I went to algebra, then we had assembly, and in assembly, I found out what was wrong. Joan had worn her add-a-pearl necklace to the potluck. It had thirteen pearls on it and was very valuable, though Mr. Canning didn't say how much it was worth. Joan had been careless with the necklace, Mr. Canning admitted that—she hadn't noticed until she was in the girls' bathroom that it was no longer around her neck. Everyone had looked high and low. The necklace could not be found, and so it could only be assumed that someone had picked it up. That someone was expected to turn it in. Once again, I was glad I hadn't gone to the potluck.

For lunch, I had a sandwich made of a slice of the pot roast Mom had made for the prayer meeting. That was good, too.

Gloria and Stella agreed that they couldn't figure out why that necklace was such a big deal. Joan, of course, said they were real pearls rather than cultured pearls, but whose mother would let her wear real pearls to a potluck? And heels. Joan had also worn heels—two inch. "It was a potluck!" said Stella. "Why be overdressed? It's much worse to be overdressed than under-dressed for a party. My mom says that's practically a law."

Gloria nodded as if, in spite of the red boots and cowboy shirts and all, she understood this law perfectly.

This went on for all day Thursday. Joan's mother even came Thursday afternoon—I saw her enter the building and then go into the principal's office. But, to be perfectly frank, since I hadn't been at the potluck, I didn't think it was any of my business. When I got home Thursday afternoon, it didn't even occur to me to tell Mom about it, and if it had occurred to me, then I would have had to tell her about the missions, so I wouldn't have told her anyway.

Maybe because of the nice service we had had, Daddy was in a good mood all of Thursday and Friday morning. He helped me with everything, whistled a few tunes, ruffled my hair. And the weather was good. When we got up in the morning, it was already light. We had gotten past Mom's daffodils and well into the tulips, and even the irises were starting to bud out. Jack wandered around with the geldings as if he had been living with them for years. He spent most of his time not far from Black George, and they made a beautiful pair when they pricked their ears and trotted around. Black George was only four, actually, so he seemed to remember what it was like to be a colt. He and Jack would lift their tails and trot big and snort or pretend that crows taking off from the fence rail were exciting and run off leaping and kicking. Socks George and Ornery George didn't play with them much, but once in a while for a few moments they would pick up a gallop and take off across the pasture.

By Friday afternoon, the necklace thing was a big deal. In a special assembly, Mr. Canning told us in his sternest voice that Joan's parents were very upset, and that the sheriff knew about it, and that there would be repercussions if the person or persons who had the necklace did not come forward "of his or her own accord." I, of course, had my suspicions, but I didn't tell them to anyone, especially not Gloria and, when I got home, especially not Mom. Mom was a complete believer in "coming forward" because it was "in the end the kindest thing to do" and "a form of witnessing." But in seventh grade, a person who came forward was known as a snitch, and that would be the end of that person.

On Saturday morning, another beautiful day, I was up and dressed to ride by seven. Jem Jarrow appeared during breakfast. Mom asked if he would like some pancakes, which is what we were having, but he settled for a glass of water and drank it on the front porch. I gobbled down my pancakes and went out.

As we walked to the gelding paddock, he said, "You seem ready to go, Abby."

"I am. I couldn't wait for today."

He smiled. He said, "Horses are like that, too, you know. If you finish the lesson with a horse wanting to do more of what you want to teach him, he'll always be happy in his work."

The first horse we tacked up was Black George. While we were cleaning him and putting the English saddle and bridle on him, Jack stood at the gate, ears pricked, watching us. After I had mounted and we were walking toward the arena, Jem said, "That's good. That means he's got a friend."

"Black George is pretty nice with him. He plays a little."

"He's a good-natured fella."

"Daddy says he could be a show horse."

Jem didn't say anything, but not in a way that meant he disagreed, just in a way that meant it wasn't his place to have an opinion on that. We went into the arena.

I did everything Jem told me to do, in order—stepping over several times on each side until Black George was really moving along, loose and agreeable, but full of energy, too. Then I asked him to halt and then go forward a few times. Jem said I was to try and feel which leg was stepping forward first when I asked him to walk, and pretty soon I could feel that it was one of the hind legs, which meant that his whole body moved at the same time—if a front leg goes first, then the hind legs get left behind, but if a hind leg goes first, then it pushes the whole body ahead of it, and everything keeps together. Halt to walk, walk to trot, halt to trot. Black George felt springy and happy, not to mention comfortable. Then I did some work at the trot—trotting forward, holding back, turning in loops and circles. Black George kept his neck arched and his mouth soft— all I had to do to change the speed or direction was to twitch the reins, and he did what was asked. When we cantered, it was like silk.

When we were finished, Jem said, "That's the easy one. That's the one I want you to think about when you're riding the hard one. You were riding English, so I'll tell you a story. I was training a horse last year, a big Thoroughbred, an old racehorse with lots of experience. Not an educated horse in some ways. We were loping, and I started thinking a thought, and the thought was that there was an elastic band attaching my elbow to his hocks, easy and soft but keeping us together in the best way possible. And while I was thinking that thought, I asked that horse to pivot. Now, this was a big horse, seventeen hands, and long, too. But when I turned him, thinking that thought, he did a perfect pivot, da dum, da dum, da dum, a hundred and eighty degrees, and off in the other direction.

"I also knew a fella who showed up early at the barn out on the coast to try a bay horse over some jumps. So he tacks her up, gets on her, takes her out in the ring, and jumps the course easy as you please. When he gets back to the barn, he finds out he was on the wrong bay horse—not the fancy jumper he meant to buy, but a three-year-old just off the track not more than a week. Never jumped a fence in her life. Now what am I telling you?"

"That all my wishes will come true?"

"Yes, Abby, but more importantly than that, if you have a real feeling in your mind of what you want the horse to do, your own body will communicate to the horse how to do it. This is a good, athletic, and cooperative horse. The feeling he gives you is the one you want from the others."

"So my main job is to remember that feeling?"

"I would say so, yes."

When we put Black George back into the paddock, Jack came over to meet him, and they trotted around for a moment, kicking up. Then they settled to the same pile of oat hay.

We saddled up Ornery George, and then I went to put on the bridle, but Jem stopped me. He motioned toward Jack's empty pen, and I saw that I had to start with the groundwork. I made myself remember what Jem had done earlier in the week—lead him on a loose line, don't let him crowd me, stop suddenly and then move on, lift the end of the rope and insist that he back off. Jem said, "He's actually not a terribly ill-mannered horse, but he's a little ill-mannered. You need to ask him to do it really right, not sort of right."

It took us ten minutes to walk over to the pen, because I

tried to correct George every time he did a wrong thing, but when we got there, George might as well have been heeling and sitting like a dog, he was paying attention that well.

I stood in the center and sent him around me, to the left and the right. When he did what he wanted to do, I made him do more of it until he wanted to stop, and then I made him do what I wanted him to do. He tossed his head and switched his tail, but only a few times. After a while—say, by the time we were both sweating—his ears were flopped and his eye was soft. He was moving his shoulder away from me whenever I asked him to, and that made his body as soft as could be.

I got on.

I did from the saddle just what I had been doing from the ground, all the time trying to keep the Black George feel. It wasn't easy. Ornery George was stiffer and less springy than Black George. Whereas Black George could go all the way around the circle without stiffening, Ornery George could only go three or four strides, but three or four strides was enough. Once I got the feel of those, I could get him to do it for five, and then six, and then back the other way. I was busy. He was busy. I realized that he wasn't thinking about bucking, and then I realized that I wasn't thinking about him bucking—I was too busy thinking about other things that I wanted him to do.

When I was a little out of breath, I halted him, and Jem called out to me to ride him over to the arena. He was fine in the bigger space, too. Finally, I asked for the lope, and off we went, rocking back and forth, not terribly fast, but going where we wanted to go. Jem motioned with his hand, and I turned Ornery George on a circle and brought him to a halt.

Then we trotted off again, the other direction, and did the canter, just a few strides, again. We cantered halfway around the arena, and then Jem motioned me to the middle. I did that circle again, but in the other direction, and came to a halt. Jem said, "That's enough, I think. Stop while it's still fresh in your mind . . ."

"Just one more canter?"

He grinned—the first real grin that I'd ever seen—and said, "Do you think he would like that?"

"Yes."

"Save it for tomorrow. He'll have something to look forward to. Your assignment for today is very small."

"What is it?"

"Remember what you felt this morning on these two horses."

"I will."

"And get off now and walk him out so nothing gets in the way of that."

I was off in two seconds. George gave me a look of surprise. I'd been on him maybe twenty minutes, but I knew without Jem telling me that a good twenty minutes was plenty.

At lunch, Daddy said, "I was watching you. You looked good."

I had been concentrating so hard, I hadn't even seen him.

The next day, at our chapel, those Greeley kids sat still for half an hour, through four straight readings of *The Little Engine That Could*, and then the baby fell asleep and slept for the rest of the afternoon. We had strawberry shortcake, the cake kind, with whipped cream, and we really did give thanks.

* * *

Monday morning was rainy and cold, and I had to admit to Mom that I'd left my heavy sweater at school. She suggested that the fact that I was shivering inside my raincoat was something I would think about the next time I didn't bother to bring home my sweater.

The bus was late, and there was a bit of a crush at my end of the lockers. My raincoat was wet, and Joan said, "Ugh," as I pressed past her. I said, "Sorry, it's really raining," as if she didn't know that. She looked at me and wiped her hand across her skirt to get the rain off.

Stella said, "Were the bus windows open or something?" And then I took the lock off my locker and opened the door. The first thing I saw was my sweater, navy blue, right where I'd left it, and the next thing I saw was a string or something, and then Joan said, "Hey!"

And Stella said, "Oh, wow!"

And Mary A. said, "There's Joan's necklace!"

She dove for it, then held it up, and then Joan grabbed it out of her hand. The two of them ran down the hall.

This didn't take more than a couple of moments. Stella said, "Oh, Abby! Now what? You'll be in so much trouble."

"For what?"

"That's the necklace!"

"I never saw that necklace before. I didn't even know what it was. I thought it was a piece of string."

Then the bell rang. I put on my sweater, even though I wasn't cold anymore. I walked slowly to algebra, and when I went through the door, the Big Four gave me four big dirty looks.

I suppose some kids would have gone up to the Big Four

and declared right there that they had never seen the necklace and hadn't taken the necklace, but I didn't think of that. I just sat in my seat all through algebra going back and forth between wondering how the necklace got into my locker, since it was locked, and wondering what kind of trouble I was in. I couldn't really think straight, because it was all such a mystery. It's very hard to go from being the last person in the world to find out about something to the person everyone is sure did that thing. It made me stupid (I couldn't answer any of Mr. Jepsen's questions), and it gave me a headache. I kept looking at my sweater in a dumb way, as if something about it would tell me how the necklace got there. I knew I had left the sweater in my locker on Thursday around lunch, noticed it a few times after that, forgotten it Thursday afternoon, and forgotten it again Friday. I hadn't hung it up on the hook, because Mom said sweaters were to be folded, not hung, so a book or two had been on top of it once in a while. I should have folded it and set it on the upper shelf, but then—These were the thoughts I kept thinking, but I just couldn't make it out.

In the middle of second period, I was called out of social studies to the principal's office. As soon as I went in there, I saw the necklace on Mr. Canning's desk, and then he said, "Well, Abby, I'm very disappointed in you."

I didn't say anything.

"What do you have to say about this?"

I didn't say anything, then I said, "I don't know."

"Since I wasn't there this morning, I have to ask you, Abby, whether this necklace was found in your locker?"

I nodded.

"How did it get there?"

"I don't know."

He shook his head. He said, "I am going to ask you again, Abby, how did the necklace get into your locked locker?"

"I don't know."

"Does someone else know the combination to your lock?"

"I don't know. I don't think so."

"Well, that leaves you up a crick, doesn't it?"

"Yes, sir."

"I'm going to ask you again how the necklace got into your locker."

"I don't know, Mr. Canning. I didn't even go to the potluck."

"Well, Abby, we do know that the necklace was lost at the potluck, but we don't know that it was found at the potluck."

I said, "Yes, sir."

"I have called your mother."

I didn't say anything.

"I'm sorry you've decided to be obdurate on this, even if you are protecting someone else. But it is a valuable necklace, and everyone in school was warned about keeping it quiet and everyone was asked to come forward, so everyone has had a chance to be honest."

I stood there.

"Do you understand what I mean?"

"Yes, sir."

What was I thinking through all this? I don't know. I was looking at the shelves behind Mr. Canning's desk and at the stuff on his desk (a small stuffed bear because he went to UCLA, a picture of his son in a football uniform, a picture of his dog). Mostly I was scared, and it didn't make me less scared that Mom was on her way to school. I didn't for a moment think that Mom would think I stole the necklace, but I did think she would make a fuss about the missions. Mr. Canning said, "Well, Abby. I was hoping you would be more forthcoming. I'm disappointed."

I said, "Yes, sir."

"You may go now." I went out of his office.

The bell rang and it was time for English, but instead I went out onto the steps and waited until our car drove up to the door. I could hear Mom talking even before I could see her, saying, "—and what could all this about suspension possibly mean? I don't understand a word of this! I can't believe you've left me in such ignorance, young lady! What are the missions?"

"Please don't talk to him about the missions."

"What are the missions?"

"It's a school project where we learn about the California missions, and everyone has to build one, so I—"

"You built a Catholic mission?"

"We all did."

"Daniel did not."

"I'm sure he did, Mom. If you ask him."

But by now we were at the door of the principal's office. We knocked and walked in.

Mr. Canning said what he had to say, which was that a valuable necklace had been taken and hidden and then found in my locker, but I was not revealing anything about it, either because I had taken it or because I was "protecting a friend very unwisely."

And Mom said what she had to say, which was that I could not have possibly taken the necklace and it was highly unlikely that I would protect anyone, because I was a good girl and a well-taught girl and I would certainly come forward if I had any knowledge, so there was something going on, no doubt about that, and what was this about Catholic missions?

Mr. Canning explained that the misson project was a universal history project in California schools. State law.

"Never heard of it before. My son, Daniel—"

"Daniel and his partner built a very nice mission, as I remember. Was it cut-up cardboard boxes? Colorful and nicely painted. Mission San Miguel, I think." He sighed and looked down.

Mom stared at him.

The only thing they agreed on was that I would be suspended for some days or at least until the school got to the bottom of the necklace mystery.

We walked to the car, and Mom said that we would talk about it later, after she had calmed down. That was okay with me. I looked at the hall clock as we were leaving the school. Two hours had passed since the first bell, and I was leaving already. Mom walked in front of me as we headed toward the car, which was parked at the far end of the parking lot. Her shoes made a sharp thudding noise on the tarmac, and even the back of her head and her shoulders looked mad. I wondered if I could remember the last time Mom had gotten mad—usually that was Daddy's department. I tried to imagine what would happen next and what I would do about it, but I couldn't.

Cowboy Hat

Cowboy Boots

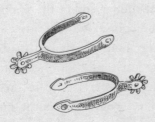

Spurs

Chapter 16

WE GOT HOME BEFORE LUNCHTIME. DADDY'S TRUCK WAS gone, which was probably a good thing. I decided to get all my horse work done, but after I had put my jeans on and gone out to the barn, I began to wonder what the point of it all was. The horses looked happy in their pastures. The three mares were standing in a straggling line on the brow of the hill, dark in the noon sunshine. Their pasture was big enough to still have some grass, and one of the mares was grazing, but the other two were standing ears to tail not far from the biggest oak tree, their heads down, idly switching flies. In the gelding pasture, I didn't see Jack for a moment, and then I saw him lying flat out, asleep in the sunlight. Black George was grazing about halfway between him and the other two. Ornery George was methodically licking the bottom of a bucket that was tied to the fence—Jack's bucket, in which Mom had probably fed him his morning mixture of bran and milk—and Socks George was over by the water trough, pushing his nose into the water, then shaking his head, then pawing the ground with his left front hoof. He did this three times, and even though I knew that Daddy didn't like the horses playing in the water, he looked like he was having fun.

I stood there, and I have to say that I didn't know what in the world to do. I wasn't used to having Mom mad at me, I knew that Stella wasn't my friend anymore, and that only left Gloria. But Gloria was lost, too—without even realizing it at the time, I had noticed Gloria that morning, and now that came back to me. Just after Stella saw the necklace, Gloria, who was standing behind her, didn't look shocked or upset, she just turned away for a moment and then looked back, like a person staring in a crowd, not like the best friend you've had for your whole life. She looked, in fact, like she didn't care. I realized that she was going to use what happened as a way to drop me without having a fight or saying anything at all. I looked back at the house. I couldn't see Mom anywhere, so I opened the mares' gate, closed it behind me, and headed down to the crick. I skirted way around the mares so as not to bother them. Blue Jewel turned her head and looked at me, but no one moved. I headed down the hill. The oaks along the crick looked inviting—shady dark green in the damp grass—so I headed there.

The crick was sometimes high and mostly low. This time of year, the water ran over the stones, not through them, but, except in one pool, it wasn't more than six inches deep. It was pretty, though, shining, clear, and ripply, making wrinkles and rivulets over all the stones. The shadows of the leafy branches above danced over the water, and the grass, long and moist, draped over the banks. The sand along the bottom of the pool was gray and rough—not like beach sand. The water in the pool was about a foot and a half deep. I threw a few pebbles into it, skipping them the way Danny had taught me, but the pool was wide enough only for one skip. Then I took off my boots and socks and rolled up my jeans. The rocks were slippery to get to the pool, and then the water in the pool was cold. I dug my toes into the gray sand, which felt good, and then wiggled them to go deeper. It was all too easy to imagine having no friends at school ever again. That was the difference, I realized, between one real friend and none. Your one friend surrounded you and made you feel like everything was normal so that you never even thought about the fact that there was only one. But when she was gone, you were stuck with the truth.

I swished around in the pool until my whole body was cold, and then I walked up onto the bank in a sandy part. The sand was sunny and warm, which felt good on my cold feet. Then I went over to one of the trees and sat down on a lower branch where it dipped away from the trunk and then grew upward. It was a thick branch and didn't even bend with my weight. I turned a little and leaned my back against the trunk. I could hear the breeze ruffle through the upper leaves. I closed my eyes. There were lots of noises, but they were all low ones—skittering in the grass, creaking in the tree, indistinguishable wind sounds. Silence.

When I woke up, the mares were practically on top of me, or so it seemed the first moment. But they weren't really. Really, they were just standing in front of me, Blue Jewel in front of the others, her nose about two inches from my knee, Star Jewel next to her, maybe a foot back, and Roan Jewel behind them but with her head up and her ears pricked, like a person trying to see in a crowd. I yawned a couple of times, the way you do when you've been asleep, and Blue Jewel stuck out her nose and sniffed my hands, which were crossed in my lap. Then she nosed my leg. Instead of saying, "No treats," which is what I usually said when they poked around my hands and pockets, I said, "I'm all right."

Star Jewel blew out of her nostrils, as if to say, "Okay, then." I laughed. Roan Jewel then whinnied, and there was something uncanny about the whole thing. I lifted my hand and petted Blue Jewel on the nose, then down the face. She took a half step closer. I put out my other hand and then stroked her around the eyes on both sides, starting up by her cowlick, then stroking outward and downward over her cheeks. She stretched her head out, flopped her ears, and sighed. Then I sighed. The other two came closer. Star Jewel sniffed my jeans and then lowered her head and sniffed my foot. I put my fingers in the mane hair just behind her ears and tickled. She cocked her head as if she was enjoying it. Then Roan Jewel had a thought. While I was petting the others, she went around the tree and came behind me and snuffled the back of my neck and my shirt. Her breath was warm and made my hair lift. I was surrounded.

I knew I could wave them off. I knew I *should* wave them off. At the very least, horses are so unpredictable that a squirrel or a snake suddenly spooking them could make them forget where I was completely in their rush to get away. And I was barefoot—my boots were on the bank fifteen feet away. But I didn't move. I petted them and tickled them and let them sniff me all over, ruffling my hair, investigating my hands, poking their noses under my ear, pushing lightly against me. And then Blue Jewel did an odd thing—she began to lick my shirt, right under my collarbone and over my shoulder. She licked and licked, long after any flavors I would have thought were there would have been licked away. Then she moved up to my neck, then my chin and cheek. Her licks were firm and moist, but not hard or pushy. I realized that this was what it must be like to be a foal and to have your dam lick you.

The other two mares seemed to watch Blue Jewel do her licking—their ears were forward, as if they were saying, "Why is she doing that?" But they didn't mind it. We all relaxed. After she had licked me to her heart's content, Blue Jewel sighed a deep sigh. Roan Jewel had already given up on the back of my neck and now went down into the crick for a drink from the pool. Then the two others followed her. I watched them for a moment, then fetched my boots and socks and put them on.

At the house, Daddy's truck was parked next to the car and the door was closed. I got the halter and long lead rope out of the barn and went to the gate of the gelding pasture. Jack was up by now, and he came right to the gate with a nicker. I wasn't thinking those thoughts about school or Gloria anymore. School seemed quite far away. I knew I would have to think about it later, so why think about it now?

Jack and I went into his old pen and I closed the gate behind us. I walked to the middle and stood there long enough to think about each thing that Jem would want me to do with Jack—make him go around me, make him step over, make him back up, make him go around me the other direction, make him turn his head and neck and soften them, make him relax his neck and put his head down, make him curve his body away from me as he did each movement. Then I asked him to do all those things, and he did them nicely, for no more than fifteen minutes, if that. When we were finished, I got him to stand while I ran the chamois over him from ears to tail, then I picked up his feet, one by one. He made it all seem as though nothing was a big deal. I left him in that pen while I worked with Black George.

The mares came up the hill. One by one, I made my way through all of them, grooming them, picking their feet, tacking them up, taking them to the arena. Then I moved to the geldings. I made sure to begin Ornery George with some groundwork in Jack's pen, but that was the only difference. I had saved him for last, so it was almost suppertime when I was starting with him. Since there was no one around to tell me what to do, I worked at my own speed, but steadily. When I brushed the horses and picked out their feet, I thought about how all of the new horses had gotten better-looking since coming from Oklahoma—shinier and sleeker, with their manes combed and their feet neatly trimmed. Ornery George himself looked as good as I had ever seen him, so I spent some extra time brushing his white points.

When I led him into the pen, he neither pulled nor lagged back, but just walked along with me. Nor was he giving me any looks—he was looking where we were going. I thought, right then, that we were ready. But when I opened the gate, he moved past me as if he didn't care about me, and when I gave the halter rope a jerk and said, "Hey! Pay attention to me, George," he was still oblivious. My heart sank. I thought, Thirty-six dollars down the drain. Something more I would have to talk about with Daddy.

Afterward, I wasn't quite sure why I did what I next did, but what I did was to unclip the halter rope and let him go. When he moved away from me, I swung the rope, and he began to trot around the periphery of the pen, his tail up and his ears pricked, not like he was in a bad mood, but like he was in a good mood. I shook the rope. He bucked and kicked out, then started to gallop. I shook the rope again. He bucked and kicked out again. But he went around me at a safe distance. After two circuits of the pen, I stepped over to my right, just to try it, and Ornery George turned toward me, then went the other direction, bucking and kicking. I then made a little mistake and stepped sort of in front of him—not in front of him literally, but in front of his gaze, even though I was still in the middle of the pen. He slid to the halt, spun, and went back the other direction. It was like we were playing a game, so I kept playing, stepping to the right or the left or toward him, just to see what he would do. He didn't always do anything, but sometimes he did—speeding up, spinning, sliding to a halt and going the other direction. I realized that he was watching me and his moves were reactions to me. Finally, after about ten minutes of this activity, he turned toward me and stopped, and when I stepped toward him, he stepped backward, two neat steps, made as if he meant them. I turned my back and stepped away. I heard him come up behind me and felt his breath on my arm. It was as if he were saying, "Time to go for a ride."

I believed him.

Our ride wasn't that big of a deal. We walked, trotted, cantered, halted, backed, made some large, medium-sized, and small circles in both directions, trotted from the halt, halted from the trot, stood quietly for a while while I rested my hand on his haunches. He sighed. No big deal.

That was why it was a big deal.

I walked him out. When I got back to the barn, Daddy was finishing up the evening work. He had filled all the water buckets and put out all the hay, hung up all the tack, and put away the bridles. Without saying anything, he helped me untack Ornery George and brush him off, then put him away. The very fact that he wasn't saying anything let me know that while he appreciated my efforts, there were things to talk about—things that required a family meeting and praying to the Lord for guidance, things that were much too serious to talk about as we were making our way from the barn to the house. The horses had sort of lulled me, hadn't they? But now my stomach started to hurt.

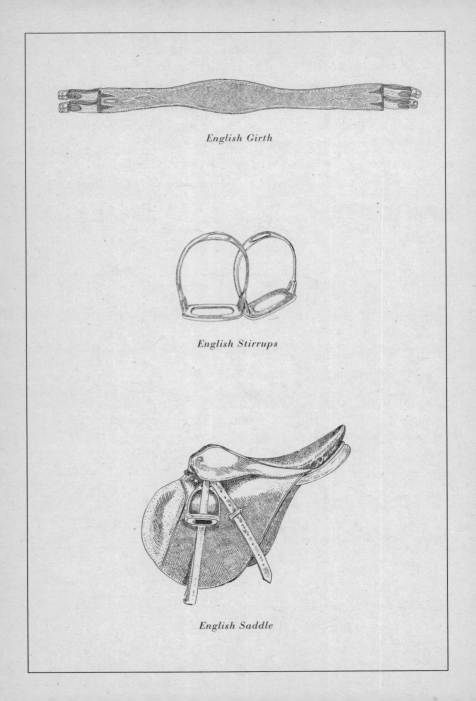

English Girth

English Stirrups

English Saddle

Chapter 17

IT DIDN'T OFTEN HAPPEN IN OUR HOUSE THAT MOM AND DADDY
had a quiet conversation over supper. Usually Daddy was excited about something and Mom went along with it, whether it
was a good thing or a bad thing. Sometimes, supper was lively
and funny, with lots of jokes and a song or two. Other times,
supper was loud and not funny at all, because Daddy was right-
eously angry or resolute in his determination or dedicated to
rectifying evil. All the Lovitts were big talkers. But our supper
that night was much more like a supper at Gloria's house,
where Gloria's mom kept up a steady, soothing patter and Gloria's dad ate first the vegetable, then the meat, then the starch,
never letting any one of those touch any of the others. Gloria's
house was very neat—even the fringes of the rugs looked like

they were combed out straight. We had spaghetti. Thinking again about Gloria, I didn't eat much.

I noticed that our house was very neat, too. That's what Daddy and Mom had been doing while I was out with the horses—turning over a new leaf. In our house, a new leaf always started with the vacuum cleaner and ended up with me going to bed at nine on the dot.

After supper, Daddy went to his desk in the living room, opened his Bible at random, and read a verse. The verse was, "And a certain man found him, and, behold, he was wandering in the field: and the man asked him, saying, What seekest thou?" I saw Mom purse her lips a little and sigh. There was a long pause, and I knew they were trying to figure out what to make of this verse. I said, "I guess they were seeking Joan's necklace for about four or five days." I tried to sound helpful.

Daddy said, "Tell me about this necklace."

I said, "It's an add-a-pearl. Every year on her birthday, her grandmother gives her a pearl, and they string it on with the rest of them."

"So there are twelve pearls?"

"Thirteen. I guess there was one to grow on."

"How valuable would a necklace like that be?"

I shrugged.

Mom said, "At least a hundred dollars. Maybe more depending on the chain and the pearls."

I said, "I didn't take the necklace."

"We don't think you did, honey," said Mom.

I looked at Daddy. He said, "But when the evidence is against you, it's hard to prove a negative. It looks to me like if they suspended you, they feel they've got a pretty good circumstantial case. How could the necklace have gotten into your locker?"

"I don't know, unless somebody knows the combination to my lock. But I haven't told it even to Gloria. They would have to be watching me open it."

"That could be anyone," said Daddy.

We listened to the clock tick for a while, then Daddy said, "I see we are at the mercy of the Lord. May his mercy be upon us."

Mom said, "Amen."

Daddy said, "Now, Abby, you have kept from us this mission-building project, and I wonder if I have been remiss in explaining to you certain facts about the Roman Catholic Church."

I said, "I don't know."

"The thing is, the Roman Catholic Church is a great and powerful enemy. *Our* great and powerful enemy. It has done many things over the centuries to our people and to its own people that are not easy to speak about."

"It was a school assignment. Danny had to do it, too."

"Reminding me that your brother may have been sneaking around behind my back does not make me happier that you have been doing the same thing."

I bit my lips and tried to think of something. I looked at Mom, but it was clear she wasn't going to help me. I knew I was right on the edge between asking a question and sassing back. Daddy didn't seem mad so far, but he could get there in no time. I kept my mouth shut, and he did what he always did, which was to expand on his previous statement. This could be dangerous, too. He said, "Who helped you with this project?"

"Kyle Gonzalez. We made it out of clay, but we didn't fire it. We just let it dry and then painted it."

"Did this boy who has a Mexican name and therefore is probably Roman Catholic witness to you while you were working together?"

"He told me who the missions were named for. Saints. Things like that."

"Which was your mission?"

"San Juan Bautista."

"John the Baptist."

"Yeah."

"At least he's in the Bible," said Mom. "He himself wasn't Roman Catholic like Francis of Assisi or Agnes. You could have ended up with someone else, a real Roman Catholic. Abby, you—"

I said, "Danny did San Miguel. That's the archangel Michael."

They looked at me a moment, letting this remark pass, then Daddy continued, "You need to ask us how to walk this narrow path."

They had been talking for sure. They were a united front. I said, "What should I ask you?" hoping this didn't sound sassy.

Daddy said, "I think I have to go to the school. I think I have to go personally to the school and look over the curriculum and discuss what Abby will be allowed to study and what she won't be allowed to study."

Mom nodded.

My heart sank. I loved my family. Both Daddy and Mom made the other parents I knew look stiff and sad. Everything they did, they did all out. There was never a moment when Daddy didn't mean what he said and say what he meant—most of the time he said what he meant until you couldn't stand to hear it anymore. Mom was prettier and more fun than any other mother—she was prettier and more fun than I was, in fact. But the idea of Daddy and Mom and Mr. Canning and my other teachers never seeing eye to eye was terrifying, because Daddy would keep after them and after them. He didn't know how to stop because he didn't think it was right to stop. He would certainly bring his Bible to school and lay it on Mr. Canning's desk and quote from it every chance he got. I wondered if it might be better, after all, just to get expelled. I could do that if I confessed to stealing the necklace.

Daddy said, "Why don't you bring your books down, Abby, and let me have a look at them. I've been remiss, I see." He sighed.

I got up and went to my room. After putting the books on his desk, I went out to check the horses. Everyone was fine. Blue Jewel was lying down near the fence, sleeping. I looked at her in the moonlight for a while and thought of her licking me, then I went back in the house. Daddy and Mom were still up. Mom said, "It's almost nine, Abby."

I put my hand on the banister and my foot on the step, and then I just said it. I said, "I want to name the horses. I want to name Blue Jewel 'Sapphire' and Ornery George something nice, like 'Rally.' Black George can stay Black George because it's sort of like a pirate and makes me laugh. I'll think of the others by morning."

I went up the stairs. They didn't say anything, and so I had no idea whether this qualified as sassiness or not. But it did seem as though I had nothing to lose.

The next day was only Tuesday. Imagine that! And then I remembered that we were coming up on spring break, anyway, so I was going to be out of school for a long time. Long enough, I thought, for the school to forget about me completely. Tuesday wasn't bad. Over breakfast, I wrote out the names I had come up with—Jack, Rally, Sapphire, Black George, "Sprinkles" for Roan Jewel, "Sunshine" for Star Jewel, "Webster" for Socks George (I had been stuck for a name, and then my school dictionary was the first thing I laid eyes on when I got up in the morning). I read the names aloud to Mom, and she didn't say that now I was going to get attached to them, she said, "Maybe when we name them, we're really seeing something in them that will help us train them the best way we can."

Maybe. I did like the names. I could see each one in my mind's eye very clearly now. I said, "I think I'm going to get a notebook and write each name on one of the pages, and then I can keep track of things I need to remember about them."

Mom treated me not like she was mad at me, but like she had been mad at me, which was a different thing completely, because Mom always hated getting mad at anyone and felt remorse afterward, so she would make it up in little ways, like giving me a cut-up banana with my Cheerios or opening the apricot jam even though we weren't finished with the strawberry jam. After breakfast, since Daddy was gone into town, she helped me get the horses ready and she let me do Jack first, even though our usual motto was work before pleasure. She stood and watched us, and when he paid attention to me the whole time, keeping his eyes on me and his ears in "learning position"—that is, sort of flopped to either side—she said, "He's learning. You're doing a good job with him." After fifteen minutes of training and some rubbing with the chamois, I put him out with Black George, Rally, and Webster. I watched them for a bit and then went around to each one and patted him and said his name, then gave each of them a piece of carrot. I did the same for the mares, Sapphire, Sprinkles, and Sunshine.

No mention that Daddy had returned from town. In the afternoon, I started with Ornery George—Rally. I went through everything that Jem told me to do—stepping over, stepping back, being sure he was soft through the shoulder, making sure he would turn his head to either side and soften. When he didn't seem quite ready, I got him to run around the pen on his own a bit. Then I walked him to the arena, where I mounted from the fence. I looked at his eye before I got on. He was looking at me, and his eye said, "Who, me?"

Daddy drove in while we were working and came over to the fence. I rode Rally for half an hour, and we did everything Daddy asked us to do, no problem. It was time-consuming, all the steps to getting Rally to do his work without a fuss, but he did it. And I had all the time in the world, didn't I? Afterword, Daddy said, "Abby, you did a very good job on that horse. I'm impressed."

I said, "Rally likes some playtime before his work time."

"Some do," said Daddy.

"But," I said, "you'd better ride him yourself, because if

you're going to tell Mr. Tacker that a grown man can ride him, you'd better be sure."

Daddy frowned as if I were sassing him but then smiled in spite of himself, and I have to say that I laughed as I went into the barn to put away the bridle.

We had a baked chicken for supper, and then I read some of *A Midsummer Night's Dream*, a play we were reading for English. It wasn't bad. I even stopped looking at the page numbers. Just before I went to bed, Mom came into my room and gave me my new notebook. It was smaller than a school notebook and nicer, too, with heavy green covers. She also gave me a Paper Mate pen—green and silver. She kissed me on the forehead. After she went out, I set them on my desk, and then I put myself to sleep thinking about what I would write in the notebook about each of the horses. The notebook had eighty-eight pages. That was eighty-eight horses. It was fun to think of what I would be writing on the last page.

On Thursday, the only horse we worked in the morning was Rally. I hadn't seen Daddy ride much for several weeks, just because either I was at school or he was making me ride the horses. Now that I had spent so much time with Jem and thinking about Jem, I saw that Daddy was more like Uncle Luke than I had realized, and almost as soon as he began working with Rally, they began arguing. I kept my mouth shut while he was tacking Rally up, even though I thought his brush strokes were too quick and his movements around the horse too brusque. It wasn't that he was doing anything mean, but compared to Jem, he seemed not to think that the horse had any feelings. At first, Rally was his new self, the self I had come to know in the last week or so, paying attention and acting interested. But by the time Daddy was leading Rally to the arena, I saw that Rally's eye was ornery again, and I realized that he was insulted. And maybe that had been the problem all along.

When we got to the arena, Daddy tightened the girth with a jerk, and Rally's ears went back. I said, "I wouldn't get on him just yet if I were you."

"Why not?"

"I would check to see if he's loosened up any or if his back is tight."

"I don't have time. . . ."

"Well, look at his face. He looks a little mad."

"He always looks a little mad."

I went up to Daddy and put my hand on his arm. I looked him in the eye and I said, "No, he doesn't. After Jem started working with him, he stopped looking mad."

"If Jem's training did the trick, then the horse . . ."

"Then it won't be worth the thirty-six dollars we spent if we wreck what he did."

"Are you sassing me, young lady?"

I took a deep breath and then said, "No. I'm being honest and saying what's in my heart."

We looked at each other for a long moment, then he took a deep breath, too, and said, "Well, missy, what do you want me to do?" Now he grinned down at me.

I have to say that I felt a little bossy as I took the rein out of his hand and showed him how to soften Rally by turning his head and his neck, asking him to step back and step over and then go around us in both directions. Then I patted Rally on the face and the neck. I said, "He doesn't like to be treated like a car or something. The others don't mind so much, but he does."

Then Daddy said, "I'm sorry. I guess I wasn't thinking." It sounded like he meant it. He took the rein and did some of the things I had done and then put his foot in the stirrup and got on the horse. It was just about then that Mom came out and checked on us the first time. She was smiling to beat the band but didn't say anything. She passed us and went over to the mares' pasture, where she pretended to do something, then she waved as she went back to the house.

Daddy walked Rally around a little bit and then stopped in front of me. He said, "What now?"

"Well, I would walk him and trot him, changing direction a bunch of times."

I showed him how to lift the inside rein and get the horse to shift his weight and step under. Then I said, "When you're lifting the rein, be sure he steps under right away. Then he won't get lazy and stiff."

Daddy tried this for a few minutes. He was good at it because he could feel the difference in the horse's willingness to do what he was being told between before Rally stepped under and after. Pretty soon he was trying a little of everything— loping, trotting some figure eights, a couple of sliding halts, a long looping gallop around the outside of the arena. Daddy was a good rider the way people are when they learn to ride at an early age and know all the moves without thinking too much about it. Probably most of the horses he had ridden over the years had decided the best thing to do was just go along with him and his ideas, because he was strong and quick and why not let him be the boss? But that didn't work with every horse, as Rally would be the first to tell you.

Mom came out again, just when Daddy was doing some figure eights at the lope, with a change of lead in the middle. She smiled and went back into the house.

I sat on the railing of the arena, looking around our place—at Jack and Black George and the mares, then up at the hawk curving through the blue sky, then over at the house, where purple and white irises were crowding against the porch, then at the dark edges of the mountains across the floor of the valley. Maybe there were a lot of things to wish for, but right then, I couldn't be bothered to wish for anything else than what I saw around me.

Daddy trotted over to me. He said, "I bet we can get at least a thousand for him."

I said, "Mr. Tacker did like him a lot. You could call him and ask how Ruby is doing."

Daddy nodded.

I jumped down off the fence and stroked Rally's nose. Daddy said, "He's a good horse."

I said, "I think he is."

We stood there for a minute, looking at Rally, and then Daddy gave me a squeeze around the shoulders.

Mom came out to check a third time, and I saw that she saw that everything was fine.

After Rally, we did the other horses, but we didn't give them much work—they had done well all week and we expected two good long days Friday and Saturday. By the time we were sitting down to a late lunch of chicken rice soup and ham sandwiches, it seemed like all of us had forgotten about school completely.

Certainly, I had. So, for a moment, I didn't even recognize Gloria's mom's car when it pulled up behind the truck. Then Gloria threw open the door and jumped out shouting, "Abby! Abby! Wait till you hear!"

Mom opened the door, and Gloria ran in and hugged me. I said, "Hear what?" I remembered the way her face went blank when she saw the necklace in my locker on Monday, and I decided I wasn't going to fall for just any old story. But it was hard to resist how she was now—jumping up and down and grinning. She exclaimed, "Kyle came back!"

"Kyle came back from where? Kyle Gonzalez?" I sounded a little doubtful, I know. But Kyle?

"Yes! He saved you!"

"Where was he?"

"He was home sick! He had pinkeye or something gross like that, so he was out Friday, Monday, and Tuesday. And you know no one talks to him much, so when he got back yesterday, he didn't know what happened to you until the end of the day, and then he told!"

Mom asked Gloria's mom to sit down and have a cup of coffee or tea, and she did, but Gloria was just jumping around the table, she was so excited. Daddy said, "Gloria, what did he tell?"

Gloria's mom said, "Settle down, Glow. One thing at a time!"

But she didn't settle down. She exclaimed, "He was fixing the bells! He was fixing the bells on your mission so they would ring better or something, and when he stood up, he saw her pick up the necklace off the floor!"

"Who?"

"Stella. It was Stella who found the necklace on the floor

of the lunchroom, and then, *she said*, she was coming out of the lunchroom to turn it in, and she saw that it belonged to Joan, and so she was afraid to do anything with it because of the anonymous note."

Gloria's mom said, "What anonymous note?"

"Well, it's not anonymous anymore. Debbie admitted that she sent it."

I said, "Debbie!"

"Yes! Debbie saw Stella put the ink cartridge on Joan's chair and she thought Joan should know, but she was afraid of Stella."

"You should never do anything anonymously—" began Mrs. Harris.

"Stella didn't see Debbie—she's so quiet. But she knew *you* had been sitting behind her, so she thought you—"

"Abby would never send an anonymous note!" exclaimed Mom. "Would you?"

"I did see it," I said.

"You should have come forward," said Mom.

But Gloria rushed on, so I didn't have to answer her. "She kept the necklace all day Thursday and all day Friday, and she was scared to death the whole time, because Mr. Canning was so mad and talking about the police, so—"

"So—"

She sat down and leaned toward me as if she was telling the punch line. "So, *she said*, she waited until the end of school, after the bus left Friday, and she pushed it through the air vents of your locker."

"Why my locker?"

"Well, *she said*, she was trying to get it into that empty

locker near yours, but she miscounted and pushed it through your vents instead."

Mom said, "Is there an empty locker near yours, Abby?"

"Mine is six from the end of that row, and the fourth one is the empty one."

"Is it locked?" said Daddy.

"They're all locked," said Gloria. "But she was mad about the anonymous note. I think she knew perfectly well that it was your locker."

Mom and Mrs. Harris shook their heads.

Daddy said, "Why didn't Kyle come forward last week?"

"Why does Kyle do anything?" said Gloria. "He said that he didn't think the necklace was any big deal on Thursday, but then when he found out that you got blamed, he had to tell."

"That sounds like Kyle," I said. "He did a good job on our mission." I glanced at Daddy. "He doesn't do anything if he can't do it right."

"Well," said Daddy. "That's a virtue in anyone."

Now Gloria sat down in a chair beside me and put her elbows on the table and her chin in her hands, staring at me. She said, "So, you're going to come to school tomorrow, right?" She looked like she always had, just Gloria, my friend. I decided I was wrong about that other look I thought I'd seen. She grinned. I grinned back at her.

Mom said, "We haven't heard anything from Mr. Canning, Gloria."

"I'm still suspended."

And then the phone rang. It was Mr. Canning, unsuspending me.

* * *

In the end, I didn't go back to school the next day, since vacation was almost here and nothing much was going on anyway, but over the weekend, Gloria brought me my assignments, and we worked on them together. When you are suspended, you can't do that work, and so you get Fs on it, so for once I was relieved to have homework.

On Monday, Mr. Tacker came by, and on Wednesday, he brought his trailer to take Rally away to his ranch. He said he would get Jem Jarrow to help prepare Rally for the big summer parade. He paid Daddy a thousand dollars, and Daddy gave me fifty for myself. Mom took me to town and we opened a savings account. Mr. Tacker said he would keep his name, Rally. I said I would come to the parade and watch him.

On Tuesday, Stella called and said that she was really sorry and that she hoped I would forgive her and still be her friend. She had learned her lesson. I said, "What lesson?" I'm sure I sounded grumpy.

Stella sounded, as Mom would have said, "truly repentant." She said, "Well, lots of them. Way too many. I guess—" There was a long pause. "I guess the main one is, well, I don't want to be mean, really. I get mean sort of not really intending to, but I know I shouldn't be mean. I have a mean thought, and then I get carried away. I guess the main lesson is not to get carried away. Don't you know what I'm talking about? Something you shouldn't say comes into your head and you just say it, even though you know you shouldn't?"

I told her I knew what she was talking about. I still wondered if she had pushed that necklace through my locker vents on purpose, but it seemed mean, as long as we were talking about being mean, to ask.

I told her I would still be her friend.

She said, "Thank you, Abby."

It sounded like she meant it. What I meant, I have to admit, was We'll see. But I decided that was a private thought.

On Wednesday, Miss Slater called and said that she had entered me and Gallant Man in four classes in the spring show; would I come out Saturday and sit on him for an hour or so? That night, I had a little free time, so I sat down with my notebook and wrote the names in my best handwriting. Under the name Rally, I wrote everything I had learned about him, and then, at the bottom, I wrote, A *little girl can ride him*.

ERIC KNIGHT

LASSIE
COME-HOME

illustrated by
MARGUERITE KIRMSE

HENRY HOLT AND COMPANY
NEW YORK

To
DR. HARRY JARRETT
A Man Who Knows a Dog

Henry Holt and Company, LLC
Publishers since 1866
175 Fifth Avenue
New York, New York 10010
mackids.com

Printed in the United States of America by R. R. Donnelley & Sons Company, Harrisonburg, Virginia

Henry Holt® is a registered trademark of Henry Holt and Company, LLC.
Square Fish and the Square Fish logo are trademarks of Macmillan and are used by
Henry Holt and Company under license from Macmillan.

Our books may be purchased in bulk for promotional, educational, or business use. Please contact your local
bookseller or the Macmillan Corporate and Premium Sales Department at (800) 221-7945 ext. 5442 or by
e-mail at MacmillanSpecialMarkets@macmillan.com.

Lassie Come-Home was so popular a short story in the *Saturday Evening Post* that it was expanded, and was
published in book form by the John C. Winston Company in 1940. Since then, the book has gone through
countless printings and has been published in numerous languages throughout the world.

Library of Congress Cataloging-in-Publication Data
Knight, Eric Mowbray, 1897–1943.
Lassie come-home.
Summary: A collie undertakes a thousand-mile journey in order
to once again meet her former master at the school gate.
1. Dogs—Legends and stories. [1. Dogs—Fiction.]
I. Kirmse, Marguerite, 1885–1954. II. Title
PZ10.3.K753Las 1978 [Fic] 78-3570

Originally published in the United States by Henry Holt and Company, LLC.
First Square Fish Edition: 2007
75th Anniversary Edition: 2015
Square Fish logo designed by Filomena Tuosto

ISBN 978-1-62779-321-6 (Henry Holt hardcover)
1 3 5 7 9 10 8 6 4 2

ISBN 978-1-250-06288-8 (Square Fish paperback)
1 3 5 7 9 10 8 6 4 2

AR: 5.4 / F&P: T / LEXILE: 780L

CONTENTS

CONTENTS

ILLUSTRATIONS

Introduction

In the early 1960s, the best night of television, as far as my younger sister, Jane, and I were concerned, was Sunday. *The Ed Sullivan Show* aired at eight, but even better was what came on an hour earlier: *Lassie*. Adventures about the beautiful and noble collie, Lassie, and her boy, Timmy, held Jane and me entranced from the first note of the whistled theme song until the final credits rolled. Our family didn't have a dog, but every Sunday night we had Lassie.

The Lassie I saw on television, an American Lassie living with an American farm family, had been inspired—although I didn't know it then—by the book *Lassie Come-Home*, which was published in 1940. Lassie's creator, British-born author Eric Knight, died just three years later, at the age of forty-five. He didn't live to see the TV Lassie I knew or to hear from the legions of passionate fans his canine character attracted.

In 2015, Knight's readers will observe the seventy-fifth anniversary of the publication of *Lassie Come-Home*, an enthralling tale about—no—not a collie living with Timmy Martin and his farm family, but a collie living with Joe Carraclough and his parents in a tiny cottage on the outskirts of the village of Greenall Bridge in northern England. On the very first page of the book, we learn that "nearly every man in the village agreed [Lassie] was the finest collie he had ever laid eyes on." But of course there's much more to Lassie than her lush tricolor coat and her "aristocratic bearing." Lassie has a sense of time (the people in Greenall Bridge maintain that you can set your clock by her), and every afternoon, rain or shine, she arrives at Joe's school at four o'clock, just as the doors open to release the students, and then she and Joe walk back to their cottage together.

Lassie's tale is one of loyalty and devotion, of bravery and determination. When Joe's father, who has fallen on hard times, sells Lassie to a wealthy duke, Lassie wants nothing more than to continue to be able to meet "her boy" at four o'clock every afternoon and walk home with him. Time after time, Lassie escapes from the duke, who then moves her north to his estate in Scotland. Eventually, Lassie breaks free of him for good and begins the long journey south—hundreds of miles—back to Greenall Bridge and Joe.

Why do our hearts sing—or break—when we read about dogs? In part because of Lassie herself. She's portrayed as a creature that will do anything to be reunited with the human she loves most in the world. She faces wild animals and men with guns. She falls ill; she walks until her paws bleed. And all to reach Joe. Eric Knight created a fictional dog so real, so breathtakingly alive, that we are caught up in her quest. And what leads Lassie on that quest are all the qualities of the best sort of hero.

Because of the Lassie I saw on TV every Sunday night, I fell in love with dogs, or the idea of dogs. Who wouldn't love a creature as noble and brave and principled as Lassie? Whose heart wouldn't sing when a dog—any dog—risked her life to save another life, human or animal? Whose heart wouldn't break when that same dog faced a cruel hand, felt the crack of a stick across her back? And whose heart wouldn't sing once more when that abused dog was brave enough to trust and love another person?

I would be forty-two years old before I got a dog and forty-eight before I began working on my first book about a dog. But I felt as if I had known dogs most of my life, starting with Lassie. My own dog, Sadie, was a gentle soul, as sweet as Lassie, but not, I have to admit, nearly as brave. Still, the emotional connection I had with Sadie, a connection that had been awakened decades earlier as I watched Lassie's adventures, informed my own stories.

There are many scenes in *Lassie Come-Home* that make readers catch their breath—scenes that illustrate Lassie's courage or the sense of justice that leads her to fight to protect a man she barely knows. But the image of Lassie that most speaks to me is subtler, the image of a dog following her heart. "And the heart was gallant and the instinct was true. And so the dog went, day after day, steadily south in the Highlands, over bracken and heather, through hill-land and plain, through stream and woodland—ever going steadily, always south."

Toward her boy.

—Ann M. Martin

CHAPTER ONE

Not for Sale

Everyone in Greenall Bridge knew Sam Carraclough's Lassie. In fact, you might say that she was the best-known dog in the village—and for three reasons.

First, because nearly every man in the village agreed she was the finest collie he had ever laid eyes on.

This was praise indeed, for Greenall Bridge is in the county of Yorkshire, and of all places in the world it is here that the dog is really king. In that bleak part of northern England the dog seems to thrive as it does nowhere else. The wind and the cold rains sweep over the flat moorlands, making the dogs rich-coated and as sturdy as the people who live there.

The people love dogs and are clever at raising them. You can go into any one of the hundreds of small mining villages in this largest of England's counties, and see, walking at the heels of humbly clad workmen, dogs of such a fine breed and aristocratic bearing as to arouse the envy of wealthier dog fanciers from other parts of the world.

And Greenall Bridge was like other Yorkshire villages. Its men knew and understood and loved dogs, and there were many perfect ones that walked at men's heels; but they all agreed that if a finer dog than Sam Carraclough's tricolor collie had ever been bred in Greenall Bridge, then it must have been long before they were born.

But there was another reason why Lassie was so well known in the village. It was because, as the women said, "You can set your clock by her."

That had begun many years before, when Lassie was a bright, harum-scarum yearling. One day Sam Carraclough's boy, Joe, had come home bubbling with excitement.

"Mother! I come out of school today, and who do you think was sitting there waiting for me? Lassie! Now how do you think she knew where I was?"

"She must have picked up your scent, Joe. That's all I can figure out."

Whatever it was, Lassie was waiting at the school gate the next day, and the next. And the weeks and the months and the years had gone past, and it had always been the same.

Women glancing through the windows of their cottages, or shopkeepers standing in the doors on High Street, would see the proud black-white-and-golden-sable dog go past on a steady trot, and would say:

"Must be five minutes to four—there goes Lassie!"

Rain or shine, the dog was always there, waiting for a boy— one of dozens who would come pelting across the concrete playground—but for the dog, the only one who mattered. Always there would be the moment of happy greeting, and then, together, the boy and the dog would go home. For four years it had always been the same.

Lassie was a well-loved figure in the daily life of the village. Almost everyone knew her. But, most of all, the people of Greenall Bridge were proud of Lassie because she stood for something that they could not have explained readily. It had something to do with their pride. And their pride had something to do with money.

Generally, when a man raised an especially fine dog, some day it would stop being a dog and instead would become something on four legs that was worth money. It was still a dog, of course, but now it was something else, too, for a rich man might hear of it, or the alert dealers or kennelmen might see it, and then they would want to buy it. While a rich man may love a dog just as truly as a poor man, and there is no difference in them in this, there is a difference between them in the way they must look at money. For the poor man sits and thinks about how much coal he will need that winter, and how many pairs of shoes will be necessary, and how much food his children ought to have to keep them sturdy—and then he will go home and say:

"Now, I had to do it, so don't plague me! We'll raise another dog some day, and ye'll all love it just as much as ye did this one."

That way, many fine dogs had gone from homes in Greenall Bridge. But not Lassie!

Why, the whole village knew that not even the Duke of Rudling had been able to buy Lassie from Sam Carraclough— the very Duke himself who lived in his great estate a mile beyond the village and who had his kennels full of fine dogs.

For three years the Duke had been trying to buy Lassie from Sam Carraclough, and Sam had merely stood his ground.

"It's no use raising your price again, Your Lordship," he would say. "It's just—well, she's not for sale for no price."

The village knew all about that. And that was why Lassie meant so much to them. She represented some sort of pride that money had not been able to take away from them.

Yet, dogs are owned by men, and men are bludgeoned by fate. And sometimes there comes a time in a man's life when fate has beaten him so that he must bow his head and decide that he must eat his pride so that his family may eat bread.

CHAPTER TWO

"I Never Want Another Dog"

The dog was not there! That was all Joe Carraclough knew.

That day he had come out of school with the others, and had gone racing across the yard in a rush of gladness that you see at all schools, all the world over, when lessons are over for the day. Almost automatically, by a habit ingrained through hundreds of days, he had gone to the gate where Lassie always waited. And she was not there!

Joe Carraclough stood, a sturdy, pleasant-faced boy, trying to reason it out. The broad forehead above his brown eyes became wrinkled. At first, he found himself unable to realize that what his senses told him could be true.

He looked up and down the street. Perhaps Lassie was late! He knew that could not be the reason, though, for animals are not like human beings. Human beings have watches and clocks, and yet they are always finding themselves "five minutes behind time." Animals need no machines to tell time. There is something inside them that is more accurate than clocks. It is a "time sense," and it never fails them. They know, surely and truly, exactly when it is time to take part in some well-established routine of life.

Joe Carraclough knew that. He had often talked it over with his father, asking him how it was that Lassie knew when it was time to start for the school gate. Lassie could not be late.

Joe Carraclough stood in the early summer sunshine, thinking of this. Suddenly a flash came into his mind.

Perhaps she had been run over!

Even as this thought brought panic to him, he was dismissing it. Lassie was far too well trained to wander carelessly in the streets. She always moved daintily and surely along the pavements of the village. Then, too, there was very little traffic of any kind in Greenall Bridge. The main motor road went along the valley by the river a mile away. Only a small road came up to the village, and that became merely narrow footpaths farther along when it reached the flat moorland.

Perhaps someone had stolen Lassie!

Yet this could hardly be true. No stranger could so much as put a hand on Lassie unless one of the Carracloughs were there to order her to submit to it. And, moreover, she was far too well known for miles around Greenall Bridge for anyone to dare to steal her.

But where could she be?

Joe Carraclough solved his problem as hundreds of thousands of boys solve their problems the world over. He ran home to tell his mother.

Down the main street he went, racing as fast as he could. Without pausing, he went past the shops on High Street, through the village to the little lane going up the hillside, up the lane and through a gate and along a garden path and then through the cottage door, to cry out:

"Mother? Mother—something's happened to Lassie! She didn't meet me!"

As soon as he had said it, Joe Carraclough knew that there was something wrong. No one in the cottage jumped up and asked him what the matter was. No one seemed afraid that something dire had happened to their fine dog.

Joe noticed that. He stood with his back to the door, waiting. His mother stood with her eyes down toward the table where she was setting out the tea-time meal. For a second she was still. Then she looked at her husband.

Joe's father was sitting on a low stool before the fire, his head turned toward his son. Slowly, without speaking, he turned back to the fire and stared into it intently.

"What is it, Mother?" Joe cried suddenly. "What's wrong?"

Mrs. Carraclough set a plate on the table slowly and then she spoke.

"Well, somebody's got to tell him," she said, as if to the air.

Her husband made no move. She turned her head toward her son.

"Ye might as well know it right off, Joe," she said. "Lassie won't be waiting at school for ye no more. And there's no use crying about it."

"Why not? What's happened to her?"

Mrs. Carraclough went to the fireplace and set the kettle over it. She spoke without turning.

"Because she's sold. That's why not."

"Sold!" the boy echoed, his voice high. "Sold! What did ye sell her for—Lassie—what did ye sell her for?"

His mother turned angrily.

"Now she's sold, and gone, and done with. So don't ask any more questions. They won't change it. She's gone, so that's that—and let's say no more about it."

"But Mother . . ."

The boy's cry rang out, high and puzzled. His mother interrupted him.

"Now no more! Come and have your tea! Come on. Sit ye down!"

Obediently the boy went to his place at the table. The woman turned to the man at the fireplace.

"Come on, Sam, and eat. Though Lord knows, it's poor enough stuff to set out for tea . . ."

The woman grew quiet as her husband rose with an angry suddenness. Then, without speaking a word, he strode to the door, took his cap from a peg, and went out. The door slammed behind him. For a moment after, the cottage was silent. Then the woman's voice rose, scolding in tone.

"Now, see what ye've done! Got thy father all angry. I suppose ye're happy now."

Wearily she sat in her chair and stared at the table. For a long time the cottage was silent. Joe knew it was unfair of his mother to blame him for what was happening. Yet he knew, too, that it was his mother's way of covering up her own hurt. It was exactly the same as her scolding. That was the way with the people in those parts. They were rough, stubborn people, used to living a rough, hard life. When anything happened that touched their emotions, they covered up their feelings. The women scolded and chattered to hide their hurts. They did not mean anything by it. After it was over . . .

"Come on, Joe. Eat up!"

His mother's voice was soft and patient now.

The boy stared at his plate, unmoving.

"Come on, Joe. Eat your bread and butter. Look—nice new bread, I just baked today. Don't ye want it?"

The boy bent his head lower.

"I don't want any," he said in a whisper.

"Oh, dogs, dogs, dogs," his mother flared. Her voice rose in anger again. "All this trouble over one dog. Well, if ye ask me, I'm glad Lassie's gone. That I am. As much trouble to take care of as a child! Now she's gone, and it's done with, and I'm glad—I am. I'm glad!"

Mrs. Carraclough shook her plump self and sniffed. Then she took her handkerchief from her apron pocket and blew her nose. Finally she looked at her son, still sitting, unmoving. She shook her head sadly and spoke. Again her voice was patient and kind.

"Joe, come here," she said.

The boy rose and stood by his mother. She put her plump arm around him and spoke, her head turned to the fire.

"Look Joe, ye're getting to be a big lad now, and ye can understand. Ye see—well, ye know things aren't going so well for us these days. Ye know how it is. And we've got to have food on the table and we've got to pay our rent—and Lassie was worth a lot of money and—well, we couldn't afford to keep her, that's all. Now these are poor times and ye mustn't —ye mustn't upset thy father. He's worrying enough as it is—and—well, that's all. She's gone."

Young Joe Carraclough stood by his mother in the cottage. He did understand. Even a boy of twelve years in Greenall Bridge knew what "poor times" were.

For years, for as long as children could remember, their fathers had worked in the Clarabelle Pit beyond the village.

They had gone on-shift, off-shift, carrying their snap boxes of food and their colliers' lanterns; and they had worked at bringing up the rich coal. Then times had become "poor." The pit went on "slack time," and the men earned less. Sometimes the work had picked up, and the men had gone on full time.

Then everyone was glad. It did not mean luxurious living for them, for in the coal-mining villages people lived a hard life at best. But it was a life of courage and family unity, at least, and if the food that was set on the tables was plain, there was enough of it to go round.

Only a few months ago, the pit had closed down altogether. The big wheel at the top of the shaft spun no more. The men no longer flowed in a stream to the pit-yard at the shift changes. Instead, they signed on at the Labor Exchange. They stood on the corner by the Exchange, waiting for work. But no work came. It seemed that they were in what the newspapers called "the stricken areas"—sections of the country from which all industry had gone. Whole villages of people were out of work. There was no way of earning a living. The Government gave the people a "dole"—a weekly sum of money—so that they could stay alive.

Joe knew this. He had heard people talking in the village. He had seen the men at the Labor Exchange. He knew that his father no longer went to work. He knew, too, that his father and mother never spoke of it before him—that in their rough, kind way they had tried to keep their burdens of living from bearing also on his young shoulders.

Though his brain told him these things, his heart still cried for Lassie. But he silenced it. He stood steadily and then asked one question.

"Couldn't we buy her back some day, Mother?"

"Now, Joe, she was a very valuable dog and she's worth too much for us. But we'll get another dog some day. Just wait. Times might pick up, and then we'll get another pup. Wouldn't ye like that?"

Joe Carraclough bent his head and shook it slowly. His voice was only a whisper.

"I don't ever want another dog. Never! I only want— Lassie!"

CHAPTER THREE

An Evil-tempered Old Man

The Duke of Rudling stood by a rhododendron hedge and glared about him. He lifted his voice again.

"Hynes!" he roared. "Hynes! Where has that chap got to? Hynes!"

At that moment, with his face red and his shock of white hair disordered, the Duke looked like what he was reputed to be: the worst-tempered old man in all the three Ridings of Yorkshire.

Whether or not he deserved this reputation, it would seem sufficient to say that his words and actions earned it.

Perhaps it was partly due to the fact that the Duke was exceedingly deaf, which caused him to speak to everyone as if he were commanding a brigade of infantry on parade, as indeed he had done, many years ago. He had also a habit of carrying a big blackthorn walking stick, which he always waved wildly in the air in order to give emphasis to his already too emphatic words. And finally, his bad temper came from his impatience with the world.

For the Duke had one firm belief: which was that the world was going, as he phrased it, "to pot." Nothing ever was as good these days as it had been when he was a young man. Horses could not run so fast, young men were not so brave and dashing, women were not so pretty, flowers did not grow so well, and as for dogs, if there were any decent ones left in the world, it was because they were in his own kennels.

The people could not even speak the King's English these days as they could when he was a young man, according to the Duke. He was firmly of the opinion that the reason he could not hear properly was not because he was deaf, but because people nowadays had got into the pernicious habit of mumbling and snipping their words instead of saying them plainly as they did when he was a young man.

And, as for the younger generation! The Duke could—and often would—lecture for hours on the worthlessness of everyone born in the twentieth century.

This last was curious, for of all his relatives, the only one the Duke could stand (and who could also stand the Duke, it seemed) was the youngest member of his family, his twelve-year-old granddaughter, Priscilla.

It was Priscilla who came to his rescue now as he stood, waving his stick and shouting, beside the rhododendron hedge.

Dodging a wild swish of his stick, she reached over and pulled the pocket of his tweed Norfolk coat. He turned with bristling moustaches.

"Oh, it's you!" he roared. "It's a wonder somebody finally came. Don't know what the world's coming to. Servants no good! Everybody too deaf to hear! Country's going to pot!"

"Nonsense," said Priscilla.

She was indeed a very self-contained and composed young lady. From her continued association with her grandfather, she had grown to consider both of them as equals—either as old children or as very young grownups.

"What's that?" the Duke roared, looking down at her. "Speak up! Don't mumble!"

Priscilla pulled his head down so that she could speak directly into his ear.

"I said, *Nonsense!*" she shouted.

"Nonsense?" roared the Duke.

He stared down at her, then broke into a roar of laughter. He had a curious way of reasoning about Priscilla. He was convinced that if Priscilla had pluck enough to answer him back, she must have inherited it from him.

So the Duke felt in a much better temper as he looked down at his granddaughter. He flourished his long white moustaches, which were much grander and finer than the kind of moustaches that men manage to grow these days.

"Ah, glad you turned up," the Duke boomed. "I want you to see a new dog. She's marvellous! Beautiful! Finest collie I ever laid my eyes on."

"She isn't so good as the ones they had in the old days, is she?" Priscilla asked.

"Don't mumble," roared the Duke. "Can't hear a word you say."

He had heard perfectly well, but had decided to ignore it.

"Knew I'd get her," the Duke continued. "Been after her for three years now."

"Three years!" echoed Priscilla. She knew that was what her grandfather wanted her to say.

"Yes, three years. Ah, he thought he'd get the better of me, but he didn't. Offered him ten pounds for her three years ago, but he wouldn't sell. Came up to twelve the year after that, but he wouldn't sell. Last year offered him fifteen pounds. Told him it was the rock-bottom limit—and I meant it, too. But he didn't think so. Held out for another six months, then he sent word last week he'd take it."

The Duke seemed pleased with himself, but Priscilla shook her head.

"How do you know she isn't coped?"

This was a natural question to ask, for, if the truth must be told, Yorkshiremen are not only knowing about raising dogs, but they are sometimes alleged to carry their knowledge too far. Often they exercise devious secret arts in hiding faults in a dog: perhaps treating a crooked ear or a faulty tail carriage so that this drawback is absolutely imperceptible until much later, when the less knowing purchaser has paid for the dog and has taken it home. These tricks and treatments are known as "coping." In the buying and selling of dogs—as with horses—the unwritten rule is *caveat emptor*—let the buyer beware!

But the Duke only roared louder when he heard Priscilla's question.

"How do I know she isn't coped? Because I'm a Yorkshire-man, too. Know as many tricks as they do, and a few more to boot, I'll warrant.

"No. This is a straight dog. Besides, I got her from Whatsis-name—Carraclough. Know him too well. He wouldn't dare try anything like that on me. Indeed not!"

And the Duke swished his great blackthorn stick through the air as if to defy anyone who would have the courage to try any tricks on him. The old man and his grandchild went down the path to the kennels. And there, by the mesh-wire runs, they halted, looking at the dog inside.

Priscilla saw, lying there, a great black-white-and-golden-sable collie. It lay with its head across its front paws, the delicate darkness of the aristocratic head showing plainly against the snow-whiteness of the expansive ruff and apron.

The Duke clicked his tongue, in signal to the dog. But she did not respond. There was only a flick of the ear to show that the dog had heard. She lay there, her eyes not turning toward the people who stood looking at her.

Priscilla bent down and, clapping her hands, called quickly: "Come, collie! Come over here! Come see me! Come!"

For just one second the great brown eyes of the collie turned to the girl, deep brown eyes that seemed full of brooding and sadness. Then they turned back to mere empty staring.

Priscilla rose.

"She doesn't seem well, Grandfather!"

"Nonsense!" roared the Duke. "Nothing wrong with her. Hynes! Hynes! Where is that fellow hiding? Hynes!"

"Coming sir, coming!"

The sharp, nasal voice of the kennelman came from behind the buildings, and in a moment he hurried into sight.

"Yes, sir! You called me, sir?"

"Of course, of course. Are you deaf? Hynes, what's the matter with this dog? She looks off-color."

"Well, sir, she's a poor feeder," the kennelman hurried to explain. "She's spoiled, Hi should say. They spoils 'em in them cottages. Feeds 'em by 'and wiv a silver spoon, as ye might say. But Hi'll see she gets over it. She'll take her food kennel way in a few days, sir."

"Well, keep an eye on her, Hynes!" the Duke shouted. "You keep a good eye on that dog!"

"Yes, sir. I will, sir," Hynes answered dutifully.

"You'd better, too," the Duke said.

Then he went muttering away. Somehow he was disappointed. He had wanted Priscilla to see the fine new purchase he had made. Instead, she had seen a scornful dog.

He heard her speaking.

"What did you say?"

She lifted her head.

"I said, why did the man sell you his dog?"

The Duke stood a moment, scratching behind his ear.

"Well, he knew I'd reached my limit, I suppose. Told him I wouldn't give him a penny more, and I suppose he finally came to the conclusion that I meant it. That's all."

As they went together back toward the great old house, Hynes, the kennelman, turned to the dog in the run.

"Hi'll see ye eat before Hi'm through," he said. "Hi'll see ye eat if Hi 'ave to push it down yer throat."

The dog gave no motion in answer. She only blinked her eyes as if ignoring the man on the other side of the wire.

When he was gone, she lay unmoving in the sunshine, until the shadows became longer. Then, uneasily she rose. She lifted her head to scent the breeze. As if she had not read there what she desired, she whimpered lightly. She began patrolling the wire, going back and forth—back and forth.

She was a dog, and she could not think in terms of thoughts such as we may put in words. There was only in her mind and in her body a growing desire that was at first vague. But then the desire became plainer and plainer. The time sense in her drove at her brain and muscles.

Suddenly, Lassie knew what it was she wanted. Now she knew.

CHAPTER FOUR

Lassie Comes Home Again

When Joe Carraclough came out of school and walked through the gate, he could not believe his eyes. He stood for a moment, and then his voice rang shrill. "Lassie! Lassie!"

He ran to his dog, and in his moment of wild joy he knelt beside her, plunging his fingers deep into her rich coat. He buried his face in her mane and patted her sides.

He stood again and almost danced with excitement. There was strange contrast between the boy and the dog. The boy was lifted above himself with gladness, but the dog sat calmly, only by the wave of her white-tipped tail saying she was glad to see him.

It was as if she said:

"What's there to be excited about? I'm supposed to be here, and here I am. What's so wonderful in all that?"

"Come, Lassie," the boy said.

He turned and ran down the street. For a second he did not reason out the cause of her being there. When the wonder of it struck him, he pushed it away.

Why question how this wonderful thing had happened? It was enough that it had happened.

But his mind would not stay at rest. He quieted it again.

Had Father bought the dog back again? Perhaps that was it!

He raced on down High Street, and now Lassie seemed to catch his enthusiasm. She ran beside him, leaping high in the air, barking that sharp cry of happiness that dogs often can achieve. Her mouth was stretched wide, as collies so frequently do in their glad moments and in a way that makes collie owners swear that their dogs laugh when pleased.

It was not until he was passing the Labor Exchange that Joe slowed down. Then he heard the voice of one of the men calling:

"Eigh, lad. Wheer'd tha find thy dog again?"

The tones were spoken in the broadest Yorkshire accent, and it was in the same accent that Joe answered. For, while in school all the children spoke "pure" English, it was considered polite to answer adults in the same accents that they used.

"She were bi' t' schooil gate," Joe shouted.

But after that he knew the truth. His father had not bought the dog back again, or else all the men would have known it. In a small village like Greenall Bridge everyone knew the business of everyone else. And certainly, in that particular village, they would have known about any such important matter as the resale of Lassie.

Lassie had escaped! That was it!

And so young Joe Carraclough ran gladly no more. He walked slowly, wonderingly, as he turned up the hillside street to his home. By his door he turned and spoke to the dog sadly.

"Stay at heel, Lassie," he said.

With his brow furrowed in thought, he stood outside the door. He made his face appear blank of expression. He opened the door and walked in.

"Mother," he said. "I've got a surprise."

He held out his hand toward her, as if this gesture would help him get what he most desired.

"Lassie's come home," he said.

He saw his mother staring at him. His father looked up from his place by the fire. Then, as he came into the cottage, he saw their eyes turn to the dog that followed obediently at his heel. They stared but they did not speak.

As if the collie understood this silence, she paused a moment. Then she walked, going head down as a dog will when it feels that it has done something—it does not know what—that is wrong. She went to the hearth rug and wagged her tail as if in signal that no matter what sins had been committed, she was willing to make up again.

But there seemed to be no forgiveness, for the man turned his eyes from her suddenly and stared into the fire. That way the man shut his dog from his sight.

The dog slowly coiled herself and sank to the rug, so that her body touched the man's foot. He drew it away. The dog lay her head across her paw and then, like the man, stared into the depths of the fire, as if in that golden fancy-land there would be an answer to all their troubles.

It was the woman who moved first. She put her hands on her hips and sighed a long, audible sigh—one that was eloquent of exasperation. Joe looked at her and then, to try to soften their stoniness, he began speaking, his voice bright with hope.

"I was coming out of school, and there she was. Right where she always is. Right at the gate waiting for me. And you never saw anyone as glad to see you. She wagged her tail at me. She was that glad to see me."

Joe spoke on, the words racing from him. It was as if as long as he could keep on talking, neither his mother nor father could say the dread words that he expected to hear. With his flood of speech, he would hold back the sentence.

"I could see she was that homesick for us—for all of us. So I thought I'd bring her right along, and we could just . . ."

Lassie paused, then walked head down.

"No!"

It was his mother, interrupting loudly. It was the first word that either of the parents had spoken. For a second Joe stood still, and then the words flooded from him again, making a fight for what he wanted and what he dared not hope he could have.

"But she's come home, Mother. We could hide her. They wouldn't know. We could say we hadn't seen her and then they'd . . ."

"No!"

His mother's voice repeated the word sternly.

She turned away angrily and continued to set the table. Again she found relief, as the village women did, in scolding. Her voice ran on, with the words coming cold and sharp, to cover up her own feelings.

"Dogs, dogs, dogs!" she cried. "I'm fair sick o' hearin' about them. I won't have it. She's sold and gone and done with, and the sooner she's out of my sight the better I'll be pleased. Now get her out of here. And hurry up, or first thing you know we'll have that Hynes comin' 'round here. That Mr. Know-It-All Hynes!"

Her voice sharpened with the last words, for she pronounced them in imitation of Hynes's way of speaking. The Duke of Rudling's kennelman was from London, and his clipped Southern British accent always seemed to irritate the local people, whose speech was broad-vowelled and slow.

"Now, that's my say," Joe's mother went on. "So you might just as well put it in your pipe and smoke it. She's sold, so take her right back to them that's bought her."

Feeling there was no help coming from his mother, Joe turned to his father sitting before the fire. But his father sat as if he had not heard a word spoken. Joe's underlip crept out stubbornly, as he sought for some new means of argument. But it was Lassie who argued for herself. Now that the cottage was silent she seemed to think all trouble was passed. Slowly she rose and, going to the man, began nudging his hand with her slim muzzle, as a dog so often will when it wants attention and comfort from its master. But the man drew his hand away from the dog's reach and went on staring into the fire.

Joe watched that. He turned a soft argument on his father.

"Eigh, Father," he said, sadly. "Ye might at least bid her welcome. It isn't her fault, and she's that glad to be home. Just pat her."

Joe's father gave no sign that he had heard his son's words.

"Ye know, happen they don't care for her right up at the kennels," Joe went on, as if speaking to the open air of the cottage. "D'ye think they understand how to feed her properly?

"Now, for instance, look at her coat. It does look a bit poorly, doesn't it? Father, don't ye think just a bit o' linseed strained through her drinking water would bring it up a little? That's what I'd do for a dog that could stand a bit brighter coat, wouldn't ye, Father?"

Still looking in the fire, Joe's father began nodding slowly. But if he did not seem aware of his son's attack, Mrs. Carraclough understood it. She sniffed.

"Aye," she stormed at her son, "tha wouldn't be a Carraclough—nor a Yorkshireman—if tha didn't know more about tykes than breaking eggs with a stick."

Her voice droned on in the cottage.

"My goodness, sometimes it seems to me that the men i' this village think more o' their tykes than they do o' their flesh and blood. That they do. Here's hard times, and do they get work? No. They go on the dole, and I swear some of 'em will be quite content to let their own children go hungry as long as the dog gets fed."

Joe's father shifted his feet uneasily, but the boy interrupted quickly.

"But truly, Mother, she does look thin. I'll bet you anything they're not feeding her right."

"Well," she answered pertly, "at that I wouldn't put it past Mister Know-It-All Hynes to steal best part of the dog meat for himself. For I never saw a skinnier-looking, meaner-faced man in all my life."

During this flow of words her eyes had turned to the dog. And suddenly her tone changed.

"By gum," she said. "She does look a bit poorly. Poor thing, I'd better fix her a little summat. She can do with it, or I don't know dogs."

Then Mrs. Carraclough seemed to realize that her sympathies were directly opposed to the words she had been speaking five minutes before. As if to defend herself and excuse herself, she lifted her voice:

"But the minute she's fed, back she goes," she scolded. "And when she's gone, never another tyke will I have in my house. All ye do is bring 'em up and work over 'em—and they're as much trouble as raisin' a child. And after all your work's done, what do you get for it?"

Thus, chattering angrily, Mrs. Carraclough warmed a pan of food. She set it before the dog, and she and her son stood watching Lassie eat happily. But the man never once turned his eyes toward the dog that had been his.

When Lassie had finished eating, Mrs. Carraclough picked up the plate. Joe went to the mantlepiece and took down a folded piece of cloth and a brush. He sat on the hearth rug and began prettying the dog's coat.

At first, the man kept his eyes on the fire. Then, despite his efforts, he began to turn quick glances toward the boy and the dog beside him. At last, as if he could stand it no longer, he turned and held out his hand.

"That's no way to do it, lad," he said, with his rough voice full of warmth. "If ye're off to do a job, ye might as well learn to do it right. Sitha—like this!"

He took the brush and cloth from his son and, kneeling on the rug, began working expertly on the dog's coat, rubbing the rich, deep coat with the cloth, cradling the aristocratic muzzle carefully in one hand, while with the other he worked over the snow white of the collie's ruff and artistically fluffed out the "leggings" and the "apron" and the "petticoats."

So for a spell, there was quiet happiness in the cottage. The man lost all other thoughts as he gave his mind over to the work. Joe sat on the rug beside him, watching each turn of the brush and remembering it, for he knew, as in fact every man in the village knew—that there was not a man for miles around who could fix up a collie either for workday or for show bench as Sam Carraclough, his father, could. And his greatest dream and ambition was to be, some day, as fine a dog-man as his father was.

It was Mrs. Carraclough who seemed to remember first what they had all driven from their minds, that Lassie no longer belonged to them.

"Now please," she cried, in exasperation. "Will you get that tyke out of here?"

Joe's father turned in sudden anger. His voice was thick with the Yorkshire accent that deepened the speech of all the men of the village.

"Ye wouldn't have me takking her back lewking like a mucky Monday wash, would'ta?"

"Look, Sam, please," the woman began. "If ye don't hurry her back . . ."

She paused, and they all listened. There was the sound of footsteps coming up the garden path.

"There," she cried, in exasperation. "It's that Hynes!"

She ran toward the door, but before she reached it, it opened, and Hynes came in. The small, thin figure in its checked coat, riding breeches, and cloth leggings halted for a moment. Then Hynes's eyes turned to the dog before the hearth.

"Ow, Hi thought so," he cried. "Hi just thought as 'ow Hi'd find 'er 'ere."

Joe's father rose slowly.

"I were just cleaning her up a bit," he said ponderously, "and then I were off to bring her back."

"Hi'll bet ye were," Hynes mocked. "Ye were going to bring 'er back—Hi'll bet ye were. But it just so 'appens that Hi'll take 'er back myself—since Hi 'appened to drop in."

Taking a leash from his pocket, he walked quickly to the collie and slipped the noose over her head. At the tug she rose obediently and, with her tail down, followed the man to the door. There Hynes halted.

"Ye see," he said, in parting. "Hi wasn't born yesterday, and Hi 'appen to know a trick or two myself. You Yorkshiremen! Hi know all about yer and yer come-home dogs. Training 'em to break loose and run right back 'ome when they're sold, so then ye can sell 'em to someone else. Well, it won't work with me. It won't. Because Hi know a trick or two myself, Hi do . . ."

He halted suddenly, for Joe's father, his face deep red with anger, had started toward the door.

"Er—Good evening," Hynes said quickly.

Then the door closed, and Hynes and the collie were gone. For a long time there was silence in the cottage, and then Mrs. Carraclough's voice rose.

"I won't have it, I won't," she cried. "Walkin' into my house and home without so much as by your leave, and keeping his hat on as if he thinks he's the very Duke himself. And all on account of a dog. Well, she's gone, and if you ask me, I say good riddance. Now happen we can have a little peace. I hope I never see her again, I do."

As she scolded, her tongue running on, Joe and his father sat before the fire. Now both of them stared into it, unmoving and patient, each burying his own thoughts inside himself as the North-country people do when they are deeply troubled.

CHAPTER FIVE

"Don't Come Home Any More"

If Mrs. Carraclough thought that everything was settled, she was mistaken, for the next day Lassie was at the school gate, keeping her faithful tryst, waiting for Joe.

And again Joe brought her home. On his way, he planned to fight for his dog. To him the course was simple. He felt that when his parents saw the dog's faithfulness, they would relent and let her stay with them again, and thus reward her. But he knew it would not be easy for him to persuade them.

Slowly he walked up the path with the dog and opened the door. Everything in the cottage was as it had been before—

his mother getting the evening meal ready, his father brooding in front of the fire as he did for hours these days since there was no work.

"She's—she's come home again," Joe said.

All his hopes fled at his mother's first words. There was no surrender in them.

"I won't have it. No, I won't have it," she cried. "Ye can't bring her in—and it's no use begging and plaguing me. She's got to go right back! Right this minute!"

The words cascaded over Joe. In the strict bringing-up of his Yorkshire home, with its stern kindness, it was rare that he "answered back," as the saying is, to his parents. But this time he felt he must try, must make them understand.

"But Mother, just a little while. Please, just a little while. Let me keep her just a little while!"

He felt that if he could only keep her there a short time, the hearts of his parents would soften. Perhaps Lassie felt that, too, for as Joe talked she walked in and went to her accustomed place on the hearth rug. As if she knew the talk was of her, she lay down, turning her eyes from one to another of the humans who usually spoke so quietly, but whose voices now were harsh.

"It's no use, Joe. The longer ye keep her here, the harder it's going to be to take her back. And go back she must!"

"But Mother—Father, look, please. She doesn't look well. They don't feed her right. Don't you think . . ."

Joe's father got up and faced his son. The man's face was blank and emotionless, but his voice was full of understanding.

"That won't work this time, Joe," he said, ponderously. "Ye see, lad, it's no use. We maun take her back right after tea."

"No! Ye'll take her back this very minute," Mrs. Carraclough cried. "If ye don't, ye'll have that Hynes round here again. And I won't have him walking into my house as if he owned it. Now put on your cap and go this very minute."

"She'll only come back again, Mother. Don't ye see, she'll only come back again. She's our dog . . ."

Joe stopped as his mother sank down in a chair in a movement of weariness. She looked at her husband, and he nodded, as if to say Joe was right.

"She comes back for the lad, ye see," the father said.

"I can't help it, Sam. She's got to go," Mrs. Carraclough said slowly. "And if it's the lad she comes back for, then ye must take him with ye. Let him go with ye, and he must put her in the kennels and tell her to stay. Then if he bid her rest there, happen she'd understand and be content, and not run away home any more."

"Aye, there's sense to that," the man said, slowly. "Get thy cap, Joe, and come wi' me."

Miserably Joe got his cap, and the man made a soft whistling sound. Lassie rose obediently. Then the man, the boy, and the dog left the cottage. Behind him, Joe could hear his mother's voice still going on, but full of weariness, as if she would soon cry from her tiredness.

"If she'd stay, then happen we could have a little peace and quiet in the home, though heaven knows there's not much chance of that these days, things being what they are . . ."

Joe heard her voice trail away as silently he followed his father and Lassie.

"Grandfather," Priscilla said, "can animals hear things that we can't?"

"Oh, yes. Yes. Of course," the Duke roared. "Take a dog, now. Hears five times as well as a human being. For instance, my silent dog whistle. It isn't silent, really. Makes high frequency sounds, but we don't hear them. No human can. Dog hears them, though, and comes running. That's because . . ."

Priscilla saw her grandfather start and then begin waving his blackthorn stick menacingly as he went down the path.

"Carraclough! What're ye doing there with my dog?"

Priscilla saw down the path a great, tall, village man and beside him a sturdy boy, who stood with his hand resting lightly on the mane of a collie. She heard the dog growl softly, as if in protest at the menacing advance of her grandfather, and then—the low voice of the boy quieting the dog. She followed her grandfather toward the strangers.

Sam Carraclough, seeing her coming, lifted his cap and poked his son to do likewise. This was not in any sense a servile gesture, but because many of the rough village people prided themselves in being well brought-up and conducting themselves with politeness.

"It's Lassie," Carraclough said.

"Of course it's Lassie," the Duke boomed. "Any fool can see that. What're ye doing with her?"

"She's run away again, and I'm bringing her back to you."

"Again? Has she run away before?"

Sam Carraclough stood silent. Like most of the village people, his mind moved very slowly. From the Duke's last words, he realized that Hynes had not told of her previous escape. And if he answered the Duke's question, he felt that in some way he would be telling tales on Hynes. Even though he disliked Hynes, he could not tell on him, for, as he phrased it in his own honest mind, he "wouldn't like to do a man out of his job." Hynes might be discharged, and jobs were hard to get these days. Sam Carraclough knew that.

He solved his problem in a typical Yorkshire way. Stubbornly he repeated his last words.

"I'm bringing her back—that's all."

The Duke stared at him menacingly. Then he lifted his voice even louder.

"Hynes! Hynes! Why does that man always run away and hide every time I want him? Hynes!"

"Coming, sir—Coming," came the nasal voice.

Soon Hynes came hustling from behind the shrubberies beside the kennels.

"Hynes, has this dog broken away before?"

Hynes squirmed uneasily.

"Well, sir, hit's this way . . ."

"Did she or didn't she?"

"In a way, sir, she did—but Hi didn't want to disturb Your Grace about 'er," Hynes said, fingering his cap nervously. "But Hi'll jolly well see she doesn't get away again. Can't think 'ow she did it. Hi wired hup all the places she dug underneath, and Hi'll see . . ."

"You'd better!" the Duke shouted. "Utter nincompoop! That's what! I begin to think ye're an utter nincompoop, Hynes! Pen her up. And if she breaks out again, I'll—I'll . . ."

The Duke did not finish explaining what dire things he intended to do, but instead went stumping away in an evil temper without so much as a "thank you" to Sam Carraclough.

Priscilla somehow felt that, for she started to follow her grandfather but then halted. She turned and, standing quietly, watched the scene he had left. Hynes was stirring angrily.

"Hi'll pen 'er hup," he muttered. "And if she hever gets away again, Hi'll . . ."

He did not finish the sentence, for as he spoke he made as if to grasp Lassie's mane. But he never reached the dog, for Sam Carraclough's heavy, hobnailed boot trod on Hynes's foot, pinning him to his position. The man spoke slowly.

"I brought my lad wi' me to pen her up this time," he said. "It's him she runs home for, and so he'll pen her up and bid her stay."

Then the cumbrous Yorkshire voice lifted, as if Sam Carraclough had just noticed something.

"Eigh, now I'm sorry. I didn't hardly notice I were standing on thy foot. Come along, Joe, lad. Unlatch the kennel for us, Hynes, and we'll put her in."

Priscilla, standing still beside the aged evergreens, saw the dog come through from the kennel to the run. As the boy came by the wire, she lifted her head and then walked to him. The collie pressed against the wire, and for a long moment the boy stood there, his fingers reaching through the mesh to touch the coolness of the dog's nose. The man ended the silence.

"Come on, Joe, lad. Now get it over with. There's no use stretching it out. Bid her stay—tell her we can't have her coming home no more."

Priscilla saw the boy by the kennels look up at his father and then glance around, as if there would be some help coming from somewhere.

But there was none. There was no help anywhere for Joe, and he swallowed and started to speak, his words coming slowly, in a low tone, but getting faster and faster as he spoke.

"Stay here and bide happy, Lassie," he began, his voice hardly audible. "And—and don't come home no more. Don't

run away no more. Don't come to school for me no more.
Stay here and let us be—because—ye don't belong to us no
more and we don't want to see thee—ever, again. Because
tha's a bad dog—and we don't love thee no more, and we don't
want to see thee. So don't plague us and come running home—
and stay here forever and leave us be. And—and don't never
come home again!"

The dog, as if it understood, walked to the far corner of the
kennel and lay down. The boy turned savagely and started
away. And because it was hard for him to see where he was
going, he stumbled. But his father, who was walking beside
him with his head very high and his gaze straight ahead,
caught him by the shoulder and shook him and said roughly:

"Look where tha's going!"

Joe trotted beside his father, who walked quickly. He was
thinking that he would never be able to understand why grown-
ups were so hard-hearted just when you needed them most.

He ran beside his father, thinking that, and not understanding that the man wanted to get away from the sound that
followed them—the sound of a collie, barking bravely, calling
to her master not to desert her. Joe did not understand that.

And there was another who found many things hard to
understand. It was Priscilla, who came closer to the run where
the collie now stood, her eyes fixed unmovingly to the spot
where she had last seen her master turn the corner down the
path, her head lifting with the signal bark.

Priscilla watched the dog until Hynes came from the front of the kennels. She called to him.

"Hynes!"

"Yes, Miss Priscilla?"

"Why does the dog run home to them? Isn't she happy here?"

"Why, bless yer 'eart, Miss Priscilla, of course she's 'appy —a fine kennel like she's got. She just runs 'ome because they've trained 'er to do it. That's the way they do—steal 'em back and sell 'em to somebody else before ye could say Bob's yer uncle."

Priscilla wrinkled her nose in thought.

"But if they wanted to steal her back, why did they return her themselves?"

"Now just ye don't worry yer pretty 'ead about it," Hynes said. "Hit's just ye can't trust none o' them down in that village. They're always hup to tricks, they are—but we're too smart for 'em."

Priscilla thought a while.

"But if the boy wanted his dog back, why did they ever sell her in the first place? If she was my dog, I wouldn't sell her."

"Of course ye wouldn't, Miss Priscilla."

"Then why did they?"

"Why did they? Because yer grandfather paid 'em a bloomin' good price for 'er, 'e did. That's why. A bloomin' good price.

'E's too easy on 'em, that's what. If Hi 'ad my way—Hi'd make 'em step round a bit. That Hi would, indeed!"

Satisfied with his solution, Hynes turned to the dog, which still stood, barking its signal.

"Quiet, now. Gwan—down wiv yer! In yer kennel and lie down. Gwan!"

As the dog made no sign of having heard him, Hynes strode nearer and lifted his hand in a striking gesture.

Slowly Lassie turned, and from her chest sounded a bass rumbling, and the lips crept upward so that the great teeth shone whitely. Her ears drew back, and the mane on her neck rose slowly. The rumbling growl sounded louder.

Hynes halted, and he rolled his tongue between his gaping front teeth.

"Oh, so ye'd get nawsty, would yer?" he said.

Then Priscilla walked before him.

"Look out, Miss Priscilla. Hi wouldn't go too near if Hi were you. She'd just as leaf take a bite out o' yer as look at yer, if Hi knows dogs. Which Hi do! But Hi'll 'ave the fine lady stepping around afore Hi'm through with 'er, that Hi will. So you keep away from 'er, Miss."

And Hynes turned away. For a long time Priscilla stood. Then slowly she walked to the wiring. She put her fingers through so that they were close to Lassie's head.

"Come here, then, girl," she said, softly. "Come to me. Come on! I wouldn't hurt you. Come on!"

The dog's growling subsided, and she sank to the ground. For one second her great brown eyes met the blue ones of the girl. Then the dog ignored her, and with a sort of suffering aristocratic majesty, lay in the pen. Her eyes did not blink, and her head did not turn. She lay there, staring steadily at the spot where she had last seen Sam Carraclough and his son.

CHAPTER SIX

The Hiding Place on the Moor

The next day Lassie lay in her pen, the early summer sunlight streaming on her coat. Her head rested on her paws. It was pointing in the direction that Sam Carraclough and his son had gone the evening before. Her ears were lifted, thrown forward, so that, although her body was at rest, her senses were awake to any sight or sound or smell that might mean her masters were returning.

But the afternoon was quiet. There was the hum of early bees in the air, the smell of the damp English countryside. That was all.

The afternoon deepened, and Lassie began to stir. There was some impulse warning her faintly. It was indistinct, indefinable, perhaps as when an alarm clock rings to disturb but dimly a still-sleeping human being.

Lassie lifted her head suddenly and scented the breeze. But this did not give her any quieting answer to the vague stirrings within her.

She got up, walked slowly toward the kennel, and lay down in the shade. That did not bring her any ease. She got up again and went back to the sun; but that was not the answer. The curious urging in her mind drove more strongly. She began walking about the pen, circling around, walking by the stout mesh-wire. The force within her drove her to walking round and round, going circle after circle about her cage. Then in one corner she halted, and with her paw she clawed the wire.

As if that were the signal, now she suddenly understood her desire. It was time! Time to go for the boy!

It was not that she thought this plainly, as a human being might. She knew it only blindly. But the impulse held her entirely and drove everything else away from her feeling or awareness. She only knew that it was time to go to the school, as she had gone every day for so many years.

She clawed vigorously at the wire, but she made little impression. Memory told her she had escaped there before, clawing, tearing at the wire, then digging and squeezing underneath, lifting with her powerful neck and back muscles so that she could be free.

But Hynes had cut off that path to escape. He had reinforced the mesh of the pen with even stouter wire, and had driven stout stakes of wood into the ground beside it. No matter how Lassie clawed and fought it was no use. As if her defeat and the passing of time forced her to even more energy, Lassie raced about inside the pen. She scratched at places where her instinct told her there might be a path to safety, but Hynes had reinforced them all.

Frantically she lifted her head to bark in frustrated anger, and then, tentatively, she reared and stood on her hind legs against the wire, looking up.

If you could go under a thing, you might go over it!

Dogs can know these things not by logical thought processes, or because someone has told them it must be so. Even the very smartest dogs know them only slowly and by hazy instinct and by training they have had in their own short lives.

So, dimly, and then more clearly, the new idea came into Lassie's mind. She leaped, and fell back again. The fence was six feet high, much too high for a collie to leap. A greyhound or a borzoi could have sailed over it easily. Dogs have been bred through the years to develop types for varying needs. Collies are of that group called working dogs, raised for centuries to work with man, to understand his words and signs, to be intelligent and to help him, and in these things they excell; but they cannot leap or race as can other types of dogs that have been perfected for these qualities alone.

Lassie's leaping, therefore, brought her nowhere near the top of the wire. She turned back the length of her pen and raced in a running start, but each time she fell back.

It seemed impossible, but with the courage and persistence of a good animal, she tried again and again, leaping at different spots, as if one place might be more accessible than another.

And one place was!

She jumped right at the corner, where the mesh joined at a right angle, and, while she was in the air, her driving hind legs found some support in the angle of the fence.

She tried again and this time, almost like a man climbing a ladder, she scrambled higher in a wild flurry of energy. She was almost at the top, and then she fell back.

But she had learned quickly. She turned and ran again, this time held against the angle of wire by her own driving rush. Her feet clawed at the wire in that instant when the force of gravity was overcome. She struggled higher and higher, and her front paws reached the top. For a single second she hung there. And then slowly she pulled herself upward. She teetered a moment, uncertainly. The top of the wire clawed at her belly. But she did not feel it. Only one thought was in her mind. It was time, the time to keep faith at a meeting place.

She launched herself out and dropped to the ground outside the pen. She was free!

Now that she had achieved it, it seemed that all angry energy had left her. She had a clear way, yet instinct drove her to a new action. As if she knew that she would be captured again if she were seen, she moved warily as a dog can when it is hunting or being hunted.

With her belly close to the ground, she slid across the path silently to the rhododendron thicket. The heavy foliage swallowed her. A second later she was gliding like a ghost in the shadow of a wall far away. Her memory of terrain, like that of most animals, was perfect. She went silently, but with amazing speed, to a spot where the wall ended and the iron-paling fence began. There was a hole under the fence there that she had found before. She slid through it.

As if she understood that this was the limit of a sort of enemy territory, her way of going now changed. She became normal again. She trotted calmly, her head erect, her full tail flowing behind in a graceful continuation of the curving lines of her body. She was just a glorious collie, trotting along happily, going through a routine of life without fuss or excitement.

Joe Carraclough had never expected to see Lassie any more. After he had bidden her stay, after he had scolded her for running home, he had really believed that she would never come to meet him any more at school.

But somewhere, down far in the depths of his hopes, he had dreamed of it, without ever believing his dream would come

Then slowly she pulled herself upwards.

true. And when he came from school that day and saw Lassie waiting, exactly as usual, he felt that it was not true—he was only living in his dreams.

He stared at his dog, his broad, boyish face full of amazement. Then, as if his silence were a sign that her behavior had been worthy of disapproval, Lassie dropped her head. She wagged her tail slowly, asking forgiveness for the unknown sin she had committed.

Joe Carraclough dropped his hand to touch her neck.

"It's all right, Lassie," he said slowly. "It's all right."

He did not look at the dog. For his mind was racing, going far, far away in thought. He was remembering how, twice before, he had brought his dog home. And yet, despite all his hopes and pleadings, she had been taken away.

So he did not hurry gladly toward his home this time. Instead, he stood, his hand resting on the neck of his dog, his forehead wrinkled as he tried to puzzle out this problem of his life.

Hynes thundered at the cottage door and walked in without waiting for an answer.

"Come on, where is she?" he demanded.

Mr. and Mrs. Carraclough stared at him, and then their glances turned toward each other. The woman, with troubled eyes, seemed to pay no attention to Hynes.

"So that's why he's not home!" she said.

"Aye," the man agreed.

"They're together—him and Lassie. She's got away again and he's afraid to come home. He knows we'll take her back. He's run away with her so's we can't take her back."

She dropped into a chair, and her voice became unsteady.

"Oh, my heavens! Shall I *never* have any peace and quiet in my home? Never any peace any more."

Her husband rose slowly. Then he went to the door. He took his cap from the peg and went back to his wife.

"Now don't thee worry, lass," he said. "Joe'll not have gone far, just up on the moors he'll head. And he won't get lost—both him and Lassie knows the moors too well for that."

Hynes seemed to ignore the despair of the people in the cottage.

"Now, come on," he said. "Where's that there dog o' mine?"

Slowly Sam Carraclough turned to the little man.

"That's what I'm off to find out, isn't it?" he said mildly.

"Well, Hi'll just go along wiv yer," Hynes said. "Just to make sure there ain't no monkey business."

For a moment, a great anger surged in Sam Carraclough, and he strode toward the other man. Hynes quailed quickly.

"Now don't ye start no trouble," he piped. "Ye'd better not start no trouble."

Carraclough stared down at the smaller man, and then, as if scorning one so beneath him in size and spirit, he went to the door. There he turned.

"Ye'll just go right home, Mr. Hynes," he said. "Thy dog'll be back to thee, just as soon as I find her."

Then Sam Carraclough went out into the dark evening. He did not go to the village. Instead he went up the hill on the side street, until he had reached the great, flat table-land that stretched, foreboding and bleak, for mile after mile over the Northern country.

He tramped forward steadily. It was soon dark, but as if by instinct his feet kept to the lightly worn paths which men had made in the hundreds of years of their going and coming over the wild country. A stranger might soon be lost in that land where there seemed no landmarks for guidance, but not any of the village men.

All their lives—when children at play—they had learned their country. They knew every inch of the moorland, and a twist in a path spoke to them as surely of their whereabouts as a street sign on a corner does to a city dweller.

Surely then, Joe's father strode, for he knew where to look for his son. Five miles over the moor the land broke into what was an island in the flatness, an island of outcropping rocks, great sharp-edged blocks which looked much as if in some strange long ago a giant child had begun to pile up building-block towers and then had deserted the game while it was only half finished. For it was there that the village people often wandered in their hours of trouble. The gaunt, forbidding rock towers, with their passages and caves, formed a place where one could sit in the vast silence and puzzle upon the problems of the world and of life without being disturbed by anyone.

And it was there that Sam Carraclough strode. He walked steadily through the darkness. The night rain began sweeping over the moor, fine and mist-like and insistent, but he did not slacken his step. At last the stone pile half loomed in the dark. And then, as his feet stepped on the first echoing stones, Sam Carraclough heard a sharp bark—the bark of a dog on watch, sounding a warning.

Climbing up on a path he remembered well from his own childhood, the man went toward the sound. And there, in the lea of a rock that sheltered them from the drive of the rain, he found the dog and his son. For a moment he stood, and there was only the sound of his breathing. Then the man said:

"Come, Joe."

That was all.

Obediently the boy rose, and in miserable silence he followed his father. Together with the dog they went along the paths over the tangled heath grass, the paths they both knew so well. When they were near the village again, his father spoke once more.

"Go right home and wait up for me, Joe. I'm taking her back to the kennels. Then, when I get home, I want a word with thee."

What that "word" would be, Joe knew well. He knew he had offended the life of the family by running away. And how deeply that offence had cut his parents by the actions of his mother, he fully realized when he reached the cottage. She did not speak as he took off his soaking coat and set his shoes to dry by the hearth. She set food before him, a bowl of steaming tea. But still she did not speak.

Then, at last, his father was back again, standing in the cottage, his stern face glistening with the dampness of rain, and the light of the lamp cutting sharp reflections over his nose and cheekbones and chin.

"Joe," the man began, "tha knows what tha's done wrong by running away wi' Lassie—done wrong to thy mother and to me?"

Joe looked steadily at his father. He lifted his head and spoke clearly.

"Aye, Father."

His father nodded and took a deep breath. Then he put his hands to his waist and unbuckled his thick leather belt.

Joe watched silently. Then, to his surprise, he heard his mother speaking.

"Ye'll not," she cried. "I say ye'll not."

She was standing now, facing his father. Joe had never seen his mother quite like that before. She was standing there, face to face with his father. She turned quickly.

"Joe, go right upstairs to bed. Off ye go."

As Joe went obediently, he saw her turn back to his father and speak clearly.

"There's things to talk of first," she was saying. "And I'm off to speak 'em right here and now. I think it's time someone did."

The two were silent, and then as Joe passed his mother on the way to the stairs, she took him by the shoulders and for a second smiled into his face. She pressed his head quickly against her and then, with a kind motion of her hand, pushed him toward the steps.

As Joe went upstairs he was wondering why it was that grownups sometimes were so understanding, just when you needed them most.

The next morning at breakfast nothing was said of the matter while his father was there.

Joe remembered that after he had gone upstairs the night before, long after he was in bed, his father and mother had talked. Once he had wakened to hear them still talking below. In the stoutly built cottage he had not heard the words—only the sounds of the voices: his mother's urgent and persistent, and his father's, low and rumbling and patient.

But when his father had finished breakfast and had gone out, Joe's mother began:

"Joe. I promised thy father I'd talk to thee."

Joe bent his gaze to the table and waited.

"Now tha knows tha did wrong, lad, doesn'ta?"

"Aye, Mother. I'm sorry."

"I know, but being sorry afterwards doesn't help at the time, Joe. And it's very important, for tha mustn't worry thy father. Not at this time, tha mustn't."

She sat, plump and motherly, at the table, looking into Joe's face. Then her gaze seemed to go beyond him.

"Ye see, things ain't like what they used to be, Joe. And ye must remember that. Thy father, well, he's got a lot on his mind these days with things as they are. Tha's a big lad now, tha's twelve years old—and tha's got to try to understand things as if tha's more grown up.

"Now, it's hard just now making things go right in a home. And it does take a lot to feed a tyke, to feed it properly, that is. She had a very good appetite, Lassie did, and it's hard work to feed 'em properly these days, things being as they are. Now do ye understand?"

Joe nodded slowly. In a way he half understood. If grownups could only see it the way he did, he wanted to say that. But his mother was patting his arm, patting it with the hand that was so clean and shiny and plump, the hand that kneaded the bread and moved so quickly when there were stockings to knit, and that danced over the needle when there was darning.

"That's a good lad, Joe."

Her face brightened.

"And happen some day, things'll all be changed again—and it'll be like old times again—and then, first thing ye know, we'll get another dog, shall we?"

Joe did not know why, but it seemed as though the oatmeal were stuck in his throat.

"But I don't want another dog," he cried. "Not ever. I don't want another dog."

He wanted to say too:

"I only want Lassie."

But he knew somehow that this would hurt his mother. So instead he took his cap and ran from the house, down the street to where the others were going to school.

CHAPTER SEVEN

Nothing Left but Honesty

It was just as his mother had said. Things were not as they used to be. Joe felt that more and more as the days passed. For one thing, Lassie came no more to the school. It seemed that at last the Duke's kennelman must have invented some manner of surrounding her with obstacles which even she could not surmount.

Each day when Joe came out of school, hope would run high for a moment, and he would turn his eyes to the place by the gate where she had always sat. But she was never there.

During the hours in school, Joe would try to think of his lessons, but his mind went to Lassie. He fought off his own thoughts. He would decide not to expect her to be there any more. But always, after he had crossed the schoolyard at the close of the day, his eyes would turn to the place beside the gate, despite his promises to himself never to expect her any more.

She was never there, so things were not as they used to be.

But it was not only Lassie. Joe began to feel that many other "things" were not as they used to be. He felt that his parents now scolded him about matters that had never angered them in the old days. Sometimes, for instance, at meals, his mother would watch as he spooned the sugar into his tea. She would press her lips and sometimes now she would say:

"Now ye don't need to use all that sugar, Joe. It's—it's— well, it isn't good for you to eat so much sugar. It isn't healthy."

His mother seemed to be always so short tempered these days, another of the "things" that were not as they used to be.

One day when she had been setting out to do the week-end shopping, she had acted so strangely. And it was only because he had suggested that they have a roast of beef.

"Why don't we have a roast o' beef for Sunday, Mother— and some Yorkshire pudding? We haven't had any for quite a time. Eigh, now I talk of it I'm rare hungry for some."

Once his mother and father had been proud of his appetite. They had laughed about it and joked about it, and said he could eat enough for an elephant—and had always given him still more. But this time his mother had not laughed or even answered him. She had stood a moment, and then dropped her string marketing-bag, and without a word had run upstairs to the bedroom. And his father had stared at the stairs for a moment and then, without explanation, had jumped up and taken his cap and gone out, slamming the door behind him.

There were even more "things" that were not as they used to be. Often now when he came in, he would find his mother and father looking angrily at each other. They would stop talking the moment he arrived, but he could tell by their faces and their manner that they had been arguing.

Once, late at night, he had wakened and had heard them in the kitchen room below. It was not a pleasant drone of voices such as there used to be in the old days. The tones were puzzled and angry. And then, rising, Joe could hear the words his father was speaking:

"I tell thee I've walked my feet off for twenty miles round here, and there's not a thing . . ."

Then the voice had quieted, and Joe heard his mother's voice, suddenly low and in a warm and comforting tone.

Many "things" were not as they used to be. In fact, so many of them that Joe felt nothing was as it used to be. And to him it all added up to one thing: Lassie.

When they had had Lassie, the home had been comfortable and warm and fine and friendly. Now that she was gone nothing went right. So the answer was simple. If Lassie were only back again, then everything once more would be as it used to be.

Joe thought much about that. His mother had asked him to forget Lassie, but he could not. He could pretend to, and he could stop talking about her. But in his mind Lassie would always go on living.

He kept her living in his mind. He would sit at his desk at school and dream of her. He would think that perhaps some day—some day—like a dream come true, he would come out of school, and there she would be, sitting at the gate. He could see her just as if she were there, the sable and white of her coat gleaming in the sun, her eyes bright, her tipped ears thrust forward toward him so that she could hear the sound of a voice that tells a dog its master is near much sooner than its poor eyesight can. Her tail would move in welcome, and her mouth would be drawn back in the happy "laugh" of a dog.

Then they would race home—home—home—running through the village together, running gladly together.

So Joe dreamed. If he could not talk of his dog, he would never stop dreaming of her and hoping that some day . . .

The early, North-country English dusk was settling as Joe came in. He saw his mother and father look up at him.

"What made thee so late?" his mother asked.

Her voice sounded hard and short. Joe felt that they had been talking again—talking as they did these days, with impatience to one another.

"I were kept after school," he said.

"What did tha do wrong to get kept for?"

"Teacher told me to sit down and I didn't hear him."

His mother put her arms akimbo.

"What werta doing, standing up?"

"I was looking out of the window."

"The window? What werta looking out the window for?"

Joe stood silent. How could he explain to them? It would be better to say nothing.

"Tha hears thy mother?"

His father was standing angrily. Joe nodded.

"Well then, answer her. What werta looking out the window for in school hours?"

"I couldn't help it."

"That's no answer. What dosta mean, tha couldn't help it?"

Joe felt the hopelessness of everything flooding over him—his father, who was so understanding usually, now angry at him. He felt the words beginning to race from his mouth.

"I couldn't help it. It was near four o'clock. It was time for her. I heard a dog barking. It sounded like her. I thought it was her, truly I did. I couldn't help it. I didn't think what I was doing, Mother. Truly. I was looking through the window to see if it were her, and I didn't hear Mr. Timms tell me to sit down. I thought it were Lassie—and she weren't there."

Joe heard his mother's voice rising in impatience.

"Lassie, Lassie, Lassie! If I ever hear that name again. Is there never to be any peace and quiet in my home . . . ?"

Even his mother didn't understand!

Joe felt that most of all. If only his mother had understood!

The moment was too much for him. He felt hotness rising in his throat. He turned and ran to the door. He ran down the garden path into the deepening evening. He kept on running, up onto the moor.

Things would never be right again!

It was dark on the moor when Joe heard the sound of footsteps and his father's voice.

"Is that thee, Joe, lad?"

"Aye, Father!"

His father didn't seem to be angry any more. Joe suddenly felt comforted by the nearness of the tall, strong figure that loomed up beside him.

"Been walking, Joe?"

"Aye, Father," Joe said.

Joe knew it was hard for his father to "get talking" as he phrased it. It took his father such a long time to get the words going.

He felt his father's hand on his shoulder, and together they went along across the flat space. For a long time nothing was said. It was as if they were content to be together. Then Joe's father began.

"Now walking, Joe. That's a champion thing to do, isn't it, Joe?"

"Yes, Father."

His father nodded, and seemed quite happy with both his statement and his son's answer. He walked along freely, and Joe tried to stretch his legs so that he could match his father's firm, powerful stride. Together, unspeaking, they went up a rise, and then their feet rang on stone, and they were at the rocks. At last, by the edge of a slab, they sat. A half moon came from the rack of sky, and they could see the moor stretching away before them.

Joe saw his father put his short clay pipe in his mouth, and then absent-mindedly begin patting pocket after pocket, until his mind came to what he was doing. Then his hands ceased, and he began sucking his empty pipe.

"Haven't ye no tobacco, Father?" Joe asked.

"Why nay, lad. It's just—well, times being what they are— I've given up smoking."

Joe wrinkled his brow.

"Is it because we're poor, Father, and you can't buy any tobacco?"

"Nay, now lad, we're not poor," Joe's father asserted, firmly. "It's just—times is not like they used to be and—well, anyhow, I smoked too much. It'll be good for ma health to stop for a while."

Joe sat in thought. Sitting there beside his father in the dimness, he knew that his father was "making it easy for him." He knew that his father was protecting him from worries that grownups had. Suddenly Joe felt grateful to his father, who was big and strong and who had followed him up to the moor to try to comfort him.

He put out his hand to touch his father's.

"You're not angry at me, are you, Father?"

"Nay, Joe, a father can't get truly angry at his own lad—ever. It's just he wants him to understand how things are.

"That's what I wanted to say. Ye mustn't think we're over hard on thee. We don't want to be. It's just—well—back of it all, a chap's got to be honest, Joe. And never thee forget that, all thy life, no matter what comes. Ye've got to be honest."

Joe sat still. Now his father was talking, almost as if to himself, not gesticulating, but sitting perfectly still, speaking out toward the dim night.

"And sometimes, when a chap don't have much, Joe, he clings to being honest harder than ever—because that's all he does have left. At least, he stays honest. And there's a funny thing about honesty; there's no two ways about it. There's only one way about it. Honest is honest. D'ye see?"

Joe didn't quite understand what his father meant. But he did know that it must be something very important to his father, to make him go into such long sentences. His father usually said only "Aye" or "Nay," but now he was trying to talk. And somehow, Joe could feel the importance of what his father was trying to show him.

"It's like this, Joe. Seventeen year I worked in that Clara-belle Pit. Seventeen year, good time and bad time, full time and slack time, till she shut down for good. And a good collier I was, too, as any of my mates would vouch. In that seventeen year, Joe, butties I've had by the dozen, working alongside of me. But, my lad, there's not one can say that in all that time, Sam Carraclough ever took what wasn't his, nor spoke what wasn't true. Remember that, Joe. In all this West Riding there's not a man can stand up and say a Carraclough was ever mishonest.

"And that's what I mean by clinging to what ye've got. Honest is only one road. It can't be two. And ye're big enough to understand now that when ye've sold a chap owt, and ye've taken his brass for it, and ye've spent it; well then, done's done. And Lassie was sold and that's all . . ."

"But, Father, she . . ."

"Now, now, Joe. Ye can't alter it. No matter how many words tha says, tha can't alter it that she's sold, and we've taken the Duke's brass and spent it, and now she belongs to him."

For a while Sam Carraclough sat silent. Then he spoke again, as if to himself.

"And happen it were for the best at that. No two roads about it, she were getting hard to feed. A dog like that eats most as much as a good-grown child."

"We always fed her before."

"Aye, Joe, but ye've got to face things. Now, before, I were working. But now I'll have to face ye with it—I'm on the dole,

And ye can't feed a dog right on that—ye can't feed a family right on it. So she's better off.

"Why look at it this way, lad. Ye wouldn't want Lassie going around looking peaked and pined and poorly. Ye wouldn't have her looking like the road some chaps round here keep their tykes, would'ta?"

"We wouldn't pine her, Father. We could manage. I don't need to eat so much . . ."

"Now, Joe, that ain't the road to look at it."

They were silent, and then the man began again.

"Think on it this road, lad. Now ye're rare fond o' the tyke, aren't ye?"

"You know I am, Father."

"Well then, if that's so, tha should be truly happy because now she's so well off. Just think, Joe, now Lassie's got lots to eat—and a private kennel all to herself—and a fine big run—and everybody to care for her. Why, lad, she's just like a sort of princess living in her own palace and garden. That's it, she's just like a varritable princess now. Ain't that nice for her?"

"But Father, she'd be happier if . . ."

The man blew out his breath in exasperation.

"Eigh, Joe! There's no pleasing thee! Well then, I might as well let thee have it straight from the shoulder. Tha might as well put Lassie clean out o' thy mind, because tha's never off to see her no more."

"But she might get away . . ."

"Nay, lad, nay! She's run away her last time, and that were once too often. She'll never run—never any more!"

Joe forced the words from him.

"What did they do to her?"

"Well, last time I took her back, the Duke got angry at me and Hynes and the whole lot. And I got mad at him, for I don't owe him a penny, Duke or no Duke, and I said if she got away again, he'd not see her no more, and he said if she ever got away again I was welcome to her, but he'd see she didn't. So he's taken her up to his place i' Scotland with him. He's off to get her ready for the shows. Hynes has gone up wi' her and half a dozen more likely show dogs. But after the shows, she goes back to Scotland, and she's never to be kept down here i' Yorkshire any more.

"So there she stays for good, so it's good-bye, and good luck to her. She's not coming home no more. Now I weren't off to tell thee this, but it's happen best tha should know. So there it is, and put it in thy pipe and smoke it.

"Now what can't be helped in this life must be endured, Joe lad. So bide it like a man, and let's never say another word about it as long as we live—especially i' front o' thy mother."

Then Joe found himself stumbling down the path from the rocky crags, and they were going over the moor. His father did not comfort him but merely walked along, still sucking his empty pipe. It was not until they were near to the village and could see the windows shining that the man spoke again.

"Just afore we go in, Joe," he said. "I want thee to think on thy mother. Tha's growing up, and tha must try to be like a man to her and understand her.

"Now women, Joe, they're not like men. They have to stay home, women do, and manage as best they can. And what they haven't got—well, they've got to spend time in wishing for.

"And when things don't go right, well, they have to take it out in talk and give a man hot words. But if a man's really got any gumption, he gives 'em that much. For he knows a woman really doesn't mean owt by it when she natters and nags and lets her tongue go. So tha mustn't mind it when thy mother talks hard at me, or if she sometimes snaps at thee. She's got a lot to put up with these days, and it tries her patience.

"So it's us that has to be patient, Joe. Thee and me. And then—some day—well, happen things'll pick up again and times'll be better for all on us. D'ye understand, lad?"

Joe's father reached over and pressed his son's arm quickly, in a gesture of encouragement.

"Yes, Father," Joe said.

He stood for a while looking at the lighted village.

"Father. Is it very far to Scotland?"

The man stood, his head sunk on his broad chest. He breathed deeply and sadly.

"A long, long road, Joe. Much farther than tha'll ever travel, I'd say. A long, long road."

Then, sadly, they went together down to the village.

CHAPTER EIGHT

A Captive in the Highlands

It is, as Sam Carraclough had said to his son, "a long, long road" from the village of Greenall Bridge in Yorkshire to the Duke of Rudling's estate up in the Scottish Highlands. Much farther than you would wish to walk.

To get there you would go almost directly north—first out across the moors and the flatlands of Yorkshire. Twining east, you would go past wild land, then through rich farming districts. If you were going by train, you would soon look through the windows at the right and see the North Sea, shining down beneath the high cliffs. There would be on your left the spires of ancient cities, and then the pall of grime over the industrial centers of Durham, where the great shipways stand along the river mouths, and the coal goes pouring by train to the docks of the seaports.

Dark night falls early as you travel, for this land is in a high latitude where the sun sinks early and rises late. But your train would go on and on, screaming in the darkness as it raced over the bridges, crossing rivers, crossing at last the Tweed River, which means that you are leaving England behind.

Through the night the train would race on, clattering past the industrial towns of Lowland Scotland, where the furnaces and forges glow brighter in the darkness than by day. During the night your train would go over mighty bridges, carrying you across the very wide river mouths that the Scottish people call "firths."

In the morning your train would still be racing, only now the country would have changed. There would be no more cities belching smoke. Instead you would see the beautiful Scottish land that the poets have sung about for centuries, the blue mountains and green-bordered lakes, and the rolling land where the shepherds watch their flocks.

On and on the train would go, and the land would become wilder and wilder, the hills more rugged, the lochs more closely enclosed by woodlands. It would be lonelier and lonelier—now great expanses of heatherland where men are seldom seen, where the deer still roam. On and on you would go, right up to the tip of the northern land.

And there, in that farthermost point, is the great Scottish estate of the Duke of Rudling, the frowning stone house that looks out over the sea toward the Shetland Islands—those strange rock-bound dots of land where life is so hard and the weather so severe that nature seems to have adjusted most forms of life in a new manner so that they may survive; where the horses and dogs have become tiny, but also extraordinarily sturdy, so that they may continue to live in a stern land with a stern climate.

And there, far away in that northern land, was Lassie's new home. There she was fed and tended carefully. The food she was given was of the best. Each day she was combed and brushed and manicured and taught to stand in a perfect position so that some day soon she might go to the big shows and win more renown for the Duke of Rudling and his kennels.

She submitted patiently to all the handling of Hynes, as if she knew there were no use making any protest, but each day, just before four o'clock in the afternoon, something waked in her, and the training of a lifetime called her. She would tear against the wires of her pen or dash at the fence and try to leap it.

She had not forgotten.

In the clear, healthy coolness of the Highland air, the Duke of Rudling rode down the trail. Beside him, on her frisky cob, rode Priscilla. Her horse arched its neck and bucketed gaily.

"Hands," the Duke boomed. "That's what does it. Collect her now lightly. Good hands."

Priscilla smiled. For her grandfather considered himself such an authority on all animals that he could not ride without keeping up a stream of admonitions. But really he was quite proud of Priscilla's riding, and she knew it.

"That's what nature gave you hands and legs for," he roared. "Legs to push a horse forward, hands to collect him. Legs and hands does it!"

The Duke sat erect and proceeded to give an example, but his sturdy grey hack ambled along patiently with no change of gait or carriage. Truly, if the Duke had had his way despite his age, he would still have gone riding on the most spirited saddle horses available; but his entire family, in what amounted to an alliance, had conspired to limit him to the safe and uninspired hack that he now rode. Priscilla knew that too, so she nodded her head as if his plodding horse had just broken into proud carriage and mincing gait.

"Oh, I understand now what you mean, Grandfather," she said.

The Duke threw out his chest happily. For, in truth, he was happy. In his old age he found little to delight him thoroughly more than his granddaughter, and he could wish for nothing finer than these days during which they rode or walked about his northern estate.

"Just look at this weather! Marvellous! Wonderful!"

He shouted it with an air of proud ownership, as if he alone, the Duke of Rudling, were responsible for the tang in the air and the gentle warmth of the sun.

"All summer here," he announced gladly. "All summer. Then in autumn, back to Yorkshire. Then we'll have some more good times together."

"But in the autumn I'm going away to school. I'll be far away in Switzerland, Grandfather!"

"Switzerland!"

The Duke roared the word in such thunderous tones that Priscilla's cob skipped nimbly a half dozen feet sidewise.

"But I've got to go to school, Grandfather."

"Poppycock," the Duke thundered. "Sending girls to school in foreign lands—teaching them to jabber away in foreign languages like monkeys. Never could understand why they have such things as foreign languages—or if they have 'em, why anybody with any sense should wish to jabber 'em. Look at me. English is good enough for me. Never spoke a word of any other language in all my life, and I've got along well enough, haven't I?"

"But you wouldn't want me to grow up uneducated, would you, Grandfather?"

"Uneducated! You're educated enough. All this modern nonsense isn't education—teaching a girl to jibber-jabber away in some sort of senseless language that only a foreigner knows how to understand. Modern nonsense, that's what I call it!

"In my day, we educated people properly."

"What's properly, Grandfather?"

"Teach you how to run a house, that's what. In my day girls were brought up to do their duty—run a home properly. Nowadays they fill their heads full of nonsense. Pooh—this modern generation. They grow up impertinent. Always contradicting their elders. No respect for age, that's what. You contradict me—well, I forbid it. I won't have any more impertinence! For you are impertinent, aren't you?"

"Yes, Grandfather."

"Yes? Yes? You dare to say yes right to my face?"

"I had to, Grandfather. You just told me not to contradict you, and if I said no, then I would be contradicting you, wouldn't I?"

"Hrrumph!" the Duke said. "Hrrumph!"

Then he brushed his long white moustache triumphantly, as if he had won a battle. He looked down at his granddaughter, with her long flaxen hair tumbling from underneath the pert riding hat and cascading down onto her jersey-clad shoulders. He coughed and snorted and flourished his moustache again, and then he smiled and nodded his head.

"You're an impertinent baggage," he said. "But there's some hope for you. You know, you're just like I was when I was your age. You're like me, that's what you are. You take after me—the only one of the family that does! So there's some hope for you."

The horses clattered into the cobbled stableyard, and the Duke puffed as the groom ran out to take them.

"Don't hold his head, man," he shouted at the groom. "I hate to have anybody hold a horse's head while I'm dismounting. I can dismount perfectly without any help from anyone."

Fussing and fuming in his bad-tempered way, the Duke stood while Priscilla slackened the girth of her pony and led him toward the stall.

"That's right," he shouted, in what was his most agreeable tones. "No girl should be allowed to ride a horse who doesn't know how to feed and saddle 'em. If you don't know how yourself, you'll never be able to tell anyone else how to do it properly."

Thus, in a good temper, the old man and his granddaughter started along by the stables toward the great house. It was as they came by the low, stone building that Priscilla halted. For by the building were the runs for the dogs. In each one a dog leaped and barked a bedlam—except in one pen. In that pen was a beautiful tricolor collie. And it did not bark or leap. Instead it stood, its head turned to the south. It gazed into space.

And that was the dog Priscilla saw.

"What is it? What's up now?" the Duke said testily.

"That collie. Why is she chained, Grandfather?"

The Duke started and fixed his attention on the dog. For a second he was still, then it seemed as if some explosion had taken place in him. His voice rose so that the stables and the kennels thundered.

"Hynes! Hynes! Where is that man hiding? Where *is* he?"

"Coming, sir. Coming," came the voice of Hynes, as the kennelman trotted in from the other direction.

"Yes, sir. 'Ere, sir."

The Duke whirled.

"Well, don't sneak up behind me like that," the Duke bellowed. "What's that dog doing on a chain?"

"Well, Hi 'ad to put 'er on a chain, sir. She tears and scratches the wire away. Hi've mended it a dozen times, but hevery hafternoon she's hat it again. You told me to be sure and . . ."

"I never said a chain! No dog of mine goes on a chain— understand that?"

"Yes, sir."

"Then don't forget it. No dog—ever!"

The Duke whirled in anger, almost treading on Priscilla's toes. He looked down on her as she tugged his sleeve.

"Grandfather, she doesn't look at all well. She's had no exercise. Couldn't she come walking with us? She's so pretty!"

The Duke shook his head.

"Couldn't do that, m'dear. She'd never get in shape."

"In shape?"

"Yes. Going to show her. She's a champion. If we let her run wild with us she'd get—oh, burrs in her coat, and her leggings would get torn and spoiled. Couldn't have that, you know."

"But she ought to have some exercise, shouldn't she?"

The two of them stared at the dog behind the wire. Lassie stood, ignoring them as if she were a queen and they were beings so far beneath her that she could not see them.

The Duke rubbed his chin.

"Yes. She could do with a bit more exercise, I should say. Hynes!"

"Yes, sir?"

"She needs walking. You see she gets a good walk every day."

"She'll try to run away, sir."

"Put a leash on her, you idiot! You walk with her yourself. See she gets exercise. I want that dog in perfect condition."

"Yes, sir."

The Duke and Priscilla turned to the house. Hynes watched their backs. When they were out of sight he put on his cap savagely. He drew the back of his hand across his mouth, and then turned to the dog.

"So ye 'ave to 'ave a walk, do ye, milady?" he said. "Well, Hi'll walk ye. Not 'arf Hi won't."

But the dog paid no attention to his voice. She stood at the end of the chain, still gazing before her—gazing to the south.

CHAPTER NINE

Freedom Again at Last

It was Lassie's time sense that did it—that curious sense in an animal which tells it exactly what time of the day it is.

For had it been any other part of the day, Lassie might have followed her lifetime training to obey a spoken order and returned to Hynes as he bid her. But she did not.

It had been while on one of the newly ordered walks, with Lassie going along obediently at Hynes's heel. The leash was about Lassie's neck, but she neither tugged ahead on it nor lingered behind so that it tugged at her. She was going as a well-trained dog should go, close at the left heel so that her head almost touched Hynes's knee.

Everything was orderly as could be wished—only that Hynes had not forgotten his resentment about being forced to take exercise himself so that Lassie could be kept in good fettle. He wanted to get back to his tea—and he still wanted to show Lassie "who was boss."

And so, quite needlessly, he suddenly tugged on the leash.

"Come along wiv yer, will yer?" he snapped.

Lassie felt the sudden tug on her neck and hesitated. She was only slightly puzzled. She knew from long training that she was doing exactly what was expected of her. Obviously, though, this man expected something else. She wasn't sure what it was.

So in that moment of indecision, she slackened her pace. Almost gladly Hynes noted this. He turned and yanked at the leash.

"Come on, now. Come on when I tell yer," he shouted.

Lassie backed away from the threatening tone. Hynes yanked again. Lassie did what any dog will do: she braced herself for the tug and lowered her head.

Hynes tugged harder. The leash slipped up over Lassie's head.

She was free!

In the split second that Hynes saw that, he acted according to his nature—but not according to his own knowledge as a dog-man. He jumped to grab Lassie. It was exactly the wrong thing to do. For instinctively she jumped away to elude him.

Hynes's action had done only one thing. It had shown Lassie clearly that she wanted to keep away from him. Had he spoken to her in an ordinary manner, she might have come to him. In fact, if he had just ordered her to heel, she might have followed him back to the kennel held by nothing more than her trained habits of obedience to man.

Hynes was enough of a dog-man, however, to understand this—to see that he had made a bad mistake, that if he moved menacingly again, he might frighten the dog even more. So he began to do what he should have done in the first place.

"Here, Lassie. Come here," he said.

Lassie stood in indecision. One instinct told her to obey. But the memory of the sudden leap at her was too fresh.

Hynes saw that. He lifted his voice in a high, wheedling tone which he thought might be alluring.

"Nice Lassie. Nice dog," he chanted. "Nice dog—now stay there. Don't you move, now. Stay there."

He half knelt, and snapped his fingers to hold the dog's attention. Imperceptibly, inch by inch, he crept nearer.

"Stand still, now," Hynes ordered.

The lifetime of training that Sam Carraclough had given Lassie seemed to have its effect now. For even though Lassie disliked Hynes, she had been schooled that she must obey human beings who spoke the words of command to her.

But there was another lifetime impulse that stirred her— although only faintly. It was the time sense.

Dimly, mistily, it began to waken in her. She did not know it or reason it or think it clearly as a man would. It began to grow in her faintly. It was only a weak stirring.

It was time—time to—time to . . .

She watched Hynes creeping nearer. Her head lifted a trifle.

It was time—time to—time to go . . .

Hynes edged himself nearer. In another second he would be near enough to grab the dog—to sink his fingers into the wealth of heavy mane and hang on until he could slip the guardian leash over her head again.

Lassie watched him. The stirring was becoming plainer.

It was time—time to go for . . .

Hynes gathered himself. As if sensing it, Lassie moved. Quickly she backed away two paces from the crawling man. She wanted to be free.

"Drat you," Hynes exploded.

As if he realized this mistake, he began all over again.

"Nice Lassie, now. Stand still, there. Stand still. Stay there."

Lassie was not listening to him now, however. With only a small part of her senses she was watching the man edging nearer. All the rest of her was increasingly intent upon the stirring that was becoming clearer and clearer. She wanted time. She felt somehow that if this man reached her, she would be disappointed once more.

She stepped back again. And just at that moment Hynes leaped. Lassie dodged aside.

Angrily Hynes stood erect. He walked toward her, speaking soothing words. Lassie backed away. Always she kept the same distance between Hynes and herself—the distance an animal knows so well—the distance which places it beyond the sudden reach of an enemy.

Her instinct was saying:

"Keep away from him. Do not let him reach you. For there is something—something else. It is time—time to go—time to go for the . . ."

And then, suddenly, in that second, Lassie knew. She knew as surely and irrevocably as the hands of a clock that point to five minutes to four.

It was time to go for the boy!

She wheeled and began trotting away—trotting as if she had but to go a few hundred yards. There was nothing to tell her that the rendezvous she would keep was hundreds of miles and scores of days away. There was only the plain, unadorned knowledge of a duty to be done. And she was going to do it as best she could.

But now, behind her, she heard Hynes. He was running, shouting. She broke from her trot into a gentle lope. She was not afraid. It was as if she knew surely that this two-footed creature could never catch up with her. She didn't even need to put on speed. Her thrown-back ears told her how near Hynes was. Then, too, dogs, like most other animals, have their eyes set much more at the side of their heads than do human beings, and thus are able to see behind them with only the slightest turn of the head.

Lassie did not seem to worry about Hynes. She just kept on going in her steady lope, down the path, over the lawn.

For a second, Hynes's heart leaped with hope. Perhaps, he thought, Lassie would head back to the kennels.

But the kennels, where she had been chained and penned, were not a home for Lassie. They were a hated place. And Hynes's hope died as he saw the collie turn down the gravel path toward the front gate.

Hynes's heart gave a leap again. The gate was always closed, and the walls about the "home" part of the estate were tall, frowning granite ones. Perhaps he could corner her yet.

Priscilla and her grandfather rode up the road from the fishing village and halted by the iron gate to the estate.

"I'll open it, Grandfather," the girl said.

She slipped lightly from her saddle as the Duke began bumbling in protest. But Priscilla knew she could dismount and mount again much more easily than her grandfather. For despite all the protests, he was an old man, and climbing up into the saddle of even the quietest horse was a task accompanied by much fuming and puffing and groaning.

Linking the reins over her crooked arm, the girl drew back the bolt and, putting her weight against the wrought-iron structure, she swung it slowly back on its hinges.

It was only then that she heard the noise. Looking up the path, she saw Hynes. He was racing toward her. Before him was the beautiful collie. And Hynes was shouting:

"Close that gate, Miss Priscilla! Close that gate! That collie's loose. Don't let 'er get hout! Close the gate!"

Priscilla looked about her. Before her was the great gate. All she needed to do was swing it shut, and Lassie was trapped inside the home grounds.

She looked up at her grandfather. He was unaware of all the stir. His deaf ears had not caught the high shoutings of Hynes.

Priscilla began to pull the gate. For a second she swung her weight back on it. She half heard her grandfather beginning to roar in puzzled protest. But then she forgot that, and she saw only one picture in her mind.

It was the picture of a village boy just a little taller than herself, standing beside the meshed wire of a run, saying to his dog: "Bide here forever and leave us be—and don't never come home no more." And she knew then that while the boy was saying it, every sense and part of him was crying out to say just the opposite.

So she stood, seeing the picture in her mind, listening to the words again as if they were spoken plainly. And still she had not closed the gate.

Her grandfather was still fuming, knowing something was happening that his aged senses could not grasp. Hynes was still screaming:

"Close that gate, Miss Priscilla. Close it!"

Priscilla stood in the moment of indecision, and then quickly she began swinging the gate wide open. There was a blur that flashed past her knees and then Priscilla stood, looking down the road, watching the dog go steadily at a lope as if it knew it had a long, long way to go. So she lifted her hand.

"Good-bye, Lassie," she said, softly. "Good-bye and—good luck!"

On his horse sat the Duke, not looking down the road at the collie, but staring at his granddaughter.

"Well, drat my buttons," he breathed. "Drat my buttons."

There was a blur that flashed through the gate.

CHAPTER TEN

A Long Journey's Beginning

It was growing dusk as Lassie came down the dusty road. Now she trotted more slowly, and there was indecision in her gait. She halted and then turned back toward the direction from which she had come. She lifted her head, for she was badly puzzled.

Now the pull of the time sense was leaving her. A dog knows nothing of maps and of distances as a man does. By this time Lassie should have met the boy, and they should now be on their way home again—home to eat.

It was time to eat. The years of routine told Lassie that. Back in the kennels there would be a platter of fine beef and meal set before her. But back in the kennel also was a chain that made a dog a prisoner.

Lassie stood in indecision, and then another sense began to waken. It was the homing sense—one of the strongest of all instincts in animals. And home was not the kennel she had left. Home was a cottage where she lay on the rug before the fire, where there was warmth and where voices and hands caressed her. Now that she was lost, that was where she would go.

She lifted her head as the desire for her true home woke in her. She scented the breeze as if asking directions. Then without hesitation, she struck down the road to the south. Do not ask any human being to explain how she should know this. Perhaps, thousands upon thousands of years ago, before man "educated" his brain, he too had the same homing sense; but if he had it, it is gone now. Not with all his brain development can man tell how a bird or an animal can be crated, taken miles away in darkness, and when released, strike straight back toward its home. Man only knows that animals can do what he can neither do himself nor explain.

And in Lassie there was no hesitation. Her senses were now aware of a great satisfaction, for there was peace inside her being. She was going home. She was happy.

There was no one to tell her, and no way for her to learn that what she was attempting was almost in the realm of the impossible—that there were hundreds of miles to go over wild land—a journey that would baffle most men going afoot.

A man could buy food on the way, but what coin has a dog to pay for food? No coin except the love of his master. A man can read signs on the road—but a dog must go blindly, on instinct. A man would know how to cross the great lochs which stretch from east to west almost across the entire country, barring the way of any animal going south. And how could a dog know that she was valuable, and that in villages and towns lived hundreds of men of keen eye, who would wish to capture her for that reason?

There were so many things that a dog could not know, but by experience a dog might learn.

Happily Lassie set out. The journey had begun.

In the last of the long Northern twilight two men sat outside their cottage. It was like the other cottages of the village which lined the old, narrow street. The walls were thick with the whitewash coating of years.

The elder man, clad in rough homespun, lit his pipe carefully and lifted his head as it drew freely. He watched the puffs of smoke eddying away in the still evening air. Then he felt the sudden clasp of the younger man's hand on his arm.

"Wullie, see yonder!"

The older man looked where the other was pointing. He sat for sometime until his eyes saw more plainly in the evening. It was a dog coming toward them.

The younger man, who wore leggings and a corduroy suit, stood up.

"Looks like a good 'un, Wullie," he said.

"Aye, Geordie—a fine collie."

Their eyes followed it as it trotted near. Then the younger man stirred.

"Havers, Wullie. It looks like that fine collie belongin' tae the laird. It is! I'll sweer on it. I saw it twa days back when I were up chinnin' to McWheen aboot the salmon season. It'll be escaped, no doot . . ."

"Och, and then there'll be . . ."

"Aye, a rewarrrd for the mon that finds . . ."

"Losh, aye!"

"Hi!"

The younger man flung this last cry over his shoulder, for he was dashing out into the street. He barred the dog's way.

"Here, lass," he called. "Here, lass!"

He patted his hand on his knee in a gesture of friendliness.

Lassie looked up at him. Her ear had caught the sound which was almost her name: lass. Had the man walked toward her, she might have let him place his hand on her. But he moved too quickly. Suddenly Lassie was reminded of Hynes. She veered slightly, and without altering her trot, ran past him. The man dove at her. Her muscles flexed, and, like a football star, she put on a spurt that upset his timing. She loped a few steps and then went back to the purposeful trot.

But the man raced after her down the village street. Lassie quickened her pace again and broke into a steady gallop. The more he chased her, the more firmly it was becoming fixed in her mind that she must not let any human being put his hands on her. To chase a dog is merely to teach it to run away.

When the Scot saw that he had no chance of catching the dog by speed, he halted and picked up a loose flint. He thought he could hurl it ahead of Lassie, so that the sound of the falling stone might head her off and turn her back toward him. He drew back his arm and threw.

The aim was bad. The stone fell almost at Lassie's shoulder. Even as it was falling, she changed her gallop as a well-trained polo pony does, leading with the other forefoot. She veered away into the ditch. Belly-close, she went at an amazing speed. There was a gap in a hedge. She faded through it and shot away from the road up into the bleak back-country.

Once there, she turned south again and went back to the steady trot.

But now Lassie had learned one thing. She must keep away from men. For some reason that she could not understand, their hands were against her. Their voices now were rough and angry. They shouted and threw things. There was menace in men. Therefore, she must keep away from them. The thought stayed firmly with her. Lassie had learned her first lesson in the first day.

That first night Lassie traveled steadily. Never before in her five years of life had she been out alone at night. So there was no training to help her, only her instinct.

But the instinct within her was keen and alert. Steadily she followed a path over the heather-clad land. The path filled her with a warm satisfaction, for it was going south. She trotted along it confidently and surely.

At last she reached a rise and then, in the hollow below, she saw the dim shapes of farm buildings. She halted, abruptly, with her ears thrown forward and her nose trembling. Her magnificently acute senses read the story of the habitation below as clearly as a human being might read a book.

She read of horses standing in the barns, of sheep, of another dog, of food, of humans. She started down the slope warily. The smell of food was pleasant, and she had gone a long time without eating. But she knew she must be cautious, for men were there, too. And it was becoming fixed in her mind that she must keep away from them. She trotted down the path.

Then there came a sudden challenging bark of the other dog. She could hear him racing toward her. She stood, waiting. Perhaps he was friendly.

But he was not. He came tearing up the path, his mane erect, his ears flat. Lassie crouched to meet him. As he sprang, she stepped aside. He turned, giving loud voice in hysterical rage. His tones were saying: "This is my home—you are an intruder. It is my home and I will defend it."

Then, from the farm below, came the muffled voice of a man. "What is it, Tammie? Sic 'em up!"

At the sound of the human voice, Lassie wheeled. She trotted away. This was not *her* home. She was an outcast here.

The rough-coated shepherd charged at her as she loped away, worrying at her flanks. She turned quickly, her lip curling. As if that menace were enough, the other dog drew back.

Steadily she trotted on. The farm was soon left behind. She went over the wild country, following the animal paths. Finally in a depression she scented water. She found the small, cold stream and lapped greedily. The sky was greying in the east. She looked about her.

By a rock she scratched gently with her forepaw. She turned around three times and then curled herself up. Behind her was the protecting overhang of the rock. Her head faced outward. Now, even though she slept, her nose and ears would warn her of any approaching danger.

She put her head on her paw and sighed loudly.

Early the next morning Lassie was on her way again. She went steadily at a swinging trot that drove at the miles. Her muscles paced with inexorable rhythm, uphill, downhill. She did not pause or hesitate. Whenever a path ran to the south, she followed it. If it veered away, she left it, keeping to animal paths through the dense heather and brush.

When a path led toward a town or a farm, she shied away, circling the habitations to keep away from man. So at the places where men lived she went warily, instinctively keeping under cover, gliding like a ghost under the shadow of thicket and brush, taking advantage of any woodland.

For the most part her ground lay uphill, for ahead of her was a range of blue mountains. Unerringly she headed for the lowest dip where there would be a pass. As the day wore on and she gained higher ground and higher, the sky became overcast. The clouds looked leaden.

Then suddenly there was a flash, and thunder pealed. Lassie hesitated and whined in a quick, querulous tone. She was frightened. It is little use to blame a dog for having fear. A dog has so many braveries that its few fears do not cancel them out. And truth to tell, there are few collies that can stand thunder and lightning.

There are many dogs that do not mind such noise. There are breeds of hunting dogs that are never so happy as when a gun is sounded. But not a collie. It seems as if this breed, having worked so long as man's companion, has learned that such sharp, savage sounds may mean hurt. And the crack of a gun will send most collies running for cover. Other foes they will face, but not the unknown danger of noise.

So Lassie hesitated. The rolling peals of thunder echoed through the mountains, and the torrents of rain lashed down in one of the wild storms of North Scotland. For a long time she fought her fear, but at last it was too much. She trotted to a place on the boulder-strewn pass where overhanging ledges made a dry cave. There she crouched, pressing herself back against the rock as the thunder drummed and echoed like a barrage of guns.

But if she had halted her journey, it was not for long. As the storm went muttering away down the mountain range, she got to her feet. For a second she stood, head high, questing the breeze. Then again she started, going in that long, swinging trot.

The rain and the splashed earth now made the beautiful expanse of her coat tarnished and spotted. But she kept on going steadily, going to the south.

CHAPTER ELEVEN

The Fight for Existence

For the first four days Lassie traveled without pause, resting only briefly during the nights. The urge to travel south burned in her like a fever, and nothing could replace it.

On the fifth day a new demand began to gnaw at her senses. It was the call of hunger. The command to travel had blotted it out at first, but now it was insistent.

She had had no trouble in finding streams to quench her thirst, but the problem of getting food was one far removed from her protected life. From her first memory, food had never been her responsibility. At stated times it was provided for her. Man put it down before her in a platter. She had been taught carefully that that was her portion, and she must never eat any food that lay elsewhere. Year after year, that lesson had been driven into her. Food was not her responsibility. Man provided it.

But now, suddenly, the training and conditioning of a lifetime were useless. There was no man to put down a pan of food each afternoon. And yet this aristocratic animal must learn to exist.

Lassie found the way. She did not reason it out as a human being would. Human beings have imagination—they can picture events and circumstances before they meet them. Dogs cannot do this, they must wait blindly until the circumstance faces them and then do their best to meet it.

Yet how could Lassie meet this new problem? She had not the brain of a man to reason about it. She could not base her conduct on the past experience of others of her kind, which is another human method. A young child does not have to undergo many dangerous experiences in life to find out the result, for his parents and other older persons can tell him from their acquired knowledge what will result in such a case. No animal can pass on its own acquired knowledge to its young. Every animal must meet each new experience as if it had never faced his kind before in the history of the world. How then should Lassie learn how to feed herself?

She had that quality which is in animals that man perhaps had once, but has no longer: instinct.

With instinct, and the lessons of their own past experiences, animals manage to arrive at conclusions which man reaches by his reasoning power.

It was instinct that drove Lassie daily in one direction. It was past experience that taught her to be wary of human beings. It was instinct that told her how to keep out of their sight— to follow the low ground of ravines, to glide belly-low on the skylines. Instinct taught her to find food.

On the fifth day as she went along, traveling at her fast, swinging trot, her senses began to warn her. She halted in the half-beaten animal track through the wild heather and with head forward stood transfixed, her eyes, her ears, her nose reading the signs that came so faintly that a human being would have been insensible to them.

It was her sense of smell that deciphered the puzzle first. There was a warm, thick smell—the smell of food.

The habit of a lifetime impelled Lassie to run toward it openly. But instinct overruled habit. She dropped to a crouch, and with body low began to creep upwind toward the smell. Silently she moved through the heather, edging nearer and nearer. And then, suddenly, on the path she saw what her nose had warned her of. Coming down the path, his snakelike body undulating, was a weasel. His head was lifted high, and by his side he dragged the freshly killed body of a rabbit. His game was much bigger than himself, yet the powerfully built killer was dragging it along at a surprising speed. Then his

senses warned him, too, and he whirled in defiance. Dropping
his quarry, he turned to face the menace. His savage, white
teeth were bared, and he gave a shrill cry that sounded like
one of defiant rage.

Lassie, with head low, gazed at him. She had never seen such
an animal before. Nor was there in her breeding the instinct
of the terrier kind, which will dash more quickly than thought
of man at any form of rodent life. She was a working-dog breed,
a dog of peace—and yet instinct drove her on.

Slowly the ruff on her neck rose. The lips curled back from
her teeth. Her ears lay flat against her head. She gathered her
hindquarters under her.

But at the second she sprang, as if knowing the precise
moment when that would be, the screaming weasel flashed
aside. With lightning rapidity, he wove his way through the
tangled heather, going silently, swiftly, flowing like water.
Lassie whirled to look for him, but her senses were drawn to
something else—the warm, blood smell of the rabbit that lay
on the path.

For a long time she regarded it. She came nearer, bending
her head warily, as if ready to spring away. For, though the
blood smell of food was there, the scent of the weasel still
lingered, too. Carefully her nose came nearer and nearer until
it touched the freshly killed quarry. She drew back and walked
around it. Then she came near, bent her head, and picked up
the game. She lifted her head again and waited.

Lassie, with head low, gazed at him—yet instinct drove her on.

It was as if, in the wild land, far from all human beings, she was expecting the sudden call of the master: "No, Lassie! Drop it! Drop it!"

But no sound came.

She stood indecisively for almost a half minute, and then it was over. Carrying the rabbit, she trotted along. She quested to right and left as she went. Then she saw what she wanted— a thick tangle of gorse that made a sort of den. She walked to it, coiled herself close so that she was protected on three sides. She dropped to the ground, letting the rabbit fall before her. She smelled it again. It smelled good. It was food.

After that she had a newly acquired sense. She had learned the smell of rabbit. Instinct told her the rest. As she traveled along, whenever her keen nose told her of the nearness of game, she became a hunter. She scouted and ran and caught it, and she ate. It was the sensible law of nature. She did not kill wantonly as man often does. She killed to live, and no more.

Such food was just sufficient to sustain life, but that was all. Now there were no keen eyes to watch Lassie, to note her weight, to look at the color of her gums, to eye the quality of her coat. There was no one to say:

"She's off a couple of pounds—give her a little more beef liver in her dinner!"

"She doesn't seem quite up to snuff—better start giving her a bowl of milk in the morning. You might just drop a raw egg in it if she'll take it!"

"Hmm—I don't quite like the color of her gums. I think she'd better have a spoonful of cod liver oil once a day. That'll bring her up to condition!"

Not now all those cares for a royal dog that lies of nights in a dry kennel. Instead it was a dog with pinched, lean flanks; with coat blotched and torn; with petticoats and tail matted with burrs. But it was still a dog that had lived a life under loving care, so that it had known no sickness. And those years of care were telling now. For the frame was rugged and the muscles strong, and they drove along, mile after mile each day.

And the heart was gallant and the instinct was true. And so the dog went, day after day, steadily south in the Highlands, over bracken and heather, through hill-land and plain, through stream and woodland—ever going steadily, always south.

CHAPTER TWELVE

What a Painter Saw

The time was turning to the deepness of summer. Leslie Freeth lay back lazily in the bow of the rowboat. He puffed his pipe contentedly and watched the smoke go evenly in the cool morning air, drifting back to where McBane methodically pulled at the oars.

"It'd be better if I sat in the back, Mr. McBane," he said.

"Nay, she trims better, I've told ye, Mr. Freeth. She's a verra peculiar boat," the oarsman said.

Freeth puffed evenly and gave himself up to the day. There was no reasoning with these hard-hearded Scots. Yet if McBane wanted him in the bow . . .

His eyes took in the glory of the Scottish landscape, and Freeth was happy. The lochs—happy hunting ground of the British fishermen—meant something else to Leslie Freeth. They are the places whose beauty, long treasured by the Scotsmen, is also a magnet to English painters. And Leslie Freeth was one of those who never tired of the everlasting change of light and shadow that moved about the wide waters and the purpling hills. Each summer he came again, to paint and to resume earthy contact with the McBanes, who dourly welcomed him back to their cottage and gave him studio room in their fine stone barn.

So, content with the day, he lay back in the bow until the boat grated on the shingle of a small island. Mechanically he helped McBane unload the paraphernalia, the easel, the canvases, the metal paint boxes. He set up the canvas and the folding chair. He cocked his head on one side and regarded the unfinished painting.

"Weel, I'll be back for ye at the noon," McBane said.

"All right, Mr. McBane. I'll be several hours on this. How d'you think it's coming?"

McBane walked heavily to a position of vantage and, shutting one eye, began cocking his head from side to side. Throughout the long winters, at the small inn by the loch, McBane would argue for hours if need be that his Mr. Freeth was one of Britain's greatest landscapists, before whom all the Dutch and the French school would have bowed—if only they had been still alive to do so. But in the artist's presence McBane never let his undoubtedly prejudiced opinion show for an instant.

"Weel, sin' ye're asking me, I would say she's a wee bit on the gaudy side. T'watter's a bit too violent, and losh, but I never saw the ben that color—and yer clouds is verra startlin'. But I don't doubt she's fine elsewheres."

Leslie Freeth smiled. He was used to McBane's criticisms. Moreover, he really valued them, for the dour Scotsman had a good eye and a sound appreciation of his fair-faced land. So Freeth nodded, his eyes going from his canvas to the landscape, back and forth. He was thinking how still it all was. Not a movement anywhere, except the gentle lap of the water that slapped at the bottom of the rowboat down by the shore. Not a movement—except . . .

He shaded his eyes.

"See that, Mr. McBane—a deer?"

The Scotsman glanced at Freeth's outstretched arm pointing. His own eyes sought the shore of the northern mainland. The heavy, sandy eyebrows lowered as if they would shield the grey-blue eyes below them.

"A deer?" the artist repeated in question.

McBane shook his head without speaking. His eyes, used to the outdoors, were keener than the Englishman's.

"Weel, I never," he ejaculated finally.

"What is it?"

"A dog," the old man said.

He shaded his eyes with his hand. The artist did the same.
"So it is. I can see now."

Now that he was satisfied, Freeth made as if to turn to his painting, but the older man still gazed steadily. His attention brought the artist back to steady staring.

"A collie," McBane said. "Now what would it be doing . . ."

"Oh, probably one from somewhere around—a farm dog."

The Scotsman shook his head. Gazing steadily, he saw the animal come to the water's edge and wade in several feet. Then it backed away, ran along the bank several yards, and tried again. It kept repeating this, as if at some new spot it would find the water had disappeared and dry land was at its feet.

"Havers, Mr. Freeth. It looks as if it's seeking to cross."

"Perhaps it wants to follow us to the island."

"Nay. It's seeking to cross."

As if to remove all doubt, they heard a querulous whine—a short series of lifting cries such as a dog makes when it finds itself barred by something that surpasses its understanding.

"Aye, it's wishful to cross," the Scot repeated. "I think I'll tak' a row across by there and . . ."

As he spoke, he walked to the beach and lifted the bow of the rowboat. The shipped oars thumped in the rowlocks, and the noise went eddying across the still surface of the loch. At that moment Leslie Freeth saw the dog lift its head and then turn away.

"It's going, Mr. McBane," he called.

The Scot looked up. He straightened. The two men watched the collie turn into the underbrush. Only once in a while could they see a glimpse of the dog as it trotted steadily along the edge of the loch toward the west. It went confidently, as if now it had made up its mind.

"It's on its way the noo," McBane said. "Puir thing—it's got a long road to gang."

"You mean, it's going to walk round this loch? Why, that'd be miles and miles . . ."

"It'll ha' to gang near a hundred miles afore it can get by."

The artist stared at the older man, a little incredulously.

"You mean to tell me that a dog is going to walk a hundred miles just to get round a lake. Why . . ."

Freeth began to laugh, but McBane's tone halted him.

"Mr. Freeth, a collie is bi' origin a Scottish dog. And it has in it the courage and perrtinacity o' this land."

McBane said it reprovingly, and Freeth recognized the tone behind the words. His mind moved on.

"Mr. McBane."

"Aye?"

"What do you think it wants to cross for? Why should it?"

The Scotsman stood still a long time. Then he said:

"Now who could say? Only one thing, forebye. It's got business somewheer, and it's ganging aboot its business wi'oot asking help fra' no ither body on the face o' this airrth. And . . ."

Here McBane turned to his boat and clambered in. Then he continued:

". . . it's an example which all the rest of us micht do weel to follow."

Freeth smiled to himself. The dour old man had a habit of turning all things in nature to a stern lesson on human conduct. His mind went back to his painting, and his eye only half saw the boat, growing smaller and smaller, as McBane pulled it across the water, leaving him in solitude.

Instinct is like the flight of a bird, for its directions are in mighty, straight lines.

So Lassie, in her quest to get home, had worked almost in a beeline toward the village of Greenall Bridge, far to the south. Sometimes turning or bending her path where the obstacles of towns or impassable mountains lay before her, she had always come back to the instinctive line to the south. So she had come down through the Highlands, day after day of endless, weary travel. Her line had been straight.

But she had no way of foreseeing the land before her. She could not know that the instinctive straight line toward home would bring her to an impasse against the great lochs of Scotland.

One can look at a map and see what an obstacle these are, for they are great, long bodies of water, running almost due east and west, that almost cut the country in two. And although they look like narrow fingers on the map, they are not truly narrow in actuality. Wide, expansive bodies of water they are, and their far reaches are not to be swum by an animal. For narrow as they may be, the farther shoreline is often lost, or at best a thin, low-lying stripe of faint blue.

No, the lochs are a fearful barrier. Man can cross in his boats and ferries, but not an animal.

Yet, at the shore of the great loch, Lassie did not surrender her purpose. Her instinct told her to go south. But if the way was barred, she would seek some other way. So she started on her long trip to circle the lake. Day after day she worked west, fighting her way along, circling hamlets and villages, but always returning afterwards to the lake's edge, and working west.

Sometimes it would seem as if the barrier were circled and the way free. For a spell Lassie would trot at her unfaltering pace in the desired southern direction.

But it was always just a headland that jutted out, a headland that reached into the water. And always Lassie would work to the southermost tip and wade into the water, and with her head turned to the south would give a short, questing whine. Then always she must turn north again, back along the shore, to press west once more in her search for a way around.

Dozens of bays and headlands and just as many disappointments! A week after Leslie Freeth and McBane had seen the dog, she was still working her way west. And still the great, long loch stretched as a barrier that a dog could not understand.

CHAPTER THIRTEEN

When a Dog Is Ailing

Lassie trotted from a thicket and came to the shore. She was moving more slowly now, for the pads of her feet were bruised and sore, and in the delicate membrane between those pads on the right forefoot a thorn was festering. Nor was her head as high now, and there was less confidence in her way of going.

Often, at times, it seemed as if she had forgotten why she was on her endless journey. But this was never for long, and now her pace became steady again, and she quickened it, carrying herself so that her afflicted paw took less weight. Her head turned hopefully, for on her left now, at last, was no great impassable body of water. The loch had narrowed to a river. But it was a tumultous, fast-charging river that cascaded fiercely over the rocky bed.

Lassie came to the water's edge. She turned her head to the west again. But there, not far below her, was a town. From a bridge there were boys—fishing, shouting, filling the air with their cries. Lassie was still wary of human beings. She gazed steadily at them.

Then she looked again at the white, tumbling water. The roar of it drummed unpleasantly in her ears. Yet she hesitated only a moment. Then, boldly springing, she launched her body far out into the water.

The current caught her as a piece of paper thrown from a moving train is snatched away by the wind; so the water bore Lassie's body downstream as she landed. The power of the river tumbled her about, but she came to the surface and began striking out for the far shore. Her head was outstretched, her four feet drove steadily, pumping her along.

Again and again the current tumbled her with crushing force, and often she was submerged in swift eddies. But each time the marvellous direction sense of a dog never deserted her, and as she came up she was still fighting in the right direction. A man battered on a football field might start to carry the ball in the wrong direction, but the direction sense of an animal is not so easily defeated. Always Lassie struck out toward the southern bank.

But the stream had now carried her down toward the village. The boys on the bridge saw the spectacle of a dog being whirled by the current. They shouted and hallooed. With the cruelty of the young that sometimes gets free rein, they picked stones from the roadbed and flung them at her. As her body was whirled under the bridge, they ran across to the downstream side and continued their senseless pelting.

Lassie still fought on. Now she was at last nearing the other bank. A cascade was below her. Her driving feet raced, but they were not powerful enough. The current caught her, and she felt herself being whirled through space. Her body was driven cruelly against a rock, and the stab of pain ran like fire along her side. The current drew her down, and she disappeared.

The boys on the bridge, looking now far downstream, gave a shout, almost of insane triumph, such as the Tuscan army might have given before the moment of silence when Horatius leaped into the Tiber. Then they were still. They stood gazing at the tumbling water. At last, after it seemed that too much time had passed, they shouted again. There, in a backwater, Lassie's head broke the surface again, and she was still driving with her legs. Now the water was still, and she was able to master it. Fighting, swimming, driving with all her force, she made the landing. Her feet touched ground. The water soaked into her coat seemed to be too much of a burden, for she staggered at that moment, and her weary muscles seemed unable to hold her.

She started to drag herself clear. But now, for the first time, she became aware of another danger. The troop of boys was dashing down the river bank, sounding a wild chorus. Lassie called on her last strength. She pulled herself up the bank. She did not even wait to shake the water from her coat. She did not halt for the old pain in her forefoot nor for the new one that seared like fire along her side. Her mind held only one thing.

At last she was across. After weary days of thwarted direction sense, she was at last free—free to go south. The barrier was passed.

She broke into a clumsy lope. The noise of the lads behind her faded.

Now that the great barrier of the loch was circled at last, Lassie drove in her desired direction with clearer intensity. The village and the shouting boys were soon left behind. She dropped from the gallop to the slow trot that covered the most ground with the least effort.

The pain in her side and in her forepaw did not come into her mind. She adjusted her gait as best she could to favor the injuries.

Soon she left the road behind and set her path across meadows and flatlands. At sundown she was still traveling, as if, now that she could follow the line south again after so many days of going westward, she could not travel long enough to satisfy the urge within her. It was long past nightfall when at last she denned up where a clump of gorse arched over beside a field-wall.

She lay close to the ground. The coolness of the earth there, sheltered from all suns, felt good to the burning ache in her side. She licked at the forepaw, trying with her tongue to reach between the pads where the thorn festered. For nearly an hour she worked, but in the end the thorn still rested there.

With a sigh that was almost like that of a tired man, she crossed her muzzle over her extended foreleg and closed her eyes.

It was not yet dawn when she woke. She yawned and tried to raise herself. Her forequarters came from the ground. But her hindquarters did not move. She sat for a moment as if in surprise at this new and puzzling problem. Then again she strained, pulling with the muscles of her shoulders. For a second she managed to stand upright. She took one step forward and gave one hop with her good back leg. The other one did not work.

During the night the injury to her side had stiffened. In the last crash against the rocks in the tumbling river she had broken one rib and bruised badly the muscles and joints of her hind leg. They had now almost stiffened to immobility.

Hobbling badly, Lassie turned round in the shelter under the gorse. Then she let herself fall heavily to the ground. She curled herself up and lay silently, her eyes staring through the mass of stalks and tendrils toward the field where the first hint of dawn was showing. She could travel no farther. Instinct told her that. She must stay there.

When human beings are ill, they often make a show of their injuries and parade them so that others may see and give them sympathy. It is just the reverse with an animal living in its natural state. Asking no sympathy, deeming rather that weakness of any kind is something to be ashamed of, it crawls away into some hidden corner and there, alone, it awaits the outcome—either recovery or death.

This same force held Lassie to the den beneath the gorse. The desire to travel often wracked her, but the animal law to stay hidden during injury overcame it.

For days she lay, coiled and hidden away, her eyes bright but unmoving. Outside, the world went through its cycles. The darkness and the daylight followed each other. The birds sang. Once some field laborers passed. Sometimes the wind brought the unmistakable hot, near scent of a rabbit. Once a weasel, questing through the field, came part way through the gorse toward the den. His sharp eyes saw the coiled, furry shape. His nose trembled. For a moment he stood, unmoving; then he turned calmly and went on his way as if knowing the sick animal had no desire to pursue him.

All those things passed, but Lassie did not stir. The fever raged in her and possessed her body.

For six days she lay, almost without a move. Then, on an afternoon, as the sun was slanting lower, she lifted her head at last. Slowly, weakly, she began to lick her forepaw. Nature had done its work. From the festering sore the thorn had worked its way. Little by little, Lassie licked it clear and then cleaned the wound. She looked about her. Slowly she struggled to her feet. Her bad hind leg hung, not touching the ground. Slowly she limped from her hiding place. Hobbling across the field, she went downhill to where her nose told her there was water. She found the tiny streamlet, lowered her head, and lapped. It was the first time she had drunk for a week.

Greedily she took the water. She lay down by the stream, but her head now stayed erect. Her nose lifted, and she gave the sharp, protesting cry. She stood and faced to the south. Then she looked back to the gorse clump. At last she turned and hobbled again up the hill.

Now some of the stiffness was gone from her body and she managed to go quite freely on three legs. Returning to the gorse clump, she crawled into the shelter and lay there, patiently, waiting for the night.

For two more days she rested there, making brief trips to the stream to quench her thirst. But of food, she had none, nor did she seem to desire any.

Nine days after she had crossed the turbulent river, she came out from her den and made her way to the drinking place. Now she looked as if she were using all four feet, but the bad hind leg was carrying no weight—only going stiffly through an imitation of its function.

She lapped the clear water and, as before, raised her head afterwards and looked toward the south. In her mind something was stirring. It was the time sense.

Faintly in the depth of her mind the time sense, that had been blotted out during her illness, woke again.

It was time—time to go—time to go for . . .

Then Lassie knew once more. This was the time she should be keeping the rendezvous at the schoolhouse. But the school —it was there—in that direction. That was the way to go!

She turned her head once and looked back up the field toward the gorse clump by the wall. But it was only for a moment. Then, stiffly, she crossed the stream. Going slowly, she struck out to the south. Lassie was on her way again.

This was no proud show collie that trotted boldly now. It was a travel-stained dog, its body weak and pinched, wracked from the long days of starvation and with the fever that had passed. It was a painful shuffle rather than a proud trot that carried the dog along. And it did not last long.

Shortly after sundown Lassie halted again, this time by a snug walled-in place. It was a shooting-point in which the wealthy men stood hidden as the birds were driven over them during the grouse season; but Lassie did not know this. All she knew was that it gave her protection and warmth.

Nor did Lassie know that she had come but three miles from the den under the gorse clump. The greatness, or the smallness, of a distance do not qualify in the minds of an animal. All she knew was that she felt satisfied. She had made her way in the direction in which she wanted to go more than she wanted anything else in life. She breathed happily.

She lifted her ears, and the tip of her nose moved. The scent of rabbit came to her clearly.

Food! At last she was aware of it again and desired it. A ravening hunger woke in her, and the saliva formed in her mouth. She edged herself forward from the corner of the shooting-point. Soon she would eat again. And soon she would travel again, with recovered strength.

She edged forward silently.

If she was too weak and slow now to capture food for herself, she must die. For she would soon be weaker from starvation. If she was strong enough and quick enough now to capture food, soon she would be stronger.

She crept forward, going like a ghost toward her quarry.

CHAPTER FOURTEEN

For to Kill the Beasties

Two men crouched in a rude, stone croft. The moonlight coming through the windowless gap in the wall above them revealed them faintly. They were dressed alike, in rough homespun tweed, except that the younger one wore a peaked cap and the other a great woolen tam-o'-shanter. For a long time there was nothing but the sound of their breathing. Then the younger one stirred.

At that moment the older put out his hand to quiet him.

"Whist," he said.

They froze into stillness.

"Did ye hear aught, Andrew?" the younger one whispered.

"I thocht. . . ."

Silently they rose and stared out through the rectangular gap in the wall. Stretching away below them was the moonlit land, the grassy fields looking like those of a well-ordered park in the faint smoky-blue of a thin mist.

They stared a long time, their eyes and ears alert.

"Nay, Andrew, I don't hear a thing."

The older man nodded, so that the tuft on his tam-o'-shanter bobbed back and forth.

"I just thocht I did."

With the tension lifted, the younger man absent-mindedly took his pipe from his pocket. The other regarded him disapprovingly.

"I wadna smoke, Jock. Och, they'd smell it clear."

"Aye—that's so. But I'm dying for a smoke. And they'd smell them first, wouldn't they?"

Jock nodded his head toward a great pen in the field below. There, in the moonlight, the great flock of sheep stood unmoving and still. They were packed so close together that their backs made a sea of grey.

"And they'd hear aught long afore us," Jock continued, motioning with his head back over his shoulder. "At least, ma Donnie would."

Hearing his name, one of the two dogs in the shelter lifted his head expectantly. The other sighed and watched alertly to see if the long vigil was at last over.

"I don't see the idea o' keeping them in here, anyhow, Andrew. We should leave 'em ootside by the sheep."

"Na, na, Jock. If they're ootside, them devils'll never come. They're that canny, lad, it passes understanding."

"Aye, they maun be canny all richt," the younger agreed. "Six nichts we sit up on guard, and not a sign of 'em. The seeventh we gang to oor homes for sleep, and no sooner are oor ee's closed, nor doon they come on us, ravening and slaughtering. Seeven lambs and twa ewes! Seeven lambs, mind you! Why do they no come one o' the nichts we were ready for 'em?"

The older man ignored the last question.

"Ye should be thankful, Jock. Sixteen it was Archie Forsythe lost the Sabbath. And McKenzie thirteen the nicht afore."

"Ah, the brutes. The Sabbath and all ither days is the same to them devils. The black-hairted creatures o' Satan! If I ever caught one on 'em . . ."

The younger man left the rest unsaid.

"What makes 'em do it, Andrew?"

"Ah, lad, that's one o' those things pairhaps it's not given us to onderstand. But I suppose dogs is like humans, Jock. Most on 'em is honest and trusty. But every so often there's one born that has greed and cruelty and dishonor in his heart, and while he poses daytimes as a pairfect Galahad, as soon as dark hides him he becomes what he is—a ravening devil."

"Aye, Andrew. Ye knaw, Heaven above knaws I hae a love for dogs. Why, yon beastie o' mine, there's not a thing I wadn't

do for him, or a care I wadn't gie him—or a trust I wadn't put
in him. But they devils o' sheepkillers—they're not dogs. Ye
knaw, Andrew, what I think sometimes?"

"What, Jock?"

"Weel, ye may laugh. But times I think them sheepkillers
is not dogs, but they're the ghosts o' murderers who've been
hanged that return disguised i' the body o' animals!"

The young man said that in such an eerie tone that they
both shuddered. Then the older shook off the feeling.

"Na, na, Jock. They're just dogs—and ravening ones that's
gone bad. And we should ha' no pity on 'em."

"Ah, I'll hae no pity—if I ever see one. If I draw a bead on
one o' em . . ."

"Whist!"

They froze again as the older man gave his signal.

"There it is!"

"Where?"

"Just dipped ower the rise, Jock! Get yer gun, man. Quick!"

The younger grasped his rifle that leaned against the wall,
and they waited. The silence grew too long.

"Ah, ye're seeing things, Andrew," the younger said finally.
"there's naught. Nor will be, while we're here. The devils, they
knaw we're waiting. They knaw it!"

"Hush, Jock. Be still, will ye?"

The younger complied. But the long minutes dragged, and
the tedium was too much for him. He spoke again.

"Andrew."

"Aye?"

"Ye knaw, I were just thinking. It's curious that wi' us, a dog should be oor greatest helper and also oor greatest enemy."

"That's it, Jock. It's because they're so clever to help us, they become so clever to hurt us when they turn bad. And any of 'em can turn bad, too, Jock. Don't forget that. Even your ain beastie that ye treasure so much. Once they taste sheep-blood, they become killers."

"Not ma Donnie!"

"Nay, nor I think ma Vic, either. But it's true. Once ony of 'em kill, they're started, and they go on killing not for food, but for the joy o' bloody slaughtering."

"Ma Donnie wadn't!"

"Ye can never tell, Jock. There's some dogs, now, that'll be pairfect and upricht wi' their ain flock. Then, comes nicht, they'll travel far awa'—sometimes meeting like by appointment wi' ithers o' their kind. Then like a pack o' wolves they'll descend ravening on the flock, and they'll tear through 'em, killing and slaughtering, and they'll be awa' again afore help comes. Then they'll separate, and each steal back hame. And come the next day, they'll guard their ain flock as if butter wadn't melt i' their mouths."

"Ah, but not ma Donnie. If I thocht he did . . ."

They were silent a while. Then Jock spoke again.

"It seems sad that us wha hae the greatest fondness for dogs must destroy 'em."

"Aye—but little destroying we'll do if we keep chattering all nicht. They'd never come."

The silence settled again, and the patch of moonlight moved across the floor of the rude croft. And then, at last, the older man spoke again, this time his voice trembling with emotion.

"Here they come!"

The other jumped to position, leaning his rifle on the ledge. They both stared, breath-held, at the landscape far to their left.

"Aye, there!"

Jock sighted along his rifle. There was a movement by the stone wall. Then, beyond the lined sights of the gun he saw a dog. There was no air of stealth to it. It came over the wall and trotted plainly into view.

It was Lassie. It was a week since she had left her den, but she still traveled with a limp. She came over the field in the clear moonlight, going straight and steady as if following a compass route.

In the stone hut the older man released his pent breath.

"Let him have it, Jock," he cried, in a hoarse whisper.

The younger man cuddled his rifle, but did not fire.

"Where's the others?"

"What's the odds? Let him have it."

"It's a collie—d'ye ken wha's it is?"

"Nay. It's a stray—one o' them wild ones, forebye. Let it have it, lad. Don't miss, now."

Jock turned his head.

"I handled one o' these things in the war, Andrew. I dinna miss—not when I pay for ma own ammuneetion."

"Then let fly, Jock!"

The younger man cuddled the stock of his rifle again. He held his breath. Slowly he brought the sights in line—now he saw over the vee of the hindsight the steady, unwavering tip of the foresight. Above it was the tiny figure of a trotting collie. The collie moved, but it always stayed in the tip of the foresight as the gun followed it along.

Jock took up the slack on the trigger. He felt the "second pull" beginning to take up.

"Hurry, Jock, now!"

Jock lifted his head and laid the rifle down.

"I canna do it, Andrew."

"Shoot it, man, shoot it!"

"Na, na, Andrew. It doesna look like one o' they devils. Look, it pays no heed to aught. Let's see if it gangs near the sheep. For it seems to be paying no heed to them at all. Look."

"It's a stray. We have a richt to shoot it!"

"Let's see if it gangs near the sheep. If it does . . ."

"Och, ye gormless! Shoot it!"

The older man's voice rose in urgent tones. The cry floated over the night to where Lassie trotted. She paused in her

tracks and turned her head. Then it all struck her together—
the sound of men, the scent of them, the movement in the
window of the stone hut. It was man—man that would chain
her, man that she must avoid.

She wheeled and sprang away in a sudden lope.

"There! It's seen us! Let him have it!"

The sudden dash of Lassie half convinced the younger man
that he had misjudged the dog below. For Lassie's actions
were like those of a guilty dog.

He lifted the rifle quickly, cuddled the stock, and fired.

At the crack that shattered the night, Lassie leaped away.
The ugly whine of a bullet passing by her left shoulder made
her veer quickly to the right. She raced across the field. There
was another shot, and she felt a burning shock in her flank.

"Nay, I hit it."

"Ye didna. Look at it go!"

Inside the small shelter the voices of the men mixed with
those of the dogs, who now cried pandemonium.

"Let 'em out!"

The old man raced to the door and opened it. The dogs,
then the men, tumbled out, and raced away after Lassie's
tracks.

"Go get it! Sic 'em!" yelled Andrew.

The dogs raced along, baying at the chase. They went down
the slope, bellies flat and their bodies almost doubling in two
with the urgency of their speed. Behind them came the men,

but they were soon left behind. The dogs suddenly swerved, and bayed louder—for they had picked up the trail—the warm scent of new blood.

Ahead of them Lassie galloped. Twice she halted suddenly and snapped at the flank where the bullet had creased her leg muscles. She could hear the pursuing dogs behind, but she did not increase her pace. She had no fear of dogs. It was man she wished to leave behind, and her senses told her they were not near. But now she feared him more than ever. Not only could his hands chain and pen one up, but he could make the terrifying thunder noises that hurt the ears and that somehow reached out like a long, invisible whip and brought pain such as that which now tore at her.

Truly man was an evil menace.

Steadily she loped along, feeling that perhaps she would soon leave them all behind.

But the other dogs were fresh. They had not traveled, half-starved, for hundreds of weary miles. And they were soon within sight of her. They bayed a higher note, and despite the best speed that Lassie could attain, they were soon behind her. Then one charged at her flank, tearing it with his teeth and buffeting her with his shoulder to bring her down.

But one thing Lassie still had. She might be weary and starved. But she had no cowardice. She whirled like lightning and stood, fearless. Her mane stood erect, and her lips were drawn back from her fangs.

With her forepaw over one dog's body, Lassie faced the other dog.

Her attitude halted the other dogs in their tracks, for though of a much rougher breed, they were of collie blood, too. And they understood the warning.

Here was no cur to be chivied and chased like a rabbit.

As if she had driven away a petty worry, Lassie turned in obedience to the great driving force inside her. She must go on her way—south and ever south.

But the others took it for a signal of fear, and together they charged. They tore past her, as collies will, slashing as they went. For collies do not rush and hold. Their way of fighting is not like that of the bulldog; nor like that of the terrier which dodges and worries and shakes. They rather desire to run past an enemy, giving the long, slashing wounds that wear a foe down.

It was Lassie's own way of fighting, and instinctively she knew how to meet it. However, as she whirled to meet one adversary, the other would race in and slash from the other direction. But Lassie pivoted, waiting to meet the nearest foe. She stood, her head erect, watchful in the moonlight. The one behind her charged. She dodged it and started on her way again. But the other was racing in. She turned again—a second too late. The charge buffeted her and she half fell. The other raced in before she could regain her feet. The three became a snarling, composite pile. Lassie fought herself free. And then it began all over again—one dog charging, the other racing in as she turned to meet the first.

The battle was long, and it was still going on as the men arrived, panting from their long run. They stood and watched.

"Dinna ye shoot the noo, Jock," Andrew puffed. "Ye micht hit ma Vickie."

Jock nodded, and cradled the gun on his arm. His head was thrust forward. He watched closely the battle that the one, tired, travel-weary dog put up against the two sturdy ones, rough and heavy and hard from their years of work. And often he thought that the two must win.

But Lassie had something that the others had not. She had blood. She was a pure-bred dog, and behind her were long generations of the proudest and best of her kind.

This theory of blood lines in animals is not an empty one, as any animal lover knows. Where the cold-blood horse will quit and give no more, the thoroughbred will answer and give another burst of speed gallantly, even if he is spending the last ounce of life strength: where the mongrel dog will whine and slink away, the pure-bred will still stand with uncomplaining fearlessness.

And it was this blood that won for Lassie. As one dog charged, she met him. Unmindful of the other coming at her flank, she drove him down. He lay in a moment of surrender.

Then Lassie did a curious thing. Instead of taking an easy victory and driving at his throat, she merely placed a forepaw stiffly over his body as if holding him there as a wrestler would. As long as he remained motionless, he would not suffer.

Then, as he lay still and unprotesting, Lassie faced the other dog. She lifted her head where the fangs gleamed white, and from her chest came the slow, low rumble of challenge.

The other dog looked at her, and then he, too, lay down and began licking a wound on his paw. It was armistice.

So the dogs stood for a moment—the one prone under Lassie's stiff paw, the other cleaning himself with an air that seemed to say:

"I didn't have anything to do with this whole affair at all!"

It was only for a moment that picture remained, and then the madness of the fight left Lassie. The growl died in her throat, and she remembered what she had to do. She turned calmly and trotted away.

Only then did one of the men behind dance and lift his voice.

"Now—now Jock! Shoot it!"

But the younger man did not move. For, in his mind, he was not seeing dogs, but men. He was remembering a certain day. And as he stood the tired collie passed out of sight.

"Losh, Jock, and why did ye not shoot?"

"I could 'na, Andrew."

"And why not?"

"I were thinking o' March—March i' 1918, Andrew, when they come over us—and the regiment stood. It were like that, Andrew, yon collie. She fought the same way the Black Watch did, Andrew. I' March, back i' 1918 . . ."

"Are ye daft?"

"Nay, Andrew."

The younger man wrinkled his brow.

"March, 1918," the older man scoffed.

"Weel, it were a brave dog, anyhow, Andrew. And—and it were going somewheer—and—and—besides. I couldn'a shoot, for I forgot to load up again."

"Och, now that's something. Forgot to load. I should think a sojer would never forget to load up again after he's fired."

"Weel—we ha' so mony things to remember, Andrew," the younger man said.

Then, as they turned away, he clicked open the breech gently, took out the cartridge from the chamber of his rifle, and slipped it in his pocket silently. With the dogs following them, the men went back to the rude shelter on the moonlit slope.

CHAPTER FIFTEEN

A Captive in the Lowlands

The country had changed now. There were no more High-lands and heather; no more rolling hills and sheep pastures. Instead the country was flatter, and the only eminences were the "bings" or slag-tips where the waste from the coal mines was piled by the great industrial conveyers.

There were many more towns here and many more roads. And no longer could a dog pass unobserved around the towns, nor could it keep out of sight of men, for there were men everywhere. No matter how Lassie might try to circumvent them, she must come within sight of them to make her way south.

So she developed a new attitude toward them. She kept as far away as possible, but if she had to pass close to them, she ignored them.

Actually, she felt much easier about the men of this country, for in many ways they were like the men among whom she had grown up. Their faces were often black with grime, as they had been in Greenall Bridge. Their clothes were coated with muck, and in the men's hands or on their heads were lanterns. And more than that, the men and the towns carried about them the scent of human beings who work underground. This scent was much like that that Lassie's master had worn—but these men were not her master. They were like the others in the village, though.

And so Lassie, although now much warier, treated these men as she had treated those other men in her own village: she accepted them, but responded to none of them, nor went where they could touch her, nor answered any of their commands.

For they did command her. In the industrial lowlands of Scotland there are, as in Yorkshire, many who are knowing about dogs. They can spot good ones and tell with a glance when a dog was a stray. And so often these men would say:

"Look, Archie! A stray! And a good 'un, too. Hi, here, lass! Come here then, come, lass!"

They would stretch out their hands and snap their fingers and call in kindly tones. But although Lassie often heard in their commands a sound which was almost like the speaking of her own name, she never responded. If the outstretched hands came too near, she faded away from under the touch like quicksilver. If they pursued, she would make her weary, battered body break from the trot and drive into a lope that would soon put her beyond the reach of two-footed pursuers.

Once clear, she would go back to her trot, heading south.

That trot was slower now, for there was another thing about the changing land. There was no food. Once there had been rabbits, but these had become scarcer and scarcer until now it was seldom that her nose caught the warm smell. Lassie felt the impulse to make her muscles drive her along at any speed becoming harder and harder to command. She even felt it harder to obey the impulse to keep away from man. Her greater fatigue made her too weary to worry about him unless his hand was very near.

But one impulse did not die—to keep on going south. Never any other direction but south. So, slowly, Lassie came down through the Lowlands of Scotland. Her trail went through that black industrial country as she obeyed the unquenchable flame that burned in her—the desire to go south—always south. And behind her on that trail she left many stories—words that flowed in homes and cottages.

A young wife at the table in a home in a small mining town, watching her husband eat his evening meal, said:

"I had the oddest thing today, Ivor—with a dog."

"A dog? Whose?"

"I don't know who it belonged to. I was sitting outside with the baby, getting a few minutes of sun, when this dog came down the road. It was aye so muddy and forlorn and terrible-looking, but nice-looking in a way . . ."

"How could it be nice-looking and terrible-looking?"

"I don't know, now. But it was. And it looked so tired. It just looked like the men on the shift sometimes when they're coming off—so tired and weary, and yet—keeping going. So I called it, but it wadna come. It just stood off away and looked at me—and little Ivor. So I went in and got a dish o' water and put it doon. And it came over and lapped that up. So then I got a bowl o' scraps and put them doon. And it looked a long time and walked round one way and then another, and finally came over and smelled and then began to eat—very dainty it was, but I could swear it was half starved. It was that poor and thin.

"Then, right in the middle, as it was eating, it stopped and lifted its head and started off right down the road just as if it had remembered an appointment . . ."

"Weel what did ye want it to do? Stop and say thank you?"

"No, but to go richt off in the middle o' eating! Now why should it do that?"

"Ah, Peggy, and how should I know? All I do know is that ye'd be feeding all the stray dogs and waifs and tramps in the world if ye had your way."

Then the man laughed, and the woman laughed, too, for by the warmth of her husband's voice she knew that he was pleased with her. And so she forgot the stray dog to which she had shown kindness.

In a town fifty miles to the south a thin-faced woman wrote a letter to her husband who was away on a business trip. The letter read:

"We had a frightful experience the other day. We had a mad dog in the village. Constable Macgregor saw it first and suspected it, for it had saliva flecked on its mouth. He tried to catch it, but it eluded him. I saw it coming down the street— I had been visiting Mrs. Tamson—and a terrible creature it was, with its mouth gaping open, and galloping wildly. The constable and many of the town boys were after it. I ran into Jamison's drapery and didn't come out for nearly an hour, it gave my heart such a turn.

"I heard later that they cornered it down Fennel's Alley, and they thought they had it, but at the last moment it jumped over the rear wall, which, as you know, is at least six feet high. So it must have been mad, for no sane animal would have thought of attempting such a thing.

"Since then we have had a rabies scare, and all stray dogs are being rounded up and taken to the pound. I think they should shoot all stray dogs, for one never knows what damage they may cause. I tell you, I have been very nervous about the whole thing, so I hope you hurry back as soon as you can possibly end your trip . . ."

Stories of cowardice and fear—as well as of trust and love—lay in the long trail over which Lassie patiently fought her way toward home.

By the great Scottish industrial city the river is broad. Along its banks are high walls and fences, for space on the river frontage is valuable—almost the lifeblood of the community.

There, by the river, the towering cranes pick up gigantic pieces of metal. They move them to the frameworks where skeletons of steel arise. There the men clamber all day, drilling and riveting, adding the harsh tattoo to the mighty thumping of steam-hammers. And there the great ships that later race across the Atlantic are born.

The shipyards and the city are sprawled over every inch of the wide river. To cross from side to side there are the chugging ferries—and in the city the aged bridges that have carried traffic north and south for centuries.

And over one of those busy bridges Lassie trotted. For days she had roamed the northern bank, seeking some way to cross, but this at last was her solution—she must walk among men.

As she went along, often persons on the crowded pavement turned their heads and spoke a word to her, but she paid no attention and threaded her way along, and was soon lost to view in the crowds.

But there were two men who did not let her get out of sight. They were on a truck, crossing the bridge. One, on the front seat, merely nudged his companion who drove, and pointed toward the dog that went so intently. The other did not answer. But he nodded as if in happy agreement and set his truck at a speed which allowed them to keep Lassie in sight.

At the end of the bridge Lassie stepped forward steadily. Her trot quickened a trifle, for now she felt at peace with her desire to get south. The river was behind her. For a second a flash of vigor flowed over her, and her tail lifted a little higher so that she looked almost gay.

She went along the pavement to the south. She did not heed the truck pulling up beside her. Among the multiple dins and smells of the city there was no chance for her keen ears or nose to give her warning. Only at the last second, her animal senses warned her and she gave a leap. Something was moving through the air. She drove with her legs—but it was no use. About her was a net that strangled her efforts.

For a full minute she fought, slashing at the imprisoning web. But she was only held the tighter. And now, kneeling beside her, was one of the men from the truck. He was holding her with expert hands. A thong was being twisted cruelly about her muzzle, clamping her jaws shut. Another thong went about her neck. Still another was binding her legs together.

Lassie lay still. Now she was ringed in by people.

She felt the net being lifted. With a mighty wrench she tried to tear away. Her forefeet came free! One hind leg was free! She was getting away!

Lunging and wrenching, she fought against the man who held her. Now the other had thrown his body on her. If only she had the thong about her jaws free! She felt a strain as one man grabbed at her foreleg. Then she was being beaten over the head.

She lay half-stunned. And then the men halted their beating, for a voice came, very clear, from the crowd. It was a woman's voice, one with clipped accents:

"Here, you don't have to treat that dog as savagely as that!"

One of the men looked up from his kneeling.

"Who's a-doing this job?" he asked.

Someone in the crowd started to snicker, but the laugh died as the young woman stepped forward. Her voice was stern.

"And if you think being impertinent is going to help you, you're mistaken. I've watched this entire proceeding and I intend to report you—for both impertinence and cruelty."

When the man spoke again, his tone had changed.

"Very sorry, mum; but it's my duty, it is. And ye can't be too careful. There's a lot of mad dogs around—and a dog catcher's got to do his duty. It's public protection."

"Nonsense—this dog has no signs of rabies."

"Ye can't tell, mum. Anyhow, it's a stray—and we've got to pick up all strays. It's got no license tag."

The young woman made as if to speak, but the man beside her touched her arm.

"Chap's right, Ethelda. Can't have hordes of homeless dogs running about. Got to have some sort of control, y'know."

"That's right, sir," the dog catcher said.

The girl looked about her. Then her jaw set.

"Well, they don't have to control it that way. Get up, I'll put it in the van for you."

"It'll get away from ye, mum."

"Nonsense. Stand up."

"We'll only have to go through it all over again, mum."

"Stand up!"

The kneeling men looked at the crowd, as if to say what a hopeless thing it was to argue with a woman who had silly ideas. Then, as they rose, the girl kneeled. For a second Lassie felt calm hands touching her, stroking her gently, soothing her with a soft voice.

"All right. Give me a leash—and take that net away."

The men obeyed. The girl put the thong gently round Lassie's neck. With one hand patting and calming, she pulled gently at the lead with the other.

"Come—stand up," she said.

Lassie did what her years of training had taught her. She obeyed. She followed the gentle touch of the lead. She walked to the van. As the man opened the door, the girl lifted the thin collie in, and the grilled door clanged.

"There," she said, severely. "You don't have to treat even stray dogs like wild beasts."

She turned and strode away, paying scarcely any attention to the man beside her.

"A fearful scene to make in public, Ethelda," he said at last.

She did not answer, and they walked on across the bridge. Midway over, he looked at her and then stopped.

"Forgive me," he said. "I should be kicked. You were very fine."

They stopped and gazed in silence down the busy river.

"I wonder why it is," he said at length, "a man always has a horror of making a show in public. Often he wants to do—well, something exactly like what you did, and he doesn't. Sort of cowardice I suppose it is. Women are braver. You were very fine—and that's what I should have said in the first place."

The young woman placed her hand on his coat sleeve in a gesture of understanding.

"It isn't me. It's the dog," she said. "You know, she reminded me so much of Bonnie. You remember Bonnie, the collie we had when I was small?"

"Oh, so I do—I'd forgotten. Well, but she was a magnificent creature, Ethelda."

"So was this one, somehow, Michael. Oh, she was starved and bony, but somehow she reminded me of Bonnie. The same sort of patience and—and—as if she understood so much that it was a crime she couldn't speak to tell about it."

The man nodded and drew out his pipe. They leaned their arms on the parapet.

"What will they do with her?" the young woman asked at last.

"Who—the blighters with the van?"

"Yes."

"Oh, take her to the pound."

"I know, but what do they do there—with stray dogs?"

"I dunno. Seems to me they keep them or something—specified length of time. Then if no one shows up they, er, do away with them."

"They'll kill her?"

"Oh, it's quite humane. Gas chamber, or something like that. Absolutely painless, they say. Just like going to sleep. Law, or something, about it."

"And no one can save her—I mean if her owner doesn't hear about it?"

"I think not."

"Isn't there a law or something—if you go to the pound, you can claim a dog? That is, if you pay the costs and whatnot?"

The man puffed his pipe.

"Seems to me there is—or there should be."

He looked up at the girl beside him. Then he smiled.

"Come on," he said.

CHAPTER SIXTEEN

"Donnell! Never Trust a Dog!"

The van with its grilled door drew into a courtyard. The iron gates set in the great wall clanged behind it. The van backed up so that it was tight against a raised entrance.

Inside, Lassie lay quietly in a corner. There were other dogs in the van. During the ride through the city, they had lifted their voices in clamor. But Lassie had lain still, like a captive queen among lesser prisoners. She had lain there, only her eyes alert, shutting out the exterior world just as she had done when she lay ill beneath the gorse clump.

She did not drop this air of dignity even when the grilled backdrop of the van was opened. The other dogs of mixed

145

breeds yelped anew and darted about. The two men seized them and urged them along toward a large, concrete chamber. But Lassie did not move. Then she was the only one left in the van.

Perhaps it was her calm and regal air that misled the man. Or perhaps, too, he remembered the facility with which the young woman had placed the dog in the truck.

He entered the van with a small leash. Lassie lay quietly, and as she had been too proud to struggle and yelp for freedom as the other dogs had done, now she calmly suffered the hands to slip the thong over her head. As the lead was about to tighten she rose obediently, and as she had been taught to do from youth, began to follow the man. Down they came over the tailboard of the van and into the echoing corridor, Lassie going without either pulling ahead on the leash or dragging behind on it.

This, too, may have lulled the man, for, just as they reached the place where his assistant was holding open the barred door, he leaned down to unslip the leash.

In that flash, Lassie was free.

She leaped away like the passing of a beam of light. The man jumped to bar her path, but his human co-ordination was snail-like compared to that of the animal. Lassie turned herself in flight even as he started to move and drove herself between his legs and the wall.

Down the corridor she went, and then she pulled to a halt. Her way was blocked. There was nothing before her but the looming interior of the van which she had just left, backed so truly against the entrance that there was not an inch of space on any side.

She turned and dashed back—straight into the faces of the men who charged after her. Dodging their arms and legs, she catapulted past them again. At the left was a stairway. She raced for it. At the top a corridor stretched crosswise. One direction went south. She raced down it.

Now, behind her, the building began to echo with cries. There were people in the corridor. Hands grabbed at her as she raced along. Twisting like a football "back," she went the length of the corridor. And then she halted. The corridor ended at a blank wall. There was a window, but it was closed.

Lassie wheeled. Now, back down the long hall men were gathered. They were advancing. Lassie looked about her. There were many doors at each side of the way, but they were all closed. There was no escape.

Her captors seemed to be confident of that, for now the two men with peaked caps appeared, and the voice of the dog catcher rose.

"Stay where ye are, everyone, please. We've got her now. Just stay where ye are so's she can't get back down the corridor. She won't bite anybody. She's not a bad dog."

Slowly the man advanced. Behind him was his assistant with the net. They came nearer and nearer.

Proudly Lassie stood at bay. With head high, she waited.

And then escape came. For right beside Lassie, one of the forbidding doors opened, and a voice sounded. It was an important voice—an official voice.

"What's going on out here? Do you realize there's a Court of Law sitting . . ."

That was as far as he got. For at that moment a tawny figure streaked by him, almost upsetting him as it cannoned off his legs. His face twisted itself into an expression of horror and outraged dignity. He gave one glance of utter contempt to the two men with the net. Then he shut the door.

Now, inside the room the air echoed with sound, for Lassie was racing about, looking for some means of escape. But in that large room there seemed to be none. All the doors were closed. At last, in a corner, Lassie stood at bay. People moved away from her, leaving her isolated. The banging and scraping of chairs and the cries slowly sank, and the only noise left was that of a thumping gavel. Then a sombre voice spoke.

"Do I understand that this is the surprise witness that the defense has promised?"

Immediately the room rocked with laughter. Young men in sombre costumes smiled broadly. The imperious figure wearing the enormous white wig allowed himself to smile, too, for he was famed far and wide for his piercing wit. And, moreover, this case had been long and tedious. His remark would be repeated and reprinted in newspapers the length and breadth of the land:

"Another report comes today anent the sparkling humor of that renowned legal wit, Justice McQuarrie, sitting at . . ."

The great man nodded affably so that his wig almost came onto his forehead. At that moment, Lassie barked, once, shortly.

The great man beamed.

"I presume that is an answer in the affirmative. And I may add that this is the most intelligent witness I have had before me in twenty years, for it is the first one that can answer yes or no without equivocation."

Again the great room rocked with laughter. The young men in gowns nodded like mandarins and turned to one another.

Old McQuarrie was in excellent form today!

Now, as though deciding that he alone should decree how long laughter should last, the judge thumped with the gavel. His brow furrowed. His eyes were stern.

"Sergeant," he roared. "Sergeant!"

A uniformed man hastened before the tribunal and stood at attention.

"Sergeant. What is that?"

"It is a dog, Your Lordship."

"A dog!"

The judge turned his glance on the animal, still at bay in the corner.

"You confirm my own suspicions, Sergeant. It is a dog!" the judge said affably. Then his voice broke into a roar. "Well, what do I want done with it?"

"I think I know what is in your mind, Your Lordship."

"What is in my mind, Sergeant?"

"You wish it removed, Your Lordship."

"I do! Remove it! Remove it!"

The Sergeant looked about him in hurt amazement. In all his years as an official, such a problem had never before arisen. Perhaps it had never arisen in all the history of law. Perhaps there was no official and recognized procedure set down by any book or statute for the proper engineering of such a matter. Every other possible thing had been thought of, but—dogs? Not that the Sergeant could remember.

Dogs—from court, removal of. Perhaps it was listed somewhere. But the Sergeant couldn't remember it. And if there were no official course of action to be followed, how should one . . .

The Sergeant's face suddenly brightened. He had solved it. The stairway of authority. He turned toward the man who had opened the door and allowed Lassie to enter.

"McLosh! Remove this dog. Where did it come from?"

The red-faced guardian of the door looked reproachfully at his superior.

"Na doot she's wiggled awa' fra' Fairgusson and Donnell. They twa's oot there the noo wi' a lashin' o' ropes."

The Sergeant turned and translated in more official language to the judge.

"The dog's escaped from the pound authorities, Your Lordship. Two of them are outside now. And since the apprehension

and detention of stray dogs properly comes within the duties
of the pound . . ."

"I won't make an official ruling on that, but unofficially,
Sergeant—unofficially . . ."

Again the delighted young men in robes smiled at each
other.

". . . Unofficially I should say it is in their province. Admit
them and order them to remove this animal."

"Very good, Your Lordship."

Escaping hurriedly, the Sergeant went to the door.

"Get it oot o' here, quick. Before he loses his temper," he
whispered huskily.

Bearing the net, the two men entered the court. The legal
array stood in eager interest. It was certainly a relief from the
droning on this dull day.

The two men crept toward the corner, slowly—warily.

"We'll soon ha' her out o' here, Your Lordship," one said
in a conciliating tone.

But as he spoke, Lassie wheeled away. She knew that net.
It was a hateful enemy. She must escape it.

Again the room became bedlam. The younger men took
every advantage of the situation, and like schoolboys they
lifted their voices in hunting cries.

"Yoicks! Gone away!"

"Look! Hallo, Watson. There by the desk!"

"Tallyho! Hiii! Ow, my shin."

Cheerily they whooped, and in high glee did their best in every way to impede the men with the net—managing to upset them at every opportunity as they pretended to help corner the dog.

But at last the fun had run its course. Lassie was penned by the wall. The ring of men crept nearer. Above her was an open window. She leaped to the ledge—and then stood there in hesitation, for below her was the courtyard where the van still stood. There was a sheer drop of twenty feet to the concrete below.

The men came forward confidently. They knew that it was too far to leap. They spread out the net.

On the ledge Lassie trembled. Off to the left was the roof of the van. It was only ten feet below, but it was too far away. She crouched, her paws dancing as if to get better footing. Her muscles trembled.

For a dog is not like a cat. Like men, a dog has learned to fear heights. And yet it was the only way.

Crouching, gathering her muscles, Lassie stood. Then she leaped. Out she drove, as far as she could, toward the top of the van. Even as she went through the air, she knew she was falling short. Her sense of time and balance told her she could not land safely.

Reaching out with her forelegs, she just touched. For a brief second she hung there, as her hind legs scrambled on the side. Then she dropped to the ground heavily. And she lay, stunned.

Above, in the courtroom, the windows were lined with faces. The dog catcher gave a sharp cry.

"Now we've got her."

He turned with his companion; but they were stopped by a sharp command. The judge frowned at them, and when he spoke it was as if all humour had gone from the day.

"This is a Court of Law. You will go quietly. Gentlemen, please. I will declare a recess."

The gavel thumped, and all stood as the age-old cry of "Oyez!" sounded.

Grumbling, the two men made their way from the room. Once in the corridor they raced along.

"That bloomin' dog," the older panted. "I'll show 'er. Wait till I get . . ."

But when they got to the courtyard, they looked about in amazement. There was the van. There was the spot where Lassie had lain, stunned. But she was not there. The yard was empty.

"Well, if it isn't the end of a bloomin' perfect day, Donnell," the older puffed. "She should be dead down 'ere—and where is she?"

"Gone over the wall, Mr. Fairgusson!"

"Six foot—and she should be dead. That ain't no blasted dog, Donnell. It's a bloomin' vampire."

They went back into their quarters in the basement.

"Mr. Fairgusson. Isn't a vampire a thing wi' wings?"

"Exactly, Donnell. That's what I mean. An animal would need wings to get over that wall."

Donnell scratched his head.

"Once," he said, "I saw one o' the cinema pictures aboot a vampire."

The older spoke sternly.

"Now, Donnell, here I am trying to set my mind on this matter—important matter, it is—and ye're raving aboot the cinema. Ye'll never make headway in the sairvice o' the municipality if ye go on like that. Now the thing is, what shall we do aboot this dog?"

Donnell pulled his lip.

"I dinna ken."

"Well, think. Now what would ye do if ye were alone?"

Donnell went into a deep study. At last his face broke like a sunbeam.

"We tak' the van and go oot and aboot and look for her again!"

The other shook his head as if he despaired of mankind.

"Donnell, aren't ye ever going to learn?"

"Learn? What ain't I learning the noo?"

"Knocking off time! Knocking off time!" Fergusson said with emphasis. "How many times have I told ye? When ye're a civil servant, ye keep yer working hours. If ye start to toil all hours o' the day and nicht, firrst thing ye know they'll be expecting it all the time."

"That's richt. I forgot."

"Forgot! Ye forgot! Well, don't forget. Set yer example by me, my lad. Then ye'll get somewhere."

The young one looked shamefaced.

"Noo," said the other. "Mak' yer head save yer feet. What we do the noo, is mak' oot a report."

He got pencil and paper. For a long time he sucked the end of the pencil.

"This is hard to do, Donnell," he said, at length. "It's a sort o' black mark on the escutcheon o' the department. For twenty-two years I've been here, and never before in all ma service has a dog got awa'. And I hardly know how to report this."

Donnell scratched his head. Then inspiration came.

"Well, look. Couldn't ye just forget it? Don't say aught aboot it."

The other looked up in admiration.

"Ye micht ha' something there, Donnell. Ye're learning at last. But one verra important thing ye forget. There's yon happenings in the Court. They'll be noised aboot, wi'oot doot!"

"Aye," said Donnell, excitedly. "But ye can say we copped the beggar at that. If they wish to test it, we can say it's yon big rough beggar in there we copped this morn. Just report one less in, and then ye'll not have an escaped dog to put that blot on yer—er—escunchon."

"Donnell, ye have it!"

Vigorously the older set to work. For half an hour he wrote painfully. He had just finished when the buzzer rang. The door opened and a policeman entered. Behind him followed the young woman and man who had stood by the bridge.

"This is the pound, sir," the policeman said.

The man advanced.

"I am informed," he said, "that on payment of pound costs and license fee, I can secure any unclaimed dog here?"

"That's richt, sir."

"Well then I—er, this young lady, that is—wishes to secure that collie captured this morning."

"Collie?" Fergusson echoed, thinking fast. "Collie. No, there was no collie captured this morn, sir."

The young woman stepped forward.

"Look here, what are you trying to do now? You know very well I was present when you captured a collie this morning, and handled it roughly, you did, too. If you're up to any tricks about it, Captain McKeith here will have it looked into."

Fergusson scratched his head.

"Well, I'll tell you the truth—it escaped."

"It what?" the girl asked.

"It escaped, mum. Anyone here can tell ye aboot it. It broke loose and got up i' Justice McQuarrie's court and jumped fro' a window and got over the wall—and it's gone."

"Gone!"

For a moment the girl stared. Then a look of happiness crept over her face.

"I don't know whether you're telling the truth or not," the young man said. "But to make sure I'm going to put in a written request for that dog."

He made a note in a small pocketbook and turned away. The girl went with him gladly.

"I'm sorry, Ethelda," he said, as they went up the stairs.

The young woman smiled.

"It's all right. I'm glad. Don't you see, it's free again. Free! Even if I don't have it—it's free!"

Downstairs in the subterranean office, Fergusson blustered before his assistant.

"Now I'll have to report it escaped, for the blighters undootedly will mak' a request for it and I'll have to explain why I canna gie 'em the dog."

Savagely he tore up his painfully written false report.

"All that fine work for naught. Now let that go for to teach ye a lesson, Donnell. What conclusion would ye draw fro' all this?"

"Never mak' oot a false report," Donnell replied, dutifully.

"Och, no," Fergusson said in scorn. "Ye'll never progress in the service, Donnell. The conclusion to draw is this: Never trust a dog!

"Ye tak' that one. There she pretended to be as meek as a babe in arms as ye micht say. I trust her for just one second, and she turrrns like a ball o' fire on Judgement Day. There she ought to be afraid to jump—and what does she do?"

"She jumps," Donnell replied.

"That's richt. There she ought to be dead, and what is she?"

"She's alive."

"Richt again. Then she ought not to ha' been able to jump yon wall, and what does she do?"

"She jumps it."

"Richt once more. And so the moral is, Donnell, as long as ye 're in this job, never trust a bloomin' dog. They ain't—well —they ain't 'uman, dogs ain't. They just ain't 'uman!"

CHAPTER SEVENTEEN

Lassie Comes Over the Border

Slowly, steadily, Lassie came across a field.

She was not trotting now. She was going at a painful walk. Her head was low and her tail hung lifelessly. Her thin body moved from side to side as though it took the effort of her entire frame to make her legs continue to function.

But her course was straight. She was still continuing to go south.

Across the meadow she came in her tired walk. She paid no attention to the cattle that grazed on the green about her and that lifted their heads from their feeding to regard her as she passed.

159

The grass grew thicker and coarser as she followed the path. The track became beaten mud. Then the mud was a puddle of water, and the puddle was the edge of a river.

She stood at the trampled place. It was where the cattle came to drink and to stand for coolness in the heat of the day. Beyond her some of them stood now, knee-deep in the slow backwater. They turned and regarded her, their jaws moving unceasingly.

Lassie whimpered slightly and lifted her head as if to catch some scent from far bank. She rocked on her feet for a moment. Then, wading forward tentatively, she went deeper and deeper. Her feet now felt no bottom. The backwater began to carry her upstream. She began swimming, her tail swirling out behind her.

This was not a turbulent river like the one back in the Highlands. It was not a dirty, factory-clustered one like that now many miles back in the industrial city. But it was broad, and its current went firmly, carrying Lassie downstream.

Her tired legs drove with the beat, her forefeet pumped steadily. The south bank moved past her, but she seemed to be getting no nearer.

Weakness numbed her, and her beat grew slower. Her outstretched head came under the water. As if this wakened her from a sleep, she began threshing wildly. Her head went straight up, and her forefeet sent a splashing foam before her. She was a swimmer in panic.

But her head cleared again, and once more she settled down to the steady drive forward.

It was a long swim—a courageous swim. And when at last she reached the other shore, she was almost too weak to climb the bank. At the first place, her forepaws scratched and she fell back. The bank was too high. The backwater began carrying her upstream. Lassie tried again. She splashed and fell back again. Then the eddy carried her, and at last her feet touched a shelving bottom. She waded to shore.

As though the weight of the water in her coat were an extra load that was too much for her to carry, she staggered. Then dragging herself rather than walking, she crawled up the bank. And there, at last, she dropped. She could go no farther.

But she was in England! Lassie did not know that. She was only a dog going home—not a human being wise in the manner of maps. She could not know that she had made her way all down through the Highlands, the Lowlands; that the river she had crossed was the Tweed, which divides England and Scotland.

All these things she did not know. All she knew was that, as she crawled higher on the bank, a strange thing happened. Her legs would no longer respond properly, and, as she was urging herself forward, the tired muscles rebelled at last. She sank, plunged a moment, and then fell on her side.

For a second, she whined. With her forepaws she clawed the earth, still dragging herself south. She was in rough grass now. She pulled herself along—a yard—another foot—another few inches. Then at last the muscles stopped their work.

Lassie lay on one side, her legs outstretched in "dead dog" position. Her eyes were glazed. The only movement was a spasmodic lifting and falling of the pinched flanks.

All that day Lassie lay there. The flies buzzed about her, but she did not lift her head to snap at them.

Evening came, and across the river was the sound of the herder and the lowing of the cows. The last notes of the birds came—the singing of a thrush through the lingering twilight.

Darkness came with its night sounds, the scream of an owl and the stealthy rippling of a hunting otter, the faraway bark of a farm dog, and the whispering in the trees.

Dawn came with new sounds—the splash of a leaping trout while the river was still veiled in mist. Then the rooks rose with their eternal cry of warning as a man left the door of the farm cottage over the fields. The sun came, and the shadows danced weakly on the grass as the overhead trees shimmered in the first breeze of the new day.

As the sun reached her, Lassie rose slowly. Her eyes were dull. Walking slowly, she set out—away from the river, going south.

The room was small and humble. In a chair beside a table where the lamp glowed, Daniel Fadden sat, reading slowly from the newspaper. Nearer the coal fire on the hearth, his wife sat in a rocking chair, knitting. She teetered endlessly back and forth as her fingers flashed over the wool and needles, so that the movements all seemed related—one rock of the chair, three stitches on the needles.

They were both old people, and it seemed that they had been so long together in life that there was no longer any need to talk. They were contented just to be, sure in the knowledge the other was near.

Finally the man pushed his steel-rimmed spectacles back on his forehead and looked at the hearth.

"We'll do wi' a bit more coal on the fire," he said.

His wife nodded as she rocked, and her lips went through the noiseless form of counting. She was "turning a heel" in her knitting and wanted to keep sure count.

The man rose slowly. Taking the scuttle, he went to the sink. In the cupboard beneath was the coal bin. With a little shovel he slowly scooped some out.

"Ah, we're nearly oot," he said.

His wife looked over. Mentally both of them began to count—the cost of more coal. How quickly they had used the last hundredweight. Their lives were deeply concerned with these things. Expenses ran very close. All they had was the small pension that the Government paid for their son who had been killed in France. Then each of them drew the old-age pension of ten shillings a week given by the State. This was no wealth, but they husbanded it carefully and owed no man.

The tiny cottage, far out on the highway from any town, was a cheap place to live. In the little plot of land about it, Fadden grew a stock of vegetables. He had a flock of chickens, several ducks, and a goose "fattening for Christmas." This last was their largest and most lasting joke. Six years before Fadden had traded a dozen early hen eggs for one tiny gosling. Carefully he had raised it, boasting about what a fine plump bird it would be by Christmas time.

It had become just that—marvellous and plump. And a few days before the holiday of holidays, Fadden had taken his hatchet, and he had sat indoors a long time, regarding it. Finally his wife, understanding, had looked up patiently.

"Dan," she said. "I just don't think I'd favor goose this year. If you did a chicken instead—and . . ."

"Aye, Dally," Fadden had said. "It would be a tarrible waste—one big goose for just the two on us. Now a chicken would be just right . . ."

And so the goose was spared. Each year after that it was dutifully fattened for Christmas.

"This year it goes," Fadden would always announce. "Fattening a goose all year, just to strut and waddle round like he's king of everything. This year he goes."

And always the goose lived. His wife always knew it would. When Fadden announced belligerently that it was headed for the Yule oven, she would say dutifully, "Aye, Dan." And when he hemmed and hawed at the last minute and announced that a goose was much too big for the two of them, she would say, "Aye, Dan." Privately she often said to herself that the goose would be living long after, as she put it, the two of them were "deep under the ground and at rest."

But she would not have it otherwise. In fact, if Dan had ever gone through with his firmly announced intentions, she would have felt the world was dropping from under her.

Of course, it cost a lot to feed up a great, hungry goose, but one could save other ways. A penny here, a penny there. One could always buy carefully and save carefully, nursing the copper coins along.

So their life went, with dignity and great content—but always with the thought of precious pennies, as it was this evening, when they both reckoned up the amount of coal and how long it had lasted.

"Ah, never mind mending the fire, Dan," she said. "Just bed it up wi' ashes and we'll away to bed. We stay up too late anyhow."

"Sit ye there awhile," Daniel said, for he knew Dally dearly loved to rock and knit before the hearth for a couple of hours in the evening. "It's early yet. I'll put just a little on. For Heaven knows, it's chilly enough tonight—nasty, cold, east rain."

Dally nodded. As she rocked she listened to the wind howling at the east of the low house and the slatting of the rain on the shutters.

"It'll be coming up for autumn soon, Dan."

"Aye, that it will. This is the first o' them easters. And cold! Blaw right through a man's body to his bones. I'd hate to be oot in it long."

His wife rocked steadily, and her mind wandered. Whenever anyone talked of bad weather, she always turned her mind back to young Dannie. In those trenches they had had no warm hearths. The men had lived their lives that first winter in muddy holes in the ground—sleeping there of nights with no shelter. A body would die, you would think. And yet, when Dannie had come home on leave, there he was all glowing and healthy and fine. And when she'd asked him about being careful to keep his chest warm and his throat dry, he had laughed and held his sides—a big, booming, strong laugh.

"Eigh, after living through this winter i' France, it's never cold that'll carry me off, Ma," he had boomed.

And it wasn't cold nor illness. Machine guns, his Colonel had written in the letter that Dally still kept folded away beside her marriage license.

Ah, war—machine wars. Bullets took them all. The brave and the cowardly, the weak and the fine strong ones like Dannie. And it wasn't the dying that took bravery, then, for cowards could die. It was the living that took bravery—living in that mud and rain and cold and keeping the spirit strong through it all. That was the bravery. And how often she pictured it, when the winds blew and the cold rain slatted.

All so long ago, but she still pictured it, knitting, purling, rocking—knitting, purling, rocking.

She halted her chair and sat with head erect. For a moment she was still. Then she began again—knitting, purling, rocking, thinking . . .

Again she stopped. She held her breath to hear better—hear above the sound of the fire. There was the hiss of the coal, the spit of ashes dropping in the pit beneath the grate, the crinkle of the newspaper; farther away the tap of a shutter looser than the rest, the surging smacking of rain. Farther beyond that there was another noise, out in the sweep of the wind. Or was it imagination, from thinking of Dannie so long ago?

She dropped her head. Then she sat up again.

"Dan! There's something by the chickens!"

He sat erect a moment.

"Ah now, Dallie. Ye're allus imagining things," he reproved. "There's not a thing but the wind. And that shutter's a bit loose. I'll have to fix it."

He went back to his reading, but the little grey-haired woman sat with head erect. Then she spoke again.

"There—again! There is something!"

She rose.

"If you won't go see what's after your chickens, Daniel Fadden, I will!"

She took her shawl, but her husband rose.

"Now, now, now," he grumbled. "Sit ye down. If ye want me to go, I'll go just to make your soul content. Now I'll look around."

"Wrap your muffler round your neck first, then," she reproved.

She watched him go, then she was alone in the house. Her ears, attuned by the lonesomeness to the sounds of living, heard his footsteps go away—and a few moments later, above the noise of the storm, come back quickly. He was running. She jumped up and faced the door before it opened.

"Get your shawl and come," he said. "I've found it. Where's the lantern?"

Together they hurried out into the night, leaning against the gusts of wind and rain. Going up the road, beside the hawthorn hedge that bordered the highway, at last the old man paused and scrambled down the bank. His wife held up the lantern. There she saw what her husband had found—a dog, lying in the ditch. She watched its head turn, and for a second the light glowed incandescent in its eyes as the lamp shone.

"Puir, puir thing," she said. "And who would leave their dog oot a night like this?"

The words were torn away by the wind, but the old man heard the sound of her voice.

"It's too done up to walk," he shouted. "Hold the lantern up!"

"Shall I gie ye a hand?"

"Hey?"

She bent down and shouted.

"Shall I gie ye a hand?"

"No! I can manage!"

She saw him bend and pick up the animal. Grasping the shawl against the gale that would pluck it away, she went beside him, holding the lantern high.

"Go easy, Dan, now," she said. "Oh, puir, puir thing!"

She ran ahead of him to open the door. Panting, the old man struggled in. The door slammed. The two old people brought Lassie into the warmth of the hearth and laid her on the rug.

They stood back a moment, looking at her. Lassie lay with eyes closed.

"I doubt it'll live till the morn," the man said.

"Well, that's no reason to stand there. We can at least try. Get your wet things off, quick, Dan, or I'll have you down, too. Look at it shiver—it isn't dead. Get that sack fro' the bottom o' the cupboard, Dan, and dry it off some."

Awkwardly the old man bent, rubbing the dog's drenched coat.

"She's awful mucky, Dally," he said. "Your nice clean hearth rug'll be all muddied up."

"Then there'll be a job for you shaking it out in the morning," she answered tartly. "I wonder if we could feed it?"

The old man looked up. His wife was holding in her hand the can of condensed milk. Their unspoken thoughts went back and forth like a silent conversation. It was the last of their milk.

"Well, we'll have tea for breakfast wi'oot any," the woman said.

"Save a bit, Dally, Ye don't like your tea wi'oot milk."

"Eigh, it won't matter," she said.

She began warming the milk in water.

"I often think we just do things fro' habit, Dan," she went on. "They say i' China, now, they always drink tea wi'oot milk."

"Happen it's because they haven't learned any better," he mumbled.

He kept on rubbing the dog's cold body as his wife stirred the milk in the pan on the grate. There was silence in the cottage.

Lassie lay there, unmoving. In her half-consciousness and terrible weariness, a feeling of dim peace stole over her. So many things came from the past and comforted her. The place smelled "right." There was the mixed aroma of coal-smoke and baking bread. The hands that touched her—they did not imprison or bring pain. Instead they soothed and brought peace to sore and aching muscles. The people—they did not move suddenly or shout noisily or throw things that hurt. They went quietly, not startling a dog.

There was warmth, too—this most of all. It was a drugging warmth, one which took the senses away and made awareness slip away as if in a gentle stream that flowed on to forgetfulness and death.

Only dimly Lassie knew of the saucer of warm milk set beside her head. Her senses would not come back from their half-conscious state. She tried to lift her head but it would not move.

Then she felt her head being lifted. The warm milk was being spooned down her throat. She gulped, once—twice—three times. The trickle of hotness went into her body. It finished the lulling of her senses. She lay still, and the milk now being spooned into her mouth dribbled out again and onto the rug.

In the cottage the woman rose and stood beside her husband.

"D'ye think it's dying, Dan? It doesn't swallow any more."

"I don't know, Dally. It may live the night. We've done the best we can. All we can do is just—let it be."

The woman stared at it.

"Dan, I think I'll sit up wi' it."

"Now, Dally. Ye've done your best, and . . ."

"But it might need some help and . . . it's such a bonnie dog, Dan."

"Bonnie! That ugly mongrel of a stray . . ."

"Oh, Dan. It's the bonniest dog I ever saw."

Firmly the old woman planted herself in the rocking chair and settled herself for a night of watching.

A week later Mrs. Fadden sat in her chair. The morning sunlight streamed through the window, and the memory of the storm seemed like a dream of long ago. She looked over her glasses and beamed at Lassie, lying on the rug, her ears erect.

"It's himself," she said aloud. "And you know it, don't you?"

There came the footsteps of her husband, and then the door opened.

"Ye know, Dan, she knows your footsteps already," the woman said proudly.

"Ah," he said skeptically.

"She does," Dally maintained. "The other day, when that pedlar came, she just raised the roof, I'll tell you. My word, she let him know someone was home while you were in town! But she doesn't make a sound when she hears you coming— so she must know your footsteps."

"Ah," the man replied again.

"She's smart—and she's bonnie," the woman said—more to the dog than to the man. "Isn't she bonnie, Dan?"

"Aye, that she is."

"And first off you said she was ugly."

"Aye, but that was before . . ."

"See, I just took an old comb and did her coat all pretty."

They looked at Lassie, now lying with head erect in that lion-like posture that collies so often take. Her slim muzzle was held gracefully above the ruff that once again was beginning to show glossy white.

"Doesn't she look different?" the woman asked proudly.

"Aye, that's it, Dally," the man said dolefully.

The woman caught his ominous tone.

"Well, what's the matter?"

"Eigh, Dally. Ye see, that's just it. First off, I thought she was a mongrel. But now . . . well, she's a fine dog."

"Of course she's a fine dog," the old woman said happily. "All she needed was a bit o' warmth and a little to eat and somebody to be kind to her."

The man shook his head as if exasperated at his wife who did not see what he was driving at.

"Aye, but don't ye understand, Dally? She's a fine dog— and now she's all cleaned up and getting better, ye can see she's a very valuable dog. And . . ."

"And what?"

"Well, a valuable dog will have owners somewhere."

"Owners? Fine owners who'd leave a puir thing oot wandering and bony and starving on a night like we took her in. Owners, indeed!"

The man shook his head and sat in his chair heavily. He stuffed his clay pipe.

"No, Dally, it's no good. She's a valuable dog, and I can see it now. So don't get your heart set on her, because any day the owner might come . . ."

The woman sat, her mind worrying over this new and terrible thought. Her beautiful dog—*her* dog!

She stared at the fire and then, for a long time, at Lassie. Finally she spoke:

"Well then, if this has got to be taken away fro' us, Dan— it might as well be sooner as later. Oh, if anyone owns it! Find out, will ye, Dan? Go ask around."

The man nodded.

"It's honest," he said. "I'll go to town and ask around tomorrow."

"No, Dan, today. Go right now. For I'd never have a minute's peace nor sleep a wink till I knew. Go today and ask around everywhere, and then if she's to go, she'll go. And if nobody owns her, then we've done our duty and can rest easy."

The man puffed his pipe, but the woman gave him no rest until he agreed to go that day.

At noon he set out, walking slowly down the road to the town four miles away. All through the afternoon the woman rocked. Sometimes she went to the door and looked down the highway.

It was a long afternoon. The minutes dragged for the old woman. It was falling dusk when at last she heard the footsteps. Almost before the door opened she began:

"Well?"

"I asked all aroond the place—everywhere—and nobody seems to ha' lost her."

"Then she's ours!"

The woman beamed with joy and looked at the proud dog, still thin and pinched, but to her the perfection of canine breeding.

"She's ours," she repeated. "We gave them their chance. Now she's ours."

"Well, now, Dally. They might pass by chance and see her, so don't . . ."

"She's ours now," the woman repeated stolidly.

Mentally she was resolving that no owner should pass and ever see the dog. She would see to that. The dog should stay always beside her in the cottage. She would not have it running around loose outside for that terrible, unknown owner to see as he passed by!

CHAPTER EIGHTEEN

The Noblest Gift—Freedom

Lassie lay on the rug. Strength had returned to her in the three weeks she had been in her new home. Her senses were back to normal, and her muscles were almost as strong as ever.

Other things had come back to her, too. When she had been weak and ill, these had been like forgotten things. But now they grew each day with the return of her health—insistent and demanding.

The one driving force of her life was wakened, and it was leaving her no peace.

It always grew worse in the afternoons. As the clock moved round toward four, it became maddening.

It was the time sense.

It was time—time to go—time to go for the boy!

Lassie rose and went to the door. She whined and lifted her head.

"Ah, now, girl!"

It was the old woman.

"Ye've been oot for a nice walk wi' me on the string! Ye don't need to go oot again. So come back here and rest yourself."

But Lassie did not obey. She poked with her muzzle at the door. She walked to the window and stood on her hind legs. She dropped to all fours and went back to the door. Then, like an animal in a cage, she began pacing back and forth. She kept it up endlessly, walking to the door and turning, walking to the window and turning. She kept it up, her feet padding on the stone floor of the cottage. The click of her paw-nails went as rhythmically as the click of the old woman's knitting needles.

An hour later, Lassie ended her patrol. Slowly she went to the hearth rug. The time was past. She lay down and regarded the fire with unblinking eyes.

Animals are creatures of habit—but new habits can be formed. There was a real chance that Lassie would forget and become contented in her new home. The couple treated her with all the love of their simple life, and she obeyed them and came to them when they called and allowed them to stroke and fondle her.

But she did it with the forbearance of a dog that has only one master—and he is absent.

For Lassie did not forget. Instead, with her returning health, she remembered more and more, and her daily patrollings in the late afternoon became longer and more agitated.

Nor did the old couple fail to notice it. The old woman who so treasured this new thing of affection that had come into her life was aware of every least move that Lassie made. Such a steady occurrence as Lassie's afternoon pacing between the window and the door could not be disregarded.

The woman hoped, and almost dreamed, that the dog would forget the outside world and be content in their small, snug, humble world of the cottage and the chickens and the goose. But finally she realized that it was no use, for Lassie began to refuse her food. Then the old woman knew.

She sat long one evening and at last, out of the silence, she spoke.

"Dan!"

"What is it now?"

"She's not happy here."

"Happy? Who isn't—what're ye talking aboot?"

"You know what I'm talking aboot. Herself. She's not happy. She's fretting."

"Oh, now nonsense. Ye think more o' that dog. Every time Herself winks an eyebrow, ye're thinking she's got the measles or the plague or—or I don't know what."

The woman turned her eyes on Herself—as they had christened Lassie. She shook her head.

"No. I didn't tell ye, but the last three days, Dan, she's not eating."

The man lifted his glasses to his forehead and studied the dog. Then his regard came to his aged wife.

"Now, now, Dally. It's all richt. Ye've been feeding her so much I don't wonder she'd turn her nose up at a dinner fit for a king. That's all."

"No, it's not nonsense, Dan. And well you know it. For why do ye always keep her so tight on a string when ye take her oot last thing at nicht?"

"Well, that's just in case—well, till she gets used to this as her home. If I let her free, she micht get lost, and not knowing this countryside well, wouldn't find her way back, and . . ."

"Ah, ye know that's a tale, Dan. As well as I do, ye know that if she was free she'd be away and leaving us alone here, and never coming back."

The man did not answer. The woman went on.

"She's not happy, Dan. Ye don't see her as I do—every afternoon, window to door, door to window, until I think she'll wear a path deep in the flagging . . ."

"Oh, now, that's just a dog's way of asking to go for a walk."

"It is not, Dan. For I've tried it. I take her on the string—and not that she doesn't follow bonnie and mind me. But she does it, Dan—ye know what I think?"

"What?"

"Well, like she's just doing it because she's sorry for us. We've been kind to her, and she wouldn't want to hurt our feelings, so she just puts up with us. Like she's too polite to run unless we tell her to go . . ."

"Ah, now, no dog can be full of things like that—like human things . . ."

"Nay, my Herself is, Dan. Ye don't know that dog. Dan!"

"Well?"

The old woman's voice dropped.

"Ye see, I know aboot this dog. I know something."

"What?"

"Dan, she's going somewhere. She's on her way."

"Ah, now, woman, and what fancies are ye building in your mind!"

"I don't care, Dan. I know—me and Herself, we both know. She was on her way, Dan, and she got tired on the way and she's just stopped here like it was a hospital—or a wayside inn in a story. And now she's better, she wants to be on her way. But she's so polite and understanding, she doesn't want to hurt us. But in her heart she's for being away. She's not happy here."

The old man did not answer. He tapped out his clay pipe in the palm of his hand and looked steadily at the dog. Finally he spoke.

"Aye," he said. "All right, Dally. All right."

There are people whose hearts are so full of ugly fear that
when they see a thirsty animal pass with a fleck of saliva on its
parched jowl, they must run in terror shouting, "Mad dog!"
There are others to whom every passing creature is an enemy,
to be harried on its way with a flung stone. But, and for this
the canine world must be thankful, there are others with affection and deep understanding in their lives who bring dignity
and honor to the relationship between man and dog.

Such was the old couple, who on the next afternoon sat
watching the dog. When the time neared four o'clock, and
Lassie rose, their eyes followed her.

And when Lassie whined at the door and then paced to the
window, they both sighed.

"Well," the old man said.

That was all. They both got up. The woman opened the
door. Side by side, the old man and his wife followed Lassie
out to the road.

There for a moment, the dog stood, as if unable to realize
that at last her great urge could be fulfilled. She looked back
at the woman whose hands had patted and fondled her and
fed her.

For a second, the old woman wished to call—to call the dog
back to her and try again to wean its mind from old memories.
But she was too honest. She lifted her head, and her aged voice
came clearly.

"It's all richt, then, dog. If ye must go—awa' wi' ye."

In that sentence, Lassie caught the word "go." It was what she wanted.

She turned, looked back once as in a glance of farewell, and then started—not up the road to the east, nor down it to the west, but straight across the field. She was going south again.

She went at a trot—the same trot that had carried her bravely through the Highlands of Scotland. Not a fast one, nor a slow one, but a steady pace that ate at miles, that could be kept up for hour after hour. So she went, across the field, over a wall, and down the slope.

Back on the road, the old woman stood, her chin set firm. And she waved her hand and said:

"Good-bye, Herself. Good-bye—and good luck to ye."

Long after the dog was out of sight she stood there, until her husband put his arm around her.

"It's getting rare chilly, now, Dally," he said. "We'd better go in."

They went into the cottage, and the routine of life went on. The woman prepared the simple evening meal. She lit the lamp. They sat at the table.

But neither of them ate.

Then the man looked up and said sympathetically:

"I'll put the lamp in the window, Dally, for tonicht. Like, for chance, she just gone for a long run. And then if she wants to find her way back . . ."

He knew the dog was never coming back, but he had thought it might make his wife feel better if he told her this. However, he stopped speaking, for as he looked up he saw his wife's head bowed, and tears were falling. Quickly he rose.

"Now, now, Dally," he said. "Now, now!"

He put his arms about her and patted her consolingly.

"Eigh, now don't fret yourself, Dally. Look, I'll tell ye what. I've a couple of shillings put away, and I'll take down a few eggs and sell 'em—and then I'll go to the market, and I know a place where they sell dogs. And I'll get ye another. Eh? A fine little dog that'll stay here wi' ye, and not want to run away.

"Ah, Herself was too big, she was—and them big ones eat too much anyhow—and, and . . . a nice little one . . ."

The old woman looked up. She wanted to cry out the words that always come from a dog lover after their animal is gone: "I don't ever want another dog!"

But because of regard for her husband she never spoke the words.

"Aye, it cost a lot to feed, Dan."

"O' course it did. And a little dog—or perhaps a cat—why, it'd cost almost nothing . . ."

"That's it, a cat, Dan! If ye'd get me just a nice cat."

"Aye—one that'd stay curled up on the hearth and stay by ye. That's it! I'll get ye a fine cat—the finest cat anybody could ever want. How's that?"

The old woman looked up.

"Ah, Daniel, ye're kind to me."

Then she dashed her tears away and smiled.

"Eigh, sure. We're getting all in a stew—and here's tea getting all cold," he said.

"Oh, I couldn't eat, Dan."

"Well, then, have a nice cup o' tea."

"Aye, that's right," she said. "A good cup o' tea'll cheer us both up."

"It will, indeed. And Saturday—we'll have you the bonniest little cat ye ever did see. Won't that be fine?"

The woman smiled bravely.

"Aye, it'll be fine," she said.

CHAPTER NINETEEN

On the Road with Rowlie

Rowlie Palmer finished shaving and cleaned off his old-fashioned straight razor.

He was a little, cheery man with a red face that somehow seemed full of buttons. His eyes were like buttons, his weather-beaten lips were like buttons, there were odd bumps and warts on his forehead and chin that were like buttons.

The button-similarity went into actual practice in his clothes. He wore a knitted woolen overshirt which was dotted with pearl-shell buttons at every available place. Over that he wore a curious corduroy jacket with leather sleeves, and on that were numerous brass buttons which, if one had inspected

185

closer, would have shown plainly as one-time fasteners of tunics in His Majesty's army.

Rowlie's face and form were well known throughout the North of England, for he was a travelling potter. He lived in the horse-drawn wagon-caravan which carried his goods and traveled slowly along the roads. When he came to a village or town, he would take out a stout cudgel and begin to beat one of his largest pottery bowls—an enormous thing of brown and yellow glaze. The result would be a sound like the rich-toned chiming of a great bell.

And Rowlie would lift up his voice and chant:

"Here comes Pedlar Palmer, the Potter. Bowls and pots, I've got lots! Bring your penny or you won't get any! Bowls and pots!"

He loved to make his grand entrances into the small towns of the North, banging vigorously with a great show on the pottery bowl. He always belabored it proudly for the double reason—to signal his coming and to show how stout was his ware that could not be broken by even such lusty blows.

Once a year he covered his route. When his stock got low, he would circle back to his home village where his older brother, Mark, made the pottery. Mark would look up and nod from his potter's wheel in the great shed where he fashioned the old-fashioned utensils. Rowlie would stock up again with the wares: tiny ones small enough for a child's bowl of porridge up to the great ones nearly three feet across, which the

Northern housewives loved to use for kneading their bread dough—and often for washing the baby in.

He would load his van with the brown-and-yellow things, so shining with their crude glazes, and off he would go again. "Well—I'm off," he would say.

Mark would look up and nod—and go on working.

Then away Rowlie would start on his route, travelling by day, at night pulling Bess over to the side of the road by a good camping place.

It was a comfortable, happy life. For in his van, Rowlie had a complete home. It was incredible that in such a small space so full a life could be achieved just by compactness. Often as a great favor to a customer Rowlie would let them see the living quarters. And even the best housewives, looking in, would exclaim over the spotlessness of the van.

There was a place for everything. A place for the razor that Rowlie was putting away. A place for his washbowl. A tiny rail for his towel.

His cot was made, his breakfast finished, his dishes put away. Bess was harnessed, her oat-bag slung beneath the cart. Rowlie got to the seat.

"Hi, up, Bess!" he cried.

Once out on the road, Rowlie jumped down from the seat of his moving van and began walking alongside it. Bess had enough to pull without his extra weight. And he loved to walk, unless the weather was too bad.

But the weather was good now. Rowlie went along, with the half-mist of morning still hanging to the ground, singing:

"Oh, father, father, dig my grave,
And dig it with your garden spade,
And place on top a turtle-dove,
To show them that I died for love."

It was a sad song, but Rowlie did not mind that. In fact, he never realized it. It was just that in his lonesome life his own voice kept him company from town to town. He had no other company but Bess, the horse, and Toots. And Toots—she was a one, as Rowlie would put it. She sat on the seat now—a tiny white dog, which might have been poodle, fox terrier, Pomeranian, or Skye terrier; but was all of them.

Toots was almost as well known as Rowlie. She could stand on her hind legs on an inverted bowl and balance another smaller bowl on her nose. She could jump on a ball of wood and roll it by walking along, still balancing. She could pick up pennies from the ground and bring them to Rowlie. She could jump through hoops.

Whenever Rowlie reached a good village, he would put on a show with Toots—not as a mountebank might, to collect pence; but because he enjoyed the laughter and happiness of the children who gathered there.

Between towns Toots sat primly in the driver's seat as she sat now, regarding the road as Rowlie sang his doleful story of the hapless village maiden.

His mind was not on the words. Instead, as always, his senses were alert to the world about him. Travelling and living in the open as he did, Rowlie knew a good deal about his world. He knew where magpies nested and when the swallows came and went. And no huntsman in the land had an eye any quicker than Rowlie's for seeing the whisp of red that was a fox.

So this morning, his senses were alert, and his eyes flicked over a field, and his song halted.

He walked over beside his moving cart and stood on the step beside the shafts. Thus he rode, his body pressed against the front of his vehicle. As he went, he watched. It was a dog, coming steadily across the field, veering toward the road.

She came without halting—as if a horse-drawn van was a thing of nature, like a tree or a deer. Rowlie knew that and so kept his body out of sight. Only he muttered to himself:

"Now what are you up to, eh?"

Nearer the dog came, until, by a part of unfenced moorland, it slipped to the road, just as the cart passed.

"Well, and what do you want?" Rowlie said out loud.

The dog looked up and recrossed the ditch into the moorland.

"Don't like my company, eh?" Rowlie said.

He got down from the step and began walking again. His eyes followed the dog, now going ahead and to his left, yet travelling almost parallel. But its passage was stopped by a stream. It began moving back to the road again, where it could cross on the bridge.

Rowlie clambered into his cart, and when he came out he had in his hand a few small pieces of liver. Toots lifted her nose and wagged her nondescript tail.

"It's not for thee, my lass," Rowlie said.

He kept his eye on the dog. It would arrive at the bridge just as his wagon did.

"Well, we'll pretend not to notice thee this time," he said aloud.

He began singing, lustily:

    "My old feyther, he used to say to me,
    "Now here's a bit o' good advice I'm bahn to gie to thee.
    Th'art so simple, so varry varry dense . . ."

And then—

"Ah-gee-way, there Bess. No, not right into th' ditch. Ah-gee-whoa a bit. That's it!"

And—

    "Thy yead is full o' summat
    But it isn't full o' sense.
    Th' only time th'art intelligent at all . . ."

So singing, timing the speed of his horse, Rowlie arrived at the bridge as the dog drew near. He went on singing lustily, pretending not to notice it. The dog halted, as if to let him pass first. Rowlie did not turn his head. Instead he waved the pieces of liver in his hand so that the scent scattered in the air. Unconcernedly he dropped one. Then he passed over the bridge. Half turning his head, he looked to see what the dog would do.

Behind, by the bridge, Lassie walked slowly to the piece of meat. The aroma of it seemed to fill the air. Her hunger drove the saliva glands to work and her mouth filled with wetness. She walked nearer. She bent her nose to touch the meat.

But training of years was there, too. How carefully had Sam Carraclough taught her not to pick up strange food. He had done that by dropping small pieces of meat at various places—and in the meat was inserted cores of burning red pepper. As a pup Lassie had started to eat those bits and had soon discovered that they contained what seemed to be balls of living flame. Moreover, as her mouth burned, she had been scolded by the voice of her master.

"It's a crewel hard thing to dew," Sam Carraclough had told his son Joe, "but it's t'only way I know that can teach 'em—and I'd sooner have a pup taste hot pepper than have a raised dog dying o' poisoned meat some madman has thrown to it."

And that lesson had stayed with Lassie.

A dog must not eat stray bits of food!

Yet the hunger in her was something that went back before training. Her nose trembled. She nuzzled the piece of liver. Then suddenly she wheeled. She left the meat and crossed the bridge.

Ahead of her Rowlie Palmer, by his wagon, nodded his head.

"A good tyke and a well-brought-up one," he said. "Good for thee, my tyke. But we'll see . . ."

He walked on singing, but still waving liver in the air so that he left what was to a dog a great, broad, rich swathe of delectable aroma.

And in that smell of desired food, Lassie now travelled. Once over the bridge, her impulse was to leave the road again and go through the fields. But she did not want to leave the trail of this sweet-smelling food. She trotted along, crossed the ditch, and began travelling slightly to the rear and parallel to the van in the road.

Rowlie Palmer sang merrily to Toots on the seat:

"There's a tyke that's shy and canny,
But I think she's coming near.
Aye, she may be fearfu' canny,
But we'll overcome her fear."

"How's that for a rhyme, Toots? Eh, you'd like a companion. Well, we'll see."

So Rowlie Palmer travelled along his road. Sometimes, when he turned his head, he could see the collie in the fields behind him. Sometimes she was lost to view and gone for quite a length of time. But always she would be back again, drawn to the scent of meat, following it steadily. And each time she came back she would come a bit nearer the wagon and the man who seemed to pay not the slightest heed in the world to her.

So it went all through the morning, as they crossed flat, bleak lands. As the sun was high, Rowlie Palmer pulled off the road. He saw the dog halt behind him.

"Time for a bite, Toots," he said.

Quickly he set up a small brazier and built a fire. He boiled water and made tea. He warmed over a pot of stew. He cut up liver and put it down in a bowl for Toots. He ate. All the time he watched the collie, drawing nearer and nearer. Very ostentatiously, he fed bits of food to his little dog. He saw the collie, now sitting only twenty feet away, following with its eyes every move that his hand made. Toots barked at her, shrilly, once or twice, but Rowlie quieted his pet promptly.

When at last his meal was done, he rose.

"Now," he said, "we know a trick or two, don't we, Toots? And we'll see whether you'll eat or not."

He took from his stock a flat bowl. He filled it with bits of liver. As unconcerned as if it were something he had done every day for years, he walked halfway to the collie and set the bowl down.

"There's your dinner," he said. "Eat it up."

Lassie watched him go back to the brazier. Then, as he seemed to be taking no notice of her, she rose from her sitting position. Slowly she walked to the bowl.

A dog must not eat stray bits of food!

But this was different. It wasn't stray. It was set out in a bowl. That was it. It was in a bowl. And when a bowl or plate was set out by man, that meant a dog could eat without fear. There would be no living fire inside the food.

Gently Lassie dropped her head. With her front teeth, she lifted a piece of meat. She snapped it upwards. Then in the joy of eating again, she tore into the food. She cleaned up the bowl. She licked the bowl itself. Then she sat, looking at the man, as if to say:

"Well, for an appetizer that was all right. Now where's the real meal?"

Rowlie shook his head and spoke out loud.

"Ah, no. Ye'll come along wi' me if ye want any more. Didn't I say we knew a thing or two about tykes, Toots? Put it down in the road, and it's no go! Somebody trained thee too well, my collie friend. But put it down in a bowl—that was the secret. That made it all right. Well, up we get and on our way!"

He took off Bess's nosebags. He tipped his brazier and stamped out the fire carefully. Snugly he stowed everything away. All the time from the corner of his eye, he saw the collie, sitting, as if waiting to see whether the miracle of a fine dinner would happen all over again. And when at last he started and was on the road again, Rowlie Palmer grunted happily. For the collie was travelling with him; not in the field now, but close behind the van. It was not too close—but Rowlie didn't mind that. That would come later he very well knew.

He sang merrily:
   "They'll hang me by the neck till I am dead,
    Yes, they'll hang me by the neck till I am dead,
     They'll take me from my bed,
     To the gallows I'll be led,
    And I'll hang till I am dead—blast your eyes!"

Days later, Lassie was still with Rowlie Palmer. She trotted by the road, always a few feet behind the pottery van. Rowlie tried to teach her to swing along under the wagon behind the rear axle, as a well-trained Dalmatian carriage dog would have done in the days of traps and phaetons; but Lassie would have none of it.

She never liked the banging and shouting as they came into villages; but it was as if she put up with it, knowing it could not last long. She was content as long as Rowlie went south. Once, at a fork in the road, Rowlie turned his van east. Some sense told him that part of his animal family was missing. He looked back. Lassie was sitting at the road junction.

Every time he called to her, she came a few steps, then circled, went back, and sat down.

Finally Rowlie threw up his hands. He climbed to the seat of the van, turned Bess round and started south on the other fork.

"Eigh, I can just as well go round Godsey way as by Menlip," he said affably.

But later he turned to Toots.

"Ye see what a poor thing a man is among women. You and Bess and Her Majesty. What chance has one lone male got again' the three on ye? Bess wants to go north 'cause that's home. Her Majesty wants to go south—for the winter on the Rivveyeria, no doubt. And you—eigh, tha' content as long as tha's wi' me. Aye, Toots, tha' the only one that loves me for masen alone!"

And the little dog wagged its tail that was neither curly nor straight nor short-haired nor plumed.

It was a good life, travelling along the unfrequented lanes of the North country, far from the main highways where the trucks and lorries and motorcars that Rowlie hated so much went racing along. And Rowlie sang as the miles passed.

"Well, Your Majesty. Shall us common folks do a little vulgar business?"

Rowlie addressed the words to Lassie behind the wagon. She walked along, giving no sign of having heard.

"I know, Your Majesty," Rowlie said humbly. "It does hurt your royal ears to hear me speak of such things as money, but us humbler folks has got to live, so if you don't mind—*if* you don't mind—me and Toots will earn a little money."

Delighted with his own make-believe, Rowlie lifted his cap to Lassie and bowed low. Then he turned to his wagon and took down the largest bowl and his cudgel. He banged lustily as he approached the first house.

The bell-like din echoed in the village. Rowlie's voice lifted:

"Bowls and pots, I've got lots,
    Bring your penny or ye won't get any!
    Bowls and pots!"

The women flocked to the doors, and Rowlie greeted them. He halted his wagon by the village center, as the housewives fingered his wares and argued and joked about prices.

"They're so strong ye can't break 'em!" Rowlie chanted.

"I broke the one I got fro' ye last year," a woman cried.

"Well, I have to have 'em break once in a while," Rowlie said, his eyes gleaming. "If I made 'em absolutely unbreakable, ye'd never want any new ones and I'd do myself out of a job."

He winked broadly, and the women screamed with laughter and nudged each other and said:

"Eigh, he's a one, that Pedlar Potter Palmer!"

"Now," Rowlie said, when the buying was done. "Who wants to see the tyke do a few tricks?"

The children yelled and clapped their hands. Rowlie got out the paraphernalia from the wagon and set it up. Toots scrambled nimbly from the seat. Rowlie clapped his hands. But nothing happened. The little dog sat waiting.

"What's the matter?" Rowlie said. "Ye're waiting for someone? Eigh, I see. Her Majesty hasn't arrived for the command performance. Why, here she comes now."

Carefully trained by Rowlie, Lassie strolled before the crowd and sat down. Rowlie gave her a little bit of liver as her reward.

"Well, now Her Majesty's here at last, we can begin, can't we?" Rowlie pattered on.

At the signal with his hand, Toots barked excitedly and began her routine. She jumped through the hoops. She told how old she was by barking. She played "dead dog." She picked out the prettiest girl in the crowd—all by Rowlie's hidden signals. Then she ended with her best trick, walking on the ball of wood while she carried in her mouth a tiny national flag.

"Doesn't the collie do aught?" a child cried.

"Why, ye wouldn't expect royalty to perform, would ye?" Rowlie answered. "But it does seem like she's on a sit-down strike."

Rowlie advanced to Lassie, carrying Toots in his arms.

"Would ye like to do some work?" he asked.

Lassie sat unblinking.

"Would ye like to pick up the things after the star's finished?"

Lassie still sat.

"Pick up those things!" Rowlie ordered in a thunderous tone.

Lassie did not move, and the children screamed happily. Rowlie scratched his head in mock dismay. Then his eyes brightened. He held up his finger to the children. Then he turned to Lassie.

"May it please Your Majesty, but as a favor to me, would you *please* pick up the things?"

She ended with her best trick, walking on the ball of wood while she carried in her mouth a tiny national flag.

This time he gave the signal with his hand—for the words had no bearing on the trick—and Lassie rose proudly. She pushed the wooden ball with her slim muzzle to the van. She picked up the hoops one by one and set them in a pile by the door. Rowlie bowed to her. Lassie curtsied, stretching her front legs forward stiffly as a dog does after it has been sleeping.

"Ye see," Rowlie said to the children. "Always remember to say please, and ye'll get more in this world. Well. Off we go. Don't forget Pedlar Palmer the Potter. I'll be back next year. Good-bye."

The hands fluttered in the village, and away went the caravan. Rowlie sang happily. Toots coiled up snugly on the front seat. Bess plodded along at her steady amble. Lassie trotted unconcernedly behind. She was glad they were on the road again. She disliked the halts in the villages, and she never really liked the performances in which she played such a small part. She was unlike Toots, who delighted in the tricks and could hardly wait to go through them. Toots was a born trick dog. Lassie—she was not of that kind.

Rowlie Palmer knew that. He looked at Toots who lay half asleep.

"Aye, she's a fine dog fro' somewhere—but she'll never be as smart as thee, my sweetheart, will she?"

Toots gave an agitated squirm which was meant to be a wagging of the tail.

Rowlie finished the evening meal and made his caravan ready again.

"Aye, I know. Ye don't want to turn out again," he said to Bess. "But it's a long jump this time, and we'll get some o' the road under our feet. It's clear enough."

Rowlie turned his eyes upward again. There was a clear moon, but there was a crispness in the air, too.

"Really mucky weather ahead if I know it—and then winter'll be down on us—and we've got to head back toward home. So we'll put on steam a bit and get some done tonight."

He turned his wagon out to the road, and soon there was the steady clop-clop of Bess's hooves on the flinty way. Toots slept soundly on the front seat. Happy to be on the way again, Lassie trotted at the rear of the caravan.

Rowlie was counting in his mind. A good four hours more, and long before ten o'clock, he should be at that snug camping place beside the Apden woods. It would be cold by then. A nice cup of tea over the brazier to cheer him up and then to bed, and up and off with the sun tomorrow morning.

CHAPTER TWENTY

A Gallant Heart and a Good-bye

The two men came up along the road where the trees cast deep gloom from the moonlight.

"Well, if ye don't like it, Snickers, ye know what ye can do!"

The man who spoke was a great, thickset man. His shoulders bulged under his moleskin jacket. The peaked cap came down over a broad, square-jowled face. The man he addressed was smaller, thin faced. From the tip of his long nose hung a small crystal which seemed to be ever there, no matter how much he sniffed.

"Ye give me a pain, ye does, Snickers—allus grousing. 'Ere I lets yer be my pal—I lets yer travel with me—I fair sees ye

202

live on the bloomin' fat o' the land, and what do I get for it?
Grouse, grouse, grouse all the time. Yer tired, ye are; yer feet
'urt yer, they do; yer cold, ye are! Why, ye bloomin' . . ."

"Hey, Buckles, look!"

The big man halted his tirade and looked where the other
pointed. Through the gloom there was a glimmer of warm
light. Buckles wiped the back of his hand slowly over his
mouth. He looked about. By the roadside he saw a stout
branch of wood. He unclasped his knife and hacked viciously,
trimming away the rough ends of limb. Finally he was satisfied.
He balanced the cudgel in his hand. He saw Snickers had done
the same.

Not a word had been spoken. Buckles merely motioned with
his head, and the two stole silently down the road. Five minutes
later they were lying in a thicket. The smell of burning wood
came straight into their faces.

"Pedlar Palmer the Potter," Snickers whispered, reading
the sign on the van. "A bloomin' travelin' 'awker, that's what."

"Hawker," Buckles breathed. "Then he'll have it with him."

"That e' will, Buckles. They carries it wiv 'em."

"Come on, then!"

Buckles rose and began a stealthy advance. But before he
had gone ten paces the still night was torn with the deep
challenge of a dog, sounding a throaty alarm.

" 'E's got a dog," Snickers panted.

"What do Hi care?" Buckles said.

He stepped out boldly, now that concealment was gone, and advanced to the place where the fire glowed in the brazier.

" 'Old yer dog, mate. It's all right. We ain't doin' nuthin'," Buckles called.

As he came to the fire, Lassie bayed. He motioned at her with his club, but she faded away. Rowlie tried to grasp her, but she eluded him, too, and stood at the circle of the fire growling. And now Toots's shrill yapping rose to add to the din.

"Quiet!" Rowlie said. "Quiet, both of ye."

The dogs subsided to a rumble. Then Buckles grinned. He heard Snickers standing behind him.

"That's good o' ye, mate," Buckles went on, in what he meant to be a disarming, friendly tone. "What ye 'aving, tea? Now ain't that nice. Could ye just spare a couple of 'omeless chaps looking for work a swaller or two to warm 'em up?"

He advanced, smiled.

Rowlie rose from his seat on a log. Despite Buckles' words, he was not fooled. He had not travelled alone for so many years without learning to read the character, and lack of it, of men he met in lonesome places.

"No, yer don't!" Buckles shouted.

He leaped between Rowlie and the van toward which the pedlar had been edging. He balanced the cudgel, smiling. Now all pretence was gone.

"Come on, where is it?" he said coaxingly. "Because if yer nice and 'ands it over wivout any trouble, we won't 'urt ye, will we, Snickers?"

"No, we won't 'urt 'im."

"Of course, we won't. But—if ye want trouble, then, sorry as we are, of course, we'll give it to yer. Come on! Where is it?"

"Why, I'll give it to you," Rowlie began.

Then he broke off his own words, and with a sudden leap was beside his caravan. Now in his hand rested his own stout stick. He placed his back against the van. He spit on his hands. He did not speak, nor did he need to.

"So, ye want it the 'ard way, do ye?" Buckles breathed. "Well, all right."

He lashed out with his weapon. Rowlie parried it and slashed backhanded in return, catching the big man's knuckles. Buckles roared in anger.

"Come on, Snickers, don't stand there—get round the other side of 'im, ye bloomin' coward."

The two men rushed in together, and Rowlie, against the van, tried to keep them beyond the half circle of his reach. The blows began to fall on his head and shoulders. He was helpless.

In despair, he looked at Lassie, now baying beyond the campfire.

"Come on, get 'em," he called.

Lassie darted about, then suddenly rushed at the bigger man. He turned and smashed at her with his stick. The blow fell across her shoulder, almost rolling her over. For a second the fight stopped and the men turned to the dog. They saw her stand, looking at them.

In Lassie's mind there were conflicting impulses. But one rose to the top.

Here again were men whose hands meant evil, who could reach out to hurt and give pain. These were hands that would capture and imprison. These were the men to avoid as she had done so many times before. A dog should slip away and not be seen by them.

At that moment, Buckles made a half step toward Lassie, raising his club.

"Gwan," he shouted. "Before I give yer another."

Lassie slid away. Then she turned into the underbrush and trotted up the slope into the woods.

Buckles turned back to Rowlie.

"What a dog!" he roared. "Ye see, mate—even yer best friend won't stick by yer. Oh, what a bloomin' dog that is! Now come on, 'and it over peaceful like, and we'll let bygones be bygones."

Rowlie's eyes, which had followed Lassie up into the woods, turned back to the men. He spit on his hands again. He braced himself.

"Come and get it," he said stubbornly.

The men crept closer, swinging warily at Rowlie. They stepped about cautiously in the firelight, for the pedlar was no weakling, and with his back against the van could keep a semicircle clear before him. And as he fought, parrying and replying deftly with his club, the tiny dog, Toots, scurried about, true to her trust, defending her master.

It was pitifully little that the tiny dog could do—almost laughable the way she darted about, yapping and shrilling, a little white bundle of energy. Grimly she dashed in, and at last managed to get her tiny teeth into the ankle of the big attacker.

In a second of surprise Buckles shook the dog loose with a kick of his foot.

"You bloomin' little rat," he said.

The little dog rushed in again, and Buckles, lifting his great cudgel, smote with all his strength. The small body was knocked, lifeless and broken, into the underbrush.

Shouting in mad anger at what he had seen, Rowlie charged out, driving the men back with his frenzied onslaught. He swung his club in fury, and seemed as if he would drive the men before him.

For a few moments they were swept back; but then Rowlie's anger proved his own undoing, for he had left the protection of the van and now was attacked on both sides. Buckles, aching from the savage blows of the pedlar's club, beat down Rowlie's guard, and a crushing blow on the shoulder sent the potter to his knees. Trying to rise, he covered his head with his stick and crooked arm. He felt a blow from the rear. Turning, he clutched Snickers and hung onto the man. He would make one enemy shield him from the other until his senses cleared. He felt a trickle of warm blood coming down into his left eye and knew his scalp was badly cut.

When Lassie first vanished into the underbrush at the threat of Buckles' club, she trotted away from the fire and automatically headed south.

Yet, as she went, she no longer felt the peaceful calm that always came when she was making headway in the desired direction. Somehow—something was wrong.

She halted in her tracks and looked back. Now, barely visible through the trees, was the glow of the fire, and her ears caught plainly the cries of the men and the shrilling of Toots. It was that high yapping that seemed to call her more than anything else, for it was the alarm—a dog crying rage and defiance.

Lassie circled, gliding through the brush, and went back. At last she sat on the bank. Toots's cries sounded no more. Lassie could see the men staggering about before their giant shadows. She saw Rowlie sink to the ground.

There were two opposing forces struggling in Lassie—one to keep away from men; the other to defend her home. For the van and the campfire were her home in a sense. And this latter force was the older one in her—one that went back to her ancestors. Her shyness of men was a later thing, acquired only in the last few months of her life. And suddenly the older force won.

She had never attacked man in her life, and she was not of a ferocious breed. Yet, once the conviction held her, she did not hesitate, nor did she go warily. With a deep, ugly baying that came from her chest, with her hackles raised, she started down the bank.

The first that the men about the fire knew of the dog's return was when a furry shape came across the patch of light from the fire like a thunderbolt. She sailed through the air, striking Buckles in the chest. The force of the first charge toppled the big man over. Lassie did not stop. She went out of the circle of light, wheeled through the brush, and came back in another direction. She raced past Snickers, still clutched by Rowlie, and slashed with her teeth into his leg as she passed.

The force of her drive tore her fangs through the flesh, and the night was broken by Snickers' scream of pain.

She turned to Buckles again.

"So, you're back," he muttered.

Confident that she would run as before, he charged at her. But Lassie this time ducked the swing of the club and raced past, tearing the calf of the man's leg. On she went across the space, circled, and charged back. Each time she went across the clearing she slashed as a collie does in battle. Each time she reached the shadow of the underbrush she wheeled and came from a new direction.

Shouting his encouragement, Rowlie set to with renewed vigor and began belaboring the two footpads. He battered them about, driving them round the fire. And the two found that no matter where they turned to escape Rowlie, there was the tricolor animal that came, always from a new direction, racing out of the darkness, slashing with her keen fangs and away again before they could strike at her.

Sometimes it seemed as though there must be two or three dogs, for no matter which way the men turned there was always one charging at them from a new direction.

They were helpless against such tactics. And at last, harried and beaten, they attempted to retreat. It was Snickers who went first, not thinking of his companion. He fled in terror from the ghost that inflicted such lance-wounds on his legs. He went crashing through the brush in blind panic. And behind him, he soon heard another crashing. It was Buckles, running blindly, anywhere, any direction, as long as it was away from the foe that struck so effectively and could not be struck in return.

From the darkness behind him, Snickers could hear a horrible, worrying sound. Then he heard the voice of the pedlar.

"Come, come! Leave him alone, now. Not that he doesn't deserve anything he gets, but I wouldn't have ye kill him. Come!"

Snickers fled on. He was now alone and friendless. He didn't want to meet Buckles, who would be sure to accuse him of desertion in time of need—and he certainly had no more desire to meet the pedlar or his dog.

Snickers decided that he who travelled alone travelled fastest. He struck off to the west. And back by the campfire, Rowlie Palmer crouched beside a small white body. Lassie stood stiff-legged and touched it with her nose.

For a long time Rowlie crouched, unmoving, his mind crowded with the memories of many days when the little dog was his only companion.

At last he rose, went to the van and took out a spade. He began digging a small grave.

Lassie stood by the crossroads in the cold, driving rain. She whimpered once, and saw the van stop. The man called to her. She shifted her feet in a sort of dance, but went no nearer. At last he walked back.

"Come here then, Your Majesty," he said.

She heard the first word and walked to the man who squatted on his heels on the muddy road. For a long time he patted and fondled her.

Then he rose.

"Won't ye come, then?" he asked.

Lassie lifted her head and moved her feet in the dance but still would not follow.

"Aye," he said. "Perhaps it's best that way. I'd like to go on with ye, but stock's low, and I've got to be getting back to Mark for the winter.

"And besides—ye'd never fit in with me like Toots did— and ye'd aye be reminding me of her. Not that ye haven't been a good dog."

Lassie caught the last two words and moved her tail in acknowledgement.

"Aye, ye understand a lot, don't ye? Well, forgie me—at first I thought ye were a coward, but it's not that. There's summat else about thee, my lass, and I'd dearly love to be inside thy mind and know what it is."

The collie heard the word "lass," and barked at it. The pedlar shook his head.

"Nay, that's the pity of it. Ye can understand some o' man's language, but man isn't bright enough to understand thine. And yet it's us that's supposed to be most intelligent!

"Eigh, dear, but we had some good times going along the road together, didn't we? And now—if it's over, it's over. I'll be lonely. No thee—and no Toots. But I always did say if a man doesn't like to be alone, then he shouldn't never pick the job o' travelling pedlar for himself. It's what I must expect.

"And another way of looking at it. Sometimes I think ye didn't come along wi' me as much as ye let me come along with thee as long as our roads lay together. And now—well, ye'll be off about whatever business it is ye're on."

Lassie did not understand these words. All she knew was that the voice of the man who had fed and fondled her was a warm, soothing tone. So she muzzled his hand.

"That's good-bye, eh?" he said. "Well, may luck go wi' thee, then. Off ye go!"

Lassie caught the word "go."

She paced to the crossroad and turned away. There she looked back. The man waved.

"On ye go then, and good luck," he called.

He stood a long time watching the collie that trotted away. The cold afternoon rain beat in his weather-tanned face. He shook his head slowly, as if saying to himself that he would never be able to puzzle it out.

Soon the dog was lost from view. Rowlie went back to his van silently. He climbed aboard, clucked to Bess, and headed east. Down on another road Lassie swung along—going south. The rain streamed from her coat; the mud splashed up over her legs.

A week later Rowlie's van moved slowly along the road. He did not sing now, nor did he walk beside his moving home, for the air was thick with flying white flakes.

Rowlie sat on the front seat, a tarpaulin buttoned over his knees, his buttony face bowed against the drive of the storm. The front of him was almost solid white, and before him he could see the steam rising from the flanks of Bess, as she plodded vigorously along.

"Aye, that's right," Rowlie said aloud. "Ye know we're most home now. And glad I'll be to get there; for it's been a mucky trip back. Naught but rain, sleet, rain—and now snow. I stayed out too long on the trip—and that's what I get."

Rowlie grumbled on, and then suddenly he stopped his lonesome talk. His mind went to the dog that had left him at the crossroads.

"Aye, well," he said finally. "I'm most home. And as for thee, my friend, here's hoping that whatever ye were seeking, ye've found it. Peace—or whatever it was ye were looking for. But wherever ye are—I hope ye're snug and warm and dry.

"Sometimes I wish I'd locked ye in the van and brought ye back wi' me; but I didn't have the heart to then—for I wanted no dog again after Toots. Perhaps I shall some day, but just now I don't. She were as true as they come—but happen ye're being true to summat else. So good-bye to ye, and I hope ye're as near home as I am.

"There we are, Bess! Here's Twelve Corners. We'll be home i' time for tea wi' Mark."

As Bess plodded more vigorously and the van went toward home for the winter, many miles to the south Lassie plodded on.

Now she was crossing a great, high moor, where the wind swept without halt. The snowstorm drove from behind her, blowing the hair in sodden wisps forward from her thin flanks.

She found it hard to keep going. The snow was getting deeper, and it took more and more strength from her tired muscles to lift her feet clear of the snow at each step. At last she staggered and fell. Coiling up, she began biting the matted ice from the hair between her claws. Again she tried, but the snow was too deep. She began plunging at it like a horse, rearing and leaping forward, but before very long she found herself utterly exhausted.

She stood, her head down, the panted breath coming like white steam. She lifted her head and whined; but the snow was still there. She jumped and bucketed again, trying to leap through the drifts. Again she stopped, without power to go farther.

Then, lifting her head, she gave a long cry—the cry of a dog lost, cold, and helpless. It was a long, high call that went out over the wide moor, through the driving snow where the darkness was descending.

The snow blanketed all sounds. There was no one for miles on that flat, wild land. Even if there had been someone within a few hundred yards, it is doubtful whether or not he could have heard that snow-muffled cry.

At last Lassie sank to the ground. The white expanse of snow softly covered her. Below that white blanket she lay, exhausted but warm.

CHAPTER TWENTY-ONE

Journey's End

Sam Carraclough had spoken the truth early that year when he told his son Joe that it was a long way from Greenall Bridge in Yorkshire to the Duke of Rudling's place in Scotland. And it is just as many miles coming the other way, a matter of four hundred miles.

But that would be for a man, traveling straight by road or by train. For an animal how far would it be—an animal that must circle and quest at obstacles, wander and err, back-track and sidetrack till it found a way?

A thousand miles it would be—a thousand miles through strange terrain it had never crossed before, with nothing but instinct to tell direction.

Yes, a thousand miles of mountain and dale, of highland and moor, plowland and path, ravine and river and beck and burn; a thousand miles of tor and brae, of snow and rain and fog and sun; of wire and thistle and thorn and flint and rock to tear the feet—who could expect a dog to win through that?

Yet, if it were almost a miracle, in his heart Joe Carraclough tried to believe in that miracle—that somehow, wonderfully, inexplicably, his dog would be there some day; there, waiting by the school gate. Each day as he came out of school, his eyes would turn to the spot where Lassie had always waited. And each day there was nothing there, and Joe Carraclough would walk home slowly, silently, stolidly as did the people of his country.

Always, when school ended, Joe tried to prepare himself— told himself not to be disappointed, because there could be no dog there. Thus, through the long weeks, Joe began to teach himself not to believe in the impossible. He had hoped against hope so long that hope began to die.

But if hope can die in a human, it does not in an animal. As long as it lives, the hope is there and the faith is there. And so, coming across the schoolyard that day, Joe Carraclough would not believe his eyes. He shook his head and blinked, and rubbed his fists in his eyes, for he thought what he was seeing was a dream. There, walking the last few yards to the school gate was—his dog!

He stood, for the coming of the dog was terrible—her walk was a thing that tore at her breath. Her head and her tail were down almost to the pavement. Each footstep forward seemed a separate effort. It was a crawl rather than a walk. But the steps were made, one by one, and at last the animal dropped in her place by the gate and lay still.

Then Joe roused himself. Even if it were a dream, he must do something. In dreams one must try.

He raced across the yard and fell to his knees, and then, when his hands were touching and feeling fur, he knew it was reality. His dog had come to meet him!

But what a dog was this—no prize collie with fine tricolor coat glowing, with ears lifted gladly over the proud, slim head with its perfect black mask. It was not a dog whose bright eyes were alert, and who jumped up to bark a glad welcome. This was a dog that lay, weakly trying to lift a head that would no longer lift; trying to move a tail that was torn and matted with thorns and burrs, and managing to do nothing very much except to whine in a weak, happy, crying way. For she knew that at last the terrible driving instinct was at peace. She was at the place. She had kept her lifelong rendezvous, and hands were touching her that had not touched her for so long a time.

By the Labor Exchange, Ian Cawper stood with the other out-of-work miners, waiting until it was tea time so that they could all go back to their cottages.

You could have picked out Ian, for he was much the biggest man even among the many big men that Yorkshire grows. In fact, he was reputed to be the biggest and strongest man in all that Riding of Yorkshire. A big man, but gentle and often very slow of thinking and speech.

And so Ian was a few seconds behind the others in realizing that something of urgency was happening in the village. Then he too saw it—a boy struggling, half running, along the main street, his voice lifted in excitement, a great bundle of something in his arms.

The men stirred and moved forward. Then, when the boy was nearer, they heard his cry:

"She's come back! She's come back!"

The men looked at each other and blew out their breath and then stared at the bundle the boy was carrying. It was true. Sam Carraclough's collie had walked back home from Scotland.

"I must get her home, quick!" the boy was saying. He staggered on.

Ian Cawper stepped forward.

"Here," he said. "Run on ahead, tell 'em to get ready."

His great arms cradled the dog—arms that could have carried ten times the weight of this poor, thin animal.

"Oh, hurry, Ian!" the boy cried, dancing in excitement.

"I'm hurrying, lad. Go on ahead."

So Joe Carraclough raced along the street, turned up the side street, ran down the garden path, and burst into the cottage:

"Mother! Feyther!"

"What is it, lad?"

Joe paused. He could hardly get the words out—the excitement was choking up in his throat, hot and stifling. And then the words were said:

"Lassie! She's come home! Lassie's come home!"

He opened the door, and Ian Cawper, bowing his head to pass under the lintel, carried the dog to the hearth and laid her there.

There were many things that Joe Carraclough was to remember from that evening. He was never to forget the look that passed over his father's face as he first knelt beside the dog that had been his for so many years, and let his hands travel over the emaciated frame. He was to remember how his mother moved about the kitchen, not grumbling or scolding now, but silently and with a sort of terrific intensity, poking the fire quickly, stirring the condensed milk into warm water, kneeling to hold the dog's head and lift open the jowl.

Not a word did his parents speak to him. They seemed to have forgotten him altogether. Instead, they both worked over the dog with a concentration that seemed to put them in a separate world.

Joe watched how his father spooned in the warm liquid, he saw how it drooled out again from the unswallowing dog's jowls and dribbled down onto the rug. He saw his mother warm up a blanket and wrap it round the dog. He saw them try again and again to feed her. He saw his father rise at last.

"It's no use, lass," he said to his mother.

Between his mother and father many questions and answers passed unspoken except through their eyes.

"Pneumonia," his father said at last. "She's not strong enough now . . ."

For a while his parents stood, and then it was his mother who seemed to be somehow wonderfully alive and strong.

"I won't be beat!" she said. "I just *won't* be beat."

She pursed her lips, and as if this grimace had settled something, she went to the mantlepiece and took down a vase. She turned it over and shook it. The copper pennies came into her hand. She held them out to her husband, not explaining nor needing to explain what was needed. But he stared at the money.

"Go on, lad," she said. "I were saving it for insurance, like."

"But how'll we . . ."

"Hush," the woman said.

Then her eyes flickered over her son, and Joe knew that they were aware of him again for the first time in an hour. His father looked at him, at the money in the woman's hand, and at last at the dog. Suddenly he took the money. He put on his cap and hurried out into the night. When he came back he was carrying bundles—eggs and a small bottle of brandy—precious and costly things in that home.

Joe watched as they were beaten together, and again and again his father tried to spoon some into the dog's mouth. Then his mother blew in exasperation. Angrily she snatched the spoon. She cradled the dog's head on her lap, she lifted the jowls, and poured and stroked the throat—stroked it and stroked it, until at last the dog swallowed.

"Aaaah!"

It was his father, breathing a long, triumphant exclamation. And the firelight shone gold on his mother's hair as she crouched there, holding the dog's head—stroking its throat soothing it with soft, loving sounds.

Joe did not clearly remember about it afterwards, only a faint sensation that he was being carried to bed at some strange hour of darkness.

And in the morning when he rose, his father sat in his chair, but his mother was still on the rug, and the fire was still burning warm. The dog, swathed in blankets, lay quiet.

"Is she—dead?" Joe asked.

His mother smiled weakly.

"Shhh," she said. "She's just sleeping. And I suppose I ought to get breakfast—but I'm that played out—if I nobbut had a nice strong cup o' tea . . ."

And that morning, strangely enough, it was his father who got the breakfast, boiling the water, brewing the tea, cutting the bread. It was his mother who sat in the rocking chair, waiting until it was ready.

That evening when Joe came home from school, Lassie still lay where he had left her when he went off to school. He wanted to sit and cradle her, but he knew that ill dogs are best left alone. All evening he sat, watching her, stretched out, with the faint breathing the only sign of life. He didn't want to go to bed.

"Now she'll be all right," his mother cried. "Go to bed—she'll be all right."

"Are you sure she'll get better, Mother?"

"Ye can see for yourself, can't you? She doesn't look any worse, does she?"

"But are you sure she's going to be better?"

The woman sighed.

"Of course—I'm sure—now go to bed and sleep."

And Joe went to bed, confident in his parents.

That was one day. There were others to remember. There was the day when Joe returned and, as he walked to the hearth, there came from the dog lying there a movement that was meant to be a wag of the tail.

There was another day when Joe's mother sighed with pleasure, for as she prepared the bowl of milk, the dog stirred, lifted herself unsteadily, and waited. And when the bowl was set down, she put down her head and lapped, while her pinched flanks quivered.

And finally there was that day when Joe first realized that —even now—his dog was not to be his own again. So again the cottage rang with cries and protests, and again a woman's voice was lifted, tired and shrilling:

"Is there never to be any more peace and quiet in my home?"

And long after Joe had gone to bed, he heard the voices continuing—his mother's clear and rising and falling; his father's in a steady, reiterative monotone, never changing, always coming to one sentence:

"But even if he would sell her back, where'd Ah get the brass to buy her—where's the money coming fro'? Ye know we can't get it."

To Joe Carraclough's father, life was laid out in straight rules. When a man could get work, he worked his best and got the best wage he could. If he raised a dog, he raised the best one he could. If he had a wife and children, he took care of them the best he could.

In this out-of-work collier's mind, there were no devious exceptions and evasions concerning life and its codes. Like most simple men, he saw all these things clearly. Lying, cheating, stealing—they were wrong, and you couldn't make them right by twisting them round in your mind.

So it was that, when he was faced with any problem, he so often brought it smack up against elemental truths.

"Honest is honest, and there's no two ways about it," he would say.

He had a habit of putting it like that. "Truth is truth." Or, "Cheating is cheating."

And the matter of Lassie came up against this simple, direct code of morals. He had sold the dog and taken the money and spent it. Therefore the dog did not belong to him any more, and no matter how you argued you could not change that.

But a man has to live with his family, too. When a woman starts to argue with a man . . . well . . .

That next morning when Joe came down to breakfast, while his mother served the oatmeal with pursed lips, his father coughed and spoke as if he had rehearsed a set speech over in his mind many times that night:

"Joe, lad. We've decided upon it—that is, thy mother and me—that Lassie can stay here till she's all better.

"That's all reight, because I believe true in ma heart that nobody could nurse her better and wi' more care nor we're doing. So that's honest. But when she's better, well . . .

"Now ye have her for a little while yet, so be content. And don't plague us, lad. There's enough things to worry us now wi'out more. So don't plague us no more—and try to be a man about it—and be content."

With the young, "for a little while" has two shapes. Seen from one end, it is a great, yawning stretch of time extending into the unlimitable future. From the other, it is a ghastly span of days that has been cruelly whisked away before the realization comes.

Joe Carraclough knew that it was the latter that morning when he went to school and heard a mighty, booming voice. As he turned to look, he saw in an automobile a fearsome old man and a girl with her flaxen hair cascading from under a beret. And the old man, with his ferocious white moustaches looking like an animal's misshapen fangs, was waving an ugly blackthorn stick to the danger of the car, the chauffeur, and the world in general, and shouting at him:

"Hi! Hi, there! Yes, I mean you, m' lad! Damme, Jenkins, will you make this smelly contraption stand still a moment? Whoa, there, Jenkins! Whoa! Why we ever stopped using horses is more than any sane man can understand. Country's going to pot, that's what! Here, m' lad! Come here!"

For a moment Joe thought of running—doing anything to get all these things he feared out of his sight, so that they might, miraculously, be out of his mind, too. But a machine can go faster than a boy, and then, too, Joe had in him the blood of men who might think slowly and stick to old ideas and bear trouble patiently—but who do not run away. So he stood sturdily on the pavement and remembered his manners as his mother had taught him, and said:

"Yes, sir?"

"You're Whosis—What's-his-name's lad, aren't you?"

Joe's eyes had turned to the girl. She was the one he had seen long ago when he was putting Lassie in the Duke's kennels. Her face was not hearty-red like his own. It was blue-white.

On the hand that clutched the edge of the car the veins stood out clear-blue. That hand looked thin. He was thinking that, as his mother would say, she could do with some plumduff.

She was looking at him, too. Something made him draw himself up proudly.

"My father is Sam Carraclough," he said firmly.

"I know, I know," the old man shouted impatiently. "I never forget a name. Never! Used to know every last soul in this village. Too many of you growing up now—younger generation. And, by gad, they're all of them not worth one of the old bunch—not the whole kit and caboodle. The modern generation, why . . ."

He halted, for the girl beside him was tugging his sleeve.

"What is it? Eh? Oh, yes. I was just coming to it. Where's your father, m' lad? Is he home?"

"No, sir."

"Where is he?"

"He's off over Allerby, sir."

"Allerby, what's he doing there?"

"A mate spoke for him at the pit, I think, and he's gone to see if there's a chance of getting taken on."

"Oh, yes—yes, of course. When'll he be back?"

"I don't know, sir. I think about tea."

"Don't mumble! Not till tea. Damme, very inconvenient— very! Well, I'll drop round about five-ish. You tell him to stay home and I want to see him—it's important. Tell him to wait."

Then the car was gone, and Joe hurried to school. There was never such a long morning as that one. The minutes in the classroom crawled past as the lessons droned on.

Joe had only one desire—to have it become noon. And when at last the leaden moments that were years were gone, he raced home and burst through the door. It was the same cry—for his mother.

"Mother, Mother!"

"Goodness, don't knock the door down. And close it—anyone would think you were brought up in a barn. What's the matter?"

"Mother, he's coming to take Lassie away!"

"Who is?"

"The Duke . . . he's coming . . ."

"The Duke? How in the world does he know that she's . . ."

"I don't know. But he stopped me this morning. He's coming at tea time . . ."

"Coming here? Are ye sure?"

"Yes, he said he'd come at tea. Oh, Mother, please . . ."

"Now, Joe. Don't start! Now I warn ye!"

"Mother, you've got to listen. Please, please!"

"You hear me? I said . . ."

"No, Mother. Please help me. Please!"

The woman looked at her son and heaved a sigh of weariness and exasperation. Then she threw up her hands in despair.

"Eigh, dearie me! Is there never to be any more peace in this house? Never?"

She sank into her chair and looked at the floor. The boy went to her and touched her arm.

"Mother—do something," the boy pleaded. "Can't we hide her? He'll be here at five. He told me to tell Father he'd be here at five. Oh, Mother . . ."

"Nay, Joe. Thy father won't . . ."

"Won't you beg him? Please, please! Beg Father to . . ."

"Joe!" his mother cried angrily. Then her voice became patient again. "Now, Joe, it's no use. So stop thy plaguing. It's just that thy father won't lie. That much I'll give him. Come good, come bad, he'll not lie."

"But just this once, Mother."

The woman shook her head sadly and sat by the fire, staring into it as if she would find peace there. Her son went to her and touched her bare forearm.

"Please, Mother. Beg him. Just this once. Just one lie wouldn't hurt him. I'll make it up to him, I will. I will, truly!"

The words began to race from his mouth quickly.

"I'll make it up to both of you. When I'm growed up, I'll get a job. I'll earn money. I'll buy him things—I'll buy you things, too. I'll buy you both anything you ever want, if you'll only please, please . . ."

And then, for the first time in all his trouble, Joe Carraclough became a child, his sturdiness gone, and the tears choked his voice. His mother could hear his sobs, and she patted his hand, but she would not look at him. From the magic of the fire she seemed to read deep wisdom, and she spoke slowly.

"Tha mustn't, Joe," she said, her words soft. "Tha mustn't want like that. Tha must learn never to want anything i' life so hard as tha wants Lassie. It doesn't do."

It was then that she felt her son's hand trembling with impatience, and his voice rising clear.

"Ye don't understand, Mother. Ye don't understand. It ain't me that wants her. It's her that wants us—so terrible bad. That's what made her come home all that way. She wants us, so terrible bad."

It was then that Mrs. Carraclough looked at her son at last. She could see his face, contorted, and the tears rolling openly down his cheeks. And yet, in that moment of childishness, it was as if he were suddenly all the more grown up. Mrs. Carraclough felt as if time had jumped, and she were seeing this boy, this son of her own, for the first time in many years.

She stared at him and then she clasped her hands together. Her lips pressed together in a straight line and she got up.

"Joe, come and eat, then. And go back to school and be content. I'll talk to thy father."

She lifted her head, and her voice sounded firm.

"Yes—I'll talk to him, all right. I'll talk to Mr. Samuel Carraclough. I will indeed!"

At five that afternoon, the Duke of Rudling, fuming and muttering in his bad-tempered way, got out of a car that had stopped by a cottage gate. And behind the gate was a boy, who stood sturdily, his feet apart, as if to bar the way.

"Well, well, m' lad! Did ye tell him?"

"Go away," the boy said fiercely. "Go away! Thy tyke's not here."

For once in his life the Duke of Rudling stepped backward. He stared at the boy in amazement.

"Well, drat my buttons, Priscilla," he breathed. "Th' lad's touched. He is—he's touched!"

"Thy tyke's net here. Away wi' thee," the boy said stoutly. And it seemed as if in his determination he spoke in the broadest dialect he could command.

"What's he saying?" Priscilla asked.

"He's saying my dog isn't here. Drat my buttons, are you going deaf, Priscilla? I'm supposed to be deaf, and I can hear him all right. Now, ma lad, what tyke o' mine's net here?"

The Duke, when he answered, also turned to the broadest tones of Yorkshire dialect, as he always did to the people of the cottages—a habit which many of the members of the Duke's family deplored deeply.

"Coom, coom, ma lad. Speak up! What tyke's net here?"

As he spoke he waved his cane ferociously and advanced. Joe Carraclough stepped back from the fearful old man, but he still barred the path.

"No tyke o' thine," he cried stoutly.

But the Duke continued to advance. The words raced from Joe's mouth with a torrent of despair.

"Us hasn't got her. She's not here. She couldn't be here. No tyke could ha' done it. No tyke could come all them miles. It's not Lassie—it's—it's just another one that looks like her. It isn't Lassie."

"Well, bless my heart and soul," puffed the Duke. "Bless my heart and soul. Where's thy father, lad?"

Joe shook his head grimly. But behind him the cottage door opened and his mother's voice spoke.

"If it's Sam Carraclough ye're looking for—he's out in the shed, and been shut up there half the afternoon."

"What's this lad talking about—a dog o' mine being here?"

"Nay, ye're mistaken," the woman said stoutly.

"I'm mistaken?" roared the Duke.

"Yes. He didn't say a tyke o' thine was here. He said it wasn't here."

"Drat my buttons," the Duke sputtered angrily. "Don't twist my words up."

Then his eyes narrowed, and he stepped a pace forward.

"Well, if he said a dog of mine *isn't*, perhaps you'll be good enough to tell me just *which* dog of mine it is that isn't here. Now," he finished triumphantly. "Come, come! Answer me!"

Joe, watching his mother, saw her swallow and then look about her as if for help. She pressed her lips together. The

Duke stood waiting for his answer, peering out angrily from beneath his jutting eyebrows. Then Mrs. Carraclough drew a breath to speak.

But her answer, truth or lie, was never spoken. For they all heard the rattle of a chain being drawn from a door, and then the voice of Sam Carraclough said clearly:

"This, I give ye my word, is th' only tyke us has here. So tell me, does it look like any dog that belongs to thee?"

Joe's mouth was opening for a last cry of protest, but as his eyes fell on the dog by his father, the exclamation died. And he stared in amazement.

There he saw his father, Sam Carraclough, the collie fancier, standing with a dog at his heels the like of which few men had ever seen before, or would wish to see. It was a dog that sat patiently at his left heel, as any well-trained dog should do—just as Lassie used to do. But this dog—it was ridiculous to think of it at the same moment as Lassie.

For where Lassie's skull was aristocratic and slim, this dog's head was clumsy and rough. Where Lassie's ears stood in the grace of twin-lapped symmetry, this dog had one screw ear and the other standing up Alsatian fashion, in a way that would give any collie breeder the cold shivers.

More than that. Where Lassie's coat faded to delicate sable, this curious dog had ugly splashes of black; and where Lassie's apron was a billowing expanse of white, this dog had muddy puddles of off-color, blue-merle mixture. Lassie had four white paws, and this one had only one white, two dirty-brown, and one almost black. Lassie's tail flowed gracefully behind her, and this dog's tail looked like something added as an afterthought.

And yet, as Joe Carraclough looked at the dog beside his father, he understood. He knew that if a dog coper could treat a dog with cunning so that its bad points came to look like good ones, he could also reverse the process and make all its good ones look like bad ones—especially if that man were his father, one of the most knowing of dog fanciers in all that Riding of Yorkshire.

In that moment, he understood his father's words, too. For in dog-dealing, as in horse-dealing, the spoken word is a binding contract, and once it is given, no real dog-man will attempt to go back on it.

And that was how his father, in his patient, slow way, had tried to escape with honor. He had not lied. He had not denied anything. He had merely asked a question:

"Tell me, does this dog look like any dog that belongs to thee?"

And the Duke had only to say:

"Why, that's not my dog," and forever after, it would not be his.

So the boy, his mother and his father, gazed steadily at the old man, and waited with held breath as he continued to stare at the dog.

But the Duke of Rudling knew many things too—many, many things. And he was not answering. Instead he was walking forward slowly, the great cane now tapping as he leaned on it. His eyes never left the dog for a second. Slowly, as if he were in a dream, he knelt down, and his hand made one gentle movement. It picked up a forepaw and turned it slightly. So he knelt by the collie, looking with eyes that were as knowing about dogs as any man in Yorkshire. And those eyes did not waste themselves upon twisted ears or blotched markings or rough head. Instead, they stared steadily at the underside of the paw, seeing only the five black pads, crossed and recrossed with half-healed scars where thorns had torn and stones had lacerated.

Then the Duke lifted his head, but for a long time he knelt, gazing into space, while they waited. When he did get up, he spoke, not using Yorkshire dialect any more, but speaking as one gentleman might address another.

"Sam Carraclough," he said. "This is no dog of mine. 'Pon my soul and honor, she never belonged to me. No! Not for a single second did she ever belong to me!"

Then he turned and walked down the path, thumping his cane and muttering: "Bless my soul! I wouldn't ha' believed it! Bless my soul! Four hundred miles! I wouldn't ha' believed it."

It was at the gate that his granddaughter tugged his sleeve. "What you came for," she whispered. "Remember?"

The Duke seemed to come from his dream, and then he suddenly turned into his old self again.

"Don't whisper! What's that? Oh, yes, of course. You don't need to tell me—I hadn't forgotten!"

He turned and made his voice terrible.

"Carraclough! Carraclough! Drat my buttons, where are ye? What're ye hiding for?"

"I'm still here, sir."

"Oh, yes. Yes. Of course. There you are. You working?"

"Eigh, now—working," Joe's father said. That was the best he could manage.

"Yes, working—working! A job! A job! Do you have one?" the Duke fumed.

"Well, now—it's this road . . ." began Carraclough.

As he fumbled his words, Mrs. Carraclough came to his rescue, as good housewives will in Yorkshire—and in most other parts of the world.

"My Sam's not exactly working, but he's got three or four things that he's been considering. Sort of investigating, as ye might say. But—he hasn't quite said yes or no to any of them yet."

"Then he'd better say no, and quickly," snapped the Duke. "I need somebody up at my kennels. And I think, Carraclough . . ." His eyes turned to the dog still sitting at the man's heel. ". . . I think you must know—a lot—about dogs. So there. That's settled."

"Nay, hold on," Carraclough said. "Ye see, I wouldn't like to think I got a chap into trouble and then took his job. Ye see, Mr. Hynes couldn't help . . ."

"Hynes!" snorted the Duke. "Hynes? Utter nincompoop. Had to sack him. Didn't know a dog from a ringtailed filly. Should ha' known no Londoner could ever run a kennel for a Yorkshireman's taste. Now, I want you for the job."

"Nay, there's still summat," Mrs. Carraclough protested.

"What now?"

"Well, how much would this position be paying?"

The Duke puffed his lips.

"How much do you want, Carraclough?"

"Seven pounds a week, and worth every penny," Mrs. Carraclough cut in, before her husband could even get round to drawing a preparatory breath.

But the Duke was a Yorkshireman, too, and that meant he would scorn himself if he missed a chance to be "practical," as they say, where money is concerned.

"Five," he roared. "And not a penny more."

"Six pounds, ten," bargained Mrs. Carraclough.

"Six even," offered the Duke cannily.

"Done," said Mrs. Carraclough, as quick as a hawk's swoop.

They both glowed, self-righteously pleased with themselves. Mrs. Carraclough would have been willing to settle for three pounds a week in the first place—and as for the Duke, he felt he was getting a man for his kennels who was beyond price.

"Then it's settled," the Duke said.

"Well, almost," the woman said. "I presume, of course . . ." She liked the taste of what she considered a very fine word, so she repeated it. ". . . I presume that means we get the cottage on the estate, too."

"Ye drive a fierce bargain, ma'am," said the Duke, scowling. "But ye get it—on one condition." He lifted his voice and roared. "On condition that as long as ye live on my land, you never allow that thick-skulled, screw-lugged, gay-tailed eyesore of an excuse for a collie on my property. Now, what do ye say?"

He waited, rumbling and chuckling happily to himself as Sam Carraclough stooped, perplexed. But it was the boy who answered gladly: "Oh, no, sir. She'll be down at school waiting for me most o' the time. And, anyway, in a day or so we'll have her fixed up so's ye'd never recognize her."

"I don't doubt that," puffed the Duke, as he stumped toward his car. "I don't doubt ye could do exactly that. Hmm . . . Well, I never . . . "

It was afterwards in the car that the girl edged close to the old man.

"Now don't wriggle," he protested. "I can't stand anyone wriggling."

"Grandfather," she said. "You are kind—I mean about their dog."

The old man coughed and cleared his throat.

"Nonsense," he growled. "Nonsense. When you grow up, you'll understand that I'm what people call a hard-hearted Yorkshire realist. For five years I've sworn I'd have that dog. And now I've got her."

Then he shook his head slowly.

"But I had to buy the man to get her. Ah, well. Perhaps that's not the worst part of the bargain."

CHAPTER TWENTY-TWO

Just Like Old Times Again

When young Joe Carraclough said that you wouldn't have recognized his dog in a few days, he was right or wrong, according to what you thought his dog ought to look like.

Certainly, if you had looked for the screw-eared, gay-tailed horror that his father had coped up in his simple attempt to save the dog for his son and yet not trespass upon his stern codes of honesty, you would have never recognized it. But if you had looked for that proud, graceful, slim-headed dog known as Sam Carraclough's Lassie, you would have found her.

There she was, and as the weeks passed, under careful feeding and correct treatment, she slowly blossomed back into the dog she had once been. The gauntness and the pinched flanks disappeared, and the years of proper care that had built a strong constitution aided her now. Once more the rich coat billowed in black-sable and white, making her a delight to the eye. There was left only a slight limp where the bullet had creased her flank. The muscles had stiffened and, try as Sam Carraclough would, even with all his secrets and magics, he could never quite cure that.

But he did well with it, and massaged and rubbed the dog's muscles until the limp was so slight that only a dog expert would have noticed the tiny "favoring" of that foot as the dog went along. To the eye of all except the most expert dogman, she would have been that most beautiful thing—a perfect collie.

And each weekday, a few minutes before four o'clock, once again the shopkeepers of Greenall Bridge would look out and see that proud dog going down the street, and say, "You can set your clocks by her." And always, not long after, Joe Carraclough would come out of school and greet his dog, and they would go home together happily.

Yet, when young Joe promised the Duke that the dog would always be awaiting for him, he was wrong there, too. For there came a time when Lassie appeared no more at the school gate. Strangely enough, however, Joe didn't seem to care. He seemed perfectly happy, with a sort of secret happiness, as he went home alone.

It was one of those days as he went, whistling to himself, that as he came along the gravel path of the Duke's grounds, he saw the girl again.

Somehow Joe felt sorry for her. She did not look nice and plump and solid-boned as the little girls of the village did.

"Hello," he said.

"Hello," she answered.

There seemed nothing else to say, but he stood there.

"I've been away at school," she said.

"Have you?"

"Yes. But it's holidays now."

He thought gravely about that.

"We don't have our holidays for another week," he announced.

There was another pause, and then she said:

"How is Lassie?"

Joe smiled his warm smile. He looked around, as if to make sure no one was listening.

"You can come and see," he said, as if conferring a favor.

He led the way down the path to the cottage where the hollyhocks, gay-colored and tall, grew beside the white wall. He opened the door.

"Mother," he said. "I'm going to show her."

"Why, do come in, Miss," his mother said, smoothing her apron and then wiping an imaginary piece of dust from the white tablecloth set for tea.

Joe led the way to the cool scullery, where a great, low box was set in the dimness. And in the box was Lassie, and piled about her were seven plump, sleeping balls of fur.

"You see," Joe explained proudly, "we keep her here because she'd fret in the kennels. That's because she's a home dog, Lassie is."

The girl crouched down and touched one ball of fur with her forefinger. The little thing gave a drunken hiccup.

"Are they still blind?" she asked, as they both laughed.

Joe expanded.

"Of course not. Why, they get their eyes open when they're ten days old. These are over three weeks old now. They can run—only they like to sleep most of the time it seems to me."

He smiled as Lassie lifted her head. He stroked it gently.

"You know a lot about them, don't you?" the girl asked humbly.

"Well, she had a litter once before," Joe disclaimed, "and I remember from that time. This is just like old times—isn't it, Lassie?"

He crouched there, looking at his dog. It was like old times. He had often thought about that of late.

After the girl had gone, and polite good-byes and invitations to come and see the puppies again had been issued, Joe was still thinking about that. It was almost as if he was going to discover some sort of answer about life that, as a boy, he had never reached before.

This was like old times. Although, of course, it was a different house that they lived in now, it was as it used to be a year or so ago—in so many ways.

For example, if he took an extra big spoonful of sugar on his oatmeal in the morning, no longer did his mother snap at him and say:

"Now be careful, young man! Sugar costs money!"

Or, if he came in from the raw Yorkshire air boasting of how hungry he was, no longer did his mother's face take on that frightened, secret look, but instead she would laugh in her merry, plump way and say:

"My goodness, I don't know how to keep you full! Where do you put it all?"

But all the time she was saying it her voice would sound as if she were proud of a son who had such a great appetite, and that was just as it used to be in old times, too.

No longer did the grownups stop talking when he came in suddenly, nor did the voices go on, lifting and falling in weary argument after he was abed. No longer did his father come home each day, weary and dour and unspeaking, to sit by the fire and gaze into it.

Instead, the moment his footstep would sound out on the gravel, Mrs. Carraclough would jump up in a great bustle and cry:

"Look out! Here comes thy father now! Heads up—hot stuff coming!"

Then she would race from fire to table, whisking steaming tureens and bowls from the oven as if the most important thing in all the world was that they should all be set out in that brief space of time between the sound of his coming and the opening of the door.

Then she would stand, her arms akimbo, and say:

"Hurry up and wash, Sam! Sheep's head and dumplings tonight—and they don't wait for no man!"

That was the way it was—like old times again. And his father, too, sitting at the table, bowing his head to the food and then looking up and saying:

"Well, and how's our Joe been today? Did ye do your lessons good at school?"

Once it had been like that before. Then it had all stopped. Now it was like that again. What was the reason?

Joe pondered over this all through the meal that evening. After the meal was over, and Lassie came stalking in, he sank on the rug beside her and stroked her, and he thought he had found the answer.

It was Lassie! Of course—that was it! When she had been home, things had been right. When she was sold and gone, nothing had gone right any more. And now that she was back, everything was fine again, and they were all very happy.

"She came home and brought us luck," he thought. "She did it. She came home and brought us luck."

He made a crooning sound and pillowed his face in the dog's ruff. Lassie sighed contentedly.

Then his mother spoke:

"Now Joe, don't lie with that dog all over my rug. Getting hair all over. And what's making you so silent tonight?"

Joe smiled to himself. He still crooned to the dog.

"Ye're a come-home dog, aren't ye, Lassie?" he crooned. "Aye, that ye are. And ye brought us luck. 'Cause ye're a come-homer. Ye're my Come-home. Lassie Come-home. That's thy name! Lassie Come-home!"

But his mother stormed again.

"Did ye hear me, Joe Carraclough? Now tha'll have her all upset—and when she's got a litter to take care on. Tha should know better nor that!"

Joe edged an inch away from the fire and stroked the contented Lassie. He looked up gravely.

"Eigh, Feyther," he said, "I can feel her ribs."

His father turned his chair to the hearth and stretched his legs luxuriously, and then began lighting his pipe, smiling to himself.

"Don't ye think she's a bit poor, Feyther?" Joe went on anxiously. "I think she could stand a little more beef and a little less milk!"

"Ah, ye do, do ye?" his mother chattered on, as she piled up the steaming dishes she was washing. "Is that so? Ye think she could stand more beef. Aye, well, tha wouldn't be a

Carraclough—nor a Yorkshireman—if tha didn't think tha knew more about raising tykes nor breaking eggs wi' a stick!

"Aye—sometimes it seems to me that some folk in this village think more o' their tykes nor they do o' their own flesh and blood. Dogs, dogs, dogs—After this litter's raised, out she goes where she belongs, and never another dog will I have in my home . . ."

Just then Joe looked up at his father, who was looking down out of the side of his eyes. And his father lifted his hand and put his finger comically beside his nose.

That secret gesture had a meaning. It meant:

"Ye mustn't mind women too much, Joe. They have a hard time of it, staying home and scrubbing and scouring and cooking all day, and so they take it out in scolding, and we've got to let them do it to blow off steam. But we know it doesn't really mean anything, we men know that—we men!"

And his father smiled, and Joe grinned, and then it was so funny, this new kinship of men that let woman go on scolding, that Joe started to laugh. And his laughter rose and rose, until his mother turned.

"Aye, and now ye laugh at me, do ye! Well, I'll teach ye! I'll give ye a skelp!"

And she flicked him with the dishtowel expertly, till Joe rolled over.

"I wasn't laughing at you, Mother!"

"Well, what were ye laughing at?"

"At Father—he made a funny face!"

Mrs. Carraclough turned on her husband.

"So it were thee, eh? Well, I'll skelp thee, too!"

But as she advanced, Joe saw his father's great strong hands reach out, and one of them imprisoned his mother's shining wrists and the other arm went round her great waist, and Mrs. Carraclough was held fast. Then the father looked at Joe and smiled:

"Look at her, Joe. Who's the bonniest woman in the whole village?"

"My mother is," Joe said stoutly and with all the honesty in his heart.

Mrs. Carraclough's face broke into a beam.

"The two of ye," she said. "Ah, ye're both chips off the same stick. Ye're both saying that to blarney me."

"Nay, the lad answered an honest question honestly. And another thing—tha's bonnie—and there's plenty of thee, too!"

"Oh, so tha thinks I'm plump. Well, let me go, Sam Carraclough. I've got to finish drying them dishes!"

But his father wouldn't let his mother go, and she began boxing his ears, and he just sat there with his head bowed to protect his pipe. Then they both laughed.

That was just as it used to be long ago, too—his father and mother happy.

Joe bowed his head to the dog, and forgot them.

"You're my Lassie Come-home," he crooned.